GODDESS OF THE ROCK

About the author...

Born in Almora city in Uttaranchal mountains, T.C. Joshi is a graduate from Allahabad University and has a masters in Economics from Lucknow. Though a bright student, prolonged illness, love for nature and English literature turned him to apple farming in the heights of Nainital district where he wrote **Goddess of the Rock**. While writing his substantial third novel, he is publishing his second book **Hari Om** anytime now.

GODDESS OF THE ROCK

T.C. Joshi

NEW
NC
CENTURY

NEW CENTURY PUBLICATIONS
DELHI INDIA

NEW CENTURY PUBLICATIONS
34, Gujranwala Town, Part-2,
Delhi - 110 009 INDIA
Tel.: 7247805, 7138192
Fax: +91-11-7464774
E-mail: indiatax@del2.vsnl.net.in

ISBN: 81-7708-043-1

Printed at Print Line, New Delhi -110 002

PRINTED IN INDIA

PREFACE

Opening in May 1948, after the independence of India, the novel is centred around Nainital, a city situated on the second mountain range after the Himalayas. Since it was chosen as a summer capital of the state of U.P. by the British *Raj,* people there had come into closer contact with it. On its termination, they remembered in various ways, as they had known it. While lawyers Pathak and Sunder, horse-*wallah* Mazid, all sighed for losing some income and importance in society, domestic helper suffered from nostalgia for the British *Raj;* Bhandari remembered it for the material culture it left behind; Godhan and snub-nosed priest expressed their esteem for the English language; Joga Shah recalled a British officer who had given him a start in life. *Rajah* Narendra Pratap, though still somewhat bitter against the British *Raj,* provided boarding and lodging to his English lady, private secretary Mrs. Scott, who loved peasants in his Rasalgaon *zamindari.* But the meaning of independence was often missed, as when Godhan remarked, "As our people, so our government has become fashionable."

The above paragraph mentions some of the facts in the novel of the historical times, which broadly existed across India. But the conflict of the novel proceeds from the coming Hindu Code Bill – passed by the Indian Parliament in 1952 – and which it would always do, by conferring for the first time, two rights – inheritance and divorce – to Hindu women. The inheritance right disturbed the peace in the home of Sanwal who loved his nephew Desh as a son. But the right of divorce directly concerned to women, Lalita and Chandra, brought up in homes performing *puja, kirtan* and following *Geeta,* who passionately loved other than their husbands, Desh and Shanker. To Chandra seeking divorce in her times, when the freedom movement of women in India was unknown, looked as impossible; but none for Lalita, a firm believer of *karma* and *nirvana.*

The action of the novel is set in the scenic mountainous part of the Uttaranchal State, formerly Uttar Pradesh (U.P.), where enchanting lakes, slaty fog, heavy rains and snow seem to interact with the characters in the novel, which comprises about one hundred thousand words.

Indian words given above, in italics, are incorporated in the Concise Oxford Dictionary, new edition; while *Geeta* the philosophic treatise, is followed as much by the Hindus as the Bible by Christians and Koran by Muslims.

I am grateful to Ms. Jehanara Wasi for carefully and painstakingly going through the entire text and editing the manuscript. I am also thankful to my publisher Mr. Sandeep Sury for his valuable support and co-operation.

Dehradun T.C. Joshi
October 6, 2002

In memory of my brothers

Harish Chandra
Nabin Chandra

All characters in this novel are imaginary, and any resemblance to any person living or dead in coincidental.

CHAPTER - I

Today broke dull and heavy; an overcast sky suggested rain. A young man of spare frame was awakened from sleep by the clangings with which the train, he had boarded the night before, came to halt. He wanted to shake off the heaviness that had spread over his limbs, but he felt himself too spent to rise to his feet and look out. The examination he had sat in and the heat of the month seemed to have sapped away all his energy. In a while he heard the phuff-phuff of the engine, and the wheels under him thumping. A cool breeze fanned his face; with an effort he levered himself up and gazed out, through the twilight of the dawn at the slaty mountains forming the skyline. There, amidst them nestled his home town. Sometimes the gigantic *Paaka*r and *Seemal* trees cut off the view; but all the time he kept his eyes fastened upon the mountains, seized with longing for the cool, balmy air to breathe in, and disport about. "A year in the mountains is worth ten in the plains", he murmured to himself, as he lit his cigarette.

His attention trailed off. His eyes swept round the compartment; all the passengers occupying other bunks lay asleep. One of them, a middle aged man, taking an upper one, snored obtrusively. It reminded him of his third class travel with friends. How troublesome it was having to spend the night cramped, in an over-packed compartment. Of course, the company of friends kept him amused and lightened the journey. He was sorry that the chapter of his university career was closing. There existed people, like his brother-in-law, who considered friendship was a passing affair. It beat him how one came to drop one's friends.

And there was one in his home town, senior to him by about fifteen years. Curious enough, he came into his life not through school or university. By midday he would meet him, and then both would launch their boat over into the lake.

Some stations passed. The light outside intensified; occasionally the sun broke through clouds beating hard. The train chug-chugged laboriously over the *terai* forests abounding in wildlife; but steadily giving place to agricultural land and villages, composed of huts of sun-baked mud and straw. At the small station at Kichha, the train took intolerably long stoppage. The heat grew oppressive; the clouds brought little relief, and the overnight passengers, with back and limbs stiff with cramps and eyes narrowed down from want of sleep, looked for deliverance from the infernal journey. But in a first class compartment, two men having performed the ritual of morning toilet, lounged, throwing out their legs. The snoring one, for whom the young man had conceived a dislike, struck his acquaintance over a match box.

"Thanks", he lit his cigarette, "I am Bhandari."

"I am Desh Raj", replied the young man.

Bhandari was a powerful stocky man, who spoke with distinction that lent charm to his vague features, and well brushed grizzled hair. He was a Brahmin belonging to that part of the Punjab, now west Pakistan. With the partition of India he had moved to Delhi and then on to Kichha, where he had established himself in his old occupation of a farmer. He belittled the measures the government had undertaken to better the circumstances of the refugees from the Punjab. Desh felt like remonstrating that it had distributed land, extended loans, and granted numerous facilities to them, besides inviting claims of their properties left over in Pakistan; but his instinctive slowness at raising an argument kept him tongue-tied.

"Seen Nainital before?", inquired Desh, to change the conversation.

"Going for the first time." Bhandari shook his head." I am taking rest after a year of hard work."

A forest settlement growing into a renowned hill-station, in the course of a hundred years, exercised a singular fascination upon Bhandari, hiding for him the romance of the former English life. His face fell when Desh told him that few Englishmen, who were unable to proceed to England for one reason or the other, had reminded behind in Nainital.

"I am a realist, a modern man", declared Bhandari, "And like the Englishmen for their practical attitude towards life. They came from beyond the seven seas and ruled over us."

"We are becoming like Englishmen," agreed Desh, "More so after independence; look, we are changing our laws after theirs, giving right of divorce and inheritance to our Hindu women".

"I am glad when I hear a young man say so". Bhandari grinned in a self-congratulatory manner, on having embarked upon his enterprise in a new place. "Are you interested in farming?"

"No, not at all," Desh turned up his nose.

Bad thing! Middle-classes looked down upon agriculture. Bhandari apportioned the blame as much upon the Indians as upon the British *Raj*. He smashed the cigarette stub under the heel of his shoe.

"Your father is a government official."

"No, he was a lawyer; died long ago."

"*Arree*, sorry. You live with your mother."

"She died even before father; I live with my uncle."

The two got down at Kathgodam, the railway terminus, situated at the foot of the mountains which stood guard to the plains.

Desh was kindly disposed towards Bhandari now; he would have invited him to *chai* at Nainital, but his aunt disliked guests; she complained there were too many of them in summer.

An ultramarine state-service bus carried passengers straight into the depths of a wooded valley. Shaded with tall trees a wonderful, black road opened out in long curves; then it turned into sharp ones in the up grade, lifting them above the valley, and the south-western plain, they had come from, dropped off below them. The bus raced up and up till it gained a shoulder perilous of height; the eastern landscape spread out, as far as eye could travel, in a panorama of mountain huddled upon mountains. The bus was tooling through the untidy *bazaar* of Tallital that exaggerated the magnificence of the bungalows dotting the mountain slopes of a closed valley, opening southwards. On a sudden the bus came on a level ground, and squeaked to a stop.

An emerald lake flashed upon passengers getting out of the bus. It was shut in by mountains in a horse-shoe, with the south-eastern side, through which the traffic entered the city, knocked off.

"This is a lovely lake", exclaimed Bhandari, "But it is rather small."

"Yes, a mile long." Desh's voice was drowned in the clamour of *coolies*, soliciting jobs in a mixture of patois and *Hindustani*. "*Sahib, sahib*, I carry your luggage."

While he was busy hiring *coolies*, and entrusting them his suitcases and bedding-roll, to carry to his bungalow, Desh felt a squeeze on his right shoulder. He turned round, when his eyes rested on a tall figure.

"Shanker dear, how are you?" Desh held out his hand.

Shanker shook it demonstratively. His face with his prominent eyes, over thin fair moustaches and straight nose, was breaking all over in smiles. He was superbly dressed in a sky-blue tropical suit and blue tie.

"Where have you forgotten your felt-hat ?"

In embarrassment Shanker scratched his bare head, "It has gone away with the British officers."

Bhandari greeted Shanker in India style, *namaskar*, by joining the palms of his hands in front of his breast, while Shanker responded in his broad accent in English, "How do you do."

Bhandari took a *rickshaw* and left across the Mall road that ran over the right margin of the lake. Desh along with Shanker followed Bhandari. Shanker informed him that his uncle was confined to bed. It was easy for him to guess it; whether it rained or snowed, his uncle never failed to receive him at the motor-stand. For his absence, Desh blamed his asthma.

"You had called on my uncle."

"Yes, in January. Now it is from your sister that I got news of his illness."

"When did you meet my sister?"

"The other day I ran across her; otherwise I rarely see her. Since you left for Allahabad in October last, I should not have seen her more than three times."

"This is little in seven months."

"How do you expect me to see her more often? I can meet her only when she comes to my store for shopping."

Desh felt it was indiscreet of him to have hinted at the infrequent meetings of Shanker with his sister. His sister was a married woman; why did Shanker need to see her more often?

A *rickshaw* carried the two over the broad, straight road. It was lined on the left by the weeping willows touching the lake, and, on the right, by high class shops, which purveyed their wares through polished glass windows. Shanker lived a mile up in Mallital, the region towards head-end of the lake in a long, double-storeyed building in stone. Its ground-floor was designed for shops, and first one for residential apartments. A huge sign-board, surmounting an arched door-way of a large, fashionable shop, blazoned in long, raised, white letters: Empire Stores.

Shanker and he climbed upstairs to the drawing-room, which was sumptuously furnished. The windows gave on to the Mall road he had just come through, and the level land over the head of the lake, called Flats. Desh looked out at the peaks of mountains around that soared high over the lake.

A cool breeze of a cloudy day rushed in, twitching the curtains. It hardly seemed the month of May that he had parted with a few hours before in the plains, when the *loo*, hot wind, scratched the face and heated the body.

"What are you doing here?", shouted Shanker, "Leaning over the window, whistling to some girl passing through the Mall."

"*Arree*, sometimes you cut such jokes even before my sister."

"What then; I believe you and your sister are quite friendly."

As usual the table was laid in the sleeping-room, for the dining-room was seldom used excepting when Shanker entertained distinguished guests. Kept in inimitable order, the sleeping-room was also used as a study and office. Though it was overcrowded with furniture, boxes, registers, books, all articles were so arranged as not to cramp the space. Here too the windows looked on to the Mall road and Flats.

"*Accha*, Desh *sahib*, you arrived well", smiled with glee Dev Rama, the man-servant of Shanker. "It must be very hot in the plains now."

To Dev Rama summer in the plains exercised a terrific dread. Often cooking food on the stove, he would dream of himself being transferred there. "How do people manage to live in there," he would say afterwards, coming into himself. Twice, when he was in the service of *sahiblogs*, he had declined from accepting the situation of a government orderly, all on account of the cursed heat of the plains.

"You shall not go there again."

"*Arree*, never; why should I suffer the heat, when Goddess of the Rock has given this sweet, cool breeze."

"Right Desh *sahib*, why do you need to go there? You can earn a lot of money here like your lawyer brother-in-law."

Skinny, with downy moustache, tracing the sides of his lip for want of a shave, and stumps of thin beard roughening his scrawny face, Dev Rama stood a medium height. He flitted in and out of the room with a agility, unusual at his age of sixty, to serve them with condiments and pickles, he remembered could be available in the house.

"You like these Desh *sahib?*", he asked,

"You should not worry about food so much," scoffed Shanker, "Then putting on clean clothes."

"*Arree, sahib*' you always tell me that. Am I a young man going to my father-in-law's house that I need velvet garments."

"But, is there any harm in regularly washing your clothes?"

"These washermen and fine clothes are for the show of *sahibs* and not for us."

Dev Rama receded from the room. Being shy of his unclean clothes, which he was lazy to change quickly, any reference to them touched off the stock joke between the master and servant.

"You are not helping yourself to pickles and *chutney*".

"I do not touch them," replied Shanker.

"That is why people call you an Englishman."

"That is not true," returned Shanker in one breath, "I believe in a high standard of living than in hoarding money, unlike Joga Sah."

The way Shanker lived went beyond the ideas of Desh on decent living. Cream-coloured with dragons embossed upon it, the service-set off which the two were having lunch, rated among the finest imported crockery. It pointed to aristocracy than just decent living.

Inquired Shanker, "How about your future plans ?"

"Either I can try to enter the Administrative service or become a lawyer."

"Today students want to be engineers or doctors; wish you had a technical degree."

"That is too late now for me."

Shanker considered a law career was riddled with uncertainties.

" Then I should try the Administrative Service,"

"But remember, now people would not be sacred of you, if you are a district magistrate, as in British days, when you went out on roads and *bazaars*."

"It shall be a long time before we are not scared; perhaps the habits of mind change dead slow".

x x x

With the heaviness of over eating descending upon him, Desh extended himself across Shanker's bed. He started dozing. When he woke, the sun had set. The wind fluttered the curtains; he peeped out of the window. The clouds gathered into a thick mass, rumbled, threatening rain. He snapped a *rickshaw* and dashed off to Tallital the foot-end of the lake. Through the trees the wind whizzed sharply; all the boats had disappeared from the lake.

He walked up the bridle-road, bordered with shapely wooden uprights, painted white, and connected with several lines of iron cables. These roads criss-crossed the mountains, joining to one another edifices with gabled walls, red or green coloured, slanting multi-roofs, porticos and turrets. Erected by British officers and government, *nabobs, rajahs* and *zamindars*, they were designed after the European architecture that gave the city its characteristic looks.

Desh surveyed his large house, with varandah in front, curved out in the middle. Its unkempt grounds indicated that his uncle should have mostly kept indoors, during his absence from Nainital.

Wrapped in an off-white shawl, uncle was sitting out along with aunt in the verandah. The two folds on either cheeks of his thin face had become sharper. With his sickly face and grey cropped hair, he looked older than sixty-five. Beside him, aunt looked round as a foot-ball. Though younger than him by six or seven years, her broad face was fleshy, her arms and breasts rounded.

Desh leaned forward and in greeting touched the feet of uncle and aunt.

"You were a long time coming from Shanker's." From behind his gold-rimmed spectacles that bridged his high-nose, he fixed Desh.

Whenever he failed to appear in time, uncle came out to the verandah, waiting for him. His delay worried uncle. He had then to explain his reason of delay, and urge him to stop worrying over trifles.

Uncle lifted his eyes to the blackening rain clouds.

"It is good you came in time."

"What then, I am not made of paper to melt away in the rain."

"But you can catch cold and flue from sudden change of weather; you have come from the hot plains."

Uncle's health was a matter of concern than his own; the damp wind might aggravate his asthma. He should avoid sitting out in the verandah; but there was no telling him about it. Unmindful of bad weather, he installed himself there, devoting hours in the morning and evening on religious books, magazines, and the *Geeta*.

Uncle turned on the electric switch of the drawing room. In the light his head was snow-white, over his tall, narrow figure. He stooped a trifle as he walked.

The rain pattered over the roofs. Through the window-panes the lightening flickered in; the sky growled and the thunder crashed, rattling the whole house.

"Typical summer weather", remarked uncle.

The drawing-room, elliptical and extending the whole breadth of the house, divided it into two halves, with double rooms opening on either of its sides.

"You never sat in here since I left for Allahabad," he smiled, putting on all the electric bulbs in the chandelier.

To celebrate his arrival, uncle wanted all lights to remain burning, letting expense to go to oven. It seemed seven years had passed than seven months since his departure to Allahabad. Once or twice he felt time had never moved; it had come to a dead stop. Day in and day out, during meals or sitting out in the verandah, he would remember Desh; often worrying over his silence or delayed replay to his letters. Sometimes he wondered, whether Desh remembered him one tenth of what he did him or no.

Twice, in January and over again in April, his health had seriously deteriorated. Spasms of asthmatic coughing recurred and stayed long; his general health ran down so much so that aunt gave up all hopes of his recovery. And if he had passed away then, his soul would have haunted the earth, for it would have borne with it the unquenched desire to see his son, Desh.

"You know", uncle paused to take his breath. "He who reaches desirelessness alone gets *nirvana* from the chains of rebirth and death."

"Yes, I know", he replied with emphasis. "I have read the *Geeta* with you."

The holy book reminded uncle of evening *puja*, and aunt of *chulha*, for preparing food.

After the meals, Desh pressed the button of the table-lamp in his room and tucked himself into his bed. With his eyelids laden with sleep, he tried to read the day's newspaper. In a while his eyes riveted upon the date on the newspaper: May 26, 1948. From his hands the newspaper slipped down to the floor; the hot plains intruded into his memory; he had parted with them forever. His eyes readily closed down; sleep was coming over him. He heard someone padding in softly almost on tip-toe. The electric button clicked; the room sank into darkness. The padding faded away. "It should be uncle," he whispered to himself, dropping to sleep.

CHAPTER - II

He never really understood the life of Shanker. His friendship with him began about seven years before, when Desh was sitting in the high school examination. Both sister and himself had known Shanker as proprietor of Empire Departmental store; they had also noticed him for his handsome looks. But it was only while collecting funds for the school variety-show that he made his personal acquaintance, when Desh had been appointed social-secretary and approached prominent citizens. As a former social-secretary of the school, Shanker not only purchased the highest ticket of rupees fifty, but also extravagantly praised some of the dance and song items. Later he invited student musicians, actors and important members of school staff to an at-home. Few of them had ever seen anything as grand as that. Shanker arrayed in a lounge-suit looked unusually dapper. The twenty-three of them were accommodated in the dining and drawing-room. They all wondered where he had managed to get blooming flowers from, in the month of December, for the exquisite china vases. *Chai* with the faint aroma of rose was served by liveried waiters in starched robes, *puggaree*, and red-coloured sash. The expensive china tea-sets struck them with awe; the one used by the principal and staff members was carved in silver.

After *chai*, the party was regaled to a programme of recorded western music. They sat through it with patience, trying to follow it. Excepting two or three members of the staff, all failed to catch the words in the songs; even their omniscient headmaster seemed none the better than the students. Shanker sensing their difficulty changed the vocal to instrumental music. Its slow movement, without being understood, communicated them a feeling of pathos. For days the melodies haunted him. He overheard the headmaster telling a staff member, "I have never attended such a high tea."

Shanker warmly shook hands with everybody. Most of the students were unaçquainted with this pompous way of bidding goodbye. Shanker invited Desh to *chai* again. He would not hear of his excuses. When Desh saw Shanker again, he found a new, elaborately carved, silver tea-set had replaced the old one.

"Where is the other?" He lowered himself into a sofa.

"All that for the party I had taken from a hotel", answered Shanker. "This silver-set is mine."

Shanker seemed him a mighty influential person. What to say of procuring anything from them, he had never once visited any hotel in Nainital. After a stodgy tea, Desh smoked cigarette upon cigarette, and talked of the war. Shanker spoke in fluent English. He denounced the British government for retaining India, in the face of strong nationalist movement by might. Behind an anglicised, fine figure, Desh had expected to encounter a title-holder, a ruling-chief or a feudal lord, the staunch supporters of British government. But hearing the views a proprietor of a departmental store bearing an English name, and dealing in goods mostly made in England, with customers mostly Englishmen, astounded him.

As a student his knowledge of imperialism was poor. The talk impressed him; it indicated him the depths of knowledge Shanker possessed. With all his westernised manners, he seemed no less venerable than the white-capped congressmen, dedicated to the cause of freedom.

"You are coming for the evening meal on Sunday."

"What of Sunday, I can come even before."

"That is good; you come on Friday."

In his adoration for Shanker, he had more than readily accepted his invitation. A sense of regret at his hastiness tormented him. He informed sister of his new friendship with Shanker. He told her in detail of their conversation, of the stylish garments Shanker wore; and of his tea with the faint aroma of rose. Sister expressed surprise that Shanker, a failure at the intermediate examination, should possess remarkable command over English. She knew a good deal about him. He was the son of Durga Lal, and grandson of Dhani Lal, a close friend of her father-in-law; one of the big landlords of Nainital in his time. In recognition of his loyalty to it, the British Raj had conferred upon

Dhani Lal the title of O.B.E. On the death of his father, Durga Lal succeeded into an handsome fortune but, in a short while, he dissipated it in women and wine. When he was found dead one morning, after a night long booze, he had left for his two sons nothing more than the ancestral residential house. The early death of Durga Lal came as a godsend to his widow and minor sons in so far as it saved them from penury. They shifted to a middling house; renting out the palatial Arcadia to a British civilian. With the income of above three thousand rupees a year, proceeding from its rent, the family regained a measure of its old prestige. Shanker was eight years old, and his elder brother sixteen. Guided by the prejudice widespread in society then, that the rich ought to keep themselves above work, Shanker's brother, after obtaining a degree in arts, preferred to vegetate at home then starting some business. In the meantime he married, and the family expenses multiplied without any increase in income.

Shanker was a man of ideas. Repeated failures at the academic examinations left him undaunted; he saw ancient values were undergoing change in modern times. Idleness was no passport to respectability. With a single salesman to assist him, he started the Empire departmental store, which, in the beginning, exclusively dealt in woollen and cotton cloth. But in the course of some years, his gentle manners, noble presence, and honesty, attracted him a host of customers, both English and Indian. The business prospered; he began keeping all sorts of household articles, electrical appliances, crockery, watches, fountain-pens, and leather goods. In ten years Shanker had not only pulled himself and his brother out of bankruptcy, but had also made for himself tens of thousand; sent his brother back to live in Arcadia, and restored the family to its old footing in society.

The Friday evening when he was invited, Desh found Shanker reading a journal. The radio was tuned low to a foreign station; the room felt warm and cosy.

"Is that B.B.C. ?"

"Oh yes," replied Shanker, "You want Indian music". He changed the station, dropping the journal to the ground. "Let us have drinks."

Desh winced. His uncle and brother-in-law were teetotallers, who looked down upon drinking as an incurable vice. Whenever there occurred suicides, motor accidents, and disruption of homes, his uncle warned him of its dangers. "What a renowned family was of Dhani Lal; there was no party of governor in which he was not invited; and to what disgrace his son Durga Lal brought it," he would say, "And according to our *dharma* such sinners can never reach heaven."

He wanted to refuse Shanker's offer to drinks, but, out of ear of exposing himself a puritan, he slurred over, "Which do you prefer."

"Anything you want ? I stock almost all good liquors."

Desh, who was ignorant of them, remained dumb from embarrassment; and, on repeating the question by Shanker, replied, "Go ahead with anything you like; so far I am concerned I never drink."

Shanker gave a whimsical laugh. "Childling, you do not know the good things of life."

Shanker unlocked the cabinet, standing near the hearth, and produced a bottle. His heart throbbed as Shanker poured out the drinks into silver glasses. His uncle's warning echoed in his ears; he wished to bolt off; but he pulled himself together, and declared stoutly, "I cannot give you company; please excuse me."

Shanker fell in his estimation; he would keep off his company. From his bachelorhood, Desh had taken him for a *sadhu*. Now he saw Shanker in the guise of a knave. He had committed a mistake in going by his friend's proposing looks and bright conversation.

"Have at least one drink" pleaded Shanker. "It is chilly evening, you will enjoy it."

"No, I cannot touch it. It is a bad thing."

"Who tells you."

"My uncle says so."

"Then I shall not drink with you."

"Why should you forego for my shake."

"No, not until your views remains what they are." He put away the bottle.

He was moved by the gentlemanliness of Shanker. Far from pressing him to drink, he had appealed to his reasoning faculty.

"When I was your age, I thought exactly as you now do," resumed Shanker, "I wanted you not to lose time in gaining experience."

"My views cannot change."

Conversation broke off for a while. Dev Ram brought in one after another bowls containing rich, tasty food.

It was almost ten-thirty, when the dinner was over. Finding himself late, he bid Shanker good-bye.

"Do not run away, I am accompanying you for some distance."

On the Mall road not a soul stirred; a bitter chill pierced to their bones.

"I like this weather," said Desh.

"I cannot face this terrible cold. I am going to plains for a month."

"Where to ?"

"You know *rajah sahib* of Rasalgoan. His son Inder is my friend; he has a farm in *terai*."

The two had come to the middle of the lake. Shanker's teeth were chattering. For his sake his friend had denied himself the drinks; in the severe weather it should have kept him warm. Howsoever much superior his moral principles, his intolerance had made Desh look selfish.

"You are not angry with me," Shanker looked at him full in the face.

He shook hand with Shanker perfunctorily; turned round and walked off, without deigning last glance on his friend.

As he stole into his bed-room, he felt relieved that his uncle was not waiting for him. He sat by the electric heater he had put on; the chill had driven away sleep from his eyes. He reviewed his friendship with Shanker. Right from the day he had met him, for making sale of college variety-show ticket, his looks had exerted an unconscious influence on Desh. The more he learnt about him from his sister, the more sneaking admiration he developed for Shanker. All on a sudden a revulsion had come over him. Shanker's father had met his end in alcoholism; his brother was reputed to be an alcoholic; and he too was on the same way. He wanted to withdraw himself from Shanker's company.

Some days later he received a letter, written in a strange, slanting hand. No sooner he began reading it, he understood that it had come from Shanker. He had sent it from a *terai* farm. The life there was rough and solitary, but he liked it for a change. He missed Desh, but he would return to Nainital in twenty days. Lastly Shanker had begged his pardon for wanting him to partake of drinks with him that evening. He hoped that by the time the two would meet again, Desh would have forgotten of the unsavoury incident.

The friendly tone of the letter softened his dislike for Shanker. He read it aloud to his sister. He was amazed at her views on liquor; taken moderately, she saw nothing wrong with it. She disclosed him that their father was an addict, though, by his cleverness, he was able to make a secret of it from public. In point of fact it had caused the affliction of liver of which he died. The revelation shocked Desh. His uncle had naturally rubbed evils of alcoholism into him from his childhood. Sister advised him to make up with Shanker and invite him to lunch. Desh still felt reluctant, but she overbore him.

He remarked, "Aunt might not like it."

"Do not worry I shall look to expenses."

It went off excellently. Sister, who occasionally visited him, arrived early in the morning; and food was cooked under her supervision, which consisted wholly of vegetarian dishes, for uncle did not allow mutton to be taken to his kitchen.

Introduction was superfluous. Aunt and uncle knew not only Shanker but also every member of his family, right from his grandfather. So did sister, who could be counted among the oldest customers of Empire departmental store. Shanker too bore vivid memories of her, since her childhood; he often saw her in cinema houses, or in the lake rowing the boat.

On finishing lunch, all moved out to bask in the sun, and talked of the war and soaring prices. Sister was impressed as most Indians by German victories; she believed that Hitler would free Indian from British domination. Shanker dissipated her illusions by analysing the theory of fascism.

"We have done a lot of talking", sister looked at her watch. "Desh get us some good tea."

It tasted pleasant in the warm, afternoon sun of winter. Before taking his leave, Shanker invited sister and himself to lunch, the following Sunday. She expressed her inability to accept it.

"I am surprised; how much he knows of current politics," remarked sister, when Shanker was gone. "And look, he has never been to the university."

Desh inquired, "Why did you refuse his invitation?"

"How could I without your brother-in-law?"

That day the seeds of his everlasting friendship with Shanker were sown. Sister disarmed his suspicion that Shanker was an alcoholic; his enjoying a drink was a harmless diversion. Every vacation, in past seven years, had been spent in the company of Shanker. He was given to pictures; so was his friend. The difference was that he saw more *Hindustani*, while Shanker did English. But, coming under his spell, Desh reduced seeing *Hindustani*. Then Shanker taught him riding; it was hard to dispel his fear of it. Once it was overcome, Shanker and himself made jaunts to beauty-spots, over the mountains. The two picnicked under open skies; nature breathing on them, with the greenery of mountains around, and the lake spread below.

At the beginning of his friendship with Shanker, sister stayed away from gaieties with a person outside the family circle. But her continual seeing of Shanker along with him in Flats, whenever she came down from her house in the evening, wore off her hesitancy in accompanying the two to pictures. This effected change in their mode of outdoor life, from hiking to boating; for sister was fond of the latter. Sometimes they occupied themselves hours in rowing, taking photographs in different poses, with the lake in the background. It pleased him to note that sister chatted with Shanker in the manner of old friends. She made suitable remarks on his attire, shoes and ties. She inquired after his business; she took his help in her domestic matters. She needed a cook, servant, a good milkman, flower seeds. He too cracked jokes with her freely. "Granny is late coming down," he would say, or wish, "If you were dark complexioned, I would have called your cuckoo." "The naughty boy needs good thrashing," she would retort. At other time he would chaff her, "Do not buy such an expensive sari; Mr. Pathak might turn you out of the house." She would stare him silent.

In the company of Shanker, he grew out of the orthodox teachings imparted him by uncle. He began to regard the kitchen religion adhered to by his uncle as bunkum; only a handful men believed that touch polluted food; uncle counted in woeful minority. Casteism and untouchability took second place in uncle's articles of religious faith. Desh had got out of all such bigotry; he failed to see how one committed sin by drinking alcohol. Occasionally he did not mind swilling off a glass. He had covered a long way towards rationalism, since before he knew Shanker. With all his friendship with him, he knew little of Shanker's private life. He had made a success of life; he was suppose to earn about three thousand rupees a month. During war time it should have risen to four. Even if he parted with half of it to his brother, he could easily marry himself on the other half and beget children. He was a cultured, handsome man, with as fair a complexion as to pass off as a whiteman. Any girl would have felt proud in hooking him for a husband. It pained Desh that he should have elected to remain a bachelor. Could there be a woman hidden in his life ? Desh spent most of his time with him; but he had never seen him with anyone. Surely there seemed none. A secret could lie behind his solitary life; it seemed hard to Desh to penetrate it; one of these days he should directly question Shanker over it.

CHAPTER - III

Next morning after breakfast Desh decided to visit sister. It was a matter attended with ceremony; his attire needed press and selection; his shoes bright polish, and his face close shave. Nothing provoked a more ready rebuke from her than slovenliness. And he feared her tempers and bold eyes over-strained in anger.

Notwithstanding the rain the previous evening, the sky was clear. The sun had impregnated the air with a stimulant peculiar to mountains in summer. He would have liked to enjoy company of Shanker, rowing over the lake, but remembering that he was a proverbially late riser, Desh continued his journey to his sister's residence.

Seeing him horse *wallahs* pulled their horses out of the stand, shouting "*Sahib*, this one, very good-*wallah*; took this big show-thing; you always take my mare."

Desh responded with a benign smile to the horse *wallahs*. Before independence, like merchants on the Mall road, most of them solicited English customers, treating Indians coolly. A change in their behaviour was now apparent.

"Yes, you bring out your Mazid", called out Desh to a middle-aged man of dusky complexion, with a goatee and pointed nose. He wore a black velvet cap, gay quilted jacket, and a *dhoti* in red, green and blue check.

Desh struck uphill towards right. The groom from behind flicked the horse to a trot; by holding himself on its tail, he followed it steadily.

"Seen you after long *sahib*", began Majid.

"I was not here. How about your earnings these days."

Mazid wanted none to put him that question. It hurt him. The good old times would never, never return. Gram, on which the horse fed, cost four times as much as before the war. Wheat and rice showed similar rise; served as he had as groom to *sahiblogs*, he wore clean and nice clothes. They too were not cheaper than foodstuffs. But his income might drop. War prosperity had increased the number of horse-*wallahs*, while they had lost some valuable patrons; *sahibs* had left for England; *rajahs* were on way to extinction.

"British *Raj* was better," remarked Majid, "Things were cheap."

Inflation was its legacy; but who could explain all this to Majid.

"Am I wrong, *sahib?*. How can we know the right thing; we are uneducated men. Everybody is glad that we are free; but I do not see how."

Most of Majid's income was derived from British Officers and *zamindars*; when it was cut off, he turned mutely hostile to the change over.

"Soon you will earn more money than in the British days," said Desh in sympathy. "As our nation industrialises, more and more rich men will visit Nainital.

Desh got down from the horse in front of a buff-coloured, double-storeyed mansion, trim with flower garden. He had covered two miles ascend in under half an hour.

"Though your horse is old, it is still going strong", he paid Majid the hire.

"This is the famous horse of Nainital; *sahiblogs* always asked for it." Majid smiled. "I brought you so fast."

Desh handed him an extra rupee coin. Slipping the money in his pocket, Majid bowed with palm on his forehead.

Sister had come down to the porch. Seeing him her face lighted up; she caught hold of his right arm.

"Why did you not come yesterday, " she asked.

They walked in. A passage way through the middle of the ground storey communicated four rooms.

"Let us go up to the glass-room", he suggested.

A passage-way, corresponding to the lower one, communicated equal number of rooms in the second storey. At its head squatted, over the porch, a small square-room, glazed from three sides. It commanded a full view of mountains over the lake.

"You are looking weak." Sister took her seat.

"Natural from heat of plains; but why are you weather-beaten."

"Oh, what a severe winter we had this year. Many times I feel heat of plains is better than the long winter of Nainital .... you have not touched my feet".

Desh went through the reverential gesture in no time. Sister smiled archly, indicating that she had demanded it as no right of an elder from a younger, but merely out of fun. She was getting modern.

Sister was tall and well built, with ivory-white complexion. A brilliant, set on a pin, sparkled from the left side of her not a small, delicate nose. Her hair, turned at the end, was short and hung over her shoulders. In a muslin white-sari, she looked a swan queen.

Lighting a cigarette, Desh looked around. Ever since he remembered, an oleograph of king George V, framed in gilt-wood, hung over the doorway.

"This," he pointed out, "Has not been taken out. It is to show that your father-in-law had a title from the British *Raj*."

On independence, a year before, sister had removed all the oleographs representing the kings and queens of Britain from the walls of the house, excepting the one of king George V, which his brother-in-law wanted to be left out.

"Stand up on a chair and unhook it yourself from the wall."

"No," he replied, "This sin I will never do; let the great king rest there in peace."

The two kept chatting till the midday Desh ran over the catalogue of his doings at Allahabad. He saw only English pictures, a habit he had developed in the company of Shanker; he had visited the *Kumbha-Mela* many times in winter, though not out of faith that a dip in holy Ganges river remitted one's sins.

The dining-room, situated in the ground floor opened on to the front of the house. An old fashioned, massive round-table, surrounded by high backed chairs, occupied nearly half the space of the room. But from a copper bowl, placed at its centre, cascaded phloxes in crimson, red and white.

A fair-complexioned *chokra* brought in two electroplated *thalis,* loaded with food. He placed them before Desh and his sister. She considered the vegetables under fried and over salty; *dal* ill-cooked. She believed his brother-in-law in matters of food lacked discrimination. Answering her question in the morning, for he took meal before his departure to the law-courts, he had declared it nice. Compared to the food Desh had taken at home the previous night, the one before him tasted better, but insipid compared to Shanker's.

The boy-servant stood under the doorway leading out to the kitchen, ready to take orders from sister, which he executed swiftly and silently. Once or twice Desh remarked hint of a roguish smile crossing his eyes, as if he followed their conversation. But sister was mostly speaking in English; he could not be expected to know it.

" Your new *chokra* is smart."

"I do not like this smart *chokra*, Rama Nath; he is dissatisfied. He was in high school; but he had to give up studies for there was no money."

Having taken the meal, the two went upstairs to the sleeping-room that corresponded the dining-room in the ground floor. From an ornamented brass vase, resting on the table, behind the beds, peeped out roses fragrant and extraordinarily large. Above it, a life-size photograph of late Padma Dutt Pathak, framed in polished wood, embellished the wall. But sky-blue hangings with faded patterns of fruits and leaves, from washing of a generation, spoilt the decoration of the room.

"I thought of getting you some real pudding, cream and fruits, " she began, " But there is only Ram Nath, and it is so difficult to run the house when there is only one *chokra*. The pity is your brother-in-law does not see it."

"Your house is a bit far from the *bazaar*."

It lay not somewhat, but quite far. Sister wanted her house near the market. In following the British officers, her father-in-law had made a definite mistake in purchasing a housc situatcd near about the top of a mountain. It involved the British officers in no difficulties, when they lived in bungalows high up from congested localities and market places; for, with their enormous salaries, they could easily afford suite of menial servants and public schools for their children.

"Why should you not ask Pathak*ji* to increase the number of servants. He earns as much as British officers did."

"*Arree*, what do you talk. How many times I had to ask him before he agreed to keep a part-time gardener."

There arose a patter over the staircase; in a few moments Sanjeev and Miranda burst in.

"Why did you not come yesterday," piped Miranda.

Meeting him; faces of his nice and nephew brightened up with joy. Miranda seating herself across his knees, threw her left arm round his neck. "What have you brought for me ?

"Water melons."

He had told aunt at breakfast to send some of them to sister and Shanker.

"That is all."

"A dolly."

"What for me," struck in Sanjeev.

"An air gun".

"Uncle is making a fool of us," Miranda warned her brother. "He has brought us nothing from Allahabad."

Her guess was correct.

"No, I have," he protested, expecting to procure the toys from the local market.

Miranda slipped off his knees and seated herself beside Sanjeev, at the bottom of the bed. The brother and sister bore close resemblance to their father. Sanjeev was aged about twelve years and Miranda nine; but both were undersized. Miranda had inherited the white-complexion of her mother, but Sanjeev had been deprived of that too.

"Now," ordered sister, "You go to your room and put your books and copies in their places; have a wash and change; then come."

"Mummy, I am hungry," said Sanjeev.

"First go to your room" returned sister harshly.

Bother-in-law joined them in evening *chai;* Miranda and Sanjeev finished all the *pakoras* and pastries.

"Do not eat so much," warned brother-in-law, "Or you will not be able to take your dinner."

"After school," added Miranda," The climb makes both me and Sanjeev very hungry."

He gave his children a brilliant smile. From pressure of sister he took a bite at a pastry, then passed it to his son. His heart was not with the *chai*; he wanted to get off to his study. Bespected, with sharp nose and sallow skin, he stood below average height.

On suggestion from brother-in-law, the children, sister, and himself decided to enjoy an evening down in Flats. Sister took long time coming out of her dressing-room. She wore a chiffon-sari of pink colour with a golden border. Her tapering fingers were bedecked with diamond rings, and her ear lobes with diamond pins. A pearl string round her neck hightened the beauty of her skin.

The party started late; street lights were already up. There was scarcely time for strolling about Flats; sister wanted to meet Shanker.

He gave her a pale smile. "Is this time to come for boating ?"

"It takes ages", Desh slumped into a sofa, "For sister to get ready."

"No boating today in any case," Shanker fixed sister, and went on in a lower key. "Come; sit down here." He pointed her sofa-chair by him.

"Real enjoyment of boating," sister produced her radiant smile, "Lies in moonlight."

Never had the two indulged in night boating. Shanker had once or twice suggested it, but sister turned it down. A married woman was not free to behave as she liked, she had told him. Now a change seemed to have come over her; Shanker's gesture in wanting her to sit by him, betokened a degree of intimacy between them, never before noticed by Desh. It pleased him that in his absence of seven months from Nainital the two of them, whom he loved, had come closer to one another.

On sister's wanting him to buy them toffees, Desh along with Miranda and Sanjeev made for the *bazaar*, while sister remained behind with Shanker. The three of them spun about Flats; it was thronged with tourists to the hill-station; many in modish, western-suits, but instead of their collar-tie, the white-capped Congress-men that ran the government struck one with awe.

Rejoining sister and Shanker, Desh noticed that both of them sat in a pensive mood with their features disintegrated.

Sister had invited her classmate, Champs to *chai* on coming Sunday. She expected Shanker and him at her house by five in the evening that day.

"I am sorry," stammered Shanker, "I am busy that day; you better leave me out."

"No, you have to come: Sanjeev's father will not be at home then."

Shanker never called on sister, or accepted her invitation. He and brother-in-law, though classmates, never stood on cordial terms to one another. The later had distinguished himself as one of the bright students of the class, while the former among truants who were only interested in games and gossip. Himself a bookworm, brother-in-law had conceived an innate dislike for Shanker, a fine hockey player who led the school from victory to victory in local tournaments.

"What good have games brought to those players, reading with me in the school and college," said brother-in-law to Desh.

"But look at Shanker," He replied, "How successful he is in business."

"A mere chance; take it away; Shanker becomes a street-boy."

The distance between a good student and good hockey player had widened with years. At first knowing of the growing intimacy of Desh with Shanker, brother-in-law manifested surprise. Later he disapproved of it in a mild way; the interests of a student and a shopkeeper lay wide apart. Desh need to put all his energies to his studies then frittering them away in passing friendship. He gave no reply, for Desh avoided entangling himself in arguments. Seeing his efforts to correct him coming to naught, brother-in-law gave up talking on the matter; rather his attitude towards Shanker underwent a change. When sister and himself returned home from an evening walk, or a round of boating, he always inquired whether the two had enjoyed Shanker's company or no.

"I have become like the one in that poem, we read in school, Stay At Home," he would remark. "After courts, all my time is taken up in preparing cases; Sunday I am free, but you never take me with you."

"We would be only too glad, if you accompanied us."

The stipulated Sunday came and passed away; several others went by, but brother-in-law never offered to go out with them.

"I suspect," said Desh to sister "Shanker is in the way."

"Your brother-in-law and I have rarely gone out together," sister confided him. "So I do not agree with you; still to clear your suspicion you ask him straight away."

Desh hesitated; looked out for an opportunity, and when it came, his courage failed him.

One evening the two went out for a walk across a road that passed at stone's throw from sister's house. As decided beforehand, Shanker had climbed up on a horse to meet them.

When the two came back, inquired brother-in-law, "Where did you go for a walk ?"

"Upper Cheena Mall."

"Then, Shanker should not be with you."

"No, he was with us."

"Why should he not come here, to our house I mean."

"You never called him."

"If that is so, ask him over to *chai* this Sunday."

When Desh conveyed him the invitation of brother-in-law, Shanker screwed his eyes in amazement.

"I should be glad to meet," he smiled, curling up his upper lip, "Harikant, your sister's husband."

Sister received Shanker near the gate of her mansion. It was the time of June; her garden was running riot in sunflowers, daisies, and phloxes. He consumed full half an hour nosing from flower-bed to flower-bed, hedge to hedge. Sometimes he halted before a rose, fondled it with his fingers, sniffed at it.

"Lucky flower" remarked Shanker, "It has somebody to look after it."

"Lucky because it has met an admirer in you," she murmured, plucking it and handing it him. "Now you have to look after it."

He grinned as he inserted it in the bottom-hole of his lapel. "Oh, by plucking it, you have taken its very life."

"I am a great killer."

The two exchanged a significant smile.

When brother-in-law joined the party *chai* had already been served.

"Sorry for the delay." He greeted Shanker with a prim smile, " I am overworked these days; I am appearing in a sensational murder case."

"In that way my profession is better; I have time to go about and enjoy myself."

"But there is difference between yours and mine."

With *chai* a number of eatables sweet and salty had been provided by sister, though nobody paid attention to them; not even children. The chief host neither looked at any eatable himself, nor cared to request his guest to partake of them.

Shanker started talking with a zeal on coming independence, a topic hot all over the country. Sister and himself helped him continue it, while brother-in-law listened him with expression in his eyes, "If British went, how about my title and position!"

"Do come again", he said.

"It is now your turn to come to my house for tea."

"Whenever I am free I shall let you know through Desh."

But brother-in-law never notified him, when he would accept his invitation, even though Shanker repeated it through Desh. Moreover the welcome his host had given him signified frigidity, his manner condensation. As a result Shanker never again saw sister at her residence, when brother-in-law was present there.

CHAPTER - IV

On Sunday evening sister waited for her guests in her drawing-room, furnished with heavy, nineteenth century furniture.

"Your room is quite lighted," remarked Shanker, seating himself in one of the lounges, and taking stock of the glass-paned windows and furniture.

"This whole house is very lighted and airy," concurred sister.

"Have you not seen the upper storey?", chimed in Desh, "The glass-room is the most lighted one of the whole house."

"I am coming here a long time after; how do you think, I have seen the upper storey of a house whose inmate's upper storey is not sound."

Catching the joke sister grinned. Shanker twitched up one side of his upper lip into a crocked, playful smile.

Champa was not forthcoming; sister, to spin out time, showed Shanker round her house; her bed, *puja* and dressing-room, in the upper storey. He was attracted by the smart embroidery worked by sister on table and bed covers.

"Wish this house belonged to me," remarked Shanker, "I would have made it look heaven."

Being late Champa came in running; she greeted everybody with a luscious smile.

"Oho, is it you Desh; you have grown quite a man," she exclaimed.

"That is his right," flung out Shanker. "If you mean by grown up, Desh has grown to be a handsome man whom you would like to marry, you are correct."

Champa flushed through her dark complexion. She was much the same slim figure, Desh had seen ten years before. Her features were moulded in the oriental cast, and her hair, done in the oriental style, was parted down the middle of her head, and coiled into a bun, over the nape of her neck. She was draped in maroon-coloured sari of cheap silk.

Shanker was first to help himself with sandwiches; all fell to helping themselves with whatever they wanted. The convivial atmosphere, the clinking and jingling of plates and spoons, and the hearty way they ate the good things as intimate friends, soon rubbed the varnish of shyness off Champa. She stepped out in her true self of a school girl, enjoying without hitch, salty and sweet dainties. She smiled affectedly before she talked; she described in details of her friendship with sister. In school where one was seen, the other could be surely found out. She sighed recalling the old times, when both dressed alike and even saw dreams alike.

Having passed the high school examination, she started on the career of a school mistress, while Chandra persecuted her studies at Lucknow. During those years, whenever they met or corresponded, they pledged themselves to spinterhood. Chandra as well decided to enter her profession after her graduation; but instead, *Bhagwan* alone knew what came on her, she gave her hand in marriage. The treachery of her friend hurt her so much so that she discontinued visiting her some years. However, as she grew old, Champa realised that her behaviour was silly; her understanding of life immature: If Chandra had guided herself by the wisdom of her father, she was right.

"I wish, I had taken your advice then," sister inhaled an audible breath.

"This is the result of one being married, the other not," cut in Shanker. "Get married, you will start thinking like Chandra."

Sister would be on the look out for an eligible bachelor for her. Shanker teased Champa with names of few widowers.

"We have finished *chai* Desh, let us go out," Champa spoke in a huff.

He followed her out into the garden, while sister and Shanker remained in the dining-room.

"I have been transferred back to Nainital after so many years; look, how Shanker talks."

"*Arree*, you should not mind him, he likes making fun."

The two knocked about over the gravel. The garden had been laid out with pains. Level land was scare, but for a rectangular piece on the front of the mansion. It was symmetrically cut into geometrical flower beds, edged with greynight stones. Desh led her through them, teaching her names of various flowering-plants. She listened him abstractedly; she seemed least interested in gardening.

Abruptly she inquired, "What are you doing these days ?"

"I shall be taking advice from brother-in-law about my career."

Shanker and sister issued out of the porch. He noticed that the two had preoccupied air; their faces were strained.

"I have not seen your children." Champa roved her eyes around.

"They have gone out."

On their way down to Flats, Champa ignored Shanker; she made conversation only with him. She seemed to have taken to him; she wanted to know how he passed his time; what pictures interested him; English or Indian. On Shanker's parting with them in front of his Empire Store, Desh made appointment with Champa to see picture with her on coming Sunday evening, at Ashok Cinema, which stood over against Flats.

That evening his aunt appeared in good humour; her face was wreathed in smiles. She had received a letter from her only daughter that she was expectant. She was the age of his sister and was married for about the same number of years as her; but she had remained barren, though she had taken various kinds of treatments to cure herself of her sterility. Lately a surgeon in Indore, where her husband served as a petty officer in the railways, had operated on her with the result that, after full sixteen years of marriage, she was looking forward to be blessed with a baby.

"I do not believe in allopathy," commented uncle, over the meal, "The more I suffer from asthma, the more I get convinced I am right; but this surgery is a wonderful thing. Who believed Chitra could ever bear a child!"

That evening aunt had cooked rice and milk pudding, for which uncle had been demanding in vain. She had fried *puris* and cooked costly vegetables of the season. This was a rare occasion when aunt, blinking at expenditure, feasted them heartily.

She knotted in a piece of cloth handful of rice, black-*dal*, with coins of rupee one and a quarter. The proceeding emphasised her vow to perform *puja* of God Satyanarain on her daughter's coming into motherhood.

"Whether it is son or daughter, I will do it," she opened her arms.

"No," remonstrated uncle, "It is never done when a daughter is born."

"You spoil everything by your ill omens. You shut up."

Uncle bowed his head in silence, bending his eyes on Desh. When aunt started nagging at him, to reduce the ordeal to the minimum, he would keep his mouth closed.

x x x

Since meeting Champa, Desh felt an ache in his heart that bordered on tenderness; he wanted to see her. For the first time in his life, he had felt for a woman that way.

On Sunday the pictures, he had decided to see with Champa, was full twenty minutes in progress before she made her appearance.

"Sorry," she beamed at him. "Some domestic matter delayed me."

"What do you say," he asked, "Seeing second show of an English."

"I do not like it."

"Let us then have a walk on Thande Road."

It was cheerless, without a single shop or bungalow on it, and the mountain slope rising sheer over it; it joined Mallital with Tallital through the other side of the lake, athwart the Mall. But for the equestrians, it was little used. As the two crossed Flats, Champa bowed her head towards the spires of Goddess Nanda group of temples, crowding at the edge of the lake, where Thande road started.

"*Arree*, you are queer," he looked sideways at her, "Bowing from the open."

"Today is a Saturday, the day of the *Devi*; I am her devotee. I must bow to her from where ever I am."

Limping a few hundred yards, the two came on a small summer-house, painted green, on the side of the road over the lake.

"This reminds me of old days," she sighed.

They seated themselves on one of the hard benches placed there, and watched the boats gliding over the lake. From Flats wafted in enchanting music of a band, playing a popular film tune.

"If somebody saw me sitting with you now," she whispered, "What would he say? But I do not care."

He stole a glance at her. She was wearing an old fashioned, olive-green sari. He noticed that her chest was flat. He felt awkward sitting by a woman, years elder to him. He wanted to say something pertinent by way of making conversation; but his youthful shyness locked his lips.

"Can you sing?" he began at last, "I mean the song the band is playing."

"Yes I can, but not here; you come to my home. I shall sing you one or two."

"All right expect me on Sunday."

That was along way off. She fixed Tuesday evening. Her life was hard; his visit would mean a diversion for her. She was first to rise in the house and last to retire to bed. She conducted two tuitions in the morning; attended the school during the day; coached her youngest brother at night. For fifteen years day in and day out, she had been scraping along in drudgery and boredom. She was sick to death of her life. Beside her how lordly Chandra lived; owning a mansion and domestics. Her husband earned thousands a month, besides inheriting lakhs of rupees. God had also blessed her with a son and a daughter, and, above all, a peerless beauty. What more need a woman wish. It was not with a feeling of jealousy that she was recounting the happy lot her friend, but out of a sense of her own misery, Chandra was her true friend, and she could never harbour any evil thoughts for her.

"You know two flowers bloom together but destinies are different .... It is getting dark, let us go home."

She slipped her hand into his.

x x x

Few days later, as a consequence of a massage from sister, to see her at Mallital, the top of the lake, in the evening, Desh reached there much before the appointed time to pick Shanker up as well from his rooms. In Flats a hockey match was thrilling spectators, crowded along the boundary lines and semi-circular cement tiers, over the playing ground. The ball moved fast between the territories of contending teams, wearing red and blue shirts. The sorties of one towards the goal-mouth of the other and vice versa, in a sea-saw, oscillated the sympathies of the spectators. Shanker and himself standing on the top of the tiers, watched the game for the best part of an hour, but no team was able to net a goal. Shanker now and again clapped his hands when a player, by virtue of his stick-work, advanced the ball far.

On receiving a slap at his back, Desh turned round. "*Arree*, it is you Miranda."

"I have been looking out for you twenty minutes."

At Flats sister was waiting for them near the New Capital Cinema house, situated midway between the Thandi and Mall roads, over the edge of the lake. For having strayed away from the place of meeting, Desh shook from fear.

"Sorry for the delay," he apologised.

"What man you are ! keeping me here so long." Sister's countenance was inflamed. "We cannot see pictures now."

"Let us see the hockey match," interrupted Shanker, in a playfully modulated voice." It shall entertain you no less."

"*Aye*, let us go home; Sanjeev, Miranda, come."

She turned a deaf ear to him, and repaired for the palanquin-stand. Even as he followed her, Desh regretted being the cause of dampening the proceedings of a gay evening. There was no doing anything with her, once her temper was frayed.

He thanked Shanker in his heart, when lurching forward, he grabbed sister by the shoulder, and rolled her over. "If I have hurt you, I am sorry," he muttered through his most disarming smile. "Come; come now."

As she returned his smile, a twinkle came into her eyes. Desh was surprised at the smoothness with which Shanker had got round her.

Dev Rama served tea in Shanker's drawing-room. Noises from over the playing ground seeped in through the windows. Shanker sipped tea mechanically; his attention had been drawn to the hockey match that could be viewed standing from his room. It was evident that he was not himself. It passed sister that a commonplace hockey match should have disturbed Shanker. She gave importance to cricket.

Whenever anyone in his presence spoke flippantly of hockey, whose ungovernable passion had consumed him in his younger days, Shanker's face turned all black. From his sleeping room he brought out a number of gold and silver medals, he had won in tournaments. As a centre-forward, he had the capacity to dodge the ball through to the goal.

He was amazed that the medals, awarded in a game sister thought as vulgar, should have impressed her. She read eagerly the inscriptions on them; held all of them in her palm to guess their weight.

"For your marriage you need not buy gold." she observed facetiously. "You have just to melt these down to make ornaments."

"*Hun*, melt; not until a wife like you comes in and puts them on fire."

"Take care then, I might not do it one day."

"No, I will not allow you to take leave of your senses."

Desh went out with Miranda and Sanjeev, to buy them a doll and an air-gun. He looked in shop after shop until he singled out the most odd doll available in the city. It was an old man with white beard, bulbous nose and rosy skin, donning a bright red tunic-coat and trousers, braided in gold thread.

The expedition took about an hour. He had kept sister waiting a long time. She and Shanker were seated almost touching one another on a sofa. No sooner had the two noticed Desh and the children in the room, they separated themselves, and sister choked down her throat the words on her lips. She instantly hardened her face, and reproved Desh for the delay in his returning. It was necessary for him to accompany her to her home so that Miranda's father would know that he was responsible for her late coming.

Brother-in-law had settled down to the meal. He had not been put out by their delay; rather for having started eating, he begged to be pardoned. The world might stand on end, but his meal hour would never alter from nine both in the morning and evening. The only days round the year, he made a departure from his timings were when he performed the death-anniversary ceremony of his parents and kept fast on *Sivaratri*.

Brother-in-law turned to his children. "What did you do in Flats ?"

Sanjeev passed his hand over the barrel of his air-gun. Miranda tore off the packing paper revealing her doll; on seeing it brother-in-law coughed with merriment.

He asked, "You met Shanker Lal ?"

"At the hockey match" replied Desh.

"Aha, he has remained a school boy."

Sister left them for the kitchen. The children joined their father at the table. Their nerves were fluttered by the gifts; Miranda wanted to marry her doll. Among the school girls, Shanti possessed a unique one; but she had turned down all proposals of marriage for it, regarding them as beneath her doll. If uncle Shanker would speak to her, she being his niece, the union between her doll and that of Shanti's could be brought about.

Brother-in-law took a look at Desh. "You should not have bought such costly gun and doll."

But in his heart he shared the delight of his children. He pulled up his brow, casting glances with appreciation on the two playthings which recalled an incident of his childhood. Once he found a doll abandoned on the road-side, he brought it home and showed it his father, who, to his dismay, charged him for stealing, twirling his ear.

"Children," he said absently, "Are enjoying lots of freedom now than our day; women shall get it too when Hindu Code Bill is passed."

Brother-in-law had overstayed at the table in a post dinner chat; he regretted having wasted his time fixed for the disposal of everyday correspondence, conning newspaper.

"I am glad you came up to Hamilton house." echoed sister gratefully, "And waited to give me company for meal. How is food, not too bad."

When she came to the house, after marriage, she found her husband and father-in-law taking meals, after the orthodox Hindu style, at the kitchen *chulah*. She observed a sort of *purdah* from her father-in-law and took her food all by herself. In the company of her father, she took meal at the table without ever any idea that eating out of the kitchen rectangle caused pollution of food. Nor had she lived in *purdah*, mixed as she had freely with male sex. But in marriage she unlearnt all that she had learnt before. Eating food off the plate, with left over food by her husband, gave her the creeps. The loneliness of the chilly, drab, kitchen stirred in her strange feelings. She gradually steeled herself so much so that, when after the death of her father-in-law, her husband shifted from kitchen to table, she continued the old practice of eating separately.

The chime of the clock striking ten, gave Desh start, "Even if I run, I do not reach home before eleven." He sprang on his feet.

He tore down the Mall, jumped on a rickshaw and wheeled off. He entered his room burglariously without his uncle getting the wiser; but he might barge into the room any moment, and start sermon on his late coming.

Desh took out the matchbox from behind the two large size photographs of sister and Shanker, flanking the oleograph of Siva, placed on the mantelpiece, and lighted his cigarette. Both had been taken on her instant in a local studio in the city. Even brother-in-law, who had long accepted sister's friendship with Shanker, gave a gasp of horrified amazement at her bringing in the photograph of Shanker amidst other members of the family, to her living-room and installing it high over the mahogany cabinet. "If you do not object to our friendship with Shanker, why should you to his photograph being placed along ours," retorted sister. That settled brother-in-law, though he answered, "But what would people think of it." "What people come to my room? ended sister.

Desh had been conscious of a spice of abnormality in the friendship of sister with Shanker. There was no mistaking it, the way they bartered pleasantries, rejoiced in the sunshine of each others presence. But he had never looked upon their friendship with any degree of concern; sister never met Shanker without him; and surely in their bearing to each other there never dropped slightest hint that could arouse his suspicious. But that evening, for the first time, he had caught them in a compromising position. Both were sitting far too close in the sofa; their movement apart, not until Desh and the children had come on them, suggested their being absorbed with some matter urgent to them. He recalled how on rejoining the two, after a break, he had often notice their faces drawn and pinched. He was amazed at his own slowness in discovering the clandestine love of sister with Shanker. He was shocked that the object of her affection could be someone other than her husband. However, Desh held no oriental views on matrimony. He regarded it as an aberration of his sister, an innocent flirtation, to which either partner in marriage was exposed to in life. After all Shanker's love brought her some sort of happiness, when, even after sixteen years of marriage, she and her husband had not taken to sitting down together to meals. She and Shanker had presumed that he had spied their love, and, out of shyness, had never mentioned of it. But he would affect complete ignorance, expecting them reveal themselves.

Having finished his morning wash, Desh went to the room of his uncle. He had already performed his *puja* and having finished the recitation of a chapter from the Geeta he was waiting for his milk. He looked glum and withdrawn.

"I passed a worried night," he began, "I would have knocked on your door, but I got a few spasms, and your aunt would not allow me go to see you."

x x x

On Tuesday evening Desh walked to Mallital. The third lane, parallel to Bara-*bazaar*, was composed of dismal looking houses with jutting storeys, weather-beaten fronts which plunged him into disgust. He trudged the lane up and down, but he failed to recognise the shop of the *hakim* over which Champa lived. Towards its top, a massively built, bald-headed goldsmith, working at a bangle in his shop, pointed him the first shabby house in the lane from the bottom. Though he had seen sign-board of a *hakim* over a shop there, but he had omitted the possibility of Champa's living there.

A stripling youth wearing shirt and trousers of inferior material, came out of the house. He greeted Desh with humility. The youth conducted him up a narrow, dingy stairway; small rooms opening on it showed through gaping doors the mess inside them. Desh had to suppress a desire to flee.

Champa was evaluating examination copy-books in her attic, in the fourth storey. Seeing him her face lighted up.

"You came late," she said with constrain. She had not expected him to keep his promise; an engaging smile parted her lips.

The room in which he sat was low pitched under a slanting roof; but it was well lighted with windows in front that looked down upon the lake. It was the only room in the whole house that was well furnished and trim. Coloured prints of *Siva* and Goddess hanging on the walls chased away the malaise that had seized him on entering the miserable house, situated in the purlieu of the city.

In the setting of a scarlet-sari and heavy make up, Champa looked pretty. The smile with which she had greeted him, never vanished from her lips. "Did you like my room ?"

The naive question unembarrassed him.

Every piece of furniture, he saw in the room, was purchased by her. She wanted to live as well as her means permitted; but with her brothers and sisters to support, nothing was left to her to improve her own circumstances. She had worked her way from a junior to a senior school mistress by raising her educational qualifications.

Intervention of, the lad, who brought in *chai* and refreshments in a rude china set, turned her attention from herself to them. She had spent several rupees on his entertainment. He counted no less than six or seven varieties of sweet and salty eatables. Champa forced him taste of every thing she had got served. His tongue though cloyed as never before, he felt sorry that his visit should have taxed her little income.

"Oho, you having a big feast," a grey haired man, round of should and high cheek bones, entered the room. Desh readily recognised him as lawyer Sunder; father of Champa, and exchanged a greeting with him. His shoe was vamped over the little finger, and his black, frayed tie emphasised the ill cutting of his crumpled, woollen coat and trousers. "I am meeting you after several years. You resemble your father, Kedar Dutt."

"I think, you are his age."

"I should be six or seven years elder to him. Good men like him are summoned quick, whereas sinful like me live on." He pointed his index finger heavenwards.

"*Accha*, daughter, prepare me some hot tea." He slid his eyes over the table, heaped with refreshments.

He gulped down tea in prodigious mouthfuls, smacking his lips on it. Sweets melted away in his mouth as ice on fire. He looked droll and pitiable, gorging himself in the manner of a hungry man. Desh noticed a scowl gathering over the brow of Champa.

Sunder gave a grunt of animal satisfaction, and wiped his mouth on the palm of his hand.

She asked, "How was work at courts today ?"

"Very nice; I am holding brief of an important case," declared Sunder. "The way I cross-examined the witness, judge remained starting at me."

"You only cross-examined or got your fee too."

"Why not; I am expecting five hundred rupees from his case." Sunder steamed out of the room.

"Your father seems an able lawyer," remarked Desh, when he was sure Sunder was out of earshot.

"This is our misfortune; were he a good lawyer, my life would have been different."

He looked at Champa with a blank face.

"You are too young to understand me. Now what do you say to our going for a stroll?"

"I do not mind."

Champa refused to go further than the summer-house, in the Thandi-road. The evening walk was an excuse to get Desh alone to herself. She began to hum the song, the tune of which the band was playing over there, at Flats.

"You did not sing me one in your house, you had promised to do."

"That was a trick for calling you to my house."

"If that is so, I will never repeat my visit."

His cold-heartedness reduced Champa to tears. He was cruel; he grudged her even the morsel of happiness that his company brought her. In the short time she had met him, how much he had come to mean to her; she had fondly believed that he thought of her as much; though she knew well enough that he looked down upon her, a poor school mistress as she was.

"No, Champa, you are wrongly accusing me." He cupped his hands under his cheeks, flabbergasted at her suddenness in besieging him. "I was just joking; I shall visit your house, but do not spend so much on tea."

To reassure her, he put his arm on her shoulder. She grasped at his left hand and drew it to her lap, looking with overt, lifted eyes at him.

He was annoyed with himself for having visited Champa. The squalor of the lane and the rooms in her house made him retech. He was surprised that her circumstances were humble; her father's poor income had thrown the burden of the family on her shoulders. However, two of her brothers were on their way to finding employment; she was in a position to get herself married. Probably she had designs on him. She was older to him by eleven or twelve years; he would be called a fool, an owl, if he took her as wife. At the most he could think of a liaison with her; but he could not bring himself to like her, and the only course open for him was to cut her.

To indicate her his mind, he went to her place on Saturday evening. His nose wrinkled up as he walked down the lane. Champa looked up at him over the film magazine in her hands, but, without condescending ghost of a smile on him in greeting, she resumed reading it.

"Are you angry with me ?"

On his repeating his question, she flung the magazine aside, clenched her fists and drew herself bolt upright. "Why did you not come for so many days ? I waited every evening."

For a few moments he was at the end of his wits to invent an excuse.

"Uncle's conditions had become serious; you know he has asthma."

He marvelled that Champa instantly accepted it. The old, sunny smile, he was familiar with, slid across her lips.

"Naughty boy," she cooed.

On this occasion too, *chai* in his welcome was as grand as before. She had forgotten his advise on frugality in his entertainment, and there was no point in reminding her of it. He should stop calling on her, and save not only her wasteful expenditure but also himself from her.

Sunder timed his entry to the room with *chai*. At his breaking in upon them, a friction of dislike went over the face of Champa. His manner of drinking *chai*, and eating delicacies in no way changed from the previous turn. The voracity he displayed was amusing.

He finished tea much before Sunder, and wanted to light a cigarette; but he hesitated in front of an elderly man. He was glad, when lighting his own, Sunder offered him one.

"Champa was telling me that you are a heavy smoker; your father too was like you."

"I am not half as much as he was."

Sunder had never seen a greater chain smoker than his father. He had come across in his life scores of British Officers but none could beat him in smoking. His bills on liquor, wines and parties were enormous. He was a *pukka sahib*; even British judges acknowledged his calibre. His bane was his sneaking sympathy for Congress-*wallah*, whom he secretly gave legal advice and monetary help. The British government, which had intelligence of his being behind the scene of subversive activities in Nainital, denied him title. During that time Sunder was elected vice-chairman of the municipal board, and the title of *Rai Sahib* conferred on him.

"I never knew so much about you," retorted Desh.

"Surprising ! Those days wherever I went, people in awe left way for me."

"My uncle was telling me, a municipal commissioner was then a big man."

"I am glad," chuckled Sunder, "You know this; the local bodies in British days were places of great honour, but now I am sorry to see the very ones as seats of *thugs*, most of whom are congress-*wallah*."

Desh was taken a back. He had heard after independence people criticising members of congress-party. But never had anyone applied in his hearing such opprobrious words. He felt himself provoked to rebut Sunder; but from his childhood he had learnt, under the tirade of aunt, to postpone his anger to his tolerance. He let Sunder give full rein to his tongue.

"In my day, a municipal commissioner was not the little thing as he is getting after independence." There was an edge in his voice. "You know why the Congress government had finished titles ?"

But without waiting for reply from Desh, he continued, "Congress-*wailah* envied those who head titles; so when they have come to power, they finished them. I remember how water would come to the mouth of those who have now become ministers, when municipal Commissioners were invited to at home by the British governor."

The fellow was a jealous crank. Champa threw a quick look at him, showing Desh her boredom at her father's prattling, of which she was well aware.

"*Accha*, father," her voice was business like, "How about the case you were arguing in the courts ?"

"Very well."

"Then when shall you buy me Banarsi-silk sari."

"Why not; why not. Are you not going out for a walk ?" The suggestion came as a much awaited relief.

Champa and himself bustled out of the room, striking towards the Thandi road. He liked airing and bypassed the summer-house.

"I cannot go down to Tallital, the end of the lake," she declared, "I am feeling tired."

"You can do up to the temple of Goddess of the Rock."

"You seem to be very religious."

Beyond halfway to Tallital, over-handing the wall abutting the road, lay a huge rock, pigmented saffron. The two took out their footgear on the stairs reaching it. A somewhat grotesque, anthropoid form, naturally carved on the rock, and embellished with large, silver eyes, represented the Goddess. Entering the open air temple, Champa pushed ringing the bells, which were suspended from a bar overhead; then tossing a coin on to the shrine, engraved with words *Rama Sita* and fragments of prayers in *Sanskrit*, she got ready to pray. Joining the palms of her hands, under closed eyes, she bowed to the Goddess. For invoking her blessings, she rubbed out from the Rock, saffron paint on the tip of her finger, and made a round mark on his forehead, another on her own. From the bank of flowers at the shrine, offered by previous devotees, she picked up a rose, and shredding it into petals, put them over the crown of his and her head.

"How I wish, I had brought oil with me," she regretted, "And lighted to the Goddess my own earthen lamp."

Two young women going towards the temple met Champa and himself. Their *saris*, draped in the old style, went over their hair. One frail with white-skin, and suggestion of a hook nose, accosted Champa. The other who was somewhat plump with a serene, round face, listened to the conversation without interest. His attention was arrested by her finely chiselled forearms; he wanted to feel them.

One of the two sisters lived in Champa's lane. She might noise about that she had seen Champa in the company of Desh; and her neighbours, quick at scandal mongering, would only seize at the material provided by her.

"How do they know who I am?"

"Everybody knows you are son of the famous lawyer, Kedar Dutt, who has left you lot of money."

He hung his head in surprise.

"They talked such nonsense about your visit to my house; I wonder how my neighbours are so petty minded."

"You should not care."

"I do not," her voice rang hard, "I am educated and earn my living; I naturally have the liberty of going here and there. How can I behave like women living in *purdah*."

Through myriad summer tourists lounging in the phosphorescent light in the Flats, Champa and himself threaded their way in silence. He felt the crowds were looking at him with scorn, accompanied as he was with a woman years older than him. Communicating point-blank his thoughts now would hurt her;

before he parted with her, he made another appointment to see her.

Desh liked Champa's meretricious smile and the deep colours she wore to match her complexion. It was difficult to break from her without inflicting her pain. He wanted the advice of Shanker; he had never kept any secret from him; but discussing Champa with him was an audacious task. He might let the secret slip to sister, and she is turn to uncle. He would look pretty ridiculous; they would jeer at him as to what he saw in a dark, flat chested woman, fit to be his elder sister.

He purchased an expensive chiffon *sari*, in a shade of red, before he waited at Capital Cinema, some days later, to meet Champa. He was right in time, but she was no where to be seen. He turned into the Rink theatre, a dreary hall, festooned with multi coloured paper-chains, which was resounding with the din of gliding skates. He was taken aback to find Champa among spectators silted along two walls. Though he never felt comfortable to his horsy sport, he regarded her enthusiasm to it as commendable.

"I never knew you like games."

"I was always interested in them from childhood; my teaching job has kept it up."

It was an hour before the sun set; instead of their accustomed walk to Thandi road, Champa and himself hired a boat, from among many moored on the head of the lake. Champa took a seat at the bow; himself facing her, in the middle; he pulled the oars as she directed him. The mountains over them exaggerated their exclusiveness from the world of land; a tremor of fear mingled with exaltation ran through the two hearts.

"I am in a boat after many years; I feel overjoyed." She looked into his eyes.

As the frail craft skipped over the water surface, illuminated by the slanting rays of the sun, he realised of his mistake in fixing the tryst under a highly romantic atmosphere.

She gave a sweeping glance to the boats floating over the lake. "These men and women have come out to feel happy."

"I do not see how rowing makes one happy; you can say it gives pleasure."

"If you has worked in a school for sixteen years, you would have understood me."

"You do not like your job ?"

"When I started I loved it, but soon I knew service would not take me far."

Before meeting Champa, Desh had resolved to tell her his decision. But the drift of the talk had gone the other way about. He had completed a full round of the lake, rowing an hour, still unable to find a suitable opening to broach the delicate subject. To mitigate its unpleasantness, he thought it tactful to tear open the wrapper enclosing the sari that he had brought with him.

She was struck dumb. She felt its tissues, gazed the colour and the golden boarder embossed in Ajanta design. "It is a lovely *sari*; must be costing no less than a hundred and fifty rupees." She pressed it to her bosom.

"I am glad you like it."

"I never knew you care so much for me; I would look a girl of sixteen in this."

He pulled fast the boat to the landing stage, exasperated at himself for proceeding on a wrong tack. Better he had downright told her that she was too old for him. He jumped off the boat.

"When shall you meet me again?" she shouted from behind.

Getting no reply, she followed him. The melody of the band, being played from inside Flats summer-house, emotionalised him. Among the crowds a fair, plump lady, reminded him of the one he had seen near the temple of Goddess of Rock.

Over his shoulder, he asked Champa. "Who were the two sisters we saw on Saturday ?"

"What makes you think of them."

"I want to know by the way."

"They were daughters of Jaga Sah. But when shall you meet me."

"Not in near future," he waved his hand as he scurried off.

So the sisters were daughters of the trader, Desh knew right from childhood, who was proprietor of a large grain shop in Bara-*bazaar*. He owed his success to his fair prices and unadulterated foodstuffs; above all to his capacity to grovel before everyone who was rigged up in coat, trousers, and tie.

In Hamilton house he had gained admittance for over a generation. An intimacy subsisted between him and bother-in-law, though the latter was too cautions to allow any shade of comradeship to tinge it; still it was intimacy as between a master and his footman. Joga Sah wanted nothing beyond free access to an eminent lawyer, who turned to him for supplying him fresh foodstuffs.

That of all the men he should have liked the daughter of a beslavering shopkeeper of flour and rice, living in the downtown, in which did Champa, galled him. None the less he wanted to pass his hand over the arms of his daughter. He should have felt mighty thankful to anyone who gave him her name. Shanker belonged to her caste. Desh could glean some information about her from him so that he could hit upon a plan to meeting her.

CHAPTER - V

Shanker was bent on a English novel in his living-room. Sister and himself had contracted the habit of reading fiction from him, but Shanker finished several before they did one.

"Whenever I come", he complained, "I see you reading."

"Be seated sir," Shanker glanced him with comic expression in his eyes, "I am not so fortunate as to have companions to go about with me; I stay at home and read."

Was he hinting at his recent flirtation. Strange that the news should have already percolated as far as him. Someone had informed on Desh; Champa had rightly observed that nothing, which could serve their purpose, escaped the notice of scandal - mongers in her lane.

"Any news from sister," Desh tried to gloss over the innuendo, "I could not see her."

He felt himself too shy to put questions on Joga Sah.

"Some days ago I had a ring from Miranda; she was referring to some doll marriage; I could not understand her; she cut off the phone"

"Miranda has proposed", he explained, "Marriage of her doll with that of Shanti's."

Shanker would persuade his niece. It would be a fun watching the ceremony uniting the two dolls. He would commission priests to perform it; after the wedding a dinner would be arranged for discharging many a social obligation of his. Shanker's sister-in-law, who was bedridden for two years, would enjoy herself gossiping with women invited on the occasion and offering them sweets. For supplying them from a good confectioner in Bara-*bazaar*, he would speak over to Joga Sah.

"You mean the one who has a grain shop there," plumped out Desh.

"Yes, the very; he is cousin of my sister-in-law."

That night when he went to his sleeping-room, Desh stood in supplication before the oleograph of *Siva*; on the mantelpiece, that Shanti accept the proposal of Miranda. The plump sister might be among the ladies invited to the wedding of dolls.

Next day when he met him, Shanker told him that his niece had tentatively accepted the proposal. Groom-doll-*wallah* would provide the bride-doll complete outfit of trousseau and set of ornaments. It would be transferred to their house, but Shanti would exercise full authority over it; and if mishandled, she would, after pronouncing the marriage dissolved, resume its possession.

"Does your niece know the meaning of what she says ?"

"Yes, by all means; she is old enough to understand the meaning of marriage and divorce."

"O I see; that is why Shanti's conditions are so hard; but when is the wedding expected?"

"After four days. The wedding would take place, instead of night, four in the evening. There would be tea than dinner, otherwise the girl friends of Shanti would get too late to return to their homes."

Shanker's face was alight when Desh left.

x x x

Next day when Desh gave Miranda the information that the wedding of her doll would come off in three days, brother-in-law displayed one of his rare smiles of amusement. He remarked that once the ruling-chiefs and feudal lords were known to have wasted money on such pastime, but among the middle classes they engaged the attention of children. The disapproval coming from one who seldom voiced his opinions, upset Desh. But it was too late to cancel the wedding in which he expected to see daughters of Joga Sah.

His sister took a keen delight. To save him the expenses, she summoned a *darzi*, a small old man, and instructed him cut the skirt and head-cloth of the bride-doll from her old, embossed, Banarasi, silk-sari. To a gold-smith, who to his surprise was the massively built fellow in Champa's lane, sister gave orders to fashion set of ornaments for nose, neck, and wrists, from her thick, ancient silver-wristlets.

Two men remained indifferent to the wedding. One was, of course, brother-in-law and the other Sanjeev; otherwise everybody in the household had something to talk about and some bit of work to perform for it. To escape the sneers of people that grown ups were solemnising such an odd wedding as of dolls, sister excluded from it various items of pomp and ceremony. Desh regretted that there were no women to sing choruses and dance to the accompaniment of the *dholak* and no feast in the house of the bridegroom to high light the occasion.

The wedding function in Hamilton house started in a humdrum way. No lights were installed for illumination, no band arranged to mark the occasion; no guests invited, except their own domestic Rama Nath to follow the palanquin of the bridegroom.

But Arcadia, situated a mile up of Bara-*bazaar*, looked scene of a actual wedding. The large house in red stucco, with graceful arcades on its three sides, was decorated with paper buntings, festoons of flowers, and welcome-gates in green foliage. A bag-pipe band played a lively air. Shanker and his fourteen years old, pale looking, niece, greeted groom-*wallah*, with the traditional humility as became the members of a family giving away the hand of their daughter in wedding. *Attar* of rose and jasmine were sprinkled on them from long-necked, pot-bellied, receptacles, richly carved in silver; and sweet, perfumed *pans*, wrapped in silver-foils, choice cigarettes were handed round.

Shanker's brother came up swinging. He was a broad hipped man, with prominent eyes and oily skin that characterised his family.

"You like the reception," he grinned uncovering his even row of upper teeth, "No one can say it is not the wedding of my own daughter."

"You are very bold," brother-in-law wrinkled up his brow," Celebrating wedding of dolls with such show."

The guests were seated in a circle in front of the house. In its centre a snub-nosed priest lighted fire on sticks of wood over a raised square of brick-red, shifted earth, decorated with geometrical figures, drawn in flour. With its face veiled in head-cloth, the bride-doll, in its new costumes and ornaments including a string of black-beads, gifted by sister, was set upon a stool besides the groom-doll. Shanti and Miranda, representing parents of the dolls, performed *puja* to the God of Fire by offering it flowers, camphor. With the bride preceding the groom, the two dolls were made to circumambulate seven times the God of Fire and vow fidelity to each other through the vissicitutes of life.

The wedding had been over simplified, cut down to one act to save time. It was marked by the jovial atmosphere; bride-*wallah*, girl friends of Shanti, made game of the groom-doll, calling its face and figure ugly; they hung round its neck string of rags; splashed colour and beaten curd over it; then one of the groom-*wallah* took retaliatory measures and stopped their pranks.

Of the two sisters who were the first Desh had remarked in the crowd, the frail led the compaign of ridicule against the groom. From the very moment his eyes fell on the two, he had been looking out for a chance to scrape acquaintance with them. To his surprise the frail sister gave him a thin smile of recognition; and once or twice the other one had ogled him, though with expressionless face.

He found chance to speak with the frail sister, if he as bridegroom-*wallah* tried to parry her jokes. But he funked in pitting himself against a woman unknown to him.

The frail sister raised the veil of tassel from the face of bridegroom-doll, and howled, "Look at the nose," All the bridge-*wallah* broke into a rippling laugh.

He could now draw the attention of the frail sister towards him. He mustered up all his courage. "It is better than hawk nose."

She winced under his joke directed against her father and herself; but she rallied quickly, "If the nose of the bridegroom had glasses, it was that unique nose you once saw in life."

Bride-*wallah* giggled. She was hitting at his brother-in-law; Desh was alone, while his enemies were numerous; but how could he give in to women?

"See the lovely smile," he flourished his hand-kerchief, "On the lips of the bridegroom."

"Every ugly bridegroom smiles on getting a beautiful bride. There was never a pair as badly matched as this."

Though he lost in fencing with the frail sister, he had made a beginning towards her friendship. He wished the other sister had as well ganged up with other maids and women, who were running down bridegroom-*wallah*, belittling the ornaments and costumes, gifted to the bride, despite appreciative glances at them. But she never opened her lips; under the circumstances, her composure seemed Desh abnormal.

Sister, Shanker and himself, moved to the tables heaped with various types of salty and sweet delicacies as *chaat*, potato-chops, *rasmalai* and *gulab jamun*. Most of the guests had departed. Brother-in-law, ignoring the wedding ceremony, was chatting with some of his colleagues in the bar.

"Your doll wedding took good time," he said with a note of irritation in his voice.

"We had no idea," replied sister, " Shanker would do all this like an actual one; wish you had seen it; you would have enjoyed it."

Brother-in-law wrinkled up his brow. "I am glad you and Miranda enjoyed yourselves. For this I am grateful to Desh's friend Shanker."

Brother-in-law produced a bland smile as he took his leave from the function; Sanjeev accompanied his father.

"Let me hope," Heera Lal greeted brother-in-law with joined palms in front of his chest. "Next time your's will be the bride and ours the bridegroom."

Among all the women gathered in Arcadia, sister undoubtedly stood out as the most beautiful in her peacock-blue sari. Never had he noticed sister or Shanker as sparkling as that evening. During the wedding their eyes had constantly danced at one other, growing often soft and liquid. Now plying each other with snacks the two seemed overjoyed at having created for themselves a wonderful chance of a rendezvous.

Girls and women had started collecting in the porch to witness the pathetic scene of the wedding. As the bride was carried away along with its groom in a palanquin, the band struck up a plaintive tune; Shanti covered her face in the folds of her handkerchief and shed silent tears. Colour went out of the face of every bride-*wallah*, and many a bride-maid and woman joined Shanti in her sorrow. It seemed incredible that these very souls could have thoroughly enjoyed themselves, not long before, during the *puja* of God of Fire.

A fat woman with heavy frame and strong nose, whom Desh had noticed seated behind Shanti during wedding ceremony, limped up and addressed herself to sister.

"Please do not neglect our daughter, she had never been out of the house."

At the sham anxiety of the woman, everybody smiled the brightest smile of the wedding.

From sister be learnt that her interlocutor was wife of Heera Lal, who had been discharged from a tuberculosis sanatorium, where she had put in two years in treatment.

On their homeward journey the two sisters made constellation about his own. His sister gave hint that the full cost of the wedding was borne by Shanker, while the elder brother, Heera Lal, stole credit for it. Desh knew that his friend was a spendthrift, still he got a shock on Shanker's throwing away a tidy sum on nothing.

At top of Bara-*bazaar* in greeting him *namaskar* the two sisters held their palms together a long time, when eyes of plump sister got arrested on his own. He felt himself electrified.

Going up Hamilton, he learnt from his sister that of the two, the elder frail one was called Har Preya, and the other Lalita, who was the only daughter of Joga Sah left unmarried.

x x x

Reclining on a shallow chair, uncle was looking out for him from the verandah, anxious at his absence from home the whole day.

"Son," his voice was full of excitement, "You say your prayers quick to get ready for meal; I have a good news for you."

"Is it wire from Allahabad that I have passed LL.B."

"You got first division."

That night when light had gone out of the room of uncle, Desh sneaked to the verandah, not from thoughts of having succeeded in the last university examination he had sat in, but from sleeplessness consequent upon passing an evening full of bubble and squeak. Notwithstanding his success with the elder sister. Har Preya, it was tantalising not to have got a word out of the other, Lalita, during the walk from Arcadia down to Bara-*bazaar*. In contrast what a glib tongue Champa possessed; one had not to look out for one's chance to talk to her. Suddenly he was reminded of the appointment he had made her, for that evening at the Pink. Poor thing; she should have lingered over there, all the evening, for him. It was Saturday.

Lightening recurrently flickered over the western horizon. He walked in and closed the doors behind him.

"June is ending; rains have come; good rains," he told himself.

CHAPTER - VI

From next morning a sharp wind blew in clouds, which grew thick by the evening. All the same Desh hired the horse of Mazid and made for Hamilton. One of these days Har Preya and Lalita were coming there; he had to get regular in his visits to sister, lest he might not miss them.

"Saw you *sahib* after long."

"It is I who did not see you at the stand; you should be too busy. This year the season is good; never seen so many tourists before."

"But they stay here just a month."

Mazid was old to do much running about from one mountain to another; his few month's earnings in summer from horse were insufficient to cover his expenses of the year. To make both ends meet, he had to fall back on agriculture in off-season. From his forefathers, who tilled land, he had inherited it. Now, in pursuance to the wishes of his wife, he was cutting himself loose from it, by migrating to Pakistan. In parting from his fatherland, he was filled with grief, but he got to bow to his times. Of his two sons, who lived in Pakistan for over a year, the elder had in a letter broken him the saddest news of his life that his younger son had gone insane. But that was the will of *Allah*.

"You are not leaving India at once."

"Mother of my sons is mad to go; by the end of rains we will gave reached Pakistan."

To avoid the attention of brother-in-law, working in his study, Desh stole upstairs, for he was prejudiced against every sort of entertainment, excepting that of piling up of wealth. He would hardly say a nice word on the wedding of dolls.

Sister was chatting with her children in the glass-room.

"*Aree*", she exclaimed, "You came at right time. There is quarrel between Miranda and Sanjeev over the possession of the bride-doll; it is so beautiful."

All went to the adjoining bed-room of Miranda and Sanjeev, opposite that of sister's, where the two dolls stood on a table. With its skirt held in the pose of dance, and the coal-black pigtail gleaming across its breast, the bride was a specimen of exquisite workmanship in china. Its juxtaposition by the bridegroom with bulbous nose looked unaesthetic and bizarre.

"Sure", declared Desh, "The bridegroom belonged to Miranda; she got it married; the bride also belongs to her."

On his way home, he was caught in pelting rain; he was dripping wet when he entered his room. He resolved to arm himself with an umbrella whenever he went out, now that the monsoon had broken out.

x x x

He made many abortive attempts to meeting the two sister. In the morning he boated, keeping his eyes spread over the road for them; he spent the afternoon at Hamilton in anticipation of a visit from them; and in the evening, he promenaded about Flats on chance of meeting them. But never once he clapped eyes on them; he began to lose hopes of meeting the two sisters.

One afternoon, sister and himself were sitting in the glass-room. He was reading newspaper and sister flicking through a novel in English.

"How it is," he remarked, "You are just rushing through it today."

"The thing is I borrowed few books from Shanker on our first visit to him in May; till now I have not opened one of them; he says why I take books from him, if I do not read them."

Their talk was interrupted by Rama Nath who brought in the evening post. Excepting one to sister, all other letters were addressed to brother-in-law. She tore it open; it was sent by Champa.

"Well," chirped sister, "I know everything, you presented her a nice sari; your never give me one."

A moment he looked away from her. In his innocent flirtation with Champa, he had left out the possibility of being overtaken by the gossip; he should take a lesson of life.

Sister laid bare the past of Champa. She had ceased to look upon Champa with love or admiration. She wondered how Champa still made their old friendship a subject of talk, and fussed over it. School relationship carried different complexion later in life.

For some years even after taking teaching as her profession, Champa retained her modesty and womanly grace. Every thing about her boded well. She graduated herself privately, and rose from a junior to a senior school mistress. It was expected that she would soon go up as headmistress. Then one evening sister was shaken to know from father of Miranda that Champa was involved in a scrape. The matter had come to the notice of the head-mistress, and other officials of the education department. In those days Miranda's grandfather as a *Rai Bahadur* wielded much influence in the British *Raj*. Through his efforts the matter was hushed up, and the dismissal of Champa was changed to transfer to Lucknow. On the eve of her departure, she cried her eyes out, and solemnly declared to sister to live down her disgrace. But her words believed her actions. Before long she applied herself to her old trade, though now a wiser person, she managed her intrigues with exemplary skill.

Ten years Champa cut herself off from her home town. Once in two or three years, she corresponded with sister, but her letters left out her own news. Sometimes rumour would go around that she was engaged to be married with an army officer, or a *zamindar*. Pleased, sister would set about to confirm it, but only to know that Champa was degrading herself as a hussy. When on a sudden she returned to Nainital, sister considered it proper to invite her for old-time sake to *chai,* but the wicked woman, from the very evening, tried to seduce her own brother. That was a fine way to acquit oneself as a friend.

"Why did you not tell me all this before ?"

"I thought you should be knowing about Champa." An edge was perceptible in sister's voice." And I have always faith in you that you will never do anything wrong."

"Yes; I am never rash; I always think over a thing."

"And on such a right or wrong choice, happiness of life depends."

From that day he altogether dismissed Champa from his mind; he took in a cool breath that he was no longer fooling with her; still worry gnawed at his heart that gossip might not float up to his uncle, linking her name with his.

In the light of his talks with sister over Champa, his choice of Lalita seemed again wrong. When even after one month, he never saw her in Hamilton, his visits there began to get irregular.

One afternoon as forerunner to foggy weather, a splashing rain had given over an hour. Wanting to light a cigarette, he discovered he had smoked off all his reserve. He was forced to plod through a gloomy evening to Flats to purchase a box of cigarettes. Since Shanker was engrossed in filling in his ledgers, he decided to pass rest of the evening with sister.

In her bed room she was seated with Har Preya and Lalita. His heart made a pit-a-pat.

"Your bridegroom is well." A smile, reminiscent of the wedding of dolls, oozed out of the whole face of Har Preya, "We have come to meet it."

"Full month bridegroom kept remembering you." He instinctively returned her smile.

"We could not come out." Chimed in Lalita, "Because of mother's first death anniversary *puja*."

"Haun", he brought out, "You have no mother."

The reference touched the two sisters. The light mood of the company was spoilt. He noticed the saris of the sisters, though modern in design and glossy in material, were draped as before in old style, border and cloth adjoining it covered half the head.

"These people were going away," said sister, "But I told them you will surely come."

The sisters had reached Hamilton before the fog had started closing in. Both were disappointed by finding him absent from there. Har Preya wanted to make bit of fun at the expenses of bridegroom-*wallah* Desh. Unlike other women, the sister hardly saw pictures; they looked for entertainment in their social calls.

Har Preya was elder to Lalit by six years, and was married for about the same number of years to a draper in Bara-*bazaar*. She had a five-years old son; she lived in the same lane as Champa. Her parents-in-law having died before her marriage, she was the mistress of her own house.

"Bring also your son", added sister, "When you come next."

The fog hung thick. A trip through the murky evening required an escort for the sisters. He got an excellent excuse to return with them. Trees, houses, roads, and mountains had been blotted out in the sea of fog; visibility had been reduced to a few yards. The three of them floundered down a couple of hundred yards. Then Har Preya, who seemed to possess acuter eyes than Lalita and himself, forged ahead. She scoffed at them through the fog, calling them slow as mules and snails, and challenged them to catch her. Blindfold, the two chased Har Preya, but she had dashed out of their reach, and was lost in the fog. Suddenly, he got aware that he was walking alone with the woman, he had ached a full month to see. He outstretched his hand to Lalita to guide herself upon so that both could walk on firm foot. She declined it first; but her maidenly reserve quickly wore off; she seemed to like his gesture. She herself held his hand in her own; there was no mistaking that she did so with a press. Their pace automatically slowed down.

"It seems there is no use trying to run."

"Yes; sister has gone far ahead."

He wanted to crush her against his bosom, but his moral principles combined with his shyness of youth restrained him. He was pleased with himself that he had overcome a weak moment.

"Why did you not come to Hamilton before. I waited for you there a full month."

"I could not come out all by myself, nor tell sister I wanted to."

"I had come to the thought that I would never meet you."

"So had I".

Words issued out of her lips in a relishing roll. Her right hand that held his own, bedecked with a ring, felt large and soft; her expansive and curvy body oozed thick femaleness and animal sensuality.

"It seems once I have met you, I cannot again."

"I remain mostly in the house of sister than mine."

"Can I meet you there ?"

"I did not mean that. Your coming to the house is not proper." She paused to take a deep breath." We go to the temple of Goddess of the Rock, one or another Saturday evening."

The two saw a blurred shape, a dozen yards ahead of them. Instantly they disengaged their hands, and quickened their pace. Her Preya noticed nothing abnormal about them; she looked elated at her having out-distanced them.

He came home dazed. During meals he replied absent-minded to the questions of uncle. Walking back to his room, he stationed himself a long while before the oleograph of *Siva*. Whenever any problem needing solution beset him, he never forgot to inform *Siva* of it, though without reading a prayer. That night as he kept whispering to himself the name of Lalita, all the blood in his body seemed to have rushed to his heart. He wanted to listen to her rich voice for days on end.

x x x

Since the outbreak of monsoon he had never sat in a tete-a-tete with Shanker, smoking cigarette after cigarette.

Shanker was engaged in conversation, in his drawing-room, with a young man his age, who was blond with military moustache and greenish eyes. He was dressed as an aristocrat in an evening-suit of expensive, imported material. For a minute, Desh failed to place him.

"You know each other", said Shanker, "You have met in this very room few years ago."

There upon the young man shook hand with him in a constrained manner. Desh now fully recognised him. He was

Inder Pratap, son of *rajah* Narendra Pratap. In winter Shanker betook himself to his farm for enjoying the warmth of plains and for *shikar*.

"How is your father's gout", he asked.

"Should be well", answered Inder, giving a sideways chuck to his head." I do not think he will die."

He realised his mistake in putting the question, even though out of courtesy, to Inder, when a long-drawn dispute had estranged him from his father. He lived in Ranikhet in summer and in his *terai* farm in winter while Narendra Pratap at Nainital and his *zamindari* in Rasalgaon.

"Dev Rama," called Inder, in a far way, causal tone. He turned to Desh, "You used to have an uncle, who was a blot on your father. I suppose he was never earning."

Desh felt irritated; he had to make an effort to suppress an impulse to hit out at Inder. No one in his hearing had ever applied such unpleasant and insulting remarks on his uncle; he was universally liked and esteemed. The fact that the author of the remark himself stayed in idleness and parasitism, horrified Desh.

"No", he protested, "You have been misinformed about my uncle. He was a head-clerk; his money had put my father through his education. When my father began practice, he asked his elder brother because of his asthma to take a little earlier retirement."

He would have continued arguing in defence of uncle, but Kunwar seemed totally withdrawn into himself; he had dropped his uncle from his mind.

"Well", he returned to Shanker, "Will nothing be served in your house today ?"

Shanker pointed out facetiously, "Excepting medicines nothing is served here".

Inder went off into a guffaw.

For the sake of privacy, Shanker shut the front doors. He unlocked a cupboard; Kunwar picked up bottles one by one, and read labels on them with gusto and toyed with them. Whenever he selected out one, he blinked at Desh.

Though Dev Ram had served mutton-chops right from the frying pan; drinks had to wait until Inder had not taken a measured quantity from each bottle and mixed them in the manner of a pharmaceutical chemist. He smiled away requests for knowing the formula of his contortion. His secret, acquired after years of toil on liquors, would perish with him. The phrase toil on liquors drew a blithe laugh from Shanker.

With the heaviness of intoxication descending on him, Inder came out of his stand-office manners. He directed torrent of abuses at Desh, for he refused to give him company every time Inder poured out drink for himself. Being a trio he lacked the power of addicts to carry his liquor well. Kunwar called Desh a nincompoop, mooncalf. Slowly his voice thickened and his sentences lost connection and sense. He harped on one idea that Desh's father was a hard drinker. Themselves feeling weak under their knees, Desh and Shanker between them lifted him up from the chair, walked him to the bed, and flattened him across it. Instantly Inder fell into a coma.

He returned home far in the night, when he felt sure his uncle could be lying asleep. So long as his carousing remained a secret from him, he was not bothered to check them. He remembered with amusement how in his childhood his uncle stopped him, in the evening, from entering the room of his father, lest Desh might not see him drinking. His uncle drilled him for a puritanical life. In his younger days Desh rose early in the morning; took bath in empty stomach with cold water; and bare in *dhoti* sat cross-legged on the wooden slab in the sanctum, winding the holy-threaded he wore across his chest about his hand, and said in Sanskrit *gayatri* prayer, a twenty eight times. At night he once again said *gayatri* a hundred and eight times. On Saturday evening he accompanied uncle round the temples of the city, while on rest of week days he heard from him tales of *Mahabharat* and verses of *Ramayan*. When he was old to study in collegé, uncle read him *Geeta* and fragments from *Upanishads*.

The religion uncle professed was not the *Hinduism*, racy and original; rather it was governed by the code of *pundits* and *puja*. Though he often talked of *karma*, he believed that *nirvana* could only be attained through *puja*.

Desh had mostly discarded the doctrines his uncle had instilled into him from childhood. Under the guidance of Shanker, he had studied materialism. He started disbelieving that *puja* slid open the portals of heaven to one.

His eyes swivelled round to the coloured oleograph of *Siva*, resting on the mantelpiece of his room. It seemed to accuse him for embracing heterodox views.

x x x

The monsoon had set in; fog tightly closed in upon the valley of the lake. Every day rain fell in torrents; sometimes two or three days intermittently. These days his uncle disliked his going out of the house. He had conceived unintelligent dread of foggy and wet weather. He warned Desh of its injurious effects upon health; the humid air caused temperature and cough.

One Saturday in August, it had poured two days running. In the evening, following a cloudburst, rain came down in sluices accompanied by high wind, which sent a tempest through the placid lake; it took on a ghastly aspect, against the silhouetted mountains, dark and threatening.

He ran up and down the verandah of his house, watching the rain. Ever since his meeting Lalita, he had been tortured by her memory. The gloom of the evening sharpened it. When the fury of the rain lessened, he stole out of the house. He never expected to see, Lalita, but so long as he perambulated he forgot about her.

Near Flats, he went into a shop of a chemist to buy uncle antispasmodic to sooth his asthmatic fits. The chemist, a middle-aged, corpulent man, was absorbed in talking with two women. Seeing Desh, he gave a nod, and without his demanding the drug he wanted, he produced it him. Only when he was making the payment did he recognise the two women as Lalita and Har Preya.

His heart knocked against his ribs. Both had noticed him before he did, and both responded to his greeting with shadow of a smile.

"What makes you come here ?"

"Balu, my son is ill", replied Har Preya in a casual tone.

Seeing the sisters indifferent to continue talking to him, he felt piqued and stamped out of the shop. Ordinarily he should have made for home, but a strong desire to hear the deep and rich voice of Lalita, and gaze at her graceful figure, forced him to rein in his anger, and wait near the horse-stand.

The sisters had more or less followed him. Joining him, both produced their most radiant smiles. Their manner towards him had dramatically changed.

"Before the shopkeeper", began Har Preya gesticulating, "Who is a local man, I could not talk to you like this. When you had gone, he was asking us how we know you."

"Yes, Nainital is Nainital".

He shuffled along with the sisters towards their lane. Har Preya seemed hesitant in inviting him to her house; her neighbours were given to scandal-mongering. But foggy weather that had restricted the traffic, emboldened her. As he passed the house of Champa, he felt embarrassed. He looked up at the windows of her room; they all were shut; there existed but a little chance of her seeing him.

The ground floor of a three-storeyed house, located in the middle of the lane, was taken up by two shops. The sisters led him up over a wooden-stairway to a room in the second floor. It was poorly furnished with few grimy chairs and a bed, and was used both as a sitting as well sleeping-room. The walls were decorated with family photographs, coloured pictures of *avatar Rama, Siva* and Goddess. He felt ill at ease in a small, somewhat frowzy room. Har Preya went into an inner one to give medicine to Balu.

Facing him Lalita sat on the bed. The broad parting down the middle of her head, half hidden under the sari, glistened in the electric light. She kept staring at him with soft, tranquil eyes; his own had anchored on her full breasts and sculptured forearms. Whenever she moved them, maroon-coloured glass bangles, alternating with golden, adorning her wrists, jingled, lending her charm.

He was dying to hear her; tell him that since her parting with him in Hamilton, she had yearned for him as much as he had for her; but she sat on as dumb.

"It is twenty-one days", he whispered, breaking the silence," Since I saw you".

"*Accha*; I have not counted the days".

"You never came out of your house these days."

"It rained all the time."

"Do people not go out if it rains."

"We do not."

"At least you should have been going to college."

"I gave up studies after VIII Class."

"So you stay at home."

"Every woman has to stay at home; see your own sister, in spite of her education."

"You mean woman should not get higher education."

"The more one gets education, the better it is; but my mother thought it spoilt girls."

"How ?"

"It is difficult for me to explain it."

Har Preya reappeared, carrying brass tumblers filled with *chai*, and brass saucers with dry fruits.

"We are humble people; we do not use china cups."

"At home aunt also makes tea in brass tumblers."

In a little while Har Preya had made *chai.* She was efficient as well as laborious house-wife. She rose by sun rise, and started the day by cooking snack for her husband, followed by midday and evening meals. Tea making alone consumed much of her time, for she was much fond of it.

Before he had finished tea, rain spattered again on the tin roofs and the window-panes, that looked down upon the lane. Inside the room the noise rose deafening; they had to lift their voice to make themselves audible.

He waited for the rain to stop that he would get away; but it poured incessantly.

"Have you seen a minister", asked Har Preya. "For the first time, I saw one in June; he was giving lecturer in Flats that congress brought independence."

The naive question brought an expansive smile upon his lips.

When Har Preya left them to her kitchen, situated in the interior of the house, to start cooking, Lalita and himself were again left to themselves.

"Shall you stay here for the night or shall you go away ?"

"Some day I stay, if the rain does not stop."

"You and your sister seem to be great friends."

Lalita gave an affirmative nod.

He looked at his watch. Closing his shop, Har Preya's husband would be reaching home any moment. He wanted to avoid an encounter with him.

"I think, I shall be going; the rain is not coming to a stop."

"Wait some time more; it may."

"I am not waiting for the rain to stop. I am here because of you."

"If it is so; why delay yourself for me."

Lalita cast a spell on him. He would have kept on sitting with her, if she had wanted; but her curt reply obliged him to rise to his feet. Lalita stood herself behind him on the landing stage. It was dark and the stairs could not be made out.

"Is there no light here ?"

"It is gone out of order."

He strained his eyes on her ghostly figure, as he put his hand on her shoulders; she remained motionless.

"Shall you go the temple of Goddess of Rock on Saturday ?"

"Most probably".

"Come sure".

"I shall ask sister".

She followed him down the flight of stairs; she holding his hand.

Out in the lane, he found the rain falling in streaks. With umbrella bobbing over him in wind, he plodded through roads splotched over in puddles. Entering his room, he had hardly kicked out his damp shoes and changed, when he heard his uncle calling him from over the drawing-room.

He accompanied uncle to kitchen. Both squatted-down on their respective rectangles; having said his prayer, uncle waited for service of meal. Aunt did it in silence. At once three vegetables made Desh dumb. This unusual lavishness he put down to some piece of good news that aunt would have received, and no news was regarded by her as good, if it was unrelated with her daughter.

Inquired uncle, between chewing a *chapatti* morsel and tearing another, "When I knew you had gone out in this bad weather, I was surprised and worried."

"I am very healthy".

"No, you are weak as your father."

"I am strong in spirit to live long."

"So your father said, and it is sixteen years to his death. If he was living, how great was our family; even today we share his name and prestige."

"Probably it is because of his not obeying your advises on health that he died young."

Uncle took a deep breath.

"Death had come to him, so he died. There are few good brothers like him; he respected and loved me so much."

Uncle went on cramming the nice food cooked once in an age by aunt; he relished it as never before. He smacked his tongue on his palate, sipped the liquid, tomato vegetable with noise, and drew in, through his mouth, audible breath when pepper stung his tongue.

"Did you go towards your sister's house?"

"When I go to Hamilton I shall tell her that you remembered her."

"I am old, asthmatic and can die any day; she should not forget me."

No sooner uncle finished speaking, aunt loosened her venomous tongue."

Today of all days you are mentioning death when Chitra has sent letter that her husband has got a promotion; you are making ill-omen when you name those who are dead; and you are sending message to that Chandra, who does not care for you."

Words tumbled out of her mouth as though she was chattering in high fever.

"If a daughter does not care for her father, should the father not care for him."

"Ohe, you do not even take the name of your own daughter, while you embrace daughter of another man. I have never heard of any one like you who dies for his dead brother and his children, and never thinks of his own daughter and wife."

"Mother of Chitra, do not talk like this."

"*Accha*, I have no liberty to talk; but today I cannot be kept silent; in this house I am full of hearing always of Chandra and her father."

"What has come on you?"

Desh gathered his eyebrows in surprise at the protestation of uncle, for he rarely made it.

"Yes, something is come upon me today. I am considered a mad woman; the day I leave this house, I shall get peace. Now Chitra's husband has been transferred to Allahabad; I can go and live with her."

"Surely, you have gone mad today. You talk of going to the house of your daughter; I have never heard of anyone going to the house of one's married daughter to live with. I wish I were dead than having to hear you tell me all this."

Uncle's thin face reddened from anger. Immediately he left eating; jumping up on his feet, he walked out of the kitchen, soliloquizing, "This is limit."

By the time he reached his room, he was seized with a violent fit of coughing. He fell on his right side across his bed; his face resting upon his doubled arm. His bony frame kept on jerking; phlegm and saliva drooled out, messing the pillow-case. With their eyes glued on his face twisted in agony, Desh and aunt stroked his back, wiped clean his mouth, changed the pillow-case, and sprinkled anodyne on a handkerchief and pressed it on to his nose; but he felt little comforted. The coughing fit seemed to exhaust him; phlegm smothered his breathing apparatus. Life began to ebb out of him.

Desh bounded up the Mall to call the physician. He had never witnessed death; the idea that it was overtaking uncle, clawed at his hear. He remembered nothing of his mother, and next to nothing of his father. Being a lonely child, he had spent all his time with uncle. He rose within him; dined with him; went out with him to temples; and shared his religious emotions. The affection which his uncle lavished upon him was untouched by selfishness. He had never known of any occasion to complain to *Siva* that He had taken away his father from him in childhood. Uncle had every regard for his comforts, food, clothing. Of late anxiety over his career had seized him. He could put up with any amount of curses and hard treatment from aunt, but not a word of sarcasm could he listen against Desh or his dead brother. The flame of their love burnt high in his heart, and any attempt of aunt to blow it off excited him so much so that it set him coughing violently; pushing him to the brink of death. A short prayer rose to his lips that his uncle be saved.

The physician lived in a lofty house, a short distance above Flats. He looked up at Desh with stony eyes. He was a man of heavy frame, about fifty years old. He spoke with a slow dignified air to emphasis his status.

"It is useless for me to come in rain; continue the drugs I have recommended in past."

"May I ask you a question". Desh's tongue felt cold and stiff. "How long in your opinion my uncle can live?"

The physician again glanced him vacantly.

"No one can be definite about chronic cases of asthma. He can several years."

The physician's reply heartened Desh. He marched home through the rain. It battered over his umbrella, rain-coat, and rubber boots. A blanket of slaty fog was spreading over the valley; blurred lights outlined the black pall of the lake. It seemed a doomsday.

Aunt was sitting immobile, beside uncle, as he had left her; her face looked ashen and shrunk in. Seeing him in the room, she burst into a fit of cry.

Desh administered uncle antispasmodic and tucked him into his quilt. Slowly the drug wrecked the power behind his coughing; sleep crept over him. Though his breathing sounded hoarse, his regular heart beating suggested that he had come out of danger.

Desh looked at his watch; it was registering ten. The night was still young. He brought an English novel from his room, and seating himself in a shallow-chair, started reading it. In about an hour the breathing of uncle came soft and normal. He thanked *Siva* for saving uncle.

"He has become all right", smiled aunt. "Do you think I said anything harsh to your uncle that should have made him ill. I just told him that he should sometimes remember Chitra. What was there to be angry about such a small thing. It is for this reason I never say anything to your uncle."

He gave a wan smile to aunt at her brazen lie.

CHAPTER - VII

It happened to be a sunny Saturday on which Lalita had given Desh hopes of meeting him. He fagged up and down the Thandi road until the evening had not deepened into night, still; she was not visible. Tired, he sat down in one of the benches, inside the summer-house, he was familiar with, through Champa. He stayed on there two hours, irritated at her callousness. Even a schoolboy knew, how to keep an appointment. Lalita seemed to be an eccentric woman who made her promises to break. He wished he had never ran against her.

Next week, though the monsoon regained its fury, the evenings came out surprisingly clear; he limped towards the temple of Goddess of Rock. Since the Thandi road was unpaved with asphalt, he returned home with his shoes caked in mud. Noticing it, uncle remarked as to where he had been blindly treading.

Next Saturday evening, the tops of mountains lay capped in thick fog. A plume was rising from the head of the lake, accompanied with drizzling.

Desh enthroned himself in the summer-house, all nerves, with eyes set on the road. The rain murmured incessantly. Sometime a boat scuttled through the fog, massing over the lake and Flats.

His persistency brought him success. Seeing him, Lalita gave him shadow of smile; but Har Preya curled her lower lip in surprise.

"*Arree*, what are you doing here !"

"I had gone to temple", his voice was breaking from emotion, "While returning, I said let me rest here to smoke".

"If you come there again with us, the *Devi* will not be angry".

."Let me hope that She shall strengthen our friendship".

Taking out the *puja* things from their basket, the two lighted earthenware-lamp and cube of camphor, and offered sweets and flowers to the Goddess. Having performed the *puja,* Har Preya distributed the sweets as consecrated food.

"What did you pray", asked Lalita.

"I do not believe in temples and praying in them."

She fixed Desh a moment, "I have never heard a man talk like you."

For hiding them from public eye, the sisters and himself thanked the dense fog from their hearts of heart. Had the hour been not advanced, the three could have gadded on with impunity through the main streets that foggy evening.

"Let us go to a restaurant", he suggested, "Have some refreshment".

"You are asking us", Har Preya opened her eyes.

"You mean I talking to the fog."

"We are not the new type of women to visit restaurants".

The three had come upon the summer-house, over the lake beyond the Capital cinema, where during the summer months of May and June bands played in the evenings to entertain the tourists. Inside it about a dozen men were huddled in a circle. Seeing the crowd the sisters turned away, while he out of curiosity climbed the summer-house. A boatman had found a corpse floating over the lake in the fog and had pulled it ashore, which was of a tourist, who had committed suicide. Desh was confronted by death in its nakedness; fear overpowered him. He dashed out of the summer-house in hunt of the sisters, whom he found on the outskirts of Flats.

"We turned away", explained Her Preya apologetically. "It was hurting."

"But why you did not wait for me."

"*Dekho*, you do not get me; until Lalita is not married, we have to be a bit careful."

Har Preya regretted her frankness, if it hurt Desh. Since Lalita lived mostly with her, the responsibility of safeguarding her sister's reputation fell on her shoulders. If something happened, everyone in her family would fasten the blame upon her. Her father and husband would never forgive her. The matters of a girl were delicate. A word of rumour could mar her marriage prospects. One such case had occurred in their own lane; a college girl lost her finance for enjoying the liberty of seeing pictures with a body friend.

Har Preya led him to her house. She looked upon him as a brother; so did her husband. In his company she was getting modern.

"I have one elder sister", he lowered himself into the very chair he had occupied on his previous visit, "From now you are second".

"We are three sisters; now *Devi* has given us a brother too."

Har Preya cast a significant glance at Desh.

"*Accha*, I am your brother alright; but should I not stop visiting you."

"What I told you, I did to caution you and no more. Your visiting my house will not start gossips as easily as our going out with you."

The popping in of a child from the inner room changed the thread of their conversation. He was white complexioned but sickly, and at once ran for his mother.

"*Dekho*, Balu", beamed Har Preya, "Here is your maternal uncle. Say *Jai Hind* to him."

The child pivoted his eyes on Desh. His mother repeated her order.

"*Jai Hind*", greeted Balu.

"Come here", cooed Desh, "Sit by me."

No amount of coaxing could make Balu budge from the knees of his mother; he clung to her all the more.

When Har Preya left to kitchen, Balu followed her. Few minutes passed in silence; neither he nor Lalita uttered a word. He remembered since his previous meeting with her, how he had felt sick for a sight of her, and how, every evening, he had paraded the Thandi road in the hope of meeting her.

"You did not come out to the temple of the Goddess for so long."

"I asked sister, but she replied that Balu is not well; we shall go next Saturday."

"Why did you not insist."

"I insist on sister !"

"Then you should have made some excuse for going out."

Lalita stuck out her tongue. "I never speak a lie."

"An excuse is not a lie; you could have said you wanted wool to go out of the house."

"Is not this a lie to say you wanted wool, when you did not. Secondly how could I go downwards temple when wool is sold up in Bara-*bazaar*."

He smiled in amusement at her naivete.

"If you cannot ask your sister for going out of the house, we may not see each other from year to year."

"Try I will, but if she does not go out, what can I do. I have to follow her."

Har Preya reappeared.

"Come to my house some day", he rose to his feet.

"Sure", promised Har Preya. "But do not forget to come here regularly".

He trudged home inhaling the thick, grey fog of the rainy season. It seemed queer that it should have surrounded all his three meeting with Lalita. A shiver ran down his spine.

x x x

Next day was a Sunday. After mid-day meal, he went to the apartment of Shanker, for it was a free day for him. As he entered the drawing-room, Dev Rama greeted him waggishly, his thin lips blooming with a smile.

"*Accha*, we did not get your *darshan* you have stopped coming".

"Heavy rains this year".

"Why you act with me, "Dev Rama gave a knowing smile. "I also keep knowing things; Champa is very colourful."

He sighed with relief that Dev Rama insinuated at an old affair, and not the current one with Lalita.

"How you manage to know things Dev Rama; you keep mostly at home."

"*Accha*, keep this a secret that my *sahib* and your sister talk on phone; I keep overhearing".

"O, I see," Desh pursued his lips, "I never knew".

Shanker was sleeping in the adjoining room. On account of a sudden relapse in the illness of his sister-in-law, he had journeyed to Arcadia at night. She was suffering from high temperature and was bringing out blood. When news came, evening meal had been spread, but he was too much agitated to eat; he rushed off to see his gravely ill sister-in-law.

When Dev Rama went away to make a cup of coffee, Desh turned into his mind the conversation he had with him. He had often noted that when he had told something to sister or Shanker, meant only for one, it subtly passed on to the other. He wondered what agency the two employed to transmit information between them. He was surprised at his own slowness in guessing that for communicating to one another his sister and Shanker had but to lift the telephone receiver to their mouth, and break into speech.

Dev Rama reappeared with coffee in a magnificent china-set, bordered in dark red. Desh let his eyes dwell on it.

"I like your pots and cups", he poured out for himself the beverage." I see these for the first time."

"This is made in England", answered Dev Rama.

"Some of our sets are coming as good as these foreign makes."

"Indian things can never touch the English."

"You praise English goods because you liked *sahiblogs*".

"Probably".

"Then follow them to England."

"Oho", exclaimed Dev Rama, "How can poor like me reach there?"

Desh's mouth dropped upon. The departure of the British was greeted with mixed feelings even by people whose income and position was directly affected by it as of his brother-in-law. The love of Dev Rama for them, for their own sake, surprised him.

"With how many *sahibs* you have worked ?"

"There was Sheering *sahib*; Robert *sahib*, and many others."

"What was special about them ?"

"*Sahibs* had a good hand; they paid well. They recognised merit in a man; respected his honesty. They were just and impartial in the exercise of authority."

Desh glanced at Dev Rama over the lighted cigarette in his mouth.

"So you wish *sahibs* had remained in India."

"I cannot say that we should not have *swaraj*."

He saw some weight in the statement of Dev Rama. It differed widely from his knowledge of imperialism and colonial rule.

"Why Dev Rama", rang out Shanker, streaming in from the other room, and stretching himself, "Are you not getting food to your stomach full in my house that you are weeping for *sahibs*".

"No master", protested Dev Rama, "I have no trouble in your house." He kept scratching the back of his head. If all were like you, who would remember *sahibs*."

Dev Rama slunk off ashamed at his master's putting wrong construction to his praise of English people.

Shanker dropped heavily upon a sofa; his seraphic eyes were still laden with sleep. Few minute he kept on looking listlessly the wall before him, unconscious of Desh's presence.

"Your sister-in-law is better now", he jerked Shanker into himself.

"Everything is in the hands of *Siva*, blood is continuously coming out of her mouth."

He had never heard Shanker talk as a religious man. The relapse of his sister-in-law had awakened a reminiscent mood in him. He had passed his adolescents with her. At the time of her marriage she was his age; their possessing of similar temperament made them friends. Both saw pictures together, or played cards, or talked on into the night. Angry, his mother would remark whether new day was not dawning for them.

Considering his master would be feeling hungry for having missed two meals, Dev Rama placed before Shanker a splendid *chai*; but except drinking a cup, he touched nothing. The eatables reminded him that his sister-in-law was an excellent cook, who had always taken delight in making him tasty food. Her regard for his comforts was so much so that he had never even to take pains for lifting spoon to eat his meal.

Shanker led Desh into his bed-room. Unlocking a suitcase, he flung out sweaters pullovers, which numbered about a dozen; his sister-in-law had knitted them with consummate skill. Among them white-sweaters, with pattern of rope, were reminders of his hockey days.

Tears moistened the eyes of Shanker. He doubted whether she would get over the crisis; even if she could, he doubted in the efficacy of sanatorium treatment. His sister-in-law was an advanced case, whose prognosis of recovery was poor. His brother, nephew and niece, were performing *puja* in every temple, and distributing alms to the priests to invoke the blessings of the Goddess for her recovery.

Shanker was interrupted by a knock on the front doors. Desh instantly recognised the man, who entered the room, as Bhandari with whom he had travelled in train to Nainital. Being depressed Shanker gave the visitor hint of a nod.

"Everything with you is well", greeted Desh, "Could get no glimpse of yours since May."

Desh glided his eyes over the well knit body of Bhandari. He looked more weather beaten and jaded than before.

"I like Nainital a lot" said Bhandari.

Sitting out in the verandah of his hotel he could have kept gazing the lake and the wooded mountains around, months at a stretch. Its picturesque beauty had gone down to his heart and rested him. He was a man with retiring disposition; the bustle and promiscuous environment of the hotels went against it. In the season, they were packed with tourists of rank and substance; seeking gaiety and recreation. They tried to squeeze maximum of enjoyment off their holidays. But having sweated himself as a common labourer in his farm, Bhandari found little energy and inclination left in him for pursuits needing physical exertion in Nainital. Unlike other tourists, he disliked to climb to tops of mountains, row over the lake, or gallop a horse.

The keen sense of hospitality of Shanker, blunted down by his low spirits, reasserted itself. He who seldom allowed a friend, go from his doors, without being entertained, ordered Dev Rama to serve whisky.

"Huan", Bhandari raised his hand, "Now you have produced the right thing; *chai* and coffee are meant for school boys."

The drink gradually enlivened Bhandari; he commented on the brands of liquors he used, both imported and indigenous. Suddenly he grew pensive, leaned forward, putting his hand across his eyes. "Seen so much of bloodshed in partition of the country." Tears dropped from his cheeks, "Lost everything, my agricultural farm; liquor trade; only son and brother."

Consoled Desh, "In moments as yours, we think of our deeds in previous life; our *karma*."

"Nonsense; my shoe", Bhandari moped his tears, "We had enough of it. We should now give up this thinking that has hindered us from removing our poverty."

"Yes, you are very right", cut in Shanker.

"The colonisers have gone", continued Bhandari," But they have left behind their culture with us. They have done a great service to us; they have made us to think how to remove our poverty; they have made us modern."

While the drinks went on, Shanker joined Bhandari in praising the western culture. By nine he took his leave. Bhandari had enjoyed both drinks and talk.

He remained behind with Shanker an hour after the departure of Bhandari; he tried to cheer him up; made him eat food, which he might have gone off, if Desh would not have kept him company.

"You did not go towards Hamilton these days."

"How you know ?"

"Sometimes servants of your sister come here".

Desh knew that Shanker was lying. He often spoke with her on telephone.

"Why do you not go to see her ?"

"Rains are so heavy."

"Yes, rains this year are awful. I am too sick of them, and feel like going away from Nainital.

"Leaving your Empire store."

"*Zamindari* abolition and departure of British officers have affected my business.

"Then what would you do ?"

"I have not made up my mind; first I want to go to England, this is my long desire."

"You want to go there to be called England returned".

"No", Shanker grew pensive. "I do not think, a visit to England now will give me one twentieth of importance as in British days."

"Then why you want to go there ?"

"Just as a tourists".

Desh saw an opportunity of eliciting the reason of Shanker's bachelorhood.

"You want to go there to marry."

Shanker gave a throaty chuckle, "There ! I cannot".

He doubted whether he could be counted among the very much wealthy. This Empire store belonged as much to him as his elder brother. Above half of its income was spent in maintaining the two establishments; one his own, and the other at Arcadia. The balance was saved in a bank, but it could not be considered huge. Unless he would not embark upon a new enterprise, he wondered now the dreams lodged in his heart could ever come true.

"It is nearly ten", Desh looked impatiently at his wrist watch, "I had better take my leave; but do not forget to take me with you in your continental tour."

"O I see; you want to come with me to foreign countries, but you cannot be seen for days living in the very city. Now there is going to be Nanda *Devi* fair next week. Do not forget to take your sister there."

The rain was falling in fine drops. Desh let it trickle down his forehead and face than taking shelter under the hood of the *rickshaw*, which he had hired for reaching home. The glow of wine ran down his veins; rain felt cool and unusually exhilarating.

CHAPTER - VIII

Few days Desh felt hesitant in meeting Lalita at the house of her sister, in spite of the latter's standing invitation to him. He needed to guard himself and the woman he loved from the risk of a scandal. Any hasty action on his part would not only ruin his chances of meeting her, but also part her forever from him.

On Saturday his longing for meeting her got beyond his control. At all cost he must meet her sometime of other. After nightfall he entered the lane from top; avoiding the possibility of being seen by Champa.

As he walked down, he moved his eyes from side to side of the lane. He felt glad that no shopkeeper or passer-by seemed to take any notice of him. If once or twice anyone looked at him, his attention was engaged by his stylish dress than himself. He was glad that nobody recognised him.

He climbed the flight of narrow, dark, stairs to the third storey; his eyes thirty for a sight of the saintly beauty of Lalita. Awhile he hung suspended on the landing stage, too faint to knock at the door. How would the sisters take his coming, without intimation or business. The two might be sitting with a visitor; he should be ready with some excuse, if an eventuality like that arose. Mustering courage to his heart, he beat his knuckles on the door.

In his nervousness he felt he waited for several minutes before hearing the bolt withdrawn, and Har Preya revealing in the light projecting out of the room.

"*Aree*, it is you", she gave him an evanescent smile.

He followed her into the room, and took seat on the very chair he had done on his previous visits.

Presently Lalita materialised in the room; her face brightened into a smile.

"Sister and I looked out for you at Nanda Devi temple".

"*Achha*" He cocked his head sideways from joy.

"This morning my father gave two goats in the temple of Goddess."

"You should be taking the meat of sacrificed goat?"

"Not I, but all in my home do."

"You saw the goat being sacrificed."

"No; the sight hurts me."

Desh inquired, "Why does *Devi* want sacrifices ?"

Pop came Lalita's answer, "Goddess came down from heaven to earth to kill demons. So *Devi* is blood thirsty; She is pleased with sacrifice."

There, his memory had fallen short. His uncle had in his childhood and in later years narrated him numerous mythological tales that described the origin of multi-Gods and Goddesses.

"You seem to know lot of old things of our religion."

On receiving the compliment, Lalita craned her neck in pride.

"Who does not know about one's religion."

"I for one do not know." He looked askance at her.

Lalita snorted through her nose. She had gleaned some information about him. Her main source was her father, who had told her that Desh's uncle was a pious man; he had brought up his nephew in an intensely religious milieu.

"It was a long time ago", he declared.

"You will eat", she implored, "The temple meat I have cooked for father of Balu."

"You seem to be a strange woman; you would not eat meat, but you can cook it; you cannot see a goat being sacrificed to the *Devi*, still you worship Her."

"Do not think of me; eat the meat."

Ordinarily he should have refused to accept the off-hand invitation to dinner. But desire to taste the food done by Lalita possessed him.

The sisters went inside to fetch him their cookery. In the meantime, he contemplated the photographs hung upon the walls. A tall one, with a wreath around it and hung over the mantelpiece, looked a middle aged woman, who in her round, kindly face resembled Lalita. He guessed she was the mother of the sisters.

Instead of placing before him temple-meat curry, the sisters did the regular meal in a nickel-plated, large round *thali*. The two looked flurried the way they attended on him; they seemed awed by having him as a guest, and moved about his table with the turn of his eyes.

"You would not have liked my cooking." Lalita blushed.

"No, I do," he asserted.

"But you are eating nothing."

"I had a late *chai*."

Lalita was an indifferent cook. The meat-curry, she had taken hours in making, tasted insipid. But he liked the potato vegetable and sweetened curd. Lalita was a true daughter of *vaisya* caste, who only knew to do vegetarian food well.

He had to request for a spoon to save his fingers from getting greasy in eating. The sisters had not supplied him with one, for they themselves never used it.

"I am so glad", echoed Har Preya, "You accepted our humble invitation."

"This is an ordinary matter."

"No, this is a great thing; from today you have made this house as your own."

The words of Har Preya were pregnant with meaning. In advancing his friendship with the sisters, he had taken upon himself a responsibility about which he had remained so far unaware.

"Yes, this is my own house," he agreed.

Lalita had taken her eyes off him. Her cheeks had flushed with colour betraying her maidenly shyness.

"Is she your mother", he pointed the photograph over the mantelpiece.

Lalita nodded.

The photograph had been taken when she lay on death bed. She had never faced the camera before. Seeing her end near, she wished to leave behind her something for her daughters to remember hear by. As Lalita recounted the illness of her mother, tears filled up her eyes.

One day, about a year before, returning from the temple of Goddess of Rock, she complained of pain in her stomach. Taking it as an ordinary ailment, she got a small slab of stone heated and put over the spot of pain for fomentation. The remedy worked, pain subsided quickly at night; but next morning it broke out again sharp. For four days she was treated by the *hakim* in their lane; but the pain continued. At last her father sent for the chief physician of the main, state hospital, who administered her many medicines. But none worked. On the sixth day of the starting of the pain, she left for her heavenly abode. Lalita spoke haltingly, sometimes pausing to catch her breath.

"She might have been saved if she was brought under treatment of the hospital doctor from the very beginning, and no time lost on the *hakim*."

"No, she could never have lived; her time had come..... She had taken her last grain of corn, last drop of water on earth." Tears glided down the cheeks of Lalita; in sadness, her voice sounded all the more rich and deep.

"I made a mistake", he mumbled, "I should not have asked you about a thing that touched you. After all, it is only a year ago when your mother died."

"A mother's memory always remains fresh; what is a year" Lalita broke off.

"I have never known mother; I wish I had."

x x x

Next day, by three in the evening Desh dressed up to see the fair of Goddess Nanda *Devi*, which had been going on for three days; it was finishing in three or four hours that evening. His uncle and aunt had visited the temple the very morning the fair started to pay their homage to the Goddess; he resented Desh's laziness in doing so.

In response to a message he had sent her to meet him in the rooms of Shanker, sister had reached there before Desh. She voiced her anxiety at his dropping visits to Hamilton; she was apprehensive of resumption of Champa affair.

"I could not come, because of the bad health of uncle."

He was glad his reply allayed her fears over him.

Together with Miranda and Sanjeev, he shuffled across Flats to temple of Goddess Nanda *Devi*; sister and Shanker preferred to get *darshan* of the images of the two Goddesses when carried, over the Mall road, from the rooms. He knew that both had kept away from the company of Miranda, Sanjeev, and himself, for being left to themselves; but Desh gave no indication that he understood their mind.

The enclosure of temples was packed with citizens of Nainital and villagers of neighbourhood, who had split into many, circular groups; each sang together to the beating of *dholak* its own ballad. Flats resounded with incoherent dithyramb, issuing out of myriad throats in perfect abandon.

Stationing Miranda and Sanjeev at the end of the congregation, he elbowed his way to the temple whose double spires, over circular tin roofs, culminated in brass pinnacles. As he walked up the steps of the temple, his eyes fell upon the two Goddesses installed in a chair, nestling in flowers. Their long flat cheeks and long flat noses were made by stretching yellow cloth, over flat banana leaves; the eyes were painted elliptical and a red cloth mantled their heads. Both Goddesses looked as impressive as six years before, when he was a school boy; but the bow he now instinctively made lacked his ancient reverence to them. Still he was pleased with himself; by lowering his forehead to the Goddesses Nanda, he had fulfilled the wish of his uncle.

Kiosks had sprung up against the temple wall, retailing sweets, toys, cigarettes, *bidis*, and *pans.* Of all the kiosks one doing multi-coloured balloons bunched on poles was attracting most of the children.

"Would you like to have one", he passed his hand over a pink balloon.

"No", replied Miranda testily, "I have given up playing with toys".

"What is the matter. Recently you got your toy married to Shanti's.

"You ask the reason from my mother."

He waited till the break up of the fair. When the bagpipe struck from the temple, Miranda, Sanjeev and himself stood at a spot of vantage. The band, drummers, pipers with 'S' shaped pipes formed the head of the procession; behind them went villagers, making gestures with their hands or flourishing handkerchiefs, and singing in chorus some ballad in rough and untrained voice. Next followed inhabitants of Nainital, also singing some popular hymn to the accompaniment of harmonium and small *dholaks*. Four bearers carried the chair of the images of Goddesses on their shoulders.

Miranda, Sanjeev and himself joined the procession from the rear as it wend through the Mall and Bara-*bazaar*, where men, women, and children had lined the route, to pay homage to the Goddesses, showering flowers on them. He never once joined in the chorus even by mistake; his eyes kept roving among the crowds in search of his own Goddess Lalita, until towards the end of *bazaar* a flower struck him on the face. He lifted his eyes and saw the two sisters at the window of the house over him. Har Preya gave him suggestion of a smile.

The procession had thinned out as it slithered through the lanes and *bazaar* back to the temple, where the images of Goddesses, after a brief religious ceremony were immersed into the lake. The crowds having made their purchases of sweets and daily necessities were fleeing to their homes. A gloom was settling over the grounds of the temple, which for a day had been surcharged with the roar of singing and dancing men.

"You took a long time", complained sister, when he along with Miranda and Sanjeev walked into the apartment of Shanker.

"The fair was interesting."

Sister informed him that Miranda and Sanjeev had quarrelled over the ownership of the bride-doll. In a fit of anger Sanjeev had chipped its nose with the barrel of his air-gun gifted him by Desh. If the matter between a brother and sister had gone up as far as that, his sister as a mother would have set it right; but now it lay beyond her powers. The news that her doll had been disfigured had, through some mysterious agency, filtered up to Shanti, who had put forward her demand, under terms of marriage contract, for the return of her bride-doll.

"I am puzzled", he jerked out, "How all these home-things reached the ears of Shanti."

"I am no less puzzled than you; Miranda, poor thing; she is so much hurt that she has given up playing with toys."

"It was I", Shanker smiled roguishly "Who informed Shanti."

It was coming to eight; sister quickly left with her children; while Shanker and himself continued sitting together. He felt somewhat tired by keeping himself standing the whole evening. Shanker poured out whisky; over it, he informed Desh that no sooner the rains stopped, he would send his sister-in-law to some renowned sanatorium in south India.

x x x

For meeting Lalita, Desh waited for a rainy evening, when he could slink through the lane under cover of an umbrella.

He seated himself in the chair he always did; Har Preya took one placed at the further side of the room. Finding herself alone with him, she looked away from uneasiness. For relieving it, he focussed his attention on Balu, who clung to his mother. He showed him the box of toffees that he had bought him; he gave him other temptations fit for his age, but the child held away from him.

"He is very shy", remarked Har Preya.

"He will be all right as he grows up; this is not a matter of anxiety, rather his poor health."

"We give him most nourishing food, but *Devi* only knows why he is so thin. Doctors say he will remain so until he is not ten years old."

"He has got your thin bones."

He looked round for Lalita. If she was working two rooms farther in the kitchen, she should have heard his voice. He presumed that she was absent from the house.

"Lalita has not come from the house of father". Har Preya bent her eyes on him.

"Does she come every evening ?"

When she was alive, Har Preya regularly visited her mother; she provided Lalita with company. After her death, she stopped the practice; naturally Lalita was left alone, shut up in her room. Rather than mop at home, Har Preya advised her to spend the evening with her; but Lalita was an incurably self-willed being; she would never listen to her elder sister.

"So often I have met her; never suspected something the matter with her."

One had to know Lalita intimately to understand her behaviour; even Har Preya seemed unsure of her sister.

"*Achha*", whispered Desh, "I want to take mother's death off her mind."

"I am with you".

Har Preya wanted for Lalita a life different from her own. She was married to a draper who remained away from home from nine in the morning to nine in the evening. Even on Sunday, the weekly market holiday, Har Preya and her husband lacked the boldness for moving out together. For their neighbours considered such behaviour undignified. To people living in her lane anything could provide material for gossip and scandal-mongering, as wearing cosmetics, returning home from pictures late at night, often entertaining guests. In case her husband was an officer in government or industry, Har Preya would have been fearless of the scandal-mongers of her lane. But neither the shop nor the house of her husband would ever move out of the spots they stood.

The life of the draper's wife who neither possessed brother-in-law, nor parents-in-law was certain to remain lonely and monotonous. Naturally she was eager that her younger sister should gain from her experience.

On his previous visit to her, Har Preya had suggested him the proposal of Lalita; she was repeating it.

At home that night he lay awake a long time. He undoubtedly loved Lalita, but he had never looked upon her as his future wife. The idea of marriage had not once crossed his mind. He was young enough for it; he needed three years to attain his twenty-fifth. True his father had bequeathed him under three lakh of rupees, but unless he had not established himself in some profession, any decision towards his marriage would seem hasty and wrong. Further until his twenty-fifth year, his uncle would continue to function as executor of his father's will. Should he die before this stipulated period, his brother-in-law was to take over his place. And neither his uncle nor his brother-in-law would approve his uniting himself in matrimony to a *vaisya* family, whose caste was two notches beneath his own.

And one man could tender him a correct piece of advice, if he turned to him for it; and he was Shanker. He could feel his love for Lalita; he could understand that for hearing her mellifluous voice, until the end of his days, Desh was prepared to pay any price.

x x x

Again he waited for a rainy evening, when he could scurry through the lane without fear of being recognised by the inhabitants. But the rains were drying; in a month they would withdraw their protection.

Seeing Lalita sitting in the front room with her sister, Desh's heart throbbed with joy. She seemed in good cheer, and gave him a charming smile.

"When we met last time", she crooned, "You asked me about our mother; that day going home I saw her in dream".

"*Accha*", his eyes clung on to her.

"She told me never forget to go to *Devi* of the Rock on Saturday."

He squashed the cigarette, he had been smoking to a butt, under the heel of his shoe. Lalita looked at the proceeding with a measure of distaste.

That day she was wearing a violet silk-sari; it was admirably matching her complexion. Deep colours suited her; he wanted her to take to them.

"Until mother was alive", informed Lalita, "I mostly wore red-sari. I liked it a little too much."

With a view to measuring the impact of her mother's death on her, he formulated a question.

"Everybody's mother dies, but no one gives up putting on gay clothes; why do you?"

"Mother liked me to wear them. After her death they made me remember her much; I gave them up."

"If your mother knew that you do not wear good clothes, would she not be sorry?"

"But how ?"

"You believe in next life."

"Why not" Lalita looked intently at him, with a sort of triumphant air.

"Then you know there is an *atma* in everybody, which does not perish even after death."

"Yes".

"And *atma* has powers far wonderful than body. It can know about its children."

Amused, Lalita listened him with her eyes lifted on him. He set himself to exorcising the ghost of her mother from her.

Do you go to pictures sometimes?", he resumed, "One good picture is being shown these days".

The corners of Lalita's lips were depressed in a rudimentary smile.

"*Achha*, you want me to go to one".

"What I have told you is very plain. I not only want you to come with me, but I want you to come in a beautiful red-sar*i*. Your mother would be pleased to see you from heaven."

Lalita chuckled; she seemed to have welcomed his invitation; but instantly her face clouded over. She had put a full stop to seeing pictures since her mother died. Whenever any nice one was being exhibited in the city, she wished she had seen it, but she kept herself at home to mourn her mother.

"What you people are talking", began Har Preya, coming into the room from inside the house.

"I was asking Lalita to see pictures".

"This is very good idea", Har Preya shook her head, "What have you to say Lalita?".

"I do not like to go unless you force me".

Striking an attitude of contemplation, Har Preya kept her eyes directed at Lalita.

"*Achha* Desh, I can call you by this name now, I think", she spoke in feeble voice, "It will be improper, our going together anywhere, like this."

"What is the difficulty; when the picture is on, you can meet me inside the cinema house. Nobody can see us together."

He was feeling irritated at her hesitancy.

"We should wait; no need to hurry. Future have pictures and pictures."

"You are afraid father of Balu would not like it."

Desh had misunderstood her. She reproduced most of the conversation, that went between them, to father of Balu. Whenever Desh met her or called on her, she never made a secret of it in the house. Father of Balu had been impressed by her effecting introduction with him, and making him a family friend.

"What is your reason then, for not coming to pictures".

"It is improper for Lalita to go like this."

He tramped home pensive. Her Preya had made him understand that unless Lalita was not engaged to him, she should keep off his society in public. With all his love for her, Lalita scarcely answered to his description of a wife whom he had wanted to be a model after his sister, both in mind and body. Like her she would wear her hair short; don gorgeous saris, keep the house trim with flowers and decorations. What to tell, Lalita neither possessed the accomplishments of the mind, nor the striking looks of his sister.

It would inconsolably distress her, if he accepted Lalita's proposal. She had warned him from committing a mistake, in case of Champa; now she would consider his marriage with Lalita as an act of sheer madness on his part. But the voice of Lalita kept ringing in his ears, it seemed to exert on him far greater power than her looks.

He looked for a solution of his difficulty. Slowly a way seemed to open up. If Lalita would resume her studies, in some years, she would be through university education: and if she made good use of her time, she could be called a cultured woman. Himself, he would have attained his thirtieth year, the right age for him to marry her.

He was jolted out of his thoughts on Lalita by the voice of his uncle.

"*Arree* Desh; you have come back home for considerable time, but you have forgotten about meal."

"I do not know that I should do with my future. Pathakji advised me to try I.A.S.".

"You have nothing to think about your career. Your father was a great lawyer; you should try to be one."

CHAPTER - IX

Four or five days later, he was sitting with Shanker in his drawing-room in the evening, smoking choice brand of cigarettes. The whole room was pervaded with its aroma. Shanker liked it so much so that he was totally indifferent to its high cost.

Joga Sah came to see Shanker; he obsequiously greeted him. Desh received a queer turn on meeting the slight man, dressed in somewhat grubby frock-coat buttoned upto the neck and *churidars*, with whose daughter he was in love. Shanker offered him cigarette from the tin they had been themselves smoking.

"*Aha*, you are a *pukka sahib*, your cigarette is the thing; it is fit for being smoked by *sahibs*".

"Why worry about them; they are happy in their homes in England."

"You are right *sahib;* now have come the days of Congress-*wallahs*."

"You are forgetting that they made great scarifies to force *sahibs* out of India."

Joga Sah was disappointed in the *swaraj,* Shanker was speaking about. It had brought power to congress-*wallahs*, but nothing to men like him, rather it had driven away his patrons. The money he had collected through business had been drawn from the pockets of Englishmen, and to them he owed his success.

Few knew the antecedents of Joga Sah. He was brought up by his widowed mother from the age of six. He had attended the municipal school up to class fifth, but the necessity of fending for himself at an early age broke up his studies. He apprenticed himself to an auctioneer of fruits and vegetables, whom he served for about four years. He threw over his situation to the hazards of an independent career by pure chance. He had known a British officer and his wife from the auctioneer's shop, who, on the eve of his departure from India, preparatory to his retirement, required the services Joga Sah to get his personal effects sold out. These included books, china, garments, utensils, glass-ware, carpets and furniture. Joga Sah inquired of the officer how much he expected off the deal. "Ten bottles of whisky", wanted the officer. Joga Sah quickly raised in small amounts a loan that met the cost of ten bottles. Taking possession of the officer's effects, he disposed of them piecemeal, making thereby a profit of about one thousand rupees net. This amount he invested in a grocer's shop, which by degrees he had enlarged into wholesale business in grains.

The incident left an indelible impression on the mind of Joga Sah. He had come to worship Englishmen, to whom he had begun to supply provisions through their orderlies and servant. He revered them for their honesty, pomp and ostentation, and above all, for their aloofness.

"You did not like *sahibs*", smiled Shanker knowingly," For their character, but for the higher prices you could charge them."

Joga Sah pushed back his cap, and exhaled the cigarette smoke through his nostrils. Shanker had scored over them.

"I was not a well-wisher of the British *Raj* as some people think me out to be; I have wished my country was free as much as any other. I have helped congress-*wallahs* with money when they were in jails and their families starved."

The face of Joga Sah waxed tense. the small, the servile man carried inside him a patron's spirit.

"This congress government has brought our *Hindu* religion to danger; it is sympathiser of minority communities; it created Pakistan."

Shanker curled his fair mustache in a smile. "By the way let us know how much you made in war time, by fair or foul means."

Joga Sah was unprepared for a sudden change in the topic of conversation. He looked with vacant eyes at Shanker.

"I have made some money, but not as much as people believe."

Shanker extended his hand, "When all is not made by fair means, should you not give something in charity."

"Lalita's mother at the time of her death had asked me to build a *dharamshala*. I will fulfil her wish when I am free of Lalita; when I have married her off."

Joga Sah occasionally visited Shanker to seek advice from him about his income-tax problems. Before moving out of the room, Joga Sah joined the plans of his hands under a low bow; the *namaskar* was executed with abject humility, out of keeping to his age and standing.

x x x

From the next day started the parents-fortnight. During this period every year Desh performed the death anniversary *shradha* ceremony of his parents, so that their souls, if still detained in hell be freed from there and taken to heaven, as well they send their blessings on him. On *puja* day, he rose early in the morning and took a heavy bath. He kept a fast for performing libations of water to balls of cooked rice, made by him, representing his parents. He interspersed the libations with postures of his hands, and alterations of his holy-thread from right shoulder to the left and vice-versa. The snub-nosed priest helped him in conducting the ceremony by recitation of prayers in Sanskrit, lightening earthen-ware lamp and incense and offering flowers to the rice balls. Lastly he offered them delicious food cooked that day. After having performed the ceremony of his parents, he came out of the kitchen in nearly two hours. He was unused to sitting long cross-legged on floor; his back hurt him, and his knees felt stiff.

He waited for the guests, invited on the occasion of the death anniversary dinner. By twelve in the noon, they began trickling in. First to appear was the every jolly chap Shanker, who was followed by the two nephews of uncle, his sister's sons, along with their children and wives. The elder of them was tall and fair-complexioned, well preserved at fifty; while the younger, bearing nondescript looks, had greyed at forty. Both worked as clerks in local law-courts and seemed to be awed by Shanker's garments.

Last to arrive was his sister; brother-in-law had sent through her apology for his absence from the dinner.

After having taken off their shoes the guests, uncle and himself sat down cross-legged or squatted upon wooden slabs placed on the floor of the kitchen. Aunt had taken much pains in cooking a fine dinner which conveyed her regard to his long, dead father. He had taken his aunt as a hard hearted, unfeeling woman; her behaviour surprised him.

After having finished the dinner, the male members trooped out of the kitchen, so that females could take their turn. As the two nephews along with their wives and children made ready to depart, uncle gave them tips of money. A sister's son was worth a hundred priests, in religious ceremonies, uncle told him. Second to depart was the snub-nosed priest, who took his leave with utmost humility. Uncle gave him handsome remuneration besides coins and cloth pieces offered in the course of the ceremony.

Excepting exchanging courtesies with uncle, Shanker had sat noticeably quiet; a few times he looked at his watch, indicating his boredom. Colour came to his face when sister entered the drawing-room. Uncle had withdrawn to his living room; this day the memory of his brother made him sad. The three of them were left to themselves to talk on any subject they chose and smoke cigarettes.

"I do not know", Shanker threw a concentrated gaze at sister, "After how many years I took food in kitchen."

"But I do not mind it", remarked sister.

"I do; we should change with times; no sense in our kitchen religion."

Sister spoke of her monotony since Desh had suspended visiting her. After the departure of father of Miranda to law-courts, and the children to the school, silence reigned the house till the evening; neither anyone called on her, Hamilton being situated far at a height, nor she on anyone. Ram Nath was visible only when his master returned home. After *chai*, if the evening was free of rains, father of Miranda along with the children strolled around the front of the mansion, otherwise he made straight to his study, where he saw his clients and prepared briefs. During the evening-meal, he mostly talked with the children; then he read the newspapers until he retired to bed.

Should she not rightly feel pained, if Desh completely forgot that his sister was, in a sense, a lonely woman who looked to him for company to make herself cheerful.

"I am sorry", murmured Desh, "I did not see this".

"At least you could have come to meet me for the love I have for you".

He felt himself guilty of cold treatment to his sister, all on account of Lalita. He noticed that his sister's face had masked with suffering.

To hide her tears, sister covered her face with the hem of her plain, white, cotton-sari, she had put on to attend the *puja* on her father. Desh had never realised before that a jolly woman as her also knew unhappiness. When she let drop the sari from her face, he subjected it to scrutiny. Her skin even at the age of thirty-three retained the freshness of a girl. The white sari, her favourite colour, matched it perfectly. Grief had idealised her beauty.

"I had thought", consoled Desh, "Your education had made you strong and courageous".

"You are mistaken; inside me is the soft heart of a woman, which no education can change."

Sister went away to the room of aunt and uncle to get their blessings; while Shanker sat on with his hands clasped round his knees.

"Why did you not go to see your sister for so long ? was there something the matter ?"

Desh gave a negative shake to his head.

"Now you know something of your sister. You should not neglect her; it is for you to make her happy or unhappy. With you she can do picture or picnics; take her to a trip of Ranikhet."

Sister hired a palanquin for her conveyance, and took the bridal road, climbing over the mountain to her house. In the absence of Desh, she avoided the company of Shanker.

x x x

The rains had almost dried up. He had to risk being seen by the inhabitants of the lane, or meet Lalita never. By seven in the evening, when it grew almost dark, he entered the house where he expected to find Lalita.

"She is not here", said Har Preya in a jocular tone. "Today is the sharadh day of our mother. Lalita has stayed at home"

"*Arree*; you allow her to go out with me; she will think less of her mother."

"Lalita is neither very educated nor modern; even they will hesitate to go to pictures and all that."

"Not when the man is a gentleman."

Har Preya seemed to turn in her mind his declaration. "*Achha*, if you say so, I shall try to persuade Lalita to see pictures with you; but if you change afterwards what will become of her."

"You should trust me."

One receiving the veiled pledge of marriage with Lalita, the thin frame of Har Preya shook with delight. She had always wished her sister to choose her husband away from their business community. By the grace of Goddess it had been fulfilled. With him Lalita would live in an airy, furnished bungalow. She would enjoy perfect freedom to go to pictures, attend parties and functions, and meet his friends. She would eat food off china plates and ply knife and fork.

Compared to the future life of Lalita, Har Preya's presented a dreary picture. In a lane, full of squalor, she lived in a scrubby house, even though father of Balu was far from a poor man. He had inherited one bungalow, which yielded one and half thousand rupees a year as rent to supplement his income of six thousand rupees from his shop. From the standard of living of their family, no one could guess it earned as much money. Balu's father was unmindful whether his home was kept spick and span or in a mess. He wanted Har Preya to be good at housewifery, more so for their being a *vaisya* family, which thrived when it earned for hoarding than spending.

"Why", Desh said with emphasis, "You do not tell father of Balu to live in the bungalow himself than giving it on rent."

"Who can say this, it is useless to think that I can live grandly. I was born daughter of a *vaisya*; I shall die wife of a *vaisya*. But I want Lalita's life to be different from mine."

"If you really want so, you make her start her studies again."

"Now when she is eighteen."

"She should know English, otherwise how can she become wife of a *sahib*."

Har Preya pursued her lips. "Of that I was always afraid."

"It is only right", he advised, with extended forefinger, "That Lalita should learn English."

"I always wanted her to keep on studying, but mother was opposed to it. She thought that what more a girl needed than knowledge to write a letter in Hindi."

"In the days of your mother, what she said might be right; but now girls' education is spreading."

"*Achha,* I will try to change Lalita your way; but you have not to tell her anything."

He came home that evening exercised in his mind. He had shown an undue haste in accepting the proposal of Lalita. He ought to have consulted Shanker before It. But now there was no going back. What a shock his choice would give his sister and uncle; but he felt himself helpless. Good, the marriage would not come off for several years. By then opposition of everyone to it would soften; they would tolerate his love for Lalita.

x x x

Shortly afterwards he called on Har Preya to know how far she had met with success in sending Lalita to school for resuming her studies. But the latter was present in the house that evening; he decided to keep silent over the motive of his visit.

"Last time I was not here", regretted Lalita, "When you came; I was sorry to miss you."

"Oho, "he peered into her face, "You have lots of worries for me; I might have been dead you would never know."

"Why do you talk like this? Do I care nothing for you?"

"Yes; it is a fact."

"How can you say that?"

"*Achha*, if you cared for me you would not have refused seeing pictures with me."

Lalita gazed at him; her seductive power began to work upon him. He wanted to kiss her somewhat thick lips, and feel her rounded forearms.

I wish I could come," she sighed, "But I am not free."

"So far I am concerned," stuck in Har Preya, "You are free to go."

"You are becoming queer", Lalita turned her face towards her sister, "You want me now to start going to school, see pictures, and what not."

Har Preya reacted with a crinkled smile.

Desh lighted a cigarette, and puffed out the smoke." Then what have you to say to coming out with me to pictures."

"I have a condition."

"Blurt out."

"I shall see pictures with you, if you give up smoking."

"Why are you an enemy of my smoking ?"

Lalita's mother had planted upon her the idea from her childhood. She had also learnt from her father that though Shanker was an angel, he was given to drinking. Desh as his friend must have contacted this habit too; and nothing was more repugnant to Lalita than liquor.

"You remind me of my younger days," he disagreed, feeling hurt at her comment.

"So you once had beliefs like mine; now you have given them up."

"I have grown up."

"But so far I know sins done in childhood can be forgiven by *Devi,* but not afterwards."

"If smoking and drinking a glass is a sin, I am a sinner".

"You shall not stop doing these sinful deeds ?"

"I do not take them as such, or I would have stopped them."

Lalita glanced him with queer eyes. "You should change in my company."

"You are vain."

"If I have inner power in me, one day you shall change."

Lalita's voice raised in making her assertion, sounded him all the more deep.

"I hope", he protested, "In my company, you shall become like me than I like you."

That evening no further challengers were thrown by the two at each other. Har Preya diverted their attention to *chai.* Forgetting her argument with him, Lalita handed him a tumbler with a smile; she surprised him.

Balu, who had till then kept away, cautiously approached him, on being called by him. He was getting familiar with Desh now that he had met him often at his house.

"Do you go to school ?"

"I am so small; how can I go to school,"

"Do you read at home?"

"My mother teaches me."

"What do you know ?"

"This is eye; this nose; this is ear." Balu pointed out each organ as he spoke its name in English.

Desh addressed Har Preya. "Your child is sharp."

"Yes, he seems so", she smiled, uncovering the dazzling row of her upper teeth.

"I do not have much difficulty in teaching Balu English words".

"Now you have a bigger child to take care of." He screwed his eyes to Lalita.

"I do not know so much English as to teach Lalita; she shall have to go to school to learn it."

x x x

Desh wanted to inform Shanker of his secret decision to marry Lalita, but when he looked into the eyes of his friend, he quailed. Shanker would consider his decision as height of folly. He would remind Desh that he was gently born and was coming into a fortune. Furthermore he was highly connected and educated; a bright career lay before him. Why should he take to wife a woman with little pretentious to beauty or education?

Instead of Lalita he brought up the question of his career before his friend.

Shanker glanced at him with significant eyes. "You had talked the matter with your sister."

"Yes I did; she wanted me to try the I.A.S. competition".

Shanker advised him to enroll himself at the bar, for his entering I.A.S. would separate his sister from him, when she needed him by her at Nainital. His was the only company she could look to, and if Desh went away, she would be left perfectly lonely. If he joined the law profession, not only could he earn lots of money, but was free to contest seats in state assembly or parliament. With the money he would inherit and the guidance of Shanker, he could as well go in for business.

Politics had never charmed Desh; but he valued the opinions and counsel of his friend. He would consider them before starting his career. At present Lalita was burning his heart. Unable to see her, he wanted to forget her that evening.

"Well", he began, "Have you no drinks with you; let my career go to *chulha*."

"I have never seen you in such carefree mood as today, is something the matter ?"

"Nothing", he said hoarsely, "Get the drinks, quick".

Dev Rama put bottles of whisky and cut-glasses on a table. Desh unscrewed a dark-green squat one, and hurriedly poured out the drink for himself, and quaffed it off neat without serving Shanker.

"What is wrong with you today?", rebuked Shanker, casting a searching eye at him.

How he wished he could mention of Lalita to Shanker; but his tongue had paralysed in uttering her name.

"I am a bit tired today." He poured himself another drink.

Lalita had overpowered him. On the one hand he blamed himself for a wrong choice in her for a wife; on the other he felt himself too weak to rectify his mistake. And in panic, lest be might not give away his thoughts to Shanker, he poured himself drink after drink.

Then Shanker sensed something was abnormal in him. Stopping him from boozing, he piloted Desh to the eating-table, on which food had been spread. But he touched nothing; he was only conscious that he should reach home not before eleven o' clock, when his uncle would no longer be waiting for him.

A *rickshaw* dumped him below his house, on the road. He climbed up on tottering steps, supporting himself on the cables lining the bridle-road. When he slipped into his room he flung himself across his bed. He felt himself too giddy and sick to change his clothes. Before dropping unconscious, he spewed all the liquor that he had consumed that evening.

After several hours, he came into himself. He lay comfortably extended upon his bed, tucked under his quilt; his head resting on pillow. His shoes and coat had been taken off: his tie loosened; his scalp and hair rubbed with perfumed oil. Uncle sat on the bottom of his bed, and aunt a little farther on a chair. He understood everything.

"Uncle you go to sleep", he stammered, "I am all right". He shut off his eyes.

"Son", drawled uncle. "Is your humour good ?"

"The night must be very late now; please go to sleep".

"When my health is bad you keep awake all night."

Uncle handed him lime water, which he gulped down without sliding open his eyes. The anguish of shame had cut the power of speech from him. He saw as never before, the sympathy and love that his uncle conceived for him. Even his father, if he were alive, would have lost patience with a son ruining himself with the habit of drinking right from his youth.

Next morning he suffered from a dull headache; he lay exhausted till nine o'clock, when aunt brought him tea.

"Uncle say something",

"Nothing",

"Speak out; do not hesitate".

Said your uncle, "Thirty years ago, just like this, I learnt Desh's father drinks; and in that he finished himself. Today, his son has gone the same way. My teachings and efforts have come to naught."

He surveyed his trousers, crushed with night long sleeping; the sheet was soiled with matter ejected from his stomach; the room reeked of liquor.

The thought of weaning the habit of drinking preyed on his mind. It was not out of any change in his belief that drinking was a sin, but from a sense of remorse that he had inflicted unmitigated pain on his uncle.

Desh limped up to him, ravaged by a passion of fear in his heart. Having performed his morning devotions, uncle sat alone propped up against pillows. As he bent his listless eyes on Desh, his haggard face looked all the more haggard from grief.

"Uncle", he moaned, "From now on I will never touch this thing."

"I know son, you had sinned just for the first time."

Returning to his room, he included smoking in his vow. A heavy load was off his mind.

x x x

On his next meeting with Lalita, he was exultant. He had met both her conditions.

"*Achcha*", he appealed, "When will you come with me to pictures?".

"Never", Lalita shook her head.

"But why ?"

"I cannot believe you."

"How can I make you believe me?"

"That you can never", Har Preya edged in, "Unless she has not kept long watch on you."

Lalita seemed unaccountable. She should have kept her promise, seeing that he had stopped smoking and drinking. Her downright refusal hurt his vanity.

"So you are not coming to the pictures,".

"Apart from my believing you, I must care for society". Lalita rested her eyes on him.

"Why should you be afraid of society?"

"Excepting a mad man everyone is".

"If you do not care for it ?"

"People would laugh at me; father would say hard things to me."

"Still what is there to be afraid of?".

"You are strange, impossible."

"Some day, when you begin thinking like me", he coaxed, "You will see pictures with me."

"That I will never".

He gave a wistful smile to ease the tension in arguments.

Lalita turned her eyes to the alarm clock on the table. "I should be going home now. Last time I got very late; I had to lie to father to explain the delay."

"Then why hurry; tell another lie today."

"You want me to do it again."

To undo the sin of lying, she had not only dropped food that night, but had also prayed to Goddess of the Rock to pardon her. That was the way of her mother to absolve herself, if she happened to commit an act of sin, which of course was a rare chance, as a fit of anger.

"The more I know about you", he apostrophized, "The more surprised I feel."

After Lalita's departure, he talked her over with Har Preya. The hold of her mother on Lalita seemed by far stronger on her than of Desh.

"You persuade her", he requested, "To see pictures with me."

Har Preya's face grew tight with thought.

"It is difficult for me to persuade her, still I will try."

"And have you spoken to her about going to school."

"Not exactly; she should not object to it, but it is a matter in the hands of father."

Calculating that Lalita would prosecute her studies, he had abruptly consented to marry her. He would gladly wait no less than six or seven years to see her a lady than accepting her otherwise, shattering his dreams of a wife. In case she and her people ignored or rejected his condition, should his proposal to Lalita still stand ? If so, it would amount to his surrendering his sense of judgement and capacity of reasoning to her love. Better he would try to forget her; erase her sweet image from his heart than contracting an ill-assorted and hasty alliance with her.

"I will not see Lalita", he promised to himself, "For a fortnight, a month. Let her know that I am not a kid; I have fulfilled her condition of giving up smoking and drinking."

CHAPTER-X

From the next day commenced *Dussehra* festival, lasting ten days. It was marked with the dramatic renderings of the epic. *Ramayan*, called Ramalila, in open-air theatre. Desh had witnessed it with zeal many a year from his childhood, now it had damped. Neither he believed in the absolute morality preached in *Ramayan,* nor he enjoyed the same Ramalila enactment year after year. But on its fourth day, on chance of espying Lalita, he took Shanker with him to Bara-b*azaar*. Both arrived there nearby ten in the night; Ramalila had already commenced. Between two short intersecting *bazaars*, flooded with electric light, a permanent, cement stage had been erected. It was decorated with curtains from all sides; the drop--curtain was already rolled up so that Ramalila drama could be visible to some thousand of men, women, and children, from open, who had taken every available space, behind windows of double storeyed houses and ground space in Bara-*bazaar*. They had flocked there from a feeling of reverence to *avtar Rama*, and also from urge for recreation. Many spectators dawdled about *pan, bidi,* cigarette and *chai* stalls.

A handsome boy, over-painted, wearing saffron robes and shock of hair, thrown over his shoulders, played the role of *avatar Rama*. Another handsome boy, but frail and shorter in height, in red, silk-sari and coronet over her hair, did the role of Goddess Sita. She was pleading her husband Rama to take her along with him to jungle. The dialogues from the epic *Ramayan* were rendered by singing to the accompaniment of harmonium and *tabla*. Shouts from spectators, "Glory to Sita Rama", punctuated the action of Ramlila.

Both brother-in-law and sister kept themselves aloof from Ramalila. Brother-in-law reserved his *Dussehra* holidays for his rest; while sister being a lady considered herself above visiting it. Even Shanker, whom he had expected to sit through to the end of Ramalila that night, showed impatience with it. Lalita had escaped his roving eyes; only when he was coming away that he caught the glimpses of the two sisters, behind a window of the double storeyed house on which he had noticed them on the Nanda *Devi* fair. Seeing him Lalita gave him a glimmer of smile.

Shanker took him to his rooms, "For two hours, we stayed in Ramlila."

"Did you like it?" , asked Desh.

"It was as usual affair; seen it year after year from childhood. Then it is amateurish; actors do not get a fortnight for rehearsals."

"You mean you do not like it; you do not want Ramlila performed?"

"Rather I like it; it should be always done; I have not read Tulsidas's *Ramayan,* but I can tell it in detail, and how have I learnt *Ramayan*; just by seeing Ramalila. and most of us have learnt Ramayan by seeing it.

"Do you accept what has been said in Ramayan?" Desh looked at Shanker with questioning eyes.

"I do not understand you."

"Do you think, "explained Desh slowly, "A man should be honest as king Dusharath; a son as obedient as Rama; a brother as devoted as Laxman; a wife as faithful as Sita."

"Well, I agree and I do not; depends on circumstances. If a husband is good to his wife, she should be faithful to him, but if he is bad, should she still be faithful to him ? It is here that Ramayan is silent; at least to me."

"Take it like this," continued Desh thoughtfully, "You are good to your brother; if he comes out bad to you, should you still continue being good to him?"

"No", Shanker shook his head. "I shall stop being good to him".

"Then you do not follow the morals of Ramayan that we should be blindly honest, obedient, devoted, and faithful."

Shanker swallowed. "If Ramayan wants me not to fight for my rights, I shall not follow it. But one thing I know of *Ramayan* that Rama fought Ravana for taking back Sita from him".

"But *Ramayan* does not say to Sita to fight her husband Rama, when he wants her to stand on a stake in test of her fidelity. When she comes out of the flames untouched, she asks earth to break apart, and she lets herself into its bowels; there is no greater character of a wife than of Sita."

Shanker looked significantly at Desh. "But how often Sita's example of a wife is misinterpreted even by our educated women." Shanker turned his eyes on his watch. "The night is quite advanced; instead of going home you stay here."

Dev Rama was still away seeing Ramalila. For him Shanker fixed a bed along with his own, unrolling spare bedding over it.

Shanker readily fell into sleep, purring softy. But it had flown away from his eyes. The image of Lalita kept revolving in his mind; he burnt to meet her.

x x x

Dussehra was concluding on its tenth day. that evening sister, her children, Desh, along with Shanker, seated themselves behind the windows of his drawing-room to watch the Dussehra procession. It debauched out of Bara-*bazaar* into the Mall road a little after sun-set. It was headed with drummers and bandsmen, playing their musical instruments with skill. Then followed several, tall, effigies of ten-armed, ten faced. Ravan; his son Meghnath, and brother Kumbhakarna. Features of few effigies had been shaped grotesque; teeth protruding; noses overlong above ugly moustaches; and tongues sticking out of the mouth. But the last two of Ravan and Meghnath looked portly; their features were cast regular; their coloured, paper-costumes; frock coats, *churidars* and round caps-flashed glossy, almost resplendent. Behind the vehicles, carrying the effigies of demons, came the flower bedecked chariot of Rama and Laxman. The two actors wore the saffron robes that they did in Ramalila, and held their arrows, fixed on the bows, trained at the effigies in front of them. The rear of the procession was formed of festive crowds, who sung in one voice selected verses from *Ramayan*, in praise of Rama.

By the time the procession entered Flats, night had descended over the city. Their party comprising of five members, led by Shanker, adjourned from his room to the tier of stairs, rising above Flats, to watch the finale of the war between demons and God. Rama discharged ten arrows, timed with ten shots from a gun, at the effigy of Ravan; someone at once set on fire the tallest effigy; it blew up with sharp report; tongues of flames started licking it, brining out the hidden fire-work inside it. From a rotating wheel lakhs of sparks, silver or multi-coloured, shot out illuminating the darkness. One by one the effigies were thrown into flames; the reports, crackers, and brilliant fire-works kept the crowds entertained, which had encircled the gutting effigies from perilously close. Street urchins, in a burst of high-spirits, raced round them. The dying flames tore triumphant shouts from numerous throats, "Glory to *Rama Chandra*; Glory to *Sita Rama*".

The crowds began to disperse; they had gathered round hawkers retailing toys, balloons, and sweet and salty eatables. Children demanded from their parents whatever object caught their fancy. The chariot of Rama and Luxman wheeled back to Bara-*bazaar*; a small crowed followed it, singing together. In a while the battle scene between Rama and Ravan lay deserted.

Throughout *Dussehra* evening his sister exchanged few words with Miranda and Sanjeev; the two quietly watched the fireworks, letting their mother keep company with Shanker. She forgot to suggest Desh to buy them toys on the occasion of the festival. He regarded her behaviour towards her children as queer. He was too surprised at himself. Never once he took Miranda or Sanjeev near to the chariot of Rama for blessings, as his uncle did him in childhood; nor he felt thrilled at the victory of Rama over Ravan; but he enjoyed the Dussehra procession, its band and fireworks.

x x x

The day following the end of *Dussehra*, like all the married daughters visiting the homes of their parents, sister did uncle and aunt. She was clad in her favourite, white georgette-sari spangling with stars; she looked in good-humour, and tip-toed into the house with the agility of school girl. Ram Nath followed her, carrying a basket.

Uncle greeted her with a sunny smile, and signed her to sit beside him upon his bed. Even aunt who harboured inflexible jealousy for her, beamed with delight on meeting sister.

"Chandra daughter", pointed out uncle, "Where are you children ?"

"I had asked both to come along with me, but they went out for a walk with their father." Sister gave a vague smile as she quickly changed the topic of conversation. "Uncle your health looks good these days."

"My days are towards the cremation ground". A charming smile took away the edge of pathos from his voice.

"*Arree*, you speak like this; you always said you have to do many a deed."

"Yes, I have seen you happy and prosperous; but Desh remains."

Uncle was old and invalid; he wished before he stopped breathing, Desh was married, but to a moderately educated girl.

"Not English speaking", sister looked at uncle with gaping eyes.

"No; woman is made for home and children; English speaking girl is of little service to her husband; she wants equality with man".

Imagining that uncle was making innuendo at her, sister's face waxed sulky.

"You misunderstood me", he held poised his forefinger. "If all were like you, I would have liked for Desh English speaking wife."

The heavy countenance of sister relaxed into a smile.

"I have brought you up", continued uncle, "You are a worthy daughter and wife. I have brought up Desh also; he shall marry the girl I choose for him. He will not be affected by present nasty times when boys and girls are settling their marriages themselves than their parents. Results are inter-caste marriages. And soon our new government is bringing in our society such unholy thing as divorce; and right of inheritance to daughters."

Pulling the hem of her sari into a mantle over her crown, sister made red-*roli* mark upon uncle's forehead, touching his feet and of aunt, to express her reverence; while Desh being younger to her did her feet. Turning open the lid of the basket, she had brought with her, she offered everyone sweets and fruits. Uncle took extraordinary pleasure in smelling the apples and testing all the varieties of sweet. Taking little part in conversation, he gazed at sister; he was overcome by the love of his niece.

As sister was about to depart, uncle and himself slipped into her purse little amount of money, only ten rupees each, as token of their affection for her.

"Since your marriage," muttered uncle, his voice heavy, "I never gave you anything excepting something on festival day."

Sister fell to the feet of uncle, and rested her head upon them.

"You have married me so well; what do I need from you or Desh. All I need is your blessings."

Sister tried to stifle her sobs; she was aware death was hovering over uncle.

"Times are changing; soon daughters will be coming to their parental homes, wanting their share in properties".

"But uncle, I shall always want flowers of love from you and Desh."

He accompanied sister in her homeward journey. For making purchase of cosmetics, she walked into Empire store. It was long and spacious; its walls were lined half way with bales of cloth, while finished goods in glass cases, decorated its floor. Two salesmen stood behind counters; one of them was dressed smartly; the second, with grizzly hair and exuberant manners, produced the articles she demanded; she only selected the expensive imported makes.

"You did not buy some saris, *memsahib*", begged the head salesman, when she was leaving the store.

"Not now", replied sister dryly, "Sometimes when Shanker is here, I shall like to see them."

"But he is coming here much less".

"Something the matter".

"I could not tell you". The corners of the salesman's mouth showed an abortive smile; it suggested that he knew probably the reason.

Sister and himself climbed to the room of Shanker, whose right side of his upper lip twitched up, in a comic lift to greet them.

"You look grand in your new white-*sari*", Shanker glanced sister with admiration.

"This is one of those saris I purchased from your store in May; good you referred to them; has father of Miranda paid you their bill ?"

"Do not bother".

"He should have sent you the money by now; I had told him about the purchase long ago."

Dev Rama served them mutton-chops hot from the frying pan. Their savoury smell tempted Desh; he helped himself with a double of them; Shanker followed his example; both fell to eating them with noise.

"I like their smell", sister looked avidly at them.

"Then join us", Shanker gave sister a full eyed glance. "Devi Ram has done them so well today".

A pale smile cracked apart the lips of sister, "It is sixteen years to my marriage since when I gave up eating meat, chicken".

"You are doing self-denial, believing that it would increase your husband's income".

"I am not as superstitious as that; I gave up eating meat because I was married into a vegetarian family."

"And you cannot resume it".

"I do not suppose so".

"Even if I press you".

"It will be useless".

Desh accompanied sister half way up her home; returning to Shanker's rooms, he found him absent; Devi Rama was dusting and cleaning the drawing-room at that odd, sunset hour.

"What has happened since I left half an hour ago ?"

"Telephone came just now from Inder *sahib*".

"He seems a big friend of your *sahib*."

"Yes, very big; but now for two years some friendship has lessened".

Desh bent forward to listen to Devi Rama with attention.

"Our *sahib* has changed in his habits; he does not allow Inder *sahib* to stay with him at night, nor does he allow him to bring anyone with him."

For a few moments Desh was unable to catch the hint; when he understood, he added, "*Achcha,* that is why there are spare beddings".

"But no girl comes now".

"What should have changed your *sahib*?"

"That you should know better than me."

Presently Shanker appeared with a package under his arm, followed by Inder Pratap with a friend, a young man of about twenty-five. Both took seats on the sofa opposite him; neither Inder deigned him shadow of a smile in greeting, nor he on him. But Inder's friend invited Desh's attention. He had a droll face with idiotic, immobile eyes, under beetling brows and receding forehead. Inder began to hum an English tune, tapping his foot upon the wooden floor. Shanker had slipped out of the room to make arrangement for the dinner. Desh felt awkward sitting alone with Inder whose manners smacked of superciliousness. He walked out of the room.

"Where are you running away?", asked Inder.

"For a stroll".

"Then, take us with you".

Following the dull period in rainy months, Flats was getting crowded with tourists, who were streaming into the city in October, the month of autumn. Bedizened up ladies lounged about in company of prosperous looking gentlemen or stood with them in knots over the top edge of the lake, luxuriating in the cool breeze.

A pretty woman brushed past Inder's friend, as the three of them sauntered towards the skating-rink.

"Well, Sah", inquired Kunwar playfully, "You enjoyed her touch".

"Who would not", giggled Sah, opening wide his mouth.

Desh's attention was engaged by a women standing on profile to him, watching boats and yachts sailing over the lake. She turned square on him.

"Oho, Champa, how are you", greeted Desh aloud.

"*Arree,* it is you; whenever I come to Flats, I remember you".

"You expecting someone".

"No, none in particular", her old, lascivious smile flitted across her face.

"Then join us".

He had expected Champa to cut him, if she saw him. But her effusiveness towards him, to his utter surprise, seemed everlasting; in her behaviour he saw not a trace of complaint. She met him as graciously as though she had spent an evening with him only a day before.

Inder led Sah, Champa and himself to the restaurant, attached to Capital picture house, which opened on to Flats, the top of the lake.

"May I know", solicited Inder with regal deliberation, "The praise of the lady with you".

Champa returned a quick smile to Inder's greeting. He rattled out names of several prominent ladies he knew in the city, including two colleagues of Champa.

A dark-complexioned waiter, with flourishing moustaches, took order from Inder. He squinted once or twice at Inder as he wrote it out in his note book; he seemed well acquainted with Inder, who poured out the coffee without letting Champa do so; he wanted her to devour all the cutlets; his brusque, free and easy manners embarrassed her. Though the restaurant was a fashionable one, equipped with costly furnishings and crockery, the coffee supplied by it tasted weak.

"You know why it is bad", Inder turned up his nose, "Restaurant is using skimmed milk; good coffee you make only with pure, creamy milk".

"It is difficult", brought out Champa involuntarily in a toneless voice, "To get good milk in Nainital during tourist season".

"Yes, you are right. I am found of milk and I have best breeds of cows and buffalows in my farm."

"You run a farm", Champa cocked her eye with interest.

"Yes; we *zamindars* must do something, when all our lands are being given to our *ryot*".

Inder spoke with gusto of his five-hundred acre farm, which yielded him an annual net profit of fifty thousand rupees. He had sweated first two years in raising it; firstly in deforestation and clearance of land; secondly in breaking the virgin soil, and turning it fit for cultivation. Inder boasted of his prudence. He had sensed even before independence of the country that feudalism would go; he had started the farm on his own, without assistance from his father. The class of big *zimandars* was often held to be one of idlers, seeking pleasures; ill-adapted to fight the battle of life. But instances like his own proved that *zamindars* were rising to the changing times; they were entering industry, trade, agriculture, and service, to reinstate their elevated position in society.

"I am very impressed by your talk," remarked Champa, "I had never respected *zamindars*, for I had heard so much of their cruelties to their tenants; now, it seems, if I continue meeting *zamindars* like you, I might change my ideas.

"Sure, you are always welcome to meet me; I stay in hotel Metropole, and move out to Flats every evening."

Having paid the bill and a substantial tip to the waiter, who *salaamed* him low, Inder stamped out of the restaurant. On coming out Champa begged her leave, while male members of the contingent pottered about in the neon lights of Flats.

"I am so successful with women", Inder intimately gripped Desh's hand.

"You are dashing and rich".

"That is not enough; I have the chivalry to attract women".

"How have you learnt it ?"

"It is one of the oldest and most difficult of arts; I have learnt it in many years". Inder looked aslant him. "Now give me your word; you shall not tell Shanker of my meeting Champa, and of the income I gave of my farm."

Desh burst into a silvery laugh, "But what is the harm in telling that you met Champa."

"Because Shanker's brain is softening; he is becoming careless about his business; he gives bigger portion of his income to his brother, though I have always told him not to do so. Now he is becoming a *mahatma, yogi*. If he knows of Champa, he will begin giving me sermons".

An hour later all of the guests were seated around Shanker's dining-table, who had bought finest whisky to treat Inder. Knowing that Desh had got out of the habit of drinking, Shanker held side of his upper lip lifted up in bewilderment.

"You are going back to your childhood, its beliefs and morality".

"Not exactly, though no one can declare, one would remain the same all life."

Pouring himself drink, Inder fixed his attention on Desh. He invited him to his farm, and promised him gay time there. One or other of his friends kept visiting him; Desh could enjoy cards; indulge in secret pleasures that held the key to a truly happy life. Being an independent minded character, he had swapped his pleasures for the affection of his father, whose harangues on moral life filled him with disgust.

Meal came off late. Excepting Sah, who had also declined the drinks, no one felt much appetite. Food was slapping;

chapattis Dev Rama had baked paper thin; Sah sat bent eating; not once did he raise his eyes off food, or took part in conversation.

"Do not forget", whispered Inder, "To do my work quickly."

Shanker gave an odd jerk to his head.

"I am in such great difficulty; you got to help me."

Meal over, Desh immediately repaired for his home, without waiting for coffee or chat. On his way the first chill of winter struck through his limbs. He was seized with strong desire to smoke, which reminded him of Lalita. Every cell of his body was crying for her. He had taken a desperate decision to stop calling on her. On chance of meeting her, he could still make trips to the temple of Goddess of the Rock.

CHAPTER - XI

Desh's attempt on first Saturday came out unsuccessful. On the second, he trudged up and down the road leading to the temple of Goddess of Rock; but no sign of Lalita or her sister was visible. Disappointed, he had emerged out of the road into Flats, when he heard his name being called out from behind him. The voice sounded familiar, deep and rich. He turned round; Lalita and Har Preya stood over the stairs to the temple of Goddess Nanda.

"Why did you not come for so many days", complained Lalita.

His eyes traversed her figures; her round arms and full breasts. He wished his tongue could heap abuses on her, but he had lost his power of speech.

"Tell me, why did you not come to meet; why did you not come more than once to Ramalila ? I always looked out for you there."

He kept intently gazing at her.

"I had to look after uncle; he had got seriously ill."

"You lie, you lie", Lalita gave a radiant smile. "I know why you did not come."

"What do you know ?"

"You did not come because I did not go with you to pictures."

"I never knew you are so much intelligent".

"What have you been taking me for, a fool".

"Never!"

The road leading to the temple of Goddess of the Rock was unfrequented one; the sisters could risk going together with him across it. To save himself the trouble of taking out shoes, he went no further than the stairs of the temple.

Returning to Flats, Lalita interrogated him, "Why did you not come up before the Goddess to say your prayer?"

"I had told you once, if you can remember, that I do not believe in temples".

"At least you could bow to the Goddess."

"Even when I do not believe in prayers."

Lalita recoiled, "But why?"

With his arms behind him, he walked bemused.

"I do not know if there is a God or Goddess, who wants prayers from human beings, or is ready to answer them."

"You do not believe prayers bring prosperity and peace". Her voice was low and deadened.

"No".

"And you do not pray for your *nirvana*; you do not want to live in heaven, among stars".

"*Nirvana*; it is nonsense", words slipped out of his lips.

"You do not believe then that there is next life; soul transmigrates and is indestructible; you do not believe in *karma*". Lalita's face was inflamed and working.

He realised that his tactlessness had outraged her religious sensibility. His eyes gently glided over Har Preya with an expression." "I am very sorry for what I said; please set every thing right."

"Lalita." interposed Har Preya, "You should not be hurt by what Desh says; when you will go to college and become learned, you will also think like him."

Lalita gave her sister a dubious glance.

"There are so many learned men; but I have met no one who talks like Desh."

"He is just talking lightly to tease you".

Though the words of Har Preya cleared the tension from Lalita's face, still she remained for rest of the way, cold and unfriendly.

At the spot he had met the sisters that evening, over the steps to the temple of Goddess Nanda, he broke from their company. Lalita walked on without throwing him a parting glance. Har Preya turned round, paused, and then blinked at him indicating that she would be able to win over her younger sister.

He had moved some steps when Har Preya called out "Come soon; I have to tell you something".

x x x

Some days preceding *Diwali*, the last and most important festival of the year, Desh was busy as everyone in supervising the white washing and painting of his neglected house, and tidying up of rooms. To attract Laxmi, Goddess of wealth worshipped on the festival, aunt neatly decorated the *puja*-room, attached to her living one. She brought out the miniature Gods and Goddess from there along with ritualistic vessels, and scrubbed them bright with ash and water. She meticulously polished the frames and glasses on prints of various Gods and Goddesses hanging around the walls. Desh helped her in fixing bouquets on the altar, along with newly purchased earthenware Goddess Laxmi and *avtar Krishna*. Till about sunset he remained engaged in embellishing the *puja*-room.

His sister came to the rooms of Shanker some minutes after him. She was accompanied with Sanjeev, while Miranda had stayed back with her father.

Immediately the party of four set out, carving their way through gayly dressed crowds that paraded the Bara-*bazaar*, shining with new coat of whitewash and paints. Under blazing lights, each shop was typically decorated with its ware, while non-stop crackers were deafening the ears. Abundant marigolds and chrysanthemums, countless lights, mounds of sweets, and ubiquitous earthenware Laxmi and *Krishna*, filled *Diwali* enchantment in every heart, home and street.

In pursuance of the belief that new purchases that day invoked the blessing of Goddess Laxmi, sister did a tall, brass, vase with arabesque design on it. She walked around temporary *Diwali* stalls displaying earthware toys and Gods and Goddesses, and bought several of them.

"Sister, you seem to be very religious."

"Have you been taking me to be an atheist?"

"No, even I cannot say that for myself, but I never thought you were so superstitious."

"I am not."

By eight thirty in the evening, sister hired an open palanquin for returning to her home. While parting company, she held out her hand to Shanker for a shake.

"I cannot wish you happy *Diwali* by embracing you as men do men". Her voice was mellowed, caressing.

Shanker gripped her hand, raised it, then growing conscious let go it. Few moments sister's eyes lingered on his; she looked magnificent in an expensive brocade sari in crimson. She wore heavy make up that evening.

After the departure of sister, Desh also separated from Shanker. Most of the lights in the lane had gone out; but the room in the third storey, his legs urgently sought, was brilliantly lit with electric ones. As he climbed up the stairway be wished he had possessed enough will power to hold himself away Lalita, firm to his resolution; but he felt himself too weak to stick to it. He recalled with a sense of dismay that on Saturday he had wounded her. She might herself dislike to meet him.

Though both sisters were absent from the front room familiar to him; its looks had materially changed. With the rest of the house it had been whitewashed and painted. From the centre of the ceiling multi-coloured paper-chains diverged to all directions; bouquets and many earthen-ware Goddess *Laxmi* and God *Krishna* stood on tables, niches and every where. The decoration was crude and garish.

Hearing his cough, the sisters, who had been singing devotional song inside, burst into the room. He was struck by the finery of their skirts and *chuddar*, and load of golden ornaments on them; his eyes traversed over their necklaces and pendants, wristlets and finger-rings.

"It is about nine O'clock", Lalita undulated all over, "We had given up hopes of your coming".

He was taken aback by the hearty welcome she accorded him. He had expected her to look sullen, lumpish. Now her behaviour towards him beat his understanding of her. It was devoid of any constrain, or flavour of irascibility.

"You look lovely in *Diwali* costume".

Lalita blushed at him remark; she pulled her *chuddar* over her crown, demonstrating her love to him. Her gesture threw him into ecstasy.

"Now, do not sit that way like a fool", ordered Har Preya, "Show Desh Diwali *halwa, laddu*".

He happened to look at his watch. It was time for husband of Har Preya to come along, closing his shop.

Hitherto Desh had successfully avoided him. He fidgeted to go.

"*Arree*, why worry, father of Balu would not come home tonight."

"Why ?"

"He must gamble among his friends for two days of *Diwali*."

"Does he win or lose.

"Usually he loses. He believes by losing Goddess Laxmi is pleased; hence he will gain in trade all the year; but I believe in opposite."

"You also gamble."

"Who does not in *Diwali* to try one's luck."

"Sister", chimed in Lalita, "Let us play *Diwali* with our guest."

He took off his shoes. The three sat down on their haunches over the carpet, and heaped their money in front of them. In a friendly game highest stake was fixed at rupees five, and time limit to half an hour; and flush was preferred to dice. From a new pack, purchased for *Diwali*, Lalita dealt the first round; three cards each person. He picked up his hand, slid open the cards a bit from the top, and peered at them, taking in jack, ten, and ace of hearts. He made his first bid with rupee one; Har Preya did contesting bid, while Lalita dropped out. He enhanced his bid, Har Preya redoubled hers, staring him in the eye. Hesitating to risk higher bid, he tried to read from the face of his opponent whether she possessed a hand of higher order than his own. Moving rupees two he called out for a show; but Har Preya without exposing her cards, mixed them up into the pack, losing all her bids. He swept the pool money to himself even as he responded to the refreshing smile that Har Preya had given him. As winner, he dealt the second round. Har Preya made first bid, he dropped out; Lalita disliking to contend with her sister,dropped out too. Har Preya dealt the third round. Lalita made first bid. Finding his hand a run-seven, eight, and nine, he made contesting bid; Har Preya dropped out, clubbing with Lalita in opposition to him. He redoubled his bid. Har Preya advised Lalita to put up fight, but Lalita coolly reviewed her hand and instead called for a show. He won.

Har Preya was a slap-dash player, while Lalita a sedate one. In a short time she had lost a good amount even on moderate stakes. He and Lalita and shared it between them.

The game rolled over beyond the time limit of half an hour, fixed at the outset. The sisters banded themselves as one opponent to him. Invariably one engaged him, while the other dropped out. Har Preya mostly bid on blind cards, raising them to rupees four or five. He began losing both money and count on time, ravished by two obstreperously merry sisters who treated him with luscious glances, dazzling smiles, and tricks of the game. Within two hours he was cleaned out of all the cash on him. Har Preya offered to lend him a large amount of money, but he liked the game to close down. When he hoisted himself up, he found his legs dead.

"My legs are too sleeping", began Har Preya.

"And Balu is sleeping on the carpet for how long".

"*Arree*, poor thing; I forgot to give him food."

She lifted the child to her arms; planted two resounding kisses on his cheeks, and started dandling him.

"Now I can stretch my legs and can walk", he kept tapping them with his fingers, "I wish you happy *Diwali*".

"When you are coming again", Lalita glance him with pleading eyes.

"Again, impossible; I should not have come even today."

"Har Preya allows me to see pictures with you; still you are angry with me".

The sisters made an appointment with him to meet two days after, in the evening-show at the Ashok cinema. He should look for them in the dress-circle than outside. If the two found only strangers seated there, one of the sisters would sign him to come up, or he should take his seat away from them.

After full three hours he was returning home, when all over the city most of the *Diwali* light had gone out. Uncle and aunt would have waited for him to meals; he felt sorry for his absence from home on the most important festival. He casted about to invent an excuse for his delay, but Lalita had drugged his intelligence. He felt a strong desire to smoke.

A cold *Diwali* dinner lay on a table in his sleeping room. He started leisurely eating the stiffened *puris* with vegetables, over which a layer of *ghee* had solidified. He was finishing the meal with pieces of *rasmalai*, when his aunt walked in.

"You should not have kept awake for me; I was delayed by Shanker."

"After *puja* and food your uncle had an attack; for a while his breathing had stopped; I became so much afraid".

"I am going to call the doctor".

"You need not go; he is better now".

Aunt preceded him to the bed-room, where uncle lay on his right side, dormant; his eyes closed; his hand under his cheek. His face was covered in a film of sweat; his breathing sounded short and quick; his pulse beat firm.

"Aunt, uncle is recovering; you take rest; I shall look after him at night".

She buried her face in her hands; her body shook with her cries.

"I have always been hard on him, always", she soliloquized; "*Devi* punishing me."

Himself on the verge of tears, he sat down by her and patted her back, as though she were a child, and slurred over few comforting words, and made her lie on her bed. Tired as she was by the work of the festival, she soon fell asleep. He broke his vigil over uncle when the ghostly light of the dawn was peeping in through the windows. Not once had thoughts of Lalita distracted his attention from his job.

x x x

Sister was expecting him. Seeing him a joyous smile mantled her face. She had decked herself in a white, tissue sari, tight fitting satin *choli*, and string of pearls. Though she was her sister, he let his eyes dwell on her ivory skin and statuesque face.

Chrysanthemum, white, red and yellow, emblazoned the drawing-room where sister seated him. The flowers, wonderfully arranged, stood in an exquisite bowl over the centre-table, and in tall vases on the corners of the room. Sister should have spent few hours in setting them.

"Do Miranda and Sanjeev still quarrel over Shanti's doll ?"

"O, I had to return it to Shanti; she come here four times; I had to do so under contract of marriage."

"Then the marriage of doll is off."

"Yes, it is; but it has not pained Miranda; she is only interested in her studies. Only I felt sorry that the beautiful fairy had to be given away."

His voice drew out brother-in-law from his study to the drawing-room. From behind his thick glasses he held Desh in his implacable gaze; not once did he turn them to the artistically set chrysanthemums, or to his charming wife.

Brother-in-law wrinkled up his brow, "Seen you after months; we have been missing you."

His taking notice of Dish's absence from Hamilton seemed unlike of him.

"Your sister went out only in *Dusherra* and *Diwali* that is very little. Why do you not go out on picnics."

"We have been so often to every where in Nainital; same places do not attract."

"Hun, "Brother in-law pouted his lip. "Then go to Bhimtal, Naukuchia-tal."

Sisters seized at the idea. "These lakes are at a low height; winter is the time for going there then summer."

She preceded brother-in-law and himself to the dining-room, where Rama Nath served them *chai*. Sister rebuked him for laziness, and for putting the cups, the plates, and pots, unsystematically. Presently Miranda and Sanjeev burst into the room; both children took seats on either side of their father, and shared the refreshments with him.

Inquired brother-in-law, "What were you people doing?"

"I was memorising an English poem, "answered Miranda.

"It was difficult; I want a tutor to help me in English."

"Your mother can do so."

"Mother does not like teaching us."

"Then son, I shall engage a tutor for you and Miranda."

Sister had been listening the conversation between the father and son with studious unconcern. She drew everybody's attention to the bowl of marigold placed on the table.

"Now winters is coming; Soon I shall have no flowers for my vases."

"I notice," said Desh, "That your vases are beautiful and new, but your furniture is heavy and old fashioned."

"Yes, you are right. I do not like this round table; I have long been thinking of changing it."

"Achha, "cut in brother-in-law, "I am off to my work."

He stared Dash in the face with complaints in his eyes, over reference to furniture, that had forced him to disengage himself from the company of the brother and his sister.

"Your work seems on the increase."

"Yes; I have no time to drink water in courts. Recently I appeared as defence council in two murder cases; both were weak ones. If I had not taken so much pains on them, the accused would not have been acquitted." Brother-in-law smiled a smile of self-satisfaction." So do not forget to give company to your sister."

When Miranda, Sanjeev trooped out of the room with their father, sister turned to Desh.

"Now I want you to be a lawyer than an I.A.S officer, but do not be a lawyer of the type of your brother-in-law."

"In what sense you mean."

"In the sense that you obviously see."

He made for home. On the way thoughts of Lalita occupied him; he was meeting her that evening.

He reached Ashok few minutes before the commencement of pictures. He had delayed himself on purpose that Lalita would reach there before him. With all his love for her, he wanted to carry himself before her, with a measure of dignity and primness.

He tumbled upstairs the dress-circle. Being a festival day it was almost full. Stationing himself at the gate, he looked in for the sisters in the crowd. He took few minutes to spot them on the extremity of the last row of seats. Her Preya was waving to him; he walked over and took a seat next to Lalita. Her Preya greeted him with a brilliant smile exposing her fine row of teeth, while Lalita with a damp one.

"We were the first to enter here", Lalita screwed her neck to him. "My heart is sitting."

"Do not fear; with the pictures your heart will run." Lalita 's face looked slightly disintegrated.

"After how long you are seeing pictures today?"

"I saw one with my mother before her death."

With the ringing of bell, the lights went off, and the film show was preceded with a documentary on Mahatma Gandhi*ji*'s funeral. In the darkness he twice sought the hand of Lalita, but no sooner his touched hers, she withdrew it. In past she had let him hold her hand; her regard for her sister, he guessed, had brought about the change in her.

The film was based on a stereotyped love story, beginning with a handsome youth rescuing a comely girl from getting drowned in a lake.

After the show Balu, who had fallen asleep on the seat beside Har Preya, had to be carried away by her in arms. Desh accompanied the sisters out no more than he had them in.

CHAPTER - XII

It was time of November; winter had set in. Sunny days continued day after day, and Desh boated or moonched about Flats. While boating, he yearned Lalita. If she showed courage enough to do a film with him, she could as well accompany him in other of his expeditions. He would tell her that she should glide over the moonlit lake with him. But when he met her, Lalita brought an exercise-book from the inner room, and handed it him.

"What is it about ?"

"You open it," she answered in her velvety voice.

He turned over the pages; they contained in large hand few passages of English translations from Hindi. An uprush of joy lifted his feet from the ground. Lalita had resumed her studies. He read out two passages; both were full of mistakes in grammar and spelling. Her knowledge of English language was rudimentary.

"You took help of someone."

"From a book on translation."

Desh advised her to arrange a tutor, who would teach her, besides English, other subjects. Lalita explained him her difficulties. She was afraid of opening her mouth to her father about her renewed interest in books for he might disapprove of the visits of a tutor into the house, when he was absent.

"*Achha,* I am going," he concluded, "You meet me on Saturday in Flats summer-house. By then you tell your father that you want to start studies again."

"I shall try to see you."

"No, you must come. If you are afraid of day light, come after sunset."

As he issued out into the lane, a huge giant of a man swiftly crossed him. He perceived that man had thrown upon him a suspicious glance. To ignore him, Desh walked on; not once he turned over to see if the man was known to him.

x x x

Uncle never fully recovered after attack of asthma on *Diwali*. Under instructions of the physician he took light meal in the evening few hours before sleeping, comprised of sago in milk, which he took in bed.

Desh was late in returning home from visit to Lalita. Having finished his meal, uncle lay on bed; aunt was seated in a chair nearby, and fire of charcoal burnt in a metal-frame to keep the room warm.

"Your health in all right today." He entered the room.

"Better than yesterday; but any time cough can rise. If I get through winter, summer is no trouble."

Since uncle was confined to bed, he sat every evening with him an hour or two, talking him to sleep. Concerned over uncle's illness, he always tried to cheer him up; Desh told him that he looked healthier and fresh; his appetite had improved, and his asthmatic spasms had weakened. But however much he told him that he was mending and recouped, his lies were unequal to inspirit uncle. Fifteen years of continuous suffering had hardened him, and he had resigned himself to his lot. Mostly he brought the conversation from his ailment round to the future of Desh, and detained him over it.

"I think you should start going to court."

"I shall speak to brother-in-law."

"Hun, Desh, you hurry up speaking to your brother-in-law; I have only one last wish and that is to see you a *burra* man, and I do not have much time."

Uncle extracted a letter from his pillow, and reached it him. Desh tore it open. It was from sister, she had wanted him to fix the date for the trip that brother-in-law had proposed, to the cluster of lakes ten miles east of Nainital.

The letter of sister confirmed his suspicions about her true relationship with Shanker. He had regarded their fondness to one another, at the most, a platonic case. Now he saw the depth and nature of their feelings to one another. From long he had remarked that their faces lighted up on meeting; their manner indicated a sort of intimacy that appeared unlike friendship. Both resented his delays in visiting them, for he was instrumental in bringing them together, and as cover sheltering them from public eye. That he should continue staying in the city, both wanted him to take to law as profession then getting into I.A.S. He had further collected evidence that the two usually talked on the telephone. It had as well struck him that sister came down to Flats pretending business, while she never budged out of the rooms of Shanker. She had gone into her shell; she spent lesser and lesser time with her children and her husband, keeping herself occupied with her books, flowers, and embroidery. A likewise change had too come over Shanker. He was developing indifference to his business, and distaste to life. Surely his sister loved Shanker no less than himself Lalita.

x x x

On Saturday, Desh had to wait only few minutes for Lalita and Har Preya at summer-house. Both appeared soon after sundown, having finished their beat to the temple of Goddess of Rock. The place wore deserted looks; still, the three, to doubly secure themselves from publicity, took seats on a bench facing the lake.

"It always surprises me. "he pointed out, "You bypass the temples of *Siva*, *Krishna, Rama,* joined to that of Goddess Nanda Devi, and go down half a mile to Goddess of the Rock, whom no one knows expect people around this city."

"It is because Goddess of the Rock is special to our family; though Goddess is Goddess everywhere."

He realised that he had picked up a wrong topic on which Lalita and himself held opposite views. He had committed that mistake on a previous turn, and he was on the verge of repeating it.

"When I was small", he murmured by way of pleasing Lalita, "I went to the temple of Goddess of Rock every Saturday with my uncle."

She showed surprise that while she had remained true to her upbringing, he had repudiated it. Her mother was a staunch devotee of the Goddess of Rock, and went to Her temple every Saturday. She believed that the Goddess answered her *puja*; her impecunious husband had met with luck in trade, and her two daughters found men in affluent circumstances to marry.

"But who could tell, who would Goddess bless", words slipped out of his lips.

Lalita looked at him with open, melting eyes, "*Arree*, do you not even known that rewards of Goddess are not blindly given". She paused. "Goddess blesses one who is virtuous and good, both in this and previous lives, and prays Her sincerely."

"If one does not."

"Goddess would never bless."

"And if one is sinful and bad."

"She will curse".

He listened Lalita with the counterfeit seriousness of grown ups to the prattle of children.

"Do you really believe in what you are saying".

"You believe sun will come tomorrow morning."

"Without doubt".

"Then what I am telling you is as true as sun."

The ball of silvery moon had climbed up over the eastern horizon. The glassy lake spread out lurid, nude and inviting; soft breeze, with the first chill of winter, breathed on them; a boat in silhouette slipped by. He burnt to hold the hand of Lalita; he grew suddenly conscious of her full breasts. But she was chaperoned by her sister; he was forced to behave himself. There, sitting beside Lalita he had been anaesthetized into the very romance of a dream; it was impermanent, but it was heavenly.

"Let us boat", he suggested.

"No; it is nice sitting here; and then the hour is late and cold. If someone sees." Lalita's drowsy voice sounded piercingly sweet.

"Why bother about anyone; no one will eat you off."

"You are too simple, Desh".

Her words sank deep into his heart; he was thrilled; for the first time she had called him by his name.

"I so much wish we could boat", he insisted, "The moon is lovely."

"I too wish; I have never done night boating."

"The moon lit lake is calling us."

"Yes, it is. I feel so happy coming out for a walk today evening. I am getting back into my former self, when I ran to the school, and played long with friends."

His nerves tingled with delight. Lalita was showing signs of getting over her melancholy that had possessed her since the death of her mother.

"Let us boat, come on" he begged.

Lalita looked at her sister for approval; he disliked her complete subordination to her sister.

"In winter Balu's father closes the shop a hour before. Let us move home."

He accompanied the sisters to the lower end of the lane, when he was reminded of the huge, giant of a man who had taken note of him, while coming out of the house of Har Preya, on one of his previous visits there. He was overbourne by a vague sense of horror. At once he disengaged himself from the company of the sisters.

x x x

Bright days continued, though at night frost fell thick over the valley; and shed in winter of their leaves, weeping willows, hanging over the right bank of the lake, imparted it funereal looks. In the evening, air felt intensely cold, still Desh never carried with him his great-coat; he felt in his element in winter.

Taking his old route, he entering the lane from the upper end; since night fell early in winter, the cheap shops had closed down.

Lalita was sitting alone in the front room, and seemed in good spirits. She welcome him with a provocative smile, and indicated him his old seat.

"I looked for you every day", she told him.

"Was there something the matter ?"

"Yes; I have spoken to my father about my starting studies."

"*Achha*," he opened his eyes.

For few days she felt shy in approaching her father; she suspected that he would make fun of her idea. At last one evening she braced herself to face the trial. But it was not until her father was about to retire to bed that she could stand herself near him, and unroll her mind to him. A while he remained stupefied, too dull to understand her. Then he grinned.

"You", he laughed, "Want to be the educated girl of today."

"Yes",

"Why do you want higher education, when you have not to go to office to work. It is too late for you to think of books."

Lalita gave up pleading her case to her father. She saw that she looked ridiculous, and came away from the room.

"But", demanded Desh in a rough tone, "Why you did not speak to your father again ?"

"It would have been useless."

"Do no care about your father; go ahead with your studies."

Lalita gave him a faint smile.

He knew her constitution by now. She was a child devoted to her parents; she would easily overlook his advice that would set her at odds with her father. If he wanted to direct the course of her actions, he should use tact, employing on the quiet the agency of Har Preya.

"What is your sister doing ?"

"She is cooking; food in winter has to be ready earlier than summer; it is so cold afterwards."

"Yes, winter seems so rough this year. Rains too were heavy."

Lalita was ignorant of the scientific reasons underlying the severity of weathers. She believed that earth was groaning with the weight of false and wicked men and unchaste women; Goddess reduced sin by means of nature.

"Who tells you that ?"

"Whenever there were droughts or floods and harvests damaged, my parents said so."

"*Achha*, my uncle also tells me so from my childhood; but why bother about causes of droughts or floods. It is getting to be eight O'clock, and I am shy to meet father of Balu."

"You stay for sometime more."

"Better come to summer-house on Saturday; it is so pleasant; come after dark when no one can see you."

Though on the appointed day a cold wind blew from the morning, still Lalita arrived at Flats summer-house right in time. He was surprised that she had come all by herself. A passion of joy rushed through his veins; Har Preya was not in his way.

"Sister did not come", she patterned out all at once indicating her nervousness in meeting him. "Balu has temperature. I was also not coming, but sister wanted me to go."

"Sit down", he pointed her seat beside him on the bench. "You did well, you came", he gave a radiant smile.

"All the way I was not conscious", her face was twisted with fright.

"Do not worry; no one is about here this evening".

Whenever he had met Lalita before, desire to feel her arms and hold her hand had seized him. Now alone with her, he found it, to his surprise, sleeping in him; rather his heart throbbed.

He worked his hand towards her hand, caught at it, and began stroking her palm. It felt soft and large. Her wrists, emerging out of her shawl, were bedecked with gold bangles; her fingers with rings.

"You keep wearing lots of gold."

"These are my mother's things."

She showed him her hand and neck ornaments.

"You people have much love of gold."

"My mother had lots of gold; but she had no love of it. When she saw, she is dying, she divided it in five parts; she gave me two because I was most beloved daughter. Two she gave to my elder sisters, and the last fifth she asked my father to give in charity. Father will build *dharamshala* in the name of mother."

"Your mother was a great woman."

Lalita leaned her neck backwards in pride. "She always gave alms to *pujaris*, the poor and infirm."

The lake looked darkly luminous and turbulent; wave upon wave broke upon its upper bank. Neon lights, reflected deep into the water, softened the harshness of a blowy November evening.

Desh ached to put his hand round her waist, snuggle his face to her neck, and imprint a kiss on her lips. But he felt shy; then she might take his behaviour as clumsy. He could easily postpone caressing her, if he was often meeting her. He laboured under no hurry.

"You do not feel cold; you are not wearing sweater under your brown coat." Lalita gave him a softening glance.

"I do not feel half as cold as others in winter; only I feel desire to smoke when the wind blows." He took out the silver cigarette case that had remained in one of the pocket of his coat, and began to toy with it.

"When you carry it with you, you should be smoking," she said with a note of irritation in her voice.

He regretted his mistake in taking out the case from his pocket.

"I have neither smoked nor drank since I gave you my word."

"Now promise me one thing."

"What ?"

"Give up friendship of Shanker."

Desh threw a quick glance at Lalita. His face turned serious and hard, "I cannot give him up for what he thinks and believes in, rather I will you."

Feeling hurt, she stepped out of the summer-house. He had let slip an indiscreet remark or two. He tried to repair his mistake.

"We go to the temple of Goddess of the Rock. It is not even seven-thirty in the evening."

"Sitting with you I forgot I had come out to visit the Goddess; now it is late; she must be angry with me."

"Walk fast; you can return by eight O'clock."

Instead of going homewards, he turned left and walked on in the direction of the temple. After a while, he heard her scraping behind him. His posing himself a devout should please her.

By the double arched gates to the temple of Goddess Nanda Devi and other Gods; Lalita on a sudden came to a halt, spun round, and dived down the stairs. He was compelled to follow her, despite the knowledge that his venture was fraught with danger. The temple was situated near Bara-*bazaar* lanes, and Har Preya's neighbours were accustomed to paying homage to it. But it being a chilly late hour, he hoped to evade notice.

Stationing herself in the corridor of the temple, facing the two flat faced Goddesses with silver eyes, Lalita joined palms together before her breast, and prayed through barred doors, already locked by the *pujari*. Having finished it, she leaped towards the gates; hurried, unaware of him.

"You did not go", he called from behind, "To other temples of *Rama* and *Siva*."

"No," she shook her finger, "I am too late to return; then I am worshipper of only Goddess."

As himself and Lalita were emerging out of the arched gates, the huge giant of a man who had taken notice of him in Har Preya's lane, encountered them. He leered at Lalita a moment, then quickly turned his eyes away, and walked on towards the temple.

"O my father !" cried Lalita with in inflection of terror in her voice, "He is Jeewan Lal, Goldsmith of sister's lane."

Awhile the two paced on as though they were being hauled to the scaffold; dumbfounded. He regretted his mistake in wanting Lalita to visit temple of Goddess of Rock and instead following her to Nanda Devi temple, frequented by her acquaintances. He pulled himself together; he tried to infuse into her moral courage.

"*Dekho*," he gathered his brows, "Luck for us that the goldsmith of Har Preya's lane saw us; we cannot go always under fear of people. If your father knows about me, it is all the better; he will not only give you permission for your studies, but also for other things."

Lalita tramped on mute, looking straight in front of her.

"Do not worry", he comforted her, "Let the people know about us; who cares."

"You are a man; you can say so; Goddess of the Rock is angry with me."

"I will meet you soon; do not worry over the goldsmith. He might not have seen us; and bringing in of Goddess of the Rock is foolish."

Following her, he stopped short of her lane. Lalita casting him an agonised glance scampered away. He remained transfixed until her steps had not faded.

At home the incident sprang to his eyes. Though he had tried to act brave before Lalita, in matter of fact he trembled with fear. Jeewan Lal had of course seen both of them; he could be expected to pass on his intelligence to neighbours in his lane, who would spread it over the city in no time. People would whisper among themselves that though they had respected Desh as a gentleman, he proved to be a rascal. Few charitable to him might say that his conduct would be less blamable, if he married the girl he had been secretly carrying on. The inhabitants of the city would regard the course as unpractical, a bad example for their families, untarnished by inter-caste marriages.

He saw himself pointed out in streets. Brother-in-law wrinkling up his brow, declared, "You cannot marry out of your caste; the whole thing is unthinkable," Sister fetched up tears, "O Desh, I never thought you would be wanting to marry a girl without university education." Shanker laughed at his expense, "I thought you had eyes to choose a beautiful girl."

Lastly his uncle cast a haggard glance at him, "I had hoped that you would be a *burra* son of a *burra* father; and now you talk lightly of my beliefs, and fool with the daughter of a *vaisya*. I wish a were dead than seeing all this."

His pulse beat fast; a layer of perspiration had broken over his forehead and neck, and he shivered from cold. He wished he had secreted a bottle of whisky in one of his trunks; he felt himself thirsty for a drink.

CHAPTER - XIII

The following evening Desh dressed up to see Har Preya. In the light of the happenings of the previous day near Nanda *Devi* temple, he would talk over Lalita with her. If called upon to meet Joga Sah, he would reassure him of his sincerity to marry his daughter. But before facing Joga Sah, he should consult Shanker. He blamed himself, his shyness, in keeping the Lalita matter from him. If he had overcome it earlier, Shanker, by his wise advice, would have helped him preserve from scandal.

As he was stepping out of his bungalow, he was taken aback to see Shanker himself coming up the gate. He instantly understood the purpose of his visit; he should have known of Desh's involvement with Lalita, and wanted its confirmation from him.

Shanker's face was tense; he gave Desh a wan smile. Both walked in, and he quickly pulled the doors shut so that their talk could not be overhead.

"Is this a fact what goldsmith says?" Shanker glanced him with horror in his eyes.

He nodded shamefacedly. "How did you come to know of it?"

"Joga Sah visited me in the morning; then the whole afternoon I waited for you; when you did not come, I thought let me see you myself, and discuss the thing with you. Why did you keep all this from me?"

"Because you have kept yours from me."

"It was so obvious; there was nothing to hide from you," Shanker made a sweeping gesture with his hand. "Once or twice I asked your sister to tell you all about us, but she said that you understood everything, and required no information."

Goldsmith Jeewan Lal had been keeping a watch on Desh's visits to Har Preya's house. Seeing Lalita alone with him, at a late hour, bore out his suspicions. He quickly called on Joga Sah, and warned him if he failed to tighten his control over his youngest daughter, she would heap shame on him some day.

Jeewan Lal submitted him details of her affair with Desh, accusing Har Preya for a go-between. Joga Sah dashed to the room of Lalita, caught slaps on her cheeks; threatened her with murder if she stirred out of the house. Having taken preliminary proceedings against his daughter, Joga Sah called on Shanker His face was suffused, and he was wearing a *kurta* and *dhoti*, the two clothes in which he stood, at the time of the hearing of the dangerous news. Shanker was in the midst of his meal.

"You look troubled", observed Shanker, holding a morsel of *chapatti* between his fingers, "Something the matter?"

Joga Sah lapsed into tears, and through them he told Shanker that Desh was corrupting his youngest daughter.

"What", exclaimed Shanker in utter bewilderment, "You mean my friend".

"Yes, the very one. If he had come from an ordinary family, I would have seen him myself; but he is a *burra* man with a *burra* brother-in-law."

If the boy and the girl loved one another, Shanker saw hardly any reason for Joga Sah to come in their way to a marriage. But to the latter the advice was difficult to stomach. He was a conservative man who guided himself by the traditions and customs obtained in the society; an inter-caste marriage went contrary to them. He might have overlooked the convention by accepting Desh as his son-in-law, had not her mother herself made Lalita's engagement with a cousin of her eldest daughter's husband. The wedding would have come off long before, but for the intervention of the death of Lalita's mother. Now that the mourning period of one year had passed, Joga Sah was in correspondence with the boy-*wallahs* to fix the date that would suit them for performing it.

"If you can agree to take Desh as your son-in-law, then what is the difficulty in breaking your daughter's earlier engagement?"

"That is not done", Joga Sah wiped his nose with his *dhoti*, "Secondly that would hurt the *atma* of Lalita's mother. It is through her *puja* and *dharma* that I did great in business; I should not do anything which she would not have done herself."

If a man believed in a certain philosophy of life, in which his dead loving wife as well did, his actions and thoughts proceeded from it, and Shanker, knowing the maxim, put off provoking an argument with Joga Sah.

"Then why have you come to me?"

"Just to request you to make Desh do nothing that would harm my daughter".

"You could have yourself understood that he would do nothing, that sort of thing".

But the apprehensions of Joga Sah were by no means easy to still. A breath of scandal could spoil chances of his daughter's marriage. Shanker was an arch friend of Desh, and exerted enormous influence on him. He could easily check Desh from committing rash acts that might injure the reputation of Lalita.

"You make Desh," requested, Joga Sah, "Give up thinking of Lalita."

"I must see him before giving you that promise."

"Whatever befalls, I cannot offer my daughter to Desh. You make him stop thinking of her."

"Well, tell Joga Sah", he snapped, "I will never give up my rights on Lalita,".

"Desh, look here," whispered Shanker persuasi-vely, "You have to be very calm and cool; you have to do nothing that might cause harm to Lalita."

"Hun, you are right".

"I do not like you to marry this girl; not because of caste difference; but because I wanted you to marry a girl who is like your sister."

"I always thought like you; but once you begin to love someone as much as I do Lalita, you forget whether she has these qualities."

Shanker's eyes suddenly got riveted upon the oleograph of *Siva* on the mantelpiece.

"Yes, that is always the tragedy of life". He went on in a steady monotone, "Whom you admire is not your wife; whom you do not, is. But so far as I am concerned I give you full liberty to marry Lalita. It would pain your sister, but when she knows it makes you happy, she would not oppose it."

"I am so glad to hear you say so", Desh's voice rang heavy.

"Meet Lalita, and let me know what you two have decided, I will try to bring round Joga Sah to your side".

When Shanker was gone, Desh gave a sigh of relief that the name of Lalita and himself had escaped publicity. He was touched by the sympathy and affection of Shanker, who had promised to support his marriage with Lalita, even though he disapproved of it. Now he could safely wander about the streets, or face his uncle without fear.

By nine in the evening, he stamped up the lane. In winter the hour was advanced, and he found it silent. A short man answered his knock on the doors, while welcoming him in; Har Preya banged shut the doors. She with her husband squatted on a rug, spread over the floor around a coal-fire.

"I always knew", said Balu's father in a bass voice, "Father-in-law would never agree to give his daughter out of his caste; in a way he is right too, he is no young man with new ideas in his head. No one marries his daughter out of his caste. I had always been telling mother of Balu not to try a thing which she would not be able to do."

A young man of about thirty-two, father of Balu was enveloped in a *pashmina*. His skin looked dark about his thick lips, and his bulging eyes assumed a fixity of gaze as he spoke.

"The world is changing", said Desh emphatically, "Joga Sah should change too; hit castes with a broom; how can I forget Lalita."

"It is not so easy to change my father-in-law; I always knew he cannot change his ideas on marriage. I warned mother of Balu that she was playing with fire, but she did not listen me. Every time you came here, I knew the danger is coming near, but mother of Balu told me that Lalita would be lucky if she got a man like you. What could I say to mother of Balu; I knew she was pushing you and Lalita down a pit."

The loquacity of Balu's father irked Desh. He had come to meet Har Preya to urge her to get the engagement of Lalita broken.

"Why you kept this fact from me", he complained to her, in a tone of surprise mingled with anger.

"I was afraid, if you would know too quickly of Lalita's engagement, you would give her up. So I postponed telling you."

Har Preya regretted her mistake. She had never calculated that showdown would unexpectedly come. She was taken aback by receiving urgent summons from her father, whom she found boiling with rage. He rebuked her for spoiling Lalita, for taking her to Flats and pictures and allowing her full freedom with Desh. Her Preya fought for his case by praising his virtues and importance; and slowly she convinced her father that he was by far the right choice for Lalita.

"Then your father has agreed, "he blushed like a girl.

"No, I could not change his thinking. He feels there should be no castes, but himself he is helpless when it comes to marrying his own daughter. He has great fear of public; secondly our mother had engaged Lalita to Jagdish, and therefore he is the boy for her."

He was a draper, like Balu's father, in Ranikhet, and owned real estate. Desh had met him in the rooms of Shanker, with Inder Pratap.

"Yes, yes, "Desh gave a motion to his head, "I have met him; by his look I thought he is simpleton."

"Hun, you are right. Everyone who sees him first, thinks like that. But he is clever in business, though he is eccentric."

"Has he met Lalita? "

Her Preya gesticulated, "The marriage was settled by my mother and house-*wallahs* of my elder sister".

"Can I meet Lalita ?"

Har Preya had avoided mentioning her; it would hurt Desh to know that with her face buried in the crook of her arm, Lalita was moaning. Har Preya tried to give comfort and strength to her; she told her that she was secure from rumour-mongers; excepting father and goldsmith Jeewan Lal nobody knew about her story with Desh. It was always feared that their father might some day surprise her secret, and it was expected then that she would stand up to face him. That moment had arrived, though a little too quick. She wanted Lalita to ignore the threats and tempers of father; but the more she tried to console Lalita, the more she cried.

"When," he drawled, "Shall you see her again?"

"Tomorrow."

"Tell her I want to meet her; you also do your father again."

As he rose to his feet, father of Balu sprang upon him and pressed him down. He had stayed in two hours in his house, and must accept a glass of hot milk as refreshment, which Desh readily swilled off.

"As congressman I went to jail in 1942 quit India movement", father of Balu looked at him with pride; "In future I can be a M.L.A., a minister, you know."

"Yes, I know", added Desh disinterested, "Also that you gamble in *Diwali*".

Abruptly Desh jumped to his feet, and walked out of the room. He felt himself too exhausted and out of sorts to sustain conversation with father of Balu.

Desh went to Shanker's rooms next morning. His sister had reached there a little before him, and no sooner her eyes rested on him, they were filled with tears. As she dried them on her handkerchief, a tormented look came on her face. Even Shanker's was overcast with an expression of grief. From the drawing the three moved to the sleeping-room, where a cheerful wood fire burnt over the hearth.

"What a fate you and I had", remarked sister.

The misery in her voice overpowered Desh. A long silence intervened.

Sister drew her chair near the hearth; she warned her hands over it, often chafing them. Her long nails were manicured, and her beautiful face was painfully made up. She was invested in red, silken-sari and great-coat, chased with black and red bands. She seemed him as brilliant as he had never seen her before.

"Look here Desh;" she resumed in a slow, unmodulated voice, "Though you are very sensible, you are still young".

"Yes, no doubt about it."

"We all want to be happy, but we cannot do whatever we want to, because what makes us happy should not make others about us unhappy."

"But how to know what we should not do ?"

"Conscience, sense of duty, people's opinion tell us that."

"You mean I should not marry Lalita."

Sister gave him a speculative glance. "If it makes you happy you do, though it would be unreasonable of you. Every man can fight out his feelings; then you should think of uncle."

To keep arguing with sister was useless, when he craved Lalita every hour of the day.

Sister relapsed into a fit of crying; she put her handkerchief to her eyes. He wished he could alleviate her unhappiness. He transferred his gaze to Shanker; whose eyes too seemed misty. Suddenly Desh's own overflowed; he bowed his head and covered his face in his hands. He wished he could flee from Lalita, but he felt himself too weak to act.

"When", resumed sister with a melancholy note, "You are fixing trip of Bhimtal."

"We go no sooner my mind is at ease."

"In winter I feel so sad and cold; I read and knit; but I cannot do that all the time."

"I like Nainital in winter, when it snows. We are opposite of one another."

Shanker rigged himself up in his heavy, black, great-coat, and *Kashmiri*-fur cap as the three sallied out. Large shops, schools and colleges, picture houses and fashionable hotels, having closed down, Flats wore dismal looks. Shanker and himself stopped at the gates of Nanda *Devi* group of temples, while sister walked in to pray to multi-Gods enshrined there. Desh remembered with trepidation that two days before he had been caught by Jeewan Lal at the very spot in the company of Lalita.

"Your sister is a strange woman."

"Why ?"

"For four years I have been telling her that it is useless to go to temples, and follow conventional morality; but she never understands me. Though we are so near to each other in our hearts, we are so apart in thoughts and beliefs, which, as a matter of fact, separate us."

Shanker began playing with a pebble between his two feet.

"There are not many like me who can undo childhood teachings;"

"Yes, you are right Desh; I have completely failed in scraping out the religious lines in her mind, made by your uncle in her childhood."

Sister completed the round of temples surprisingly quick, and when she rejoined them, her features had composed, and a wistful smile played upon her lips.

"What has he been telling you, Desh," she demanded, corkscrewing her eyes round to Shanker. "He must be telling that I am a fool; I visit temples."

He responded with a crooked smile.

"I can never lose my sense of duty, "she declared solemnly." I can never lose faith in *Siva*."

Sister preceded Shanker and himself to the palanquin-stand. He felt unaccountably glad, severing from her and Shanker. Both pointed out to him his folly in accepting Lalita, and both loomed as ghostly to him as in a nightmare.

He had returned home earlier than other days, and without taking off his dress, he walked into the room of uncle, who was reclining against the head-rest of his bed. Over the *Geeta*, which he had been reading, he gave Desh a searching look.

He embraced his uncle in a concentrated gaze. He felt in himself an under-stirring of fear that his uncle might know of Lalita. But in a moment, putting aside his suspicion, Desh grinned even as he seated himself at the bottom of his bed.

"How is your cough today, elder-father."

"It is bad".

"Tomorrow I shall call the doctor."

"I am not as ill as to need a doctor. My thoughts are elsewhere; I want you now to marry. I have got horoscope of a good girl; daughter of an engineer."

"There is no hurry."

Uncle held him with cold eyes. For having rejected the advice of uncle, he felt ashamed of himself. His inter-caste marriage with Lalita would break his heart, in his old age. Sitting with uncle he wished he had the strength to dismiss Lalita from his mind.

By next evening Desh had forgotten of his meeting with his sister and Shanker. He found Har Preya all alone in her house; Balu having gone out with his father.

"There is good news", she smiled, looking up at him over her knitting.

"Tell me everything," he leaned forward from his seat, all ears.

At first her father had showed himself as much inimical to the proposal of an inter-caste marriage for Lalita as the previous day, when he had sent for Har Preya. He rightly feared that his kith and kin, and friends would feel outraged by such a marriage, remaining blind to the fact that he had attempted at social reform. His trade might suffer; he might hurt the *atma* of his daughters' mother. Her Preya sat out to break his resistance. She told him that if he really loved his youngest daughter Lalita, he should make her happy; and none other than Desh could bring her it. True, an inter-caste marriage of Lalita would kick up noise in society, but in due course of time it would go silent; the very people who criticised him would admire his progressive idea about the marriage of his daughter.

The more Har Preya lectured her father, the more he lent her a patient ear. He admitted that an intercaste marriage of Lalita with Desh was undoubtedly better, but he, at the same time, felt himself too weak in performing it. He saw that in fifty years or a hundred, caste barriers to marriage would weaken, but his knowledge was of little help to him. Har Preya refused to give in. She stressed upon him that for making Lalita happy he got to disregard anachronic customs. She put up fight for few hours before her father yielded to her. Overjoyed at the success of her mediation, Har Preya dashed to the room of Lalita.

She called out, "Do not weep no more. *Devi* has heard your prayers. Father has no objection to your choice."

She had expected Lalita to jump out of her bed, on hearing the good news, and give a shriek of exultation. But she continued lying on her bed, her eyes closed; her regular breathing was punctuated by low moaning.

"What is the matter, Lalita", she jerked out, feeling her forehead and neck, "Oho, you have some temperature."

Lalita remained motionless. Har Preya shook her from her torpor and sat her up.

"You heard what I said?"

Lalita threw her a weary glance; her swollen eye-lids drooped on her eyes, already reddish from weeping.

"The question of father does not arise", she stammered, her voice sounded as feeble as of a dying man. "I should do what is right."

Lalita looked so piteous and spent that tears rose to the eyes of Har Preya. Her hair was tangled and strayed wild; her sari and *choli* were execrably rumpled and the room she lived in smelt musty from want of ventilation. Har Preya walked her over to the bathroom; put her to a vigorous wash; changed her sari, bed-sheet and pillow case; smeared perfumed oil on her hair and combed it. She made *chai* and forced Lalita to gulp down a hot cup. It radiated energy into her limbs and body; she herself demanded a second.

"Sister", he gasped, "If you had not given me tea, I should have fainted away",

Lalita should have been fasting since Saturday, Har Preya guessed.

"Now you eat sweets to your stomach full", Har Preya uncovered the upper row of her teeth in winsome smile.

"You misunderstand me; I have told you a little before that it is not father's permission that matters."

"Then what matters? I cannot understand your things."

"What matters is the blessings of *atma* of mother and Goddess of the Rock that I take the right decision."

Perplexed, Har Preya darted a quick look at her sister.

"How are mother and Goddess going to send you blessings; and how are you coming to a right decision?" The voice of Har Preya rang in anger.

"I am praying constantly", answered Lalita with an inflection of sadness in her rich voice, "My inner soul should tell me."

The brow of Har Preya puckered up.

"I am bewildered by hearing your ideas. Father was in your way; now he has removed himself. Only you are changing".

"Mother had done my engagement you know."

"*Arree*, who cares what Desh thinks and believes in; you should see his position in society, his education, looks, and future."

"I am constantly praying that I take the right path; you come after three days; I shall tell you then of my decision."

"Get up ! Throw your madness ! I will force you to marry Desh. Now I am going; I shall tell father you are having temperature, and he should look after you."

The coldness of Lalita towards him thrust a dragger through Desh's heart. He abandoned his weight on the back of the chair he had been occupying; he felt a fainting fit coming over him.

"I always knew, I never understood Lalita".

Har Preya glanced him with sympathy. "Do not get anxious; Lalita never goes against my wishes."

Out of remorse, he put his hand on his forehead.

"I should not have talked about things that hurt Lalita; she is enraged with me."

"No Desh, there is nothing to worry; on my one sign she shall go to you. She obeys me like a child."

x x x

Desh was on tenterhooks. Lalita's behaviour upset him less, astonished him far more. He had always believed in liberty of thought and liberty of expression. He liked frankness, and had opened up his heart to Lalita that she should know him better. He wanted her to cast off her faith as himself, but if she clung to it, he nursed no grievance for her. He loved her more than his life, and he instinctly believed that she did him no less. It seemed that her mind ruled her heart. With all his pride for maturity of out look on life, his capacity to reasoning, his phlegmatic temperament, he marvelled at her self-control. How he wished she had acted as an impetuous girl; stolen into his room in the mid of night; caught him in her arms, and planting clinging kisses on his lips, entreated him to elope with her. But actual Lalita turned out the opposite. He was furious with himself that he should have exercised no restrain on his feelings for her; he wished he could tear himself loose from her. But how helpless he seemed; craving her with all his being; he was glad he was needing patience for only three days. The knowledge that he possessed an invincible weapon gave him great relief; a sign from her sister would send Lalita tumbling to him.

On the appointed evening, Desh climber up the stairs with a fainting in his heart. As he sat down on his usual chair, Har Preya gave him a forced smile, and at once showed him the design on the suitor-coat she was knitting for Balu.

"I like it; but you have used four colours, while I should have chosen only red and blue."

"I thought like you, but Balu's father wanted four."

"I see you always knitting something or other for Balu; he should have many woollens."

It delighted Har Preya to make her son look smart.

"*Accha*, Lalita is well", words slipped out of his lips.

Hearing the name of her sister, the slight, nibble frame of Har Preya stiffened, and a painful convulsion ran down it.

"What does she say?" Desh started at Har Preya stonily. "Tell me whatever she says; do not be afraid",

Tears glided down the cheeks of Har Preya.

"Tell me, tell me," he pursued, "If Lalita says no for me."

Har Preya inclined her head in a slow gesture.

A pang of humiliation tcre down his heart, warping his countenance. He felt hot all over; he tried to pull himself together; he clasped the sides of the chair he was occupying.

"I met her this afternoon", continued Har Preya, "No sooner she saw me, she started laughing; I was so pleased that she was in good cheer".

"*Arree*," exclaimed Lalita. "I was looking out for you; I have made my decision; not Desh".

"What ! You getting mad !"

"No, I am not; I kept praying to mother and Goddess; slowly my heart began telling me of the right man."

Har Preya's face reddened from exasperation.

"Do not be silly Lalita; do not reject a boy like Desh for stupid reasons."

"I think the opposite of you; mother has come to my help. I saw her in dream; she asked me to reject Desh. I will obey mother."

Silence fell over.

Har Preya's head drooped down, and muted cries issued out of her lips.

"Today is a good day sister; I have made up my choice; told it to father; he is also happy; he says wedding will come off soon. Rejoice sister today than feeling sorry."

With tears standing in her eyes, Har Preya contemplated Lalita. Her face looked extraordinarily radiant; her eyes glowed from sheer happiness. If Lalita was insane, it would have consoled Har Preya. She felt a sharp, burning sensation in her throat, and an heavy weight bearing down her shoulders. She wanted to scold Lalita to reverse her decision, but grief had overpowered her.

"I want to see Lalita just now, "Desh sprang on his feet, and started fidgeting about the small room; his fingers working.

"It is a bit late", answered Har Preya with hesitation, "Father might be coming from shop; postpone it till tomorrow."

"I got to see her now or never."

He knew the location of Lalita's house; he had seen her sitting there on two festival days. He followed Har Preya, keeping some yards behind her. She had told him to approach the house from the rear for avoiding notice. A stairway, smoothed with cement, led him up into second storey of the middling house. In the front room Har Preya offered him a chair.

He rolled his eyes in search of Lalita.

"She is in the inner room; she is dressing up to meet you."

He was satisfied by the information given by Har Preya. His anger for Lalita cooled off; he felt himself bursting with confidence that no sooner she would rest her eyes on him, Lalita would be overwhelmed; she would fall on her knees; wind her arms about his legs, and, lowering her head, cry high to reaffirm her love to him. He would then put up her face, kiss her, and forgive her.

He swept his eyes round the room. Har Preya sat on an unsettled bed; clothes of Joga Sah ranged over it against the wall. The untidiness of the room was somewhat relieved by the coloured prints of *Siva* and other gods, adorning the walls. A large-size photograph of mother of Lalita on the mantelpiece, arrested his attention. At once he took off his eyes; she seemed a frightening soul which had raised a wall between him and Lalita.

Some minutes passed; he started wringing his hands from restlessness. Lalita was slow in changing her sari. To avoid uneasiness, he wanted to meet her in the absence of her father.

"Lalita is taking time," he began scrapping his shoes in impatience against the old sheet of mat. spread over the floor.

"This is her room," pointed out Har Preya, walking over to the closed doors of the other room. She tapped them. "Lalita, hurry up; Desh is here outside for quite sometime.

Har Preya remained rooted to the spot where she stood waiting for an answer from Lalita. Few minutes passed without any response from her. Har Preya knocked at the doors.

"Lalita hurry up; Desh is so eager to meet you".

She waited again for few minutes, but the silence in Lalita's room reigned supreme.

"What are you doing? You told me you are taking two minutes in changing sari, but you have taken ten," Har Preya lifted up her voice.

Over again Lalita reacted to her sister with perfect silence.

"What has happened to you ? Why do you not say something? You want that Desh should go away without meeting you."

Sensing the behaviour of Lalita indicated oddity; he walked over to the doors and knocked at them.

"I came to meet you," he cried.

Lalita preserved silence. She was keeping him waiting to work up his keenness to meeting her.

"It is already very late." He cried again, "Hurry up; your father would be coming along any moment; I do not want to face him."

Lalita thwarted his wish to meeting her, with silence.

"Dearest, I love you ! Open the doors; I want to tell you many things;"

Lalita turned a deaf ear to his adjurations. He kept knocking at the doors that she would be forced to throw them open. He paused when his knuckles began aching.

"Come out, Lalita," he shouted, "I cannot wait very long here; if you do not want to see me, tell me so."

He waited for a response; he looked with consternation at Har Preya. Baulked by the silence of Lalita, he beat his aching knuckles upon the doors; banged them with kicks, rattled the bolt, but he failed to gain admittance into the room.

"Oh," he grumbled burning all over with the flame of wounded pride, "Who cares".

He spun round and dived down the stairs. He heard Har Preya shouting from behind, "Do not go away Desh; wait; Lalita shall open the doors; come back."

It was all one to him whether the elder sister supplicated him or no. He sped past the semi-circular road over Flats to the rickshaw-stand. He wanted to take himself away from the scene of his greatest humiliation in life.

The chill of the December night went through his limbs; and as he walked up the ascend to his bungalow, he panted. He wished he had on him a pullover to keep him warm, Food was spread on the table, but he left it untouched. He lay awake a long time; tears freely ran down his cheeks. The pain that Lalita had inflicted upon him had congealed in his heart; he resolved never again to see her.

CHAPTER - XIV

The following day Desh received a letter from Shanker. He had informed him that Joga Sah had visited him, and apprised him of the latest news. The father had expressed delight at the unexpected choice of his daughter. It all astounded Shanker, and he at once telephoned his sister that the rival of Desh had won.

His sister and Shanker well understood his plight. Both expressed their sympathy to him, feeling sorry that he should have come under the spell of a wayward girl. They hoped that he would get over the shock in a brief time; one should willingly suffer few years as a broken-heart than contract a misalliance.

In the last paragraph of his letter, Shanker had wanted him to fix immediately the date of the trip to Bhimtal and adjoining lakes. His sister felt that the trip would help him unburden his mind of Lalita, and by the time he would return to Nainital, he would find to his surprise that her memory was fading away.

In his letter Desh replied that he was suffering from low temperature and cough. His uncle would dislike his leaving the city in his bad state of health, before a week. Finally, he thanked Shanker for the piece of advice, he had tendered him in his letter. Surely, he would try to forget Lalita.

He remained in bed from weakness and temperature. Instead of regular food he took sago cooked in milk. Aunt alone gave him company, for uncle kept to his room in the evening to avoid cold wind.

"Your face looks sad."

He looked up at her in amazement that she should possess observing eyes. In the morning uncle had noticed nothing wrong with him.

"I might have some temperature".

"*Achha*, Desh," continued aunt in a meek tone, "Will your uncle live long ? I do not believe."

"Why let such bad thoughts to come to your mind."

"He is getting weaker and weaker; his coughs longer and longer."

"Have faith upon *Siva*."

Aunt left him shortly after wards. He had raised her hopes by mentioning a name he had openly renounced. He lifted his eyes to the oleograph of *Siva* resting on the mantelpiece. He wanted to smash it to the ground, and throw away the shards, but he dare not act from fear of his uncle. The seed of rationalism had been sown into him by Shanker; now it had grown into a tree, and he prided himself over it. Most of the beliefs of Lalita he considered as products of ignorance and superstitions. He recalled to himself few of them. If the beliefs of Lalita were dear to her, his own were no less to him. If Lalita spurned his doctrines, he would hers. He was trying to steel his heart against her love; in one single day, she seemed to have receded from his life. He felt with one supreme effort he could cast her off his mind. After all, she lacked the necessary qualifications to fit in as his wife.

The temperature and cough of Desh continued; he took complete rest and treated himself for bronchitis. Now in an interval of ten days since that fatal evening he had visited her, he should have almost forgotten her; but in reality his heart still ached for Lalita as before. He still longed to hold her soft, large hand, bedecked with rings.

He yearned to put his arm round her waist and press her to his bosom. Her rich, deep voice still lingered in his ears, and thrilled his whole being. He thought if he could run to her and explain her that since they had fallen apart without any reason, they should shake hands. He was prepared to marry her than lose her. But his pride came in his way to meeting her; unless she should not herself send for him, he would leave the matter where it stood.

One evening the snub-nosed priest brought a message from Har Preya that Desh should not have broken all contact with her all on account of Lalita. She would expect him to tea any of these evenings; he had called Har Preya as his sister, he should translate his word into deed. The invitation infuriated him; how was he related any more with members of the family of the heartless woman who had jilted him.

CHAPTER - XV

In about a fortnight Desh had recovered from bronchitis; now he himself felt restless for going out on a trip, that, owing to his illness, had been postponed. He badly needed a change to regain his old-self. He no longer allowed the memory of Lalita to intrude into his thoughts, or to depress him. He found reading of old trials a good trick to distract his attention from her.

One afternoon in the company of five others, in the first week of December, he set out on the over-delayed trip. Shanker had hired a taxi; it coasted down the new road, cut through the eastern mountains. It passed by a tuberculosis sanatorium where sister-in-law of Shanker had taken admission as a patient.

Sister looked out with interest. "Bhowali is a nice place; I like the pines here to our oaks."

Soon the bowel of Bhimtal opened up from south. The car sped smooth down low mountains closing in upon a glassy lake, the size of Nainital.

Few *coolies* carried their luggage to the state managed bungalow, which overlooked the lake. Shanker paid the *coolies* well; still they grumbled and lingered about. Sister was on the verge of losing her tempter, but Shanker wisely paid them a extra bit of money; and the coolies, who had taken note of them as high class customers, bidding them *salaam*, gladly went away.

"That is the habit of *coolies*, informed Shanker, "However much you pay them, they still hang on; you should not have felt angry at them."

Sister smiled broadly, showing her teeth. "I have never travelled after I was married; I have forgotten how to speak with them."

The bungalow standing over against the lake was a plain building with a corrugated, red tin roof. Its rooms were lighted with paned windows and doors, which opened on the verandah, where the tourists had balanced 'themselves on their bedding-rolls. Across the lake below them, spread as a river with a wide span, old, shabby bungalows nestled in thinly wooded mountains, while towards the side of the tourists terraced fields in stone, with clusters of small houses, made up the villages of Bhimtal.

The five tourists eagerly waited for the absent caretaker of the bungalow to give them rooms on hire. Sister blamed Shanker for forgetting to book them from Nainital. At length a middle-aged man with pleasing features and fair-skin appeared; he surveyed their luggage and clothes in one glance.

"If you are the *chowkidar* here," demanded Shanker in a stentorian voice, "We want rooms; we have been looking out for you an hour."

"I had gone out to the *bazaar*." The touch of hauteur was apparent in the manner of the *chowkidar*. "All rooms are reserved; *zilla* magistrate with his staff is coming in the evening."

Shanker, with his acumen of a business-man, sensed the motive behind the refusal of the *chowkidar*, and at once assumed his suave manners.

"Do not be afraid of the magistrate; we will see to him", he smiled fawningly, "You shall get good tip."

Sister with her children occupied one room, while Shanker and himself another. Shanker jocularly told sister that the *chowkidar* had looked with suspicion at him and her.

"I am glad," she grinned, "There is someone who thinks about us in this way."

"But he also thinks that we do not get on well, and want separate rooms." Shanker twitched his lip into a smile.

By sunset they took tea in the room of sister. It was heavy with plenty of cakes and apples. With the background of a home of their own, the faces of Shanker and sister blushed with happiness. Miranda and Sanjeev had gone out; both were playing in the compound of the bungalow with the stones of chestnut. In the absence of her children, sister looked an unmarried woman.

"Your illness Desh", sister looked at him meaningfully, "Spoilt the real joy of this trip."

"Why so ?"

"Because now my children have come along with me; fifteen days ago they could not have come; their schools would not have closed then for the winter."

He was amazed that sister should have felt Miranda and Sanjeev in her way; her sentiment was plainly unmotherly, but he dismissed the remark as a casual utterance.

The *chowkidar* reappeared. He expressed surprise that they had been sitting in darkness. He swiftly lighted the kerosene oil lamp, resting over the chest of drawers; instantly the room was filled with a glow.

"*Memsahib*, there is no electricity in Bhimtal; your eyes might feel the strain of dim light."

"No, not exactly. There will be soon electricity in Bhimtal; our government is looking to it."

The *chowkidar* crouched on the floor, near the doorway, an incarnation of meekness. His manner had incredibly changed within two hours; the tone of his speech was servile to the point of pathos; his face was set in the mould of fear, as if he was being tried for serious offences in a criminal court.

"Your servant Rama Nath," he faltered, "Comes from my village." He scratched his temple under his white cap. I did not know who you were *memsahib*, or I would have opened the room at once. Forgive my mistake; you are big people; everyone knows the name of your father and husband."

The *chowkidar* was employed as caretaker of the bungalow for over twenty years. His pay was small, but his village being near by, he as well tilled land with the help of his wife and two sons. People in his village rated him as a well to do man, though it was not true, for expenses in the village were rising with new things of fashion reaching it; for example travelling to Nainital or Bhowali in bus, than on foot, on the construction of the new road.

The views of *chowkidar* on the motor road had never occurred to Desh.

"*Achha*, your *zilla* magistrate has come ?" Sister looked at her watch with impatience for having given the *chowkidar* a long time.

"*Sahib's* programme has changed". At once chowkidar vanished from the room.

Miranda and Sanjeev had come in from outside; sister bid the two to get ready for the evening prayer. She had brought with her print of *Siva* from her home, and had placed it on the dressing table. With folded hands mother and her children stood facing the sombre looking *Siva*, who gazed at them over the cosmetics.

"Take us in your shelter", recited sister, closing her eyes, "That we may keep away from bad thoughts; O *Siva* give us strength to walk over the right path, keeping off the wrong."

Shanker and himself looked helplessly at one another. Shanker had never seen sister praying, nor had Desh for several years. Sister stood motionless; with her eyes closed above her joined palms, she looked a marble statue. She repeatedly said the prayer with fervour, and her children joined in with a voice no less charged with emotion than her own.

After quarter an hour sister resumed her seat on the chair. The post-tea brightness on her face had disappeared; it now showed sadness than serenity.

"Listening to your prayer was a piece of entertainment," remarked Shanker facetiously, "*Siva* will not only keep you away from wrong path, but will also send you *lakhs* of rupees."

Familiar with the nature of Shanker, sister glanced up at him.

"My prayer would not only keep me away from wrong path, but also others who are near me."

"Oho;" Shanker pursued his lips. "I do not want blessings; I believe that a man should manage his affairs himself."

In the beginning of their acquaintance, sister and Shanker sometimes exchanged views on religion, not with a desire to changing but knowing one another. Gradually, as time passed, she considered it as her misfortune that he should have renounced his faith even before meeting her. Still she thought that he possessed as much right to his beliefs as she to hers; neither she ventured to question them, nor tried to restore his lost faith to him. Her tolerance to his campaign of ridicule at her own, noticeable of late, was remarkable.

The prayer over, the three took a turn on the compound of the bungalow; Shanker preceding sister and
himself. The air was free of the chill of the high altitude of Nainital. The whole landscape of wooded mountains was bathed in moonlight with the lake below them, slivery and original, the better without electric lights surrounding it. The three sat down on a rickety bench. A languor came over them. Desh felt himself in the way of sister and Shanker. When they went in, they found Miranda and Sanjeev dosing; they had stayed out long, unmindful of winter evening.

"The journey has tired your children", he said.

"No, it is not the journey", replied sister, "They are sleeping because their father is not here to talk with them."

Rama Nath presently served the meals. In a short time he had cooked vegetables and *dal*-curry too. Shanker presided over the dining-table as though he was the head of the family; sister and himself took places on either of his sides; the children coming after sister. The journey had whetted their appetite, since food was delicious, Desh praised Rama Nath as a cook.

Sister pouted her lips. "You do not know his faults; he is dishonest and takes interest in my affairs."

"How ?"

"He tries to eavesdrop my talks on the phone."

"Then you get him dismissed."

Sister made a gesture with her hand, indicating her helplessness. "I cannot give this real reason to father of Miranda."

Rama Nath had built a fire with wood sticks over the hearth. After dinner they moved to it; and sipped coffee. In a while Miranda and Sanjeev fell asleep.

"Does your husband know", inquired Shanker, "I am with you in the trip."

"He did not ask me about you. He only said I would enjoy it."

The indifference of brother-in-law for Shanker had endured over the years. He discreetly left him out from his talks. He knew his family was being accompanied by Desh to Bhimtal; he could well suspect that Shanker might join it, but he took no ill to it.

"There are few husbands", Shanker poked the fire, "Who give as much liberty to their wives as your husband does you."

"It is because he knows that it makes me happy and also because he knows I shall never abuse it."

"Still it is exceptional of him among us to allow so much liberty to his wife; I could say I admire him for it."

Father of Miranda was forced to permit it to his wife. He took immense pains on cases he was retained; The more losing they seemed, the more labour he expended, and the more happy he felt in winning them. He loved his profession to the point of vice; it had blinded him to other forms of recreation. To him neither pictures existed, nor games nor even music or simple chit-chat with his wife. Sister wondered whether he had seen pictures since she was married, excepting twice during World War II that were exhibited to raise funds for it. He saw them under compulsion, for he dare not absent himself from functions organised by the officials of the British *Raj*, which had conferred a title upon his father. He knew he should continue his loyalty to the then government, if he wanted to get a title for himself too.

"Anyway I admire his sense of justice when he gives you full freedom to do what makes you happy." Shanker threw the butt of his cigarette into the hearth.

Sister glanced up at Shanker meaningfully. "One day he might know there is something between you and me."

"I should be so glad if he had known about us. My patience is exhausting."

Sister disliked the turn their conversation had taken; it killed the bliss of the moment. At Nainital herself and father or

Miranda seldom sat together by the hearth, after the evening meal. His routine went unchanged round the year. He read the newspapers in bed until he fell asleep, and saw no use of fire after meals even in winter months. He considered it as a sign of extravagance.

The three discussed their programme of visiting Naukichia lake, three miles east, and Sat lakes, the same number of miles west of Bhimtal. After a rest of a day the tourists could easily hike to them, including the children, than hiring palanquin and horses. Sister preferred walking; she wanted to see villages on the road side, and meet the folks. She had never lived in a village; she liked to know life in the country. Sitting out in the compound of the bungalow, before meal, the three had been enthralled by the profound silence that they missed in the bustle and glare of Nainital.

The fire was dying; the embers were burning down to ashes when they broke up for the night; they had sat by it near three hours after the meal. Shanker might have kept talking with sister though the night, but her complaint of some irritation in her throat, causing hoarseness, forced him to take leave of her.

Shanker and himself made to their room; changed and tucked into their beds. Shanker picked up an English novel; it was his habit to read himself to sleep. But soon he tossed it way.

"Damn it, I cannot concentrate".

"Yes, you must be feeling tired", added Desh, "We have been talking for long."

"No, that is not at all the reason. The fact is that your sister and myself have lived like this first time."

Desh looked at his watch. It was coming on to one O'clock. He blew out the lamp and tried to sleep, but for an hour or two it fled from his eyes. He had understood more or less correctly the relationship of sister and Shanker. Her prayer denoted that, with all her love for Shanker, she feared to commit adultery; she regarded it as an act of sin and treading the wrong path. But Shanker seemed to have grown intolerant of her morals. From their conversation that evening Desh inferred that she was unwilling for dissolution of her marriage, a right she would acquire soon through the forthcoming Hindu Code Bill. He was surprised to discover that his sister was an old-fashioned woman, who believed in clinging to her husband till death. In a way he was glad that his sister possessed a self-sacrificing spirit; it had poisoned the very sweetness of her life, still he liked her the more for it. Himself he had never encountered in his society a divorcee woman, married a second time. "*Siva*," he said to himself, "How odd it would look women marrying a second and third time like men."

x x x

Next morning both woke late when Rama Nath knocked at the door to serve them bed-tea. Shanker sat up with some difficulty and sipped it wholly withdrawn into himself.

"What are you thinking ?"

"*Aree* nothing; I wish my life was as happy as now. But you know your sister." Shanker spoke in a monologue.

"How could my sister do what you want."

"Why not ?"

"We are what we are; have you seen among us any woman thinking of marrying a second time; leaving her first husband."

"Your ideas are based on the thinking of only higher castes."

"Any way, the dignity of the higher castes is based on the restrain of its women."

"So you also have this false sense of dignity; you also want them to remain slaves of men."

"No, that is not so; but I do not like them to marry again like men."

Shanker looked aslant at him.

"Can you marry a woman who is divorced?"

"No", answered Desh stoutly.

"So you are like non-vegetarians in our country, who eat goat-meat, but cannot beef for cow is a sacred thing."

Shanker and himself simultaneously laughed a cynical laugh as they jumped out of their beds. The sun had rode high, and Desh was eager to start his reconnaissance of Bhimtal.

Sister having finishing morning prayer waited for them in the varandah where Rama Nath had laid the breakfast. It was delicious basking in the warm sun of winter, with the atmosphere of a newly established home in a rural setting. Miranda and Sanjeev joined in from tramping over fallow fields, with their shoes covered with dirt, but their hearts fluttering. Sister looked a little too sternly at her children, who, familiar with her temperament, quietly squeezed into one chair, and bent their faces over cups of tea. Shanker cut open a tin of canned ham and put a piece of it into his mouth. Sister and her children twitched up their noses.

"*Arree"*, I am sorry, "exclaimed Shanker spitting out the piece from his mouth; his face went rigid, and he tossed the tin over to adjoining field." If you do not like my eating meat, I give it up from just now."

Sister looked at Shanker mistrustfully. "I cannot believe you".

"What is your reason?", returned Shanker irritated.

"All right I do; but why not give up drinking too."

He nodded assent.

It seemed to Desh dramatic of Shanker to have given up meat and liquor in one go. He was a regular non-vegetarian and liked liquor too. The change that was noticeable in him of late was getting deeper, involving his whole character and thinking. Desh doubted whether under the powerful influence of sister, Shanker would not revert to his original faith, he was bred in.

After breakfast Miranda, Sanjeev and he walked out of the bungalow, while sister, who showed symptoms of flue, and Shanker stayed behind. The party of three sauntered over a track running though a village. Seeing Desh, villagers looked up at him with awe; few murmured, "*Sahib; sahib."*

Desh had never lived in a village; he had seen it through moving train or bus. To villagers his attire still stirred the same reaction as it did on seeing British officers. The memory of the white-man still hunted them. But in Nainital excepting the white-cap, frock coat, worn by political leaders, none was awed by his coat and trousers.

Miranda, Sanjeev and he continued walking eastwards; they overtook a peasant, going their way, who shuffled along rheumatically; he turned round and bowed to Desh. He was a stocky man of about seventy; his features were larger than life size, and on his cheeks grew stumps of unshaven, grey beard.

"This is a beautiful thing, "Desh pointed to a double-storied structure over the head of the lake.

"This belongs to a *maharajah*", informed the old peasant in patois." He always came here when he was alive."

It should have cost the ruling-chief few lakhs in times when a rupees purchased over eight seers of flour than as now two. All this money now seemed to have been wasted.

"Was it not foolish of the *maharajah*", remarked Desh. "To have built a palace in a village?"

"But a *maharaja* was a *maharaja*; he must live in a palace; wish you had seen his grandeur, he kept hundreds of *bilayati* pedigreed dogs."

The old peasant understood better than Desh the social structure of India in British *Raj*.

Added the peasant, "*Maharaja* has sold the palace."

"Now *maharajas* have finished; they cannot maintain palaces."

"*Arree*, still *maharajahs* are *maharajahs*.They have enough wealth to last them generations."

Undoubtedly the old peasant was right again. But the old peasant was ignorant that the ruling chiefs and big *zamindars* had come down from their exalted social scale, and had lost their autocratic power. Desh tried to explain him of the political changes, but he was unable to understand Desh, such was his reverence for the ruling-chiefs.

"From where have you come here", the old peasant bent his eyes on him.

"Nainital, I am staying here in the state bungalow. I am a lawyer."

"Have your heard the name of lawyer Sanwalji?"

"I am his son."

The old peasant opened out his hands, and grinned with delight.

"*Arree*, my *atma* had said that may be, may not be, you are son of the old Sanwal*ji*; so much you look like him."

The old peasant expressed his gratitude to his father, for getting him a parcel of land from law-court.

For the midday meal sister could eat next to nothing. She chattered with cold, and kept her eyes shut form headache. By the evening her temperature shot up, and she began to talk in delirium of her happy childhood with her father, who was extremely fond of her. Without her company he disliked taking food, or making a programme, see pictures, or call on friends. These years her life was full of freedom, as of a bird, hoping from bush to bush. She had never imagined that she would, 'fall upon the thorns of life and bleed.'

The unexpected illness of sister tormented Shanker and himself with anxiety. It spoilt the fun of the trip; only the previous evening she had been talking of it with zeal; now she lay motionless, burning with fever.

The *chowkidar* fetched the medical-officer, Dixit, in charge of the state hospital in Bhimtal. He was a young man with fleshy face and eyes of a drunkard. He took her temperature and quickly administered her an injection, which he had brought with him.

"Do not worry", he said with effort, "She is having ordinary fever; she will be all right in few days."

Desh offered him a cigarette.

"You like Bhimtal", asked Shanker.

"Not exactly, though when I got my appointment, I never thought I shall get as good a place as Bhimtal."

"But why you dislike rural areas?"

"Firstly because there is usually not much private practice; secondly because there is no life in them; thirdly no security."

"I came here yesterday, and I like Bhimtal a lot."

"You should have brought with you all those things that you need; so you are liking Bhimtal. If you live in a village, you will see its difficulties".

"O, I understand."

"Do not worry", repeated Dixit, "Over your wife; her temperature will begin coming down from tomorrow."

When Dixit was gone, said Shanker, "They all take your sister as my wife."

That night no one took food with appetite though Rama Nath had cooked it nicely. Of all of them, Miranda seemed more troubled than others. From her mother's bed where she had fixed herself, she had to be dragged to the table for eating whatever she could. The sensitiveness of Miranda came to Desh as a surprise. He had been impressed by her placid nature, for the she took little interest in outdoor life and games.

By nine-thirty he tucked her and Sanjeev into bed; he cheered them that by the following day their father would also come down to Bhimtal to look them up; their mother would soon shake off her temperature. Both the children were comforted by his words, and quickly fell asleep.

Himself and Shanker sat sister up; her temperature was showing signs of dropping; they forced her to drink a cup of tea, but she brought it out in the basin that Shanker had quickly put before her. He stroked her back, and raised a tumbler of water to her mouth; she took few draughts, then fell back to her bed. Shanker drew the quilt over her.

"Send Rama Nath tomorrow to Nainital," she ordered, "To inform father of Miranda that I have high fever."

"All right, dear," murmured Shanker.

He installed himself as night-nurse. He helped sister gulp down the tablets received from the medical officer. Within an hour sister fell asleep. Shanker opened up a novel, and advised him to retire to bed so that Desh could take his place from the morning.

Coming into his room, he changed and then slipped out into the verandah. A late moon lit the landscape; he sat down upon the flag-stone floor till he shivered with cold; he rose to his feet and softly walked towards the room of sister, and, out of curiosity, peeped through the window-panes. Sister lay asleep; Shanker was reading the novel in the same position he had left him. The shaft of jealousy penetrated his heart; he wished he were occupying Shanker's chair, and Lalita lay ill in place of sister. He would keep vigil on her, and nurse her as he was accustomed with his uncle.

He walked back to his room. As he nestled into his quilt he grew palpably aware that he loved Lalita no less than before; his ear drums resounded with her mellifluous voice, sweet as honey. The scene of his waiting for her leaped to his eyes - he beat his knuckles upon the doors until they ached; he shouted at her to unbolt them but she frustrated his attempt by her utter silence. Then he blew up with rage, and dashed out of the house, vowing to himself that he would never cast his eyes on her. Har Preya had invited him to tea, but he refused it. Now he regretted that he had not accepted it; probably she was trying to invent some plan to bring Lalita and himself together. Aha! His break from Lalita seemed so irreversible, so complete. She was unlike the wife of his dreams, either in looks, or education, or beliefs. Still he loved her beyond words; fate had wrested her from him. Tears streamed down his cheeks. He knew it was foolish of him to have shed them; only he was helpless in suppressing them.

Next day sister felt somewhat better. She had slept well at night; and in the morning she could herself wash her face, and drink a cup of tea.

As Rama Nath was leaving for Nainital, she advised, "Tell father of Miranda my temperature is getting down. He need not come here or send any doctor."

In the evening Dixit repeated the injection he had administered her the previous day. Occasionally she gave low moaning sound, out of high temperature or out of pain over her body. When he put her few questions, his eyes remained fixed at her face; she answered him disjointedly. Dixit seemed to have been impressed by her beauty.

Excepting sister all sat down round a formidable looking round-table, and drank coffee and smoked cigarettes.

"How you make private practice," began Shanker.

"It needs tact, I am learning it."

"To me there seems no little need of it."

The job of the rural medical-officer was a hard one. He attended calls from far and near, from the poor and the well-to-do. From the standard of living, clothes and houses of the two classes, it was often hard to distinguish one from the other, and to fix accordingly his fees. The second difficulty was to cope with the hospitality of the people; they lavishly offered him milk or curd, or *puris*, or just *gur* and water, and expected him to polish them off.

"If I were you, what you are telling me should have interested me a lot."

"But I have to come up against the ignorance of the people."

Shanker lighted the oil lamp, for the room was turning dark after sunset.

"Most villagers believe", went to Dixit, "Deities and ghost cause illness; so there is done *jagar* ceremony to invoke deities. Then there are quacks who earn sometimes as much as we do."

"It is this narrowness of the mind, this believe in *jagar* and quacks," Shanker banged his fist on the table, "That has brought ruin to our country. For over the last ten centuries we have neither given nor taken new ideas, thoughts from other countries."

"Yes, you are very right," concurred Dixit in a low voice, unsure of his knowledge of history.

"We are now a free nation", declared Shanker aloud, "We are getting modern; we are bringing in Hindu Code Bill; we are taking to industrialisation."

"As a nation we are rising from a great sleep", slipped out of the mouth of Desh.

x x x

That evening he had expected brother-in-law to come over to Bhimtal from Nainital, but he was surprised to see Rama Nath returning alone. Brother-in-law was over busy in criminal-suites. He thought that sister was suffering from influenza; she should get over it in a few days. With Desh at her bed-side, his presence was superfluous; if her temperature continued, he would visit Bhimtal.

"What a lawyer," exploded Shanker, looking up at sister from the chair he was occupying.

"He did not come because I had asked Rama Nath in the morning, he need not." Though sister tried to support her husband, yet a weak smile played upon her face.

Even an unloving husband should have rushed to his wife no sooner he learnt of her illness. The behaviour of brother-in-law seemed queer, even though he was attached to his wife. He was always mindful of her comforts and recreations; it was at his suggestion that they had made the trip to Bhimtal. His postponement to seeing her indicated how cool-headed was he; he knew the work on his hands was far more important than the ordinary illness of his wife.

The temperature of sister started falling from the next day, but it came down normal only after six days, and for about the same number of days her convalescence lasted. Rama Nath went to Nainital on alternate days to report to brother-in-law on the progress of sister. He saw no necessity of visiting Bhimtal, when she was recovering. Only he had been feeling lonely and called Sanjeev to Nainital to get him company; Miranda continued staying in Bhimtal.

These days sister sat out every morning for basking in sun. The *chowkidar* came round and greeted her with a bow. He squatted on the ground and talked about his family life. He had given his second son good education, and he regretted it, for the latter had picked up extravagant habits. He wore expensive clothes, kept his wife tip-top as himself, and lived separately from him. He went to Nainital to see pictures, and squandered money in tea shops. He disliked mixing with illiterate villagers, and looked upon agriculture as an occupation beneath him. He wanted to migrate to a city and enter there in some office or defence services.

"Your son is not much on the wrong", explained sister, "We are now an independent people; we have got in our hands all jobs in civil and defence vacated by the British; further we are increasing departments in administration; developing industry, creating large number of jobs year by year. These will go to educated men like your son."

"But my son does not want to live with me," the *chowkidar* gesticulated his hand.

"Since we are becoming modern, we are breaking old things like joint-family; we want separate homes."

"I had not educated my son to be such a modern man."

Sister gave a sardonic laugh.

Occasionally the *chowkidar* brought from his home curd or vegetables as gifts to sister. Gradually both she and Shanker came to like him; his servile behaviour had drawn both of them to him.

They had stayed ten days at Bhimtal, but sister never opened her mouth about returning home. In the evening he along with Miranda went out for walks, while sister and Shanker remained indoors, sitting by fire. Sometimes Desh wondered what they should be talking about, keeping themselves shut. He had noticed that sister disliked his or Miranda's intrusion before she called them for evening meal.

One evening after the walk he read to Miranda pages from Robinson Cruse; when she got tried, she stretched herself upon his bed and fell asleep, while he continued reading the novel. He had done it in childhood with his uncle, and reading it over again revived his memories. As a rule, until sister was unmarried, he had joined her in his infancy in prayers. Her fundamental faith had endured through time; she still performed her *puja* with the vigour of childhood; while he had renounced it. He wished it was the other way about; his sister would have then moved to break her marriage with brother-in-law and married Shanker.

He heard giggling in the other room. Sister and Shanker were enjoying a joke; he wanted to share in their merry-making. He looked at Miranda; she lay soundly asleep. He found himself walking towards the room of sister. The door and windows were heavily curtained, and nothing in the room was visible for the verandah. He stood there awhile; now and again sister giggled, and he overheard her whispering, "No dear, no. I can never image to be unfaithful to my husband, yet I can gladly give my life in your service."

Though sister had been taken ill in Bhimtal, and the trip could he hardly regarded as success, still it had brought her more happiness than all the lucky events of her life put together. It had created some change in her; she grew less impatient of Rama Nath or Miranda; she treated both with benign smile. Neither she spent her time in reading a novel, nor in embroidery. She wanted Shanker to sit eternally beside her, and if he took himself to his room or around the compound she resented it. Sometimes the two sat together hours without exchanging a single word; at other times sister said that she liked Bhimtal and wanted Desh to inform brother-in-law that they were extending their stay there.

"Then I should like," suggested Shanker with a tone of jest in his voice, "To buy you a house here."

"Better buy off this bungalow", returned sister, "I have actually fallen in love with it."

One evening Miranda and Rama Nath were playing with stones of chestnuts in the compound of the bungalow, and sister, Shanker, and himself were taking tea inside.

"I am writing to father of Miranda", sister told them, "That he should buy a bungalow at Bhimtal."

"I hope," replied Shanker, "I shall be allowed to live in there too."

"No," sister glanced him amorously, "You should live far away from me. I want to come here that I might not see you. At Nainital you are too close."

A tear rose to her eyes; she buried her face in the folds of her *sari* and began to sob. She was right. She had also come to an impasse; she could neither refuse Shanker, nor accept him.

That evening Desh went to a walk alone. Miranda had played enough to come along with him. He felt his legs too heavy to carry him far. He sat down under a chestnut tree, by the edge of the lake; the waves beat under him. The incident of the evening had overburdened his mind with the memory of Lalita; he felt she was leaning against him and crying as though she was meeting him after an age; his ears resounded with her rich voice, calling him back to her. He knew that some sort of communicative power existed between two loving hearts. Lalita wanted him; protesting her love to him. A petty quarrel had estranged them; no sooner he would return to Nainital, he would straighten it up; he would not allow his pride to come in the way of his meeting her. After all she loved him no less than he did her.

x x x

Next morning during breakfast sister sprang up a surprise. She told Shanker that she wanted to return to Nainital by that very evening.

"But you wanted to stay here till middle of January", Shanker looked at her with the eyes of a beast bulked of its prey.

"No, I cannot. It was stupid of me to have done these fifteen days." She kept stirring her tea. "What will people say, world say; my living here, forgetting about the comforts of father of Miranda."

"But you wanted to see villages and meet women there, and witness *jagar* ceremony."

"What for I need to see them ? I am not a politician. You please get the taxi by three in the evening today."

Desh had always believed that the joy of his sister at independence of the country was equal to that of any patriotic Indian, despite the fact that she was daughter-in-law of a title-holder. Now by her talk he suspected that at times she too regretted the end of British *Raj* in Indian, and the consequent decline in the influence of the family of her husband in society.

As every day she looked round for the *chowkidar*, who was absent that morning at the time of breakfast. Instead of him an old man visited them whom Desh instantly recognised as the peasant he had met on the first morning in Bhimtal.

"You came after many days", complained Desh.

The peasant greeted everybody by pressing his palms under a bow, and squatted down on the flag-stoned steps of the verandah.

"Twice I came up to the gate of the bungalow," pleaded the peasant.

"No, I never saw you."

"Rama Nath saw me; if he says no, I will drink your urine."

Scandalised, sister glanced at the old peasant. The unrefined language should have flared her up; but good, she kept her temper.

"I saw doctor Dixit here both times; I went away for I am his enemy."

The old peasant started praising his father's standard of living.

"He kept the name of Indians high among *sahiblogs*", continued the peasant, "If I am saying anything wrong, I am not the son of my father."

Over again the peasant used unrefined language, but since he did it to elevate their father, neither sister nor he felt hurt.

"He lived like *sahiblogs*; used knife, and fork like *sahiblogs*; spoke English as *sahiblogs*."

Pleased, sister kept swinging her foot. "Since my father's days, times have changed; we are a free country; we all can now live like *sahibslogs*".

The peasant gave throaty chuckle. "We all want to become *sahibslogs*, we want fine food and fine clothes and fine houses, even though we may not know English."

In his own way again, the old peasant understood the meaning of political independence as economic also; but he was confused in dissociating if from Englishmen. It seemed to him odd that everyone, irrespective of whether he knew English or no, craved higher standard of living. Though a rustic, his reverence for English language was deep.

"We shall now naturally live well." pursued sister interested in the talk, "We are progressing. See, there is already a motor road in Bhimtal soon after *swaraj*; and electricity is coming too."

The old peasant grinned as he pointed his finger upwards a mountain slope over which a bus was racing down.

"As our people, so our government is becoming fashionable; it is making motor roads, getting electricity; why I say," The old peasant's voice hardened in anger. "What we want are cheap grains and cloth, and not things of fashion. But who will tell all this to our fashionable government."

When the old peasant had gone, remarked sister, "Illiterate agriculturist, has no idea of our five year plans for development."

Shanker failed to procure the taxi by that after-noon; it would be available after two days. Instead of being annoyed by the delay, sister looked pleased; she found two more days to live near Shanker.

As the four were about to start the midday meal out in the sun-shine, a fat featured, dumpy man of about fifty, arrived at the bungalow. He was followed by few *coolies*, clerks and peons in regalia. They instantly understood that he was the district magistrate, for officers often moved about with their peons trailing behind them, the practice having descended from the British.

One of the peons paid off the *coolies*; the way they looked at the coins, they had received as wages, indicated that they had considered the payment as inadequate, but taking in the cold face of the district magistrate, they varnished. the chowkidar greeted him with a low bow, and at once unlocked the room at the farther end of the verandah, reserved for him. Then punctuating his sentences with the words, *burra-sahib, sarkar* he inquired of the magistrate whether he should cook him food or no.

Shanker out of courtesy walked up to the magistrate and invited him to join in the meal. He condescended a glance at Shanker, who, extending his arm, repeated the invitation. After some hesitancy the magistrate tramped up to the table. The beauty of sister combined with her position as wife of an eminent lawyer of Nainital thawed his official reserve.

"You have very fine crockery", his eyes travelled from piece to piece on the table. "This is one of the finest I have seen; it should be a foreign make."

The magistrate chewed slowly relishing the food, helping himself with quantity of rice for his wife had cut it off his meals to reduce his fat. When he dined out, he tried to enjoy his liberty.

"I do not know how I restrain myself at home, when my wife and children eat it before me."

"Excuse me," Shanker added in jest, "Not many fat men can restrain themselves as you can do before tasty food, though they all say that they do not eat rich food."

Everybody smiled including the *chowkidar* and the peons. They had begun well in their acquaintance with the magistrate, and invited him for evening tea.

The whole afternoon he worked in his room; granting interviews to village chiefs and junior-most functionaries of the civil and police service in Bhimtal.

"I have so much work," began the magistrate entering sister's room after sun-set.

As in the day-meal, so also now he praised the crockery; he picked the pots and cups and passed his fingers over them; he wished he had possessed a tea-set as grand as in front of him.

"How much would it cost?"

"About seventy-five *rupees*," replied Shanker.

I cannot afford it; I do not get the salary of British officers, for the *rupee* has gone down four times since the war."

"Have not rapid promotions after *swaraj* satisfied you?"

The magistrate shut his ears to the question of Shanker; he seemed to have taken it as an impudent one. He finished his tea, which was limited to one cup, and started smoking wearily.

"I do not know the reply to your question," he looked at Shanker with a wooden expression in his face. "But I know one thing; sometimes I feel like resigning my job."

Shanker looked at him with vacant eyes.

"You know what our ministers, M.Ps and M.L.As keep saying in public meetings," hissed the magistrate. "Congress drove out the British is the first part of their speech; then they say look at the police and revenue officers accompanying us; yesterday they ruled over the people today they are their servants."

"I do not think like that; it can be true in theory, because power comes from the people."

The magistrate gave his obese smile. "I am glad you know as much."

"Do you try to turn theory into practice?"

Over again the magistrate seemed absent-minded to the question of Shanker. He called one of his peons, who was waiting on him, and ordered him to fetch his small silver-box, containing *pans* from his room. He stuffed two of them into his mouth, and began to chew the ball protruding his right cheek.

"Before independence I cared about title holders, *zamindars* and few rich people," drawled the magistrate," Now I try to be polite to people; deal with tact the local, provincial, and central leaders forming the government; but, all said and done, I still exercise no less authority than in British days."

Next day neither they took their breakfast, nor the day meal out in the verandah, for Shanker wanted to avoid the magistrate. In the evening Desh and Miranda went out for a stroll; it was the last day of his stay in Bhimtal; neither the landscape, nor the bare chestnut trees fascinated him. He was impatient to meet Lalita. At night they had a quiet dinner, and, next morning set off to Nainital.

"You did not bid the magistrate goodbye," pointed out sister in the car.

"Bid him goodbye" replied Shanker acidly, "You saw his manners; he had not the courtesy to offer us cigarette of *pan*."

"I never saw you angry; he seems to be over worked," added sister.

"Yes, I should not have been angry with the magistrate. In the British *Raj* his post was usually the highest Indians filled in or aspired to get. Naturally he still feels he is one of the most important men."

"Right he is; by habit people still think, as in British *Raj* that police and revenue officers are the most important men in society."

Shanker smiled as he recalled when after independence an old man's grandson was made a minister, who sighed," He should have at least been made an inspector of police, he had been sent three times to jail in the struggle for *swaraj*."

CHAPTER XVI

Desh had told his uncle that he was going out of Nainital for three or four days, but he returned after a fortnight. He had sent though Rama Nath message to him that he had been detained in Bhimtal; he knew that his uncle must be feeling troubled over his absence from home.

"Your health remained well," He greeted uncle and aunt; overjoyed to see the former sitting out in the sun.

"Yes, I am well by the grace of *Siva*". Uncle's face took smiling curves to see him.

He looked healthy; he had gained strength and his spasms of cough had dropped in number; his uncle had been granted a new lease of life.

"Could you go out to the road?"

"Why, four days ago I went to Mallital. You know Joga Sah; he sent his man twice to borrow our silver for the wedding of his daughter, and invited me too."

A cloud of darkness spread before the eyes of Desh; he tried to pull himself together that his uncle and aunt might not suspect that the news had terribly hurt him.

"What a grand marriage Joga Sah did of his daughter," interposed aunt, " He gave so much gold; so many silk-saris, so many household items. There were such good bands and such good feasts. Joga Sah should have spent no less than forty thousand rupees. The weeding was worth seeing."

Uncle added innocently, " I will marry Desh with much more pomp and show than daughter of Joga Sah."

The ground under the feet of Desh began to slip; it was difficult for him to keep hearing details of the wedding without giving himself away. No sooner he entered his room, he secured all the doors, and without kicking off his shoes, fell down on his bed. He remained motionless, numb; unable to digest the news. But even his ailing uncle had attended the wedding, and his aunt talked of its splendour. Lalita was surely married; it was absurd to doubt the fact.

In spite of his hope against hope, Lalita had finally rejected him. Her Preya, who was fond of him and looked upon him as the future husband of Lalita, should have tried to dissuade her from marrying Jagdish, but she was a mule; there was no turning her away from her decision. He was stoked with rage at her having forsaken him without any consideration. In his short stay in Bhimtal he had come to forget the quarrel between her and himself, and the humiliation she had subjected him to, when he had gone to her house. Only the previous evening he was telling himself that he would meet her and tell her that they should make up.

A struggle ensued between him and his feelings; at one time he was able to compose his rage, at other it rose on the top of his conscious mind. He should have passed several hours in misery, when he heard knocking on the doors. He unbolted them but without looking out, he resumed his horizontal position on the bed. His eyes were burning, light offending them, a splitting headache made it difficult to slide them open.

"O you, get up", shouted Shanker, pushing open the doors, "Be like a man."

As a true friend he had come to comfort him; himself, with good cheer, he had endured an ill-fated love.

"But my case is different than yours, "Desh kept his eyes shut, "You knew sisters as a married woman, and should not have expected much from her."

"I expected a lot from her, though mistakenly. In that way I think you are more fortunate than myself; you have got rid of a woman who was totally unworthy of you. Now get up and came out with me than lying on bed with your shoes on."

Entering his apartment, Shanker gave him two tablets to alleviate his headache. Then he ordered Dev Rama to lay drinks on the table. He thanked Shanker and swilled off a drink, and no sooner he had finished, he poured out another.

"What is wrong with you?", scolded Shanker, thrusting his hand between Desh's mouth and the drink. "I am not opposed to your taking somewhat more, but I am to your behaving like a thirty man."

"O, do not stop me." he cried in self-pity, "I want to forget her; I got to forget her."

Shanker withdrew his hand; Desh lowered his mouth to the glass and drained it off to the last drop.

Shanker repeatedly told him that he should look upon Lalita's departure from his life as a blessing.

Desh had drank deep, still he retained his senses. The advice of Shanker seemed superfluous. He should have known that he was strong enough to blot out Lalita's memory from his mind, simply forget her. He had been enraged by her betrayal.

"Well, my dear Shanker, elders like to give advice to younger people", he felt the heaviness of liquor in his voice. "You are asking me to do what I am already trying. But I say why do you not follow your own advice in your own case? Why can you not forget sister?"

"Yes, you are right; you are right."

"You should cease thinking of sister," Desh raised his voice, "As I have done Lalita."

"All right", Shanker lifted up his forefinger, "I will try to forget Chandra, if she does not change."

"Are you earnest?" Desh looked intently at Shanker; but he could see nothing. He felt giddy as well nausea.

"Yes I am in earnest".

Desh got back home late. Shanker had pressed him to stay with him at night, but he wanted to leave himself alone to still the agitation in his mind. He sank into his bed, played out, sweating over his temples, neck. Drinking had failed to remove the painful memory of Lalita from his mind; he had fallen into the trap of a wayward, queer woman.

Next day though he took a hearty bath and several cups of hot tea to relieve the exhaustion, in the wake of a shock, he still felt himself feverish; he snuggled into his quilt. Uncle came to his room in the afternoon, concerned at his having slept over his day-meal.

"You came very late at night," uncle surveyed him "And had left the doors of your room open; I came here in the morning; it was smelling of medicine."

His heart dashed against his ribs. Uncle was dropping hint that he had broken his vow not to touch liquor. He felt his face was turning scarlet from shame, but he could not bring himself to repeat the vow. If he enjoyed liquor, he would never give it up.

He was glad that aunt changed the topic of conversation from himself to her daughter.

"Desho," she piped in, with a joyous spark in her eyes "There is a letter today from Chitra."

"Is it son or daughter," he cried, pleased.

"Son; in Goddess's world there is delay, not injustice", she raised her hand heavenwards.

Aunt would send her daughter and baby, gifts of gold ornaments, expensive saris, and money. She need not buy the ornaments; she possessed enough golden ones; she would order a goldsmith to fashion modern designs on them.

"But", chimed in uncle, "You should first do *puja* of *avatar* Satyanarayan."

Aunt nodded assent.

Until now winter was mild. Neither the harsh easterly wind blew, nor a speck of cloud rose upon the horizon; resplendent days brought warmth. But after two weeks of his return from Bhimtal, clouds spread all over the skies and right from the morning rain began to fall. By the evening snow came in fat flakes over the silent valley. From the verandah he gazed it long; without his volition, he craved that Lalita were standing by his side; her honey-sweet voice resounding in his ears. He plugged them with his fingers, still it kept on. He clenched his fists, furious not with Lalita but with the saffron Goddess the of Rock, which had taken her away from him.

Through the night snow fell in silence; it lay heavy upon the ground and roofs and trees. Bent under its thick pads, branches of an old oak tree in the front of his bungalow had snapped off.

To generate in himself a lively mood and warmth, he wanted the company of Shanker. Engulfed in great-coat and shod in rubber boots, he floundered down to the road through knee-deep snow. From there his progress upward was less slow; a gang of labourers having shovelled a track across the road.

Shanker was taken aback to see him; he still lay in bed, under two quilts. A charcoal fire in a huge iron-frame, standing in the middle of the room, reduced the intense cold weather.

"O my father," boomed Shanker, "You coming in snow," he opened his eyes. "You were not afraid of getting ill."

"I and illness are miles apart; snow fills me with energy."

"O, I hate the winter in Nainital; I wish I could get away."

"I wish I could spend my whole life here."

"If you are forced to live in plains."

"I will hate to do so,"

Shivering and chattering, Dev Rama served the breakfast.

"You are not feeling cold," Shanker curled up his lip with displeasure.

"Yes *sahib*," answered Dev Rama, "For good masters, I have always stayed in winter in Nainital."

"Who are they?"

A ray of a smile came on the lips of Dev Rama. "You know I worked forty years with British *sahibs*; they were white as snow; like them, you too are born white as snow".

"But I do not like winter here."

"Desh *sahib* does; he was come in snow; he is like *sahibslogs*".

"O Goddess, when the ghost of *sahibslogs* shall get out of you."

He rang up sister. He thought she would have been delighted by the heavy snow-fall; her reaction was the opposite.

"O Desho," she shouted from the other end. I hate this weather; I hate Nainital."

"You buy a house in plains, in Kathgodam," he suggested.

"O, you know father of Miranda; he would never do it."

"Well, when are you coming down?"

"Not until snow has melted. What Shanker doing?"

"Reading in bed."

"I wanted to send you a message through him."

"You can tell me that straight."

"All right. Did you try to meet Lalita?"

"No, no. she should be away in Ranikhet."

"I wanted to tell you that when a woman gets married, she does not remain the one you have known her as unmarried."

Desh touched off the telephone interview to cut sister short. Her words had hurt him. He firmly believed that Lalita would always love him more than her beetle-browed husband, despite rejecting him for reasons that baffled him.

After the day-meal, Desh pulled Shanker out of his bed to assist him in making a snow-man in front of the house. With his bare hands he did it; Shanker having kept away from fear of getting his hands frozen. The more Desh tried to shape its features in a pleasing, way, the more they got grotesque.

"Any name for it?, said Shanker.

"Goddess of the Rock."

"That is like a devotee".

"No," Desh growled, "That is like an iconoclast. He bashed in his fist into the head of the snow-man, breaking it from the trunk.

"You worked at it an hour," declared Shanker piteously, "Forcing me to stand in killing chill; now you do this cruel thing, you have surely taken leave of your senses."

He stayed with Shanker till the evening-meal; but neither then, nor during drinks was Desh himself. At home that night he delayed getting into his bed; he sat on in the chair facing the oleograph of *Siva* resting on the mantelpiece, contemplating its super-human beauty. It had occupied a place in his sleeping-room, since the days of his father, and it was alone fourteen years to his death. Over the years a sort of companionship had grown between him and the silent oleograph. In childhood in moments of his misgiving, how he wished *Siva* and stepped out of the oleograph and cleared them. After relinquishing his beliefs, he looked at it with tolerance; never once did he dislike its presence in his room. But that night it irritated him; he wanted to degrade it to his bath-room, but he felt prodigiously afraid of his uncle.

x x x

After the snow had melted away, and normal traffic on the roads had resumed, one evening uncle and aunt performed the *puja* of Satyanarayan.

For Aunt a few days before the *puja* were busy ones. She made many trips to the *bazaar* with Desh to make velvet costumes with braid of gold, and silver ornaments for God *Satyanarayan* and his wife Goddess *Laxmi*.

The job of decorating the *puja*-room was entrusted to Desh, who finished it, except for a red canopy over the altar, in the manner of *Diwali* festival. Large silver trays loaded with fruits, flowers, sweets, and other home-cookings were placed on tiers on one side of the altar, and Earthenware lamps on the other. The latter preserved oriental atmosphere in the *puja*-room flooded with electric lights.

By nightfall the invitees arrived; relatives and friends of uncle and aunt, including Joga Sah and Sunder, his two nephews with their wives, and few cousins; all looked shriveled but animated with religious spirit. Sister and her two children were last to appear, and made straight for the *puja*-room. Shanker and he were the only two who had stayed away in the drawing-room.

"You should attend the *puja*," advised Shanker, "Otherwise your uncle would be angry, more with me probably than with you."

"What have I done from childhood except attending *puja?* My heart is filled up now. I cannot go on deceiving myself for my uncle."

"O what are you saying Desh?" Shanker pursed his lips. "The more I know your sister, the more I see Goddess in her; I am attending *Satyanaran puja* to impress her."

Desh was startled. His *guru* had begun to renounce his philosophy. He was unable to convert sister to it, and had consequently begun to regard his failure as the failure of his philosophy.

"Sister does not love you enough, I believe; or she should have left her husband.'

Foe a moment Shanker pressed his lips tight in contemplation.

"You are wrong. She loves me terribly but she might never see me than give up her husband."

Shanker felt shy in admitting that the steadfastness of sister to her husband was compelling him to admire her. Desh was pleased. The thought of her separating from her husband, for living with someone else, always filled Desh with distaste, even though that someone was no other than his friend, Shanker.

"How can a woman break from her husband," added Desh in defence of his sister.

"How can your sister do it?" Shanker regarded him. "She is a woman belonging to a high-caste *Brahmin* family; her place is with her husband."

"A difficult faith to follow."

"Not so for a wife like your sister."

The *puja* of *Satyanarayan* had begun, and himself and Shanker were called in. In front of the alter was squatting uncle with aunt; she wore embroidered, velvet low-skirt and silken-*chuddar*, which she had pulled down over half of her face. Her love for gold was indicated by the old-fashioned, heavy necklaces, she had put on that evening; she seemed unmindful of the weight of huge rings that were pulling down her nose and ear lobes. Guests squatted or sat cross-legged over carpet spread over the boarded floor.

The snub-nosed priest conducted the *puja*, which took about two hours. He recited *Sanskrit* verses in encomium to *Satyanarayan*, and invoked his blessings for material prosperity. Aunt and uncle lighted camphor cubes and greasy cotton threads to perform *arti*. Guests joined them in the last part of the *puja*.

Shanker offered flowers and performed *arti* with a bow to *Satyanarayan*. Apparently he was regaining his lost faith. When he went through the ritual, he closed his eyes and seemed to pray in silence. Pulling open his eyes, he looked significantly at sister.

Next followed the interesting tales of Satyanarayan *puja*, which formed an inseparable part of it. The priest recited a few lines in *Sanskrit*, afterwards translated it in *Hindi*. Thus the tales proceeded; and the crowd listened them with rapt attention. The first two tales were simple. Sadanand, a poor *brahmin*, grew rich through *puja* of *Satyanarayan*. Likewise a *dalit* wood-cutter entered into comfortable circumstances. The third tale was a complicated one. It narrated the long hardships suffered by a *vaisya* named Sadhu, who kept postponing the *puja*, even after a vow, from lack of full faith in *Satyanarayan*. It was only when his wife and daughter performed it that he was blessed with happiness both in present and future lives. Similarly in the fourth tale a *rajah*, antagonist of Satyanarayan, regained his kingdom and lost sons by doing the *puja*.

The feast was spread on the floor of an empty room in large *thalis* of tucked seared leaves and earthenware cups to avoid the trouble of washing; only male guests participated in it, while females were served the feast in another room. Shanker resented this age old arrangement; he was robbed of the company of sister.

Desh had taken no note of Sunder during *puja*. In the feast he happened to take position next him; he was compelled to greet the elderly lawyer.

"Your brother-in-law was telling me," Sunder was bent on his food, "You are taking law as your profession."

"Quite so".

Sunder seemed too absorbed in eating to continue the talk. The manner of eating of some guests suggested gluttony; Sunder plainly displayed it.

"I have not seen Champa sister", observed Desh.

"She is in *terai*; she is gone there for winter vacation." Sunder's eyes remained pinned on food; never once he looked at Desh.

"*Terai*".

"She is staying with Inder Pratap". Sunder paused. "I mean with his wife; she is a great friend of Champa."

Nothing was farther from his imagination than her carrying on an intrigue with a notorious rake. Sunder was trying to shield his daughter, when on second thoughts he invented an excuse for her visiting Inder in *terai*. His sister was right when she had told him that Champa was a woman of easy virtue.

Till now Desh had turned away his eyes whenever Joga Sah looked at him; he felt abashed and self-conscious. He expected Joga Sah to exhibit no boldness to speak to him. But to his surprise, on finishing of the feast, Joga Sah sidled up to him.

"You are well *sahib*," he murmured, "Seen you after long."

"I was away," Desh felt hot behind his eyes from embarrassment.

Joga Sah interlocked his fingers. "Got so much happiness in *puja*. It is men like your uncle who have kept going our ancient *dharma*."

Desh harboured no ill-will against Joga Sah. He was not responsible for the marriage of Lalita with Jagdish. But his reference to *puja* rubbed Desh the wrong way.

"Mahatma Krishna Hare is coming to Nainital", resumed Joga Sah. "We shall have *kirtan* then; come with your elder father."

Joga Sah repeated his invitation; his supplication heightened Desh's embarrassment.

Soon the piercing chill of the advancing night sent the guest away to their homes. Shanker and sister were last to part.

"What did you say in your prayer?" asked sister.

"O, nothing," Shanker produced a wistful smile, " I said *Satyanarayan* make my sister-in-law well."

"You believed in your prayer ?"

"Is not this enough that I tried to pray and listen to the four tales with attention."

"But *Satyanarayan* wants full faith, or you will suffer like Sadhu *Vaisya* and the *rajah*."

x x x

Ever since her husband had been transferred from Indore to Allahabad, Chitra had been writing to her parents to spend the winter with her. Aunt had reminded uncle of his stay-at-home habit, several times, but to no effect.

"Why can we not go to Allahabad?" repeated aunt in a saw-like voice.

"Go to stay with my daughter; you are going insane. *Chhichhi;* how low."

"You have remained the old simpleton you were; you have no idea the world has moved from where to where. People have started visiting their daughters as sons."

Uncle shook his head.

"Why are you so old fashioned that you cannot go to the house of Chitra. Now daughters are getting equal rights with sons in property of parents; wives divorce."

Uncle snorted. "You are catching the infection of *Kalyug*. You telling to me of Hindu Code Bill."

"My father was a rich man, but what did I get. If my father had died now, I would have become rich."

"So what".

"I would have divorced you."

Uncle broke into a throaty, original laugh.

Chitra had sensed that her father was opposed to her scheme of making him and her mother live with her. Now she wrote endearing letters to aunt expressing undue anxiety over her father's ill health. The change in the tone and increase in the number of her letters to her parents in recent years, was obvious. She wanted her father to come down to Allahabad that she would be able to nurse him, keeping him a lot more comfortable than at Nainital. She had not met her parents for six long years; she missed them. But that winter uncle enjoyed much better health in

Nainital than previous ones; he disliked moving down to Allahabad for the sake of warm climate.

"Desh is here with me, that is why I am so well."

"You talk strangely," aunt pulled a face.

The letters of Chitra did not know of a break; she kept assiduously inviting her parents to Allahabad. The one and half month old *Kumbha-Mela* was coming to an end, and *Sivaratri* the holiest bathing day in river Ganges fell near. Her parents should not let slip that opportunity, when their own daughter lived in Allahabad.

Mother Ganges broke down the resistance of uncle, for it sprouted from the crown of *Siva*. He decided to take a dip in the river to absolve the sins that he might have committed. With his simple habits, he possessed a small stock of clothes, which needed half an hour to pack up; but aunt started doing so a week before the day of departure to Allahabad. She did not only her own *saris*, *cholis,* skirts, and ornaments, but also articles needed for establishing a home. Desh was amazed that she was taking with her kitchen utensils, several tin boxes, bottles and baskets, as though she was leaving Nainital for good.

"Chitra is not that Chitra now," remarked uncle, one day.

"Yes, she has become a very loving daughter," he replied.

"It is kindness of coming Hindu code bill."

x x x

Uncle survived the last part of winter in spite of snow-falls. But for suffering some minutes early in the morning from his asthmatic cough, he showed improvement in health. He slept well, ate food with appetite, and without complaining of tiredness, occupied himself for few hours with his devotions and Geeta.

On a sunny day, by the end of January Joga Sah sent in invitation to uncle and himself to participate in night *kirtan* in the hall adjoining the temple of Goddess Nanda *Devi*. The veil of mystery over such functions having lifted from over his eyes, he loathed to accompany uncle there.

"What is the matter with you?" he remonstrated, "In childhood you came running with me."

Uncle loved him not as a nephew but as his own son; rejection of his appeal would touch him on the raw; secondly successive snow-falls had restrained him within his bungalow. The picture houses were still close for winter; so did important shops on the Mall. The city lay depopulated; it would take a few months more to rouse into activity. Music sacred or otherwise would divert him in his boredom; he quietly followed his uncle.

The *kirtan* hall was constructed in tin and glass and overlooked the lake, adjoing the Nanda *Devi* temple. On the floor, separated in two groups, sat cross-legged fifty or sixty men and women around a dais on which was seated a man in high-necked coat and *dhoti*.

He possessed a velvety voice and took much pain in explaining the verses. Sometimes an ordinary couplet took quite a long time. At the end of the recitation all men and women, excepting Desh, offered flowers and coins to the *Ramayan*. It finished by sun-set, and before the start of *kirtan* a break of an hour was permitted. Most of the women departed to their homes, while the number of men swelled. Joga Sah, who had been sitting some yards away, crawled up and obsequiously greeted uncle and himself.

"This man reciting *Ramayan*," remarked Desh, "Is bony but his voice is so lusty and powerful."

"The more he does, the more his voice becomes deep", replied Joga Sah, "The recitation of *Ramayan* would continue for more than a month. You hear him on the last day, you will oscillate."

The name of the man, Joga Sah informed him was Krishna Hare. He was a teacher in a school, and, for his love of *Ramayan*, he had taken early retirement and lived a *yogi's* life on the banks of the Ganges in Allahabad; and being a famous reciter of *Ramayan*, he was invited by people from all over the country.

Abruptly Joga Sah let drop taking on Krishna Hare; moved his eyes towards the entrance, and whispered, "Har Preya is standing near the temple; she wants to meet you."

Desh was unprepared to see any member of the family of Lalita. Even in his short meeting with Joga Sah, he had been put out of countenance; all the same he struggled to his feet and carved his way through the gathering to the entrance. He felt a tremor running down his limbs and the palms of his hands perspiring from nervousness; he was touched by the officious manners of Joga Sah and consideration of Har Preya for him.

He walked towards the gates of Goddess Nanda Devi temple; Her Preya stood there all by herself. Seeing him a thin smile flickered through her lips, then her face grew small and pinched and tears welled up in her eyes; she began to cry.

"What is the use of all this now?"

"I sent for you the snub-nosed priest but you did not come." she stammered through her tears.

"What good could my meeting with you have done?"

He let the fit of her crying pass over; he felt his own eyes wet.

"How is she ?" He summoned courage to put the question gnawing his mind.

"*Arree,* what is there to ask?" answered Har Preya heavily. "She has done what she wanted to do; she has to live by her choice. There is no blame on her; all marriages are predetermined from one's *karma* of previous life."

Had Har Preya told him that Lalita was dead, the news would have hurt him less than her warning that she was bound in the ties of matrimony and must abide by its laws. This was second warning; the first having been administered by his sister. It was surprising that no one thought that Lalita was not required to cling to her mistake; she could rectify it.

"She should have come after marriage," his voice was quavering.

"Yes, just once for a short while."

"Why so ?"

"Jagdish is queer; he did not permit her to stay more than two days; come to see me sometimes."

Har Preya and himself walked back towards the *kirtan* hall; at the entrance the snub-nosed priest waited for her. He threw a knowing glance at Desh as he followed Har Preya to her home.

Presently music in the hall lifted up. To the accompaniment of cymbals and harmonium, Krishna Hare started singing in slow measure the psalm;

Jai Siva Onkara
Brahma, Vishnu, Shadasiva
Ardhange Goura.

By degrees he raised the pitch of his voice, so did the players of accompanying instruments. The audience started beating time with claps; then on a sudden Krishna Hare quickened the tempo of his solo, and the audience beat time faster and faster with their claps; the whole hall reverberated with strident music. The men with eyes half close rocked in frenzy, singing responsively; Desh alone remained unaffected by the primeval *kirtan*, but he was aware of its impetuosity and contagiousness.

He had never seen his uncle bursting with greater energy than now. He rocked conspicuously and struck the cymbals with a deft hand. His ecstasy beset Desh with a pang of jealousy; he swept his eyes around the devotees lost in singing. He tried to join them in the responses; he tried to work himself up to their mood, but he miserably failed. In an access of anger at himself, he jumped to his feet, hurried into his shoes and bounded homewards.

Aunt unbolted the door, "Your uncle did not come."

"*Kiran* is going on with full force; he would not come,"

"It can harm him."

The anxiety of aunt was right. Uncle had returned after overnight participation in *kirtan*; and for having overstrained himself a terrific asthmatic spasm in the morning had almost taken the life off him. Till late in the afternoon his wheezing was audible in the other room. The suffering of uncle agonised him; he wished he knew of some nectar sort of remedy to cure his uncle's dreadful disease.

x x x

Desh had not seen sister since Satyanarayan *puja*. One Sunday after-noon he climbed to Hamilton.

"Well," brother-in-law lifted up his face from the law-book he was reading out in the sun in front of the portico. "Seen you after long. You have stopped coming to your sister."

"Snowfalls".

Brother-in-law motioned him to one of the chairs placed in front of him, and then resumed study of the book open in his hands.

"Be with me awhile, I want to speak a word with you; your sister is sleeping.

Desh was bored stiff three quarters of an hour, sitting idle, before brother-in-law opened his mouth again, "My father had a very good practice."

"Yes, I know."

"He had great influence in the British *Raj*; it was he, among Nainital-*wallahs*, who had an easy access to the governor. Commissioners and district magistrates took legal advice from him in matters of administration; he was one of the first title-holders of Nainital."

Desh was bewildered by brother-in-law's abrupt reference to his father. But he was a wise man, who opened up his mind through subtle and indirect ways. Desh bent forward; he wanted to catch the meaning of brother-in-law.

"Still my father's life was·so simple" he continued "He never took tea, he never bothered about puddings and nice food."

"Life in his times was simple."

"It was the other way too; look at your own father; what money he spent; he had practice more than my father's, but he left you much less money than mine."

"But he died at much earlier as than your father."

"I do not think even if he had lived hundred years, he would have left you more money than he did. My father was a different kind of man; he valued his money."

"That every intelligent man should try to do."

"I wonder if children of a spendthrift father have it; you are just like him."

He understood that brother-in-law was insinuating at some of the expenditure made by sister. He waited for him to point them out, but brother-in-law had over again immerged himself into his book and took little notice of his going away.

Basking in the sun sister was teaching Miranda and Sanjeev English, on the eastern side of the bungalow. No sooner she saw him, she gave him a dry smile.

"Oho," he seated himself in a vacant chair, "You are taking much pain with your children."

"I am particular that they know good English."

"We are now replacing English by *Hindi*."

"Who denies that; but in society offices and industry English is as important as before independence."

"Seems we love English. Look at yourself, Shanker, or myself; we are mostly reading and writing English."

When he went in Desh opened his eyes wide. The old, faded hangings and lumbering furniture had gone away from the house, replaced by sumptuous, modern. The pink upholstery in the new sofas, in the drawing room, and scarlet hangings were like Shanker's, while the dining room showed sky-blue. A rectangular shining, teak wood table stood there in place of the heavy round one, surrounded by new chairs with leather-seats. The rooms in the second storey were decorated in light-green attractive hangings.

"You like my home now."

"Quite so; but you have not taken the permission of brother-in-law."

It was in his knowledge that sister wanted for long to remove the worn out hangings and out of the date furniture. Once or twice she had given her mind to Miranda's father; but the day she ordered the change, she had done so on her own.

"Quite smart of you; but brother-in-law does not seem to be pleased."

"Yes," drawled sister, "I know; these days he does not talk to me, and I do not too. If it was Shanker how glad he would have been."

Sister made tea and they sipped it without exchanging a word. Miranda and Sanjeev slipped off to join their father, who had got his tea served separately from them. He tried to read the thoughts of sister; a cloud had appeared on her face, and a tear stole down her cheeks.

"Sister", his throat was choked with emotion, "You have to be a strong, fighting human being, if you want happiness out of your life."

She gave him a flat, ghostly smile. "You are still a very young man."

At home that night he reflected upon his advice to sister. Until now the idea of her taking divorce, on the passing of the Hindu Code Bill, and remarrying Shanker was abhorrent to him. He had not known of a single woman, in the brahmin community of Nainital, who wanted to remarry; if there existed one, most probably, she would be unable to find a suitable man. But his idea on divorce was undergoing a change, and Lalita was responsible for it. Now he perfectly understood why Shanker wanted to marry an already married woman; it was not difficult for Desh to gauge the depth of his friend's yearning for sister. If after dissolving her marriage with Jagdish, Lalita wished to marry him, he would succumb to her, so compelling was his love for her.

x x x

By the end of February fell *Sivaratri*. Uncle and aunt observed fast; Desh was forced to do it too for he was afraid to reveal his true self to uncle. By mid-day aunt started getting ready for visiting the temple of *Siva* adjoining Goddess Nanda *Devi*. She put in her basket dried leaves of parijat-tree, sandal-wood paste, camphor, and coins, the articles required for offering in *puja* to *Siva*. For ill-health uncle stayed at home; he narrated to Desh the tale of deer-hunter from mythology, who unwittingly worshipped the phallus of *Siva* on the dark, holy night. When he died *Siva* remitted his sins and ordered angels to take his soul to heaven. Desh should accompany aunt to the temple to perform the exalted *puja*, not designed for gaining material prosperity, but for absolution of one's sins and *nirvana*.

"However much *Siva* is great," declared Desh, "I am not going with aunt to the temple."

Uncle knitted his brow, "You are unwell."

"I am all right, but I do not like to go."

"*Arree*, you have become an educated man now," said uncle with a heavy-heart, "You have read of things I do not know of; what do you care for an old man like me and my beliefs."

For having injured the feelings of his uncle, he felt guilty; his head hung over his hands crossed on his breast.

Uncle tried to kindle in him his true self of childhood. He knew that Desh had ceased performing *puja* and prayers. Though it broke his heart that the beloved child he had brought up with care should have gone astray, still uncle entertained hopes that as Desh would grow older, someday the merciful eye of *Siva* would fall on him and reclaim him. "I can die any day," continued uncle in a persuasive tone. "*Sivaratri* is the holiest of festivals; today all over the country people bathe in rivers, ponds, and sea, and do *puja* of Siva. You should fulfil my wish."

Desh quietly accompanied aunt to the temple. With bare feet men and women crowded around the shrine, performing *puja*, bowing to the phallus of *Siva* in black semi-precious stone. Votaries struck ringing bells suspended from the roof of the temple, accompanying their action by calling out various names of *Siva*: *Jai-Mahadev, Jai-Bambhole Nath, Jai-Shambhoo Kailashapati*. The scene was noisy. The attention of Desh was scarcely drawn by the *puja* or by the majestic names of *Siva*. Only he felt bored jostling shoulders with a train of votaries, while waiting for aunt to finish *puja*.

On his homeward march with aunt, as he was crossing the ground of the temple of Goddess *Nanda Devi*, he heard someone calling his name from behind. The voice was familiar to him, the falsetto of Har Preya. He looked over his shoulder and saw her standing few yards away from him. No sooner did her eyes fall on him, colour momentarily returned to her face and then went out.

"You did not come." her voice trailed off.

"I shall some day."

At night Desh contemplated long the gorgeously framed oleograph standing on the mantelpiece of his room. Suddenly he grew aware of the physical presence of *Siva* in his room. With an unintelligible impulse he over again vowed to himself not to touch liquor or cigarette.

For *nirvana*, Lalita would have taken fast that day; glad he was, he had done it too.

x x x

By the middle of March came the multi-coloured festival of Holi. Desh adored it for it was free from rituals, *puja* and fast. It was time when the sharpness of winter disappeared from the air, while summer still slumbered in womb, unborn. Desh pottered to and for the verandah of his bungalow, watching the eerie lake in the moon light, listening *Holi* songs in chorus, resounding Tallital *bazaar*; which depicted life of Lord Krishna. It was the groups of workingmen producing ragged music, but catching from its vigour and spontaneity. Desh enjoyed it till the advancing chill at night in mountains silenced it.

Next morning Desh gave a whistle of joy seeing his neighbour, lawyer Belwal, the sight he looked; his clothes were splashed in red colour and face and cap covered with vermilion and crimson powders. He visited uncle and himself once or twice in a year of which Holi as the sure one. Though prosaic, he came out of his shell, this day of universal bubble and mirth and riot of colour.

"You did not go to the *bazaar*," he said, "Men and boys are holding ready filled syringes; see how badly they have drenched me."

"I am waiting for you," chortled Desh, "The boys of the *bazaar* have spoilt my game."

He dashed to the farther end of the verandah where he had kept a vat of coloured water and buckets. He quickly filled one and bore down upon Belwal, who receded before his advancing steps.

"You cannot escape," he exclaimed splashing the bucketful of colour on to Belwal.

Uncle and aunt acclaimed his victory with a shout of joy.

Belwal had now known the place of colour; instantly he armed himself with a bucket, and before Desh could snatch it away, Belwal had splashed its contents over him. Everyone gave a shout of joy at this equalising victory. A ding-dong battle ensured between the Holi enemies; all the colour in the vat was emptied, spilled over the verandah. In vain uncle and aunt kept advising, "Stop, stop, water is cold," between shouts of joy. When Belwal and Desh sat down to snacks their wet clothes moulded their bodies; both felt chilly but jubilant in their hearts.

Soon a company of *Holi-wallahs*; with flaming caps and faces and clothes splotched over in multi-colours, gathered in front of the bungalow. Aunt shrunk in, while uncle and himself welcomed the *Holi-wallah* company by sprinkling over them coloured powers and offering them snacks and *pans*. The *Holi-wallahs* greeted uncle and himself in fraternal embraces after having smeared coloured powders over their faces. Then they together sang a *Holi* song to the accompaniment of *dholak* and cymbals, with Belwal, the stout man of sixty, leading.

"From when," he enquired, "You are coming to law-courts, I mean as a lawyer."

"From day after tomorrow, Belwal*ji*".

"This is very good news," grinned the elderly man of law.

Holding the palms of his hands pressed in front of his breast, uncle begged pardon from *Holi-wallah* company for his inability to join them in their tour from house to house.

"But Desh should come", demanded the crowd.

Someone bawled blessings. "In whose house comes spring this festival day."

"In the house of *burra* Sanwal*ji*" responded every Holi-wallah.

"His son Desh and family will live a lakh of years," bawled someone.

"Be that so, be that so."

By midday Desh freed himself from the company of *Holi-wallahs*; he felt lazy to greet Shanker with colour. It took him much pain to scrub it out from his hair, face, and body with hot water and soap. Having performed the last tedious rite of Holi festival, he put on his normal clothes. Day meal had been delayed, but it was cooked delicious and in plenty.

In the evening he found the road variegated in colours. Dressed in one of his lounge-suits, Desh swaggered off without fear. *Holi* playing had stopped; everyone like him had put on normal clothes.

"I waited to play *Holi* with you till two O'clock." Shanker twitched coroner of his upper lip. "Now you enjoy a cigarette till Chandra's coming; expecting you, I rang her up to come down too."

"I have again given up liquor and cigarette."

"Well I am also changing; follow me."

Desh was aghast to see a lovely print of Siva, set in a gilt frame, hanging over the bed of Shanker. A moment he disbelieved his eyes; his friend who had converted him was in need of his help.

"What am I seeing?" exclaimed Desh.

"Something good."

Desh was shaken; his mouth jerked open from apprehensions. He listened Shanker with a far away gaze in his eyes.

"When you love a woman as much as I do Chandra, she changes you."

"So I should take that you are not what you were."

"I am that way; Chandra's faith is so strong in *Siva* that it is catching me."

Now it fell on him to convert Shanker as once he did him, and pay the *guru's* debt. But for reaching his aim, it was plain, he should first attempt to convert his own sister.

Shanker rang up sister again. When she came, she was alone; it seemed unusual of her to have moved out without taking her children with her.

Dev Rama with his agile movements served coffee in a brand new, high-priced china-set with enchanting colour bands on it. Sister picked up an empty cup, and began to finger it.

"You like it," asked Shanker.

"It's lively.

"I keep it for you; there are tea and dinner services in it too."

"Buying new things would pour *ghee* into the fire; father of Miranda and myself are not in talking terms for new furnishing of the house."

It seemed impossible that she would ever get on with her husband. How opposite temperaments the two possessed, while the husband liked simple living, the wife luxurious and grand; the husband kept himself inside his world of law, the wife sought changes in experience full of excitement and colour. Moreover it was doubtful whether the husband loved his wife, who had transferred her love from him to Shanker. But the husband was unmindful of it; his time and attention were wholly taken by his profession and greed of money. Whether his wife loved him or no hardly mattered him; but his temperament had poisoned her happiness. Naturally her ever sticking to her husband reflected an undoubted infirmity of her mind.

"You should be getting tired of your lonely life", put in Desh in a tender voice with an undertone of exasperation.

"*Aree*", drawled sister, "If in my previous life I sowed barley how can I reap wheat in this; I should get fruit of my *karma*."

"You can still change your fate, if you take a leap."

"Give me time to think".

Shanker had been listening his talk with his sister with a amused expression in his eyes that brought home to Desh him mistake in giving advice to his sister.

"Make some coffee, Chandra," chimed in Shanker, "Than getting hot for nothing."

The rigidity of sister's face smoothened out. She glanced at Shanker with swimming eyes. "Today is *Holi*; you did not apply *gulal* on my forehead; first time I have come to your house on this festival. For meeting you I spoke a lie to father of Miranda;I told him I am going to see Desh."

"Your coming on *Holi* is a good omen."

Sister was invested in a blood-red, silk *sari*, with a tastefully patterned, golden border. Shanker's eyes now and again rested on her as he applied the *gulal*.

"Let us meet at *Holi*", Desh climbed to his feet.

Shanker and himself were locked in an embrace.

"Our friendship is unbreakable", declared Shanker.

Accompanied with his sister, Desh walked away from the apartment of Shanker.

That night for hours the sorrowing memory of Lalita chased away sleep form his eyes; her rich voice kept striking his ear drums. Jagdish would have smeared coloured-powder on her face. He was driven crazy.

CHAPTER - XVII

As every year the season in Nainital was in full swing in June. The city was packed with tourists from hot plains, craving gusts of cool air of mountains. Their voices echoed every where; picture-houses, shops, hotels and Flats, slumbering though the long winter months, hummed with them. Spruced men and women crowded about the motor-stand, hailed rickshaws on the road, and boated throughout the day. Desh doubted whether any one of them realised how severe the winter felt in the city that now was passing through its merriest period of the year. But they were holidaying tourists with a preponderance of young couples, many having selected Nainital for honey-mooning. Desh looked at them with envy.

One evening, the band in the Flats struck up a plaintive tune of a film song, most popular one of the year. Music having burst open the sluices of the dam of Lalita's memory in his mind, Desh sought the unfrequented Thandi road; he might run against Har Preya visiting the temple of Goddess of Rock. In the summer-house on the road, he saw a couple on a bench with hands interlocked, unmindful of him. Looking at the lake below them, both seemed too wrapped up in their own happiness than bother themselves with a passer-by.

He walked on bemused; he tried to stumble up the stairs of the temple, but he was touched by a feeling of awe on seeing the large silver eyes of the saffron Goddess. Suddenly he swung round, and made for his home. The impression that the couple in the summer-house had made on him was undeliable. If the Goddess of Rock had not cheated Lalita from him, she and himself would have occupied the very bench that evening instead of the couple.

The spring of her love in his heart, that had remained dried up and hidden, suddenly broke out. He felt a terrible choking sensation in his throat; his limbs trembled from exhaustion, and uncontrollable tears glided down his cheeks. He yearned for Lalita; he heard her sonorous voice calling him back to her. She must still love him as he did her; her marriage should not alter it. She had accepted Jagdish in a fit of insanity; she deserved pardon than vengeance. He made a mistake in ignoring the invitation of Har Preya on *Sivaratri* to visit her; as a sister she had tried to get him Lalita. He could still see her with good face; as if his relationship with her had not suffered a setback; as if Lalita was present there is the house, only she had gone in to the kitchen to make him tea.

He must meet Har Preya. He could know from her of Lalita's married life. How unhappy she was ! How often she remembered him in her letters; she should do as much as he did her walking on roads; his eyes roving, expecting her in Nainital. Would she have never come there after her marriage, strange! Six months had gone by since, but she had never been visible about the town. Was she not thinking of him? Looking forward to meeting him. Probably she had told herself that he had turned his mind away from her. After all she was a woman. How could she get ready to meet him without some clear hint from him. Every woman, whether it was his sister or Har Preya, had warned him that Lalita was now a married woman. Her home, duties and responsibilities had changed, while he had got out of her life. She must fear the cough of her parents-in-law and comply uncomplainingly to the commands of her husband. Then she must keep regard of her brothers-in-law and mind the society. Was it not natural for her to pay no visit to Nainital. By what way could she have met the man she loved, when he had been so callous as not to make inquiries after her from her sister Har Preya. "Forgive me Lalita," he said to himself, "I still love you as much as I did before."

x x x

The next morning in spite of his determination to call on Har Preya, Desh felt shy to put it to effect. How would she react to the rejected suitor of her sister. She might despise him for his visit that pointed to his abject surrender to Lalita. She had made him to understand on *Sivaratri* that Lalita was a married woman; Desh should know better that all was over between them. He should forget Lalita and behave in no way as to endanger the happiness of her married life; his visit to Har Preya could be taken by her as injurious to the reputation of her sister. It was wise for him to abandon his plan of seeing Har Preya.

But the intensity of his feelings for Lalita was too strong, almost an oven in his heart. Sometimes he thought that it would never cool down until it had not taken the very life off him. He was losing interest in everything; he never suggested Shanker to accompany him to pictures or a round of boating; rather he declined such requests from Shanker. He was giving himself to solitude. On Sunday and on days he was free early from law-courts, he climbed up the tops of mountains, and from over them gazed the country below him; his mind empty, his heart barren of inspiration. Nothing seemed to affect him; the hazards of legal profession; nerve-racking illness of his uncle; the perils attending the love of sister and Shanker.

If he could remove Lalita out of his mind; if he could loosen himself from her stranglehold on him; but it seemed impossible to him to set himself at liberty from her bonds of love. Her voice repeatedly clasped on his ear drums; he ached to feel her rounded arms and kiss her full lips. If she remained unseen in Nainital for next two or three months, he could do a trip of Ranikhet, prowl on roads there to see her.

He kept an eye on Thandi road, tormented by the total absence of the thin figure of Har Preya from there, even during the gay months of summer; she seemed to have withdrawn herself to her world. She was born and married into a family adhering to the custom of *purdha*; if she went out of house, it was done on set purpose to performing *puja* in temples, or meeting relatives specially women. It seemed that she had stopped availing herself of these one or two concessions. She might be afraid of walking upon Desh and the consequent revival of a dead affair; she might have herself advised Lalita to postpone visiting Nainital a few years to escape a possible post marriage scandal. What profit lay in Lalita's meeting him; her marriage with Jagdish was final, indissoluble. Intelligence dictated that she should always live with her man, as all women did, irrespective of whether she loved him or no. She had chosen him once for all; her marriage-knot was permanent, undoable.

One evening by the end of June Desh was buying medicines for uncle, from the fixed shop on the Mall road, when Har Preya entered, and stood at the farther end of the counter. His heart gave a thud; about a year past exactly here he had met her and Lalita. The bald-headed chemist, who was her cousin, at once attended to her, ignoring several customers. Her need supplied she left the shop. Swiftly making payment for his own purchase he followed her. He wondered whether her eye fell on his or no, for he was hidden by a row of customers, or whether she wanted to meet him or no; she might have extended invitation to him on *Sivaratri* out of a sense of courtesy. The traffic on road was heavy; she seemed lost in it. He made straight to Bara-*bazaar* than turning towards Flats; he knew she would avoid the crowds there. He had gone up few hundred yards, when he saw her ahead of him; she was hurrying home with a cloth-bag in her hand.

"*Arree*, Har Preya sister", he called in one breath.

She looked at him over her shoulder, and at once stopped, stock-still. "*Arree*, Desh", her face took on a melancholy cast "Have I not remained your sister. With Lalita you also left me. There are so many days from *Sivaratri*; you never came."

"What good of my seeing you I thought; it might have only caused harm."

"This is road; we cannot talk here. Come to my house."

"I shall come, some day."

"No, come now." Har Preya caught hold of his finger and pulled him forward as she resumed walking.

"*Achha*," he disengaged his finger, feeling awkward by her demonstration of love.

As Desh climbed the tortuous steps, he felt dull pain rising in his heart. It looked Lalita still lived there; in a minute he would find her in the room in top storey; seeing him she would jump on her feet, welcoming him with joined palms of her hands. He would respond to her with a similar gesture, staring her all the time. When the two would be seated, she would complain of his long neglect; she would tell him that without him her life was lonely, robbed of all charm. Like Sita severed from Rama, every moment, she had pined for him.

"Here it is dark, come slowly," called Har Preya, preceding him over the stairs.

He entered the room painfully familiar to him. Finding the low-chair he was accustomed to sit in missing, he took a high one; his eyes rolling and rolling round the room, searching. Photograph of the mother, coloured prints of Gods and Goddess, paper-flowers and chains, decorating the room from Diwali, lay under a sheet of dust. It appeared the room had been neglected by the family, left ownerless.

"I am so happy you have come," began Har Preya taking a seat on the bed opposite him. "I thought you would never come here." Her voice trailed off; her white hands remained resting on her lap, and her eyes bent on the floor.

Some embarrassing moments passed.

Said Desh, "If I had met you again after *Sivaratri*, I would have come here myself."

"From then I never went out of the house; Balu was ill, very ill. The doctors found his lungs weak; I got that anxious; I forget about everything; about Lalita, you."

That evening Har Preya had moved out of the house for purchasing restoratives and medicines needed by Balu, for his father was absent from home. Balu was a case of tuberculosis; she had tried every drug. Rupee, paisa had lost their value for her; if something befell Balu, Har Preya would kill herself. Since her son's illness, she had kept fasts and spent an hour every day in prayers; she had distributed copious alms to offset the effect of evil stars casting their shadow on Balu.

"You should not be anxious at all", Desh comforted Har Preya, "Tuberculosis is no longer incurable; your child will soon get well."

Balu was sleeping in the inner room. Har Preya was free to get him tea and home cooked eatables. But Desh's mind wandered far from them; be wanted to know about Lalita.

"You will not forget to come again."

"I should not." he replied in a toneless voice.

"She has been remembering you in her letters," Har Preya looked intently into his eyes.

He had died to know of the feelings of Lalita for him. He felt himself being lifted on the wings of joy.

"It is all fate," added Har Preya, "That she should have been married in Ranikhet." Her eyes overflowed; she wiped them with a languid hand. "I could have stopped the wedding; Lalita had agreed to see you. When you did not come, I again sent the priest; he returned with news that you have gone away to Bhimtal. Before I could send the priest there, everybody in the house wanted the marriage at once, to avoid public talk. Lalita, who had agreed to see you, firmly changed her mind."

"What was to happen, has happened; my seeing you would have been useless." His voice sounded almost inaudible. "I wish her a happy life."

Lalita's letters described home of her husband in detailed; her brothers-in-law and sisters-in-law disliked her eagerness to share the burden of household work. The presence of her elder sister, married to a cousin of her husband, had made her new world smooth for her.

"But what has Lalita to say about herself ?"

"Nothing excepting that her husband is a simpleton; most hard working among his brothers and cousins; he goes to cloth-shop after morning-meal and returns late in the evening. Lalita meets him only after night-meal, when he comes to his room to sleep."

She had visited Nainital once immediately after wedding, in pursuance of the custom for the bride to do so. Since then Her Preya had written her three or four times to come over to her; but she never complied to her request. She had been informed of the illness of Balu, but she refused to see him too.

"Lalita wants to forget Nainital; that is the only good thing for her to do. She remembered you in her first letter, then she never did. She is unfortunate; now nothing is possible."

Desh kept biting at his finger, unable to continue the conversation; Har Preya's words had cut deep into his heart.

"Jagdish is rich," he drawled. "Her life with him should be happy."

Har Preya shook her head. "I suspect it is not; but Lalita says nothing in her letters."

"What should be the matter ?"

Har Preya looked lumpishly at him. "Jagdish is abnormal; during the wedding he often laughed stupidly."

"*Arree*, when I met him last summer in Shanker's house, I noted his abnormal behaviour. If only I had known he would be married to ..."

Har Preya arched her eyebrows. "Jagdish was rich; nobody was worried over these small things."

He had stayed with Her Preya over two hours; he climbed on his feet.

"Listen, brother Desh; you always sat in the low chair; you remember."

"Yes; when I entered the room my eyes looked out for it."

"Lalita has taken away the low-chair with her to Ranikhet."

He looked at Har Preya amazed.

"She had no souvenir of yours; so she wanted to keep with her the chair associated with you."

"Lalita is a queer woman," he gave a deathly smile, and quickly walked away.

On his way home Desh entered into the Flats summer-house. His meeting with Har Preya had given him headache and loss of appetite. The long, multi-coloured beams of lights reflected upon the lake, the cool life-preserving breeze of summer, failed to excite him to a joyous mood. He felt himself thoroughly beaten, vanquished; he wished he could passionately weep, but not a tear collected in his eyes. Six months he had foolishly nursed hopes of meeting Lalita, when she had been separated from him as though into limbo. She would delay visiting Nainital until she had not ceased to love him, wiped his memory from her mind; and any endeavour by him to renew his contact with her would only inflame her indignation and black rage-- never should his love for her embody in action; never should his shadow fall upon her.

But she had carried the low-chair with her to Ranikhet, while she was struggling to free herself from his love. "You might never be able to do it, Lalita; my sister could not Shanker," he whispered to himself.

CHAPTER XVIII

Desh had almost suspended visiting sister. He had disliked to miss even an evening at Flats from where he kept watch on Thandi road for Lalita. Brother-in-law and advised him to come regularly to Hamilton house to get training on drafting of plaints.

"But I can do it in law-courts,"

"I want you sit beside me while I dictate them."

"I know how you do it. It's legal axiom to deny all the points of the opponent and over emphasise your own."

Brother-in-law wrinkled up his brow, "When you write them, you will see it's not all that simple."

At the beginning of July sister summoned him to Hamilton house; but he was detained about an hour by the first heavy shower of the season. A thick fog awakened into him a sad mood; he felt he was growing sensitive to rainy-weather. He would have liked to meet anyone, by far sister to buoy up his sprits.

He walked in on tip-toe to escape the notice of brother-in-law, who might have wanted his help in drafting plaints or in finding old rulings from law-books.

"You are late," sister raised her eyes from the book she was reading on to him." "I had wanted you to accompany me to pictures."

Her face was squeezed of colour; her eyes looked lusterless with depths from prolonged weeping.

"Awful rain, otherwise I should have reached here by the time of pictures."

"It is stopping now; we can see the night-show."

"You want to see the night-show", Desh strained his eyes on his sister.

"Yes, yes; I want to change."

Sister rarely stayed out of house long after sunset. She kept her boating, shopping or visits to relatives to the day; she went to pictures in the matinee.

"You want to see night-show; something the matter."

"No," tears rushed to her eyes.

She wiped them and instead of explaining herself fixed them on the novel.

"Why keep off anything from me ?"

Sister gave a slow, ironical smile. "How long to suffer Desho ! I have destroyed my life; I see no sense in living."

"But why do you feel down and out?"

"Hun; yes you have used the correct English expression to described me. I have no urge to live; I cannot bear this lonely life. Shanker will never be mine."

"But you were always a courageous woman; you hated my telling you that you should break up your marriage."

"You know if I suffered, I suffered silently; I thought I shall somehow pass remaining days of life; but now my ideas are changing; how long to suffer and why?"

"Brother-in-law is good to you; his only weakness is that he takes his profession very seriously."

Sister kept gazing at him, "You do not understand him fully; he loves money before his profession; for him neither amusement exists nor wife; sometimes he talks with children and that is all his life after his work."

Sister had resigned herself to her circumstances. She had never thought even in dream of rebelling against them, altering them. With her husband her life was dark; still she hesitated making trial with another man. Now she was showing signs of breaking up; refusing to drag on with her husband all her life.

"But you never saw night-shows."

"Yes, "she ground her teeth." "I will see pictures whenever I wish, go alone wherever I like; let the world call me bad; who cares ! My life shall be sweet."

Desh looked askance at sister; her assertion sounded hollow. She was born and bred in a Brahmin family; she might lay down her life than muster sufficient courage to declare herself independent of her husband.

"I do not believe you."

Rebuffed, sister shouted, "Why not? I had been wanting changes for home for years; when I got them, how he has behaved; no word of praise for best tapestry and furniture in Nainital."

"Why bother about his praise?"

Sister rose upon her feet and started pacing the room; she was beside herself from rage.

"That is not all; he thinks I have wasted money on them. He wants me to return them. What a humiliation." She banged the dining-table with her fist. "Tapestry has come from Shanker; he will say nothing when I return it; he will laugh. But what would the furniture-*wallah* think, tell me."

"It was better, if you had taken brother-in-law's permission."

"What permission? How long and for how many things. Have I no voice in the keeping of the house ? Instead of being glad that new tapestry and furniture have made it so well decorated, he wants me to return them. I will just leave this house for good one day than obey him."

Sister's eyes had bulged out; and her breath came quick.

"I will leave this house, I swear by *Siva* I cannot be humiliated as a slave all the time."

Coaxed Desh, "Do not be unjust to brother-in-law; he loves you. If you ask him to pay for your new furnishings, he shall do."

Sister sucked her lower lip to express her determination. "No, that I will never do, when he was still not paid last year's bill of Shanker."

Brother-in-law wrinkled up his brown in surprise and told Desh that he never meant to bilk payment. His sister was a recklessly extravagant woman who not only threw away money in superfluous, luxurious articles, but also prided herself in paying higher prices than other people. He wanted a discount from Shanker and furniture-*wallah*, and requested Desh to try it.

Shanker laughed a good humoured laugh when Desh met him. He had sent *saris* to sister the previous summer and tapestry as gifts.

"You know she cannot accept them without payment by her husband.

Shanker jumped from his seat in a ringing volley of laughter. "Tell your brother-in-law I do not want any payment; rather I will make payment to the furniture-*wallah*."

"Brother-in-law is a gentleman; he does not want that you should make payment for him. How rich you are that you want to pay for him ?"

Shanker cast his eyes on a painting in the room. "I do not have much money; from the income of Empire Store I take five hundred rupees a month."

"What about rest of income ?"

"Brother does five and balance he saves in a bank".

"If your brother cheats you of your share, what will you do?"

Shanker crossed his legs and leaned back on the sofa to show his resentment to his question. "I love my brother very much; I believe he loves me too; I do not expect such a thing from him."

Desh was surprised to see tears in the large, masculine face of Shanker; he dried them on his hand kerchief and blew his nose. "Between me and my brother his wife was a bridge; she strengthened our love. Poor thing, she has died in the sanatorium a few days ago. She had been cured of tuberculosis, but heart failure took her away; Goddess's *maya*;"

Desh was taken aback.

"Shanker, you have come to think that *Devi* manages human affairs."

"My beliefs are shaken; your sister is constantly pulling me to her side."

"But sometimes I doubt if she will herself remain the same."

Shanker interlaced the fingers of his hands to emphasise his words. "You are mistaken; the sun may not rise tomorrow I could say; but not that she will ever change."

CHAPTER - XIX

One evening Desh accompanied Shanker up the top of western mountain over which perched the yellowish-red, huge, rambling house of *rajah* Narendra Pratap, father of Inder. Flower beds in its spacious grounds were being choked by the rainy season's fast growing weeds; no one had bothered to trim the hedges. The lofty and gabled walls under slanting roofs were faded of colour; and here and there a door or window was disfigured with broken panes. Desh was overcome with a feeling of awe.

"These big people," began Desh, "Are in a poor way."

"You might as well say that their class had a longer life than it should have."

Shanker looked at the house in detail as he recalled the days he had played tennis there, fifteen years before, with Inder. Bright with paint and colour, it attracted every eye; flowers grew everywhere.

"It should have cost," continued Shanker, "So much money to maintain it; only *rajah sahib* with his love for art and flowers could do it."

Shanker led him into a long, glazed anti-room running along the middle of the huge mansion. A pair of stuffed tigers flanking the entrance frightened a visitor, but crosswise swords and knobbed shields fixed alternately on the walls heartened him. Farther a dancing lass in china beamed at him.

"These," Shanker pointed his finger to the tigers, "Were shot by *rajah sahib.*"

Having waited for some minutes for someone to announce him, Shanker looked impatiently around.

"Before coming of *zamindari* abolition, *rajah sahib* had thirty men over here; today you see the difference."

A footman, square-shouldered with wiry moustaches, appeared in a blue frock coat. He was carrying a tray.

"*Jai-hind* Shanker Lal*ji*," he greeted with a note of insolence in his voice.

Again some minutes passed before he reappeared. The footman preceded the two over the stairway to the corresponding room, in the first floor, that they had left. It was fitted with heavy curtains and wicker-chairs, four around a low-table. Elaborately carved china or metal vases but innocent of flowers stood on them. With corners decorated with bronze statues and walls with large landscapes, the room bestowed peace to a troubled heart.

"Here", told Shanker, "*Rajah sahib* gave parties"

The footman piloted them through several rooms, each revealing itself as an art museum. Bronze, china, ivory, marble ware cluttered up the dark, stately rooms; and landscapes covered the walls. One room encased silver-ware and crockery, another swords, draggers and guns, and yet another books. Hides of tigers, antelopes and other wild animals over carpets made the tread across the rooms luxurious. Shanker and himself waited in a room different than others; it was hung over with life-size photographs of the *zamindar* family with British officers, set against, blood-red wonderfully patterned Persian-carpet, velvet upholstry, bead curtains and guided ceiling. Desh felt he was sitting in a fairy land.

"This is a great place", said Desh.

"Sorry it is going to pieces."

A tall man with silvery head swung into the room. Shanker and himself stood up and greeted him. Narendra Pratap welcomed them with a smile, and signalled them to resume their seats.

"Shanker," said Narendra Pratap in bass voice, "You came after a long time."

He had long arms as was his face; it was surrounded with aura of dignity.

"Somebody about here," he clapped his hands. "*Chai, chai*"

"Thank you *rajah sahib*", responded Shanker.

"Shanker why you address we as *rajah*; I am no longer that."

"Sacked, but it's Delhi."

Narendra Pratap had ceased feeling the pride of a *rajah*. For his fabulous, net annual income of rupees ten lakhs from his lands, he would get meagre compensation in bonds payable after decades.

"I am trying," he held his hands across his chest, "To prepare myself to the change." He pointed to the cheap china-set, in which tea had been served, "I go walking down to the lake than on palanquin. I have started eating simple food in simple pots and plates; I have sold out all my cars except one; I am selling all my treasures you see in this house and in Rasalgaon." He took a deep sigh. "What is left of my social position; each year I spent a lakh of rupees in parties in Nainital alone; soon I will not have a thousand to do so."

It was touching to hear his tone of self-pity.

"There are sugar-mill owners," he resumed, "In my estate in Rasalgaon; their status in rising with their income. I remember how these fellows begged me to allow them open mills on my lands. Today these fellows look down upon me."

But unlike other *zamindars* Narendra Pratap uttered not a single word in denunciation of government policy. At first he had regarded it as wrong, but soon he realised that tens of millions of tenants would be emancipated from the hold of all manner of *zamindars*, made proprietors of the land they tilled.

Narendra Pratap lifted his wrist to see the time in his watch of solid gold. The contrast in the simplicity of his clothes and his grand living was glaring; he wore a white *kurta* and *churidars*.

"We took much of your precious time," begged Shanker.

"I have lots of time for you; I do nothing but *dhyan* and *bhajan*; my wish is that my ashes mix up in the name of *Rama*. I am very old; I can die any day."

"You have still many years to go."

"No, no; it is for this reason I called you. Inder should be writing to you from England; when is he returning ? He should be beside me at least at my death-time. Come again; when Mrs. Scott returns from Rasalgaon, I shall ring you." Narendra Pratap looked at Shanker with a smile in his eyes. "You know, she still remains my private secretary."

On the way home Shanker remarked; "There is a great change in *rajah sahib*."

He had heard Narendra Pratap mention *Rama* for the first time.

"But I do not think so," protested Desh, "If he had got over his pride, he would not have taken time in meeting us, or looked at his watch to dismiss us so quickly."

Shanker glanced at Desh with the calm, immobile eyes of a *sadhu*. "You should know that only the heart of *rajah sahib* is changing, not his habits of mind; *rajah* is *rajah*, whether he has money or no". Shanker abruptly pulled a wry face. "I do not like to see this Mrs. Scott."

x x x

Desh had advised his sister to seek dissolution of her marriage, but when she came to accepting it, he wished to retract, for saving her from social opprobrium. "Who thought Chandra could do this; wife of a high-caste *Brahmin* running away like one of a poor man." This sentence would be found on every lip. He felt hot with shame; better he had tell sister that she should cling to her first marriage than contemplate on second. She had lived about half her age; she should know that such a course for her was useless, a forlorn hope to happiness. Would she be able to forget her first home; bear separation from her children ? Would Shanker's love be strong enough to block the flow of thoughts of guilt from her mind ? Probably not; her upbringing would reassert itself. Second marriage might knock her insane. Moreover Shanker's circumstances were hardly affluent; his income of rupees five hundred a month was barely sufficient to keep him as a bachelor; but it was little if he went in for marriage and raised a family. He got to demand his share of bank deposit from his brother, or he would heap disgrace on sister for exchanging a wealthy man for an ordinary one.

He was surprised to see sister sitting over tea with Champa.

"You visited," he smiled to her in greeting, "Hamilton after more than a year."

Champa looked at him questioningly. "Now why should you always speak to me in English? Why English names continue with us?"

"British officer had made Nainital little England," he rejoined, "Here English names of schools, shops, houses, would continue."

"But", struck in sister, "You cannot change all names."

"I do not get you," replied Champa.

"I cannot change name of my daughter Miranda as easily as of lifeless object."

"But you can do of your house."

"I am habituated to call it Hamilton, and like the name. Let Sanjeev change it to Hindi when I am dead."

"You have no national pride; people like you still glue English language and names to their neck."

"You are greatly mistaken," said sister with asperity," I know more English than Hindi."

Before his departure, sister took him aside, and told him that his brother-in-law had paid off the furniture-*wallah* and Shanker. She had dropped her intention of breaking up with him; she regretted that she was intending to take a serious step. She felt supremely happy that the crisis in her married life had lasted but only some days.

Champa and he trundled down to the Mall. She kept plying him with amorous glances; she seemed ready to recommence her intrigue with him. He felt uneasy.

"You not going to England?" He asked.

It was bad in taste to poke in the reference of Inder, he knew; but he wanted her to turn her eyes away from him.

"I thought", he repeated, "You wanted to go to England."

Champa winced; but she at once recollected herself. "What to talk of England, I have no paisa even to take poison; you help me."

"How?"

Shanker's brother Heera Lal was needing tutor for his children. Champa was an applicant for the job.

"Better speak to Shanker for it."

"*Dekho*," said Champa shortly, "He came to our house in my absence and told my people about Inder; he called me a fool."

"All right see Heera Lal after a fortnight; by then I shall have spoken to Shanker about you".

x x x

Shanker and himself rode up on horses again to *rajah* Narendra Pratap's house in the beginning of August. Both had been invited to midday meal.

At the table sat with them Mrs. Scott, the English private secretary of Narendra Pratap. She had a graceful figure; neat features, weathered from long living in a tropical country. Her hair streaked with grey was meticulously done. She looked about fifty-five, but in a smart, maroon skirt, exuded youthful spirits. Her eyes lighted up on seeing Shanker.

The fare was simple. Narendra Pratap caught the eyes of Shanker searching the meat-curry, mutton chops.

"I have become a vegetarian," he pointed out "And I offer my guests only vegetarian food."

Shanker grinned, "Has Mrs. Scott become too ?"

"She is trying to; she has not remained that finicking person, you knew."

Mrs. Scott gave a radiant smile.

During and before war Shanker had witnessed the grandeur of Narendra Pratap. Then Inder lived with his father and often invited Shanker to drinks, tennis, and dinner. Only when the rupture between him and his father was complete, and he had moved his residence to Ranikhet in summer, that the visits of

Shanker to Rasalgaon house dropped off. Entertaining guests filled Narendra Pratap with a singular thrill. Though distinguished persons were hardly forgetten, bulk of his invitees were constituted of civilians, Indian and British. In his feasts expensive food and scotch whisky was so unstintly served that half of it was wasted. It was notorious that new servants grew fat, the old ones, having already gone through the process, sneered at them.

"The quiet about your table is touching," remarked Shanker.

"Times change," whispered Narendra Pratap. "Saint Kabir says beat your drum ten days, then you go; I am not bitter like other *zamindars*." He slid his eyes over Mrs. Scott and gave a grunt. "The Britishers' took away from us our fighting spirit; but by the abolition of our landed estates, we *zamindars* are coming back to ourselves. We are struggling now for jobs in government, taking to farming, industry and trade. Only Inder is an exception; he wants to sell everything I possess, than earn money."

Narendra Pratap spoke at length how *zamindars* lost their vigour in British *Raj*, grew weaklings, reduced to seeing carnal pleasures. A nationalist in his youth, he severely criticised his father for his unusually large expenditure in the entertainment of officers in general, British in particulars. A convention had established itself among *zamindars* to paying regular calls on the district magistrates and offering them presents of flowers, dry-fruits and the like. On the death of his father, when he succeeded into Rasalgaon *rajahship,* Narendra Pratap broke up the convention. Then the threat of the district magistrate to acquire his *zamindari,* took his breath away. He realised that he was a helpless creature in front of the mighty British government; indeed he decided to come to terms with the magistrate. From that time onwards he tried to dazzle British officers by his lay-out on drink parties and feasts.

"Those were difficult times." Shanker pulled a long face, "We are so soon forgetting the humiliations we suffered in British *Raj*; is this not surprising?"

Narendra Pratap's eyes involuntarily swriveled round to the chair Mrs. Scott had been occupying, but it was empty. No one was aware as to when she had slipped off the room.

"Like all Indians we *zamindars* had to suffer humiliations, though less than others. We too could not refuse to take orders from British officers, though they treated us so much inferior to themselves." Narendra Pratap lowered his voice to a whisper. "Mrs. Scott has left us for she pre-empted that I might tell you why I employed her as my private secretary. The fact was that white-skin had great value in British days. If we had an Englishman or woman in our employment, we could see the senior British officers without any difficulty, and get our official work done in no time. Similarly in a journey or party or dinner, no British officer could treat me as inferior if Mrs. Scott was beside me."

"So Mrs. Scott has done her job well."

"I know it and for this reason I have not dismissed her, when I so much reduced my staff. But now she is a white-elephant."

Mrs. Scott was the widow of an army officer saddled with two young daughters at the time she joined Rasalgaon estate. She educated her daughters in best public schools in India before dispatching the two to England to find eligible bachelors, and until both were not married, she sent them several years remittance. On the approach of the *zamindari* abolition, Narendra Pratap advised Mrs. Scott to go back to her home-land, and live with her daughters, for he could ill-afford a high paid English lady as private secretary. But Mrs. Scott refused to join her daughters, who had criminally neglected her after having extracted lumps of money from her. She was in the employment of Narendra Pratap for many years; he had treated her magnificently. She was still willing to serve him without pay, in case he provided her board and lodging, besides footing her medical bills. He agreed to her terms.

Shanker looked at Narendra Pratap with a sly, sidelong glance. "Would Mrs. Scott treat us now with a sense of equality?"

"I can say for her that she is one of those English women who is glad at our independence."

Narendra Pratap had talked long. He extended his legs and reclined on the high-backed chair; he looked tired.

"I have heart trouble; I should not have made so much exertion. It is nice meeting you. Write to Inder to return to Rasalgaon soon; I have not many days to live. After I am dead he should not start selling all my possessions. Help him earn money; you are his only friend, Shanker, son."

Instead of making straight for home, Desh was surprised that Shanker sought the room of Mrs. Scott, situated at the farther end of the mansion in the first-floor. It was fully lighted by paned-windows; one could clearly see the photographs of Mrs. Scott's family, hanging around the walls, showing her husband, a flat faced, robust man in military uniform or in mufti; her daughters from their infancy to adolescence. One was distantly pretty with large features. Mrs. Scott enumerated the occasions in which the photograph had been taken among her friends and relatives. Picnics, social-gatherings, farewell-parties were some of them.

"You remember everything."

"O yes;" murmured Mrs. Scott, "Good old times; they will never return."

"You never thought we will becomes independent so soon."

"You misunderstood me," added Mrs. Scott crisply. "I have lived most of my life here; I love India particularly simple peasants around Rasalgaon. Only, with all my countrymen having gone, I feel lonely."

A faint smile illumined Shanker's features "I am so glad to hear you say so. As a result of the peaceful way of withdrawal of your government from India, you will find no ill-will here for you."

The affection of her friends especially Narendra Pratap was holding her back from her home-land.

"Shanker, eventually I will go away; *rajah sahib* is a generous man; he will remember me in his will."

Mrs. Scott saw them to the gate of Rasalgaon house, and shook hand with them in a motherly way.

"I am glad to have met you," A ray of light shown in the eyes of Shanker.

"So am I".

A suspicion arose in Desh's mind. Shanker had stated that he disliked meeting Mrs. Scott; now he was behaving lovingly towards her.

Marching down the Mall, he inquired, "Something the matter between you and Mrs. Scott ?"

"Oh, you are becoming a sharp lawyer."

Shanker fell in love with the handsome daughter, Lucy, of Mrs. Scott, whom Desh saw in the photographs a while ago.

"You told sister about her."

"Yes".

"What does she think?"

"Your sister is glad I could not marry Lucy. After fifteen years it is not bad to think that she could not be my wife." Shanker came to a halt, turned round. "Lucy wanted me to break my business from my brother. I was hesitant to do." Shanker paused. "Then her mother came into the scene; she talked her daughter over to herself."

"How".

"By reminding her of the superiority of her white-skin."

"And Lucy changed."

"O yes, astonishingly quick."

"Now she would have changed like her mother."

Shanker resumed walking downhill. "I do not think so. I had letter from Inder in which he said that he went to see Lucky. She is married to a commonplace man who does not treat her well. Still she feels she was right in not marrying me. She still does not like mixing with Indians in England, and keeps away."

"Old habits of mind and heart are hard to change."

"Quite so."

x x x

It was the time of mid-August, when the rains came through steel grey fog, which submerged the lake and the mountains. Bulk of the tourists to the city had fled away a month before, and its trade stood dull. The divine hill-station of summer had been transformed into a boring one, where slushy rains forced people to keep indoors. Desh stayed at home, tearful; without hope of ever seeing Lalita. Flats brought depression, clouds deepening it. He felt a constant load in his heart; despite all his will power he was unable to forget her, unlike Shanker Lucy. Lalita dwelt in his eyes and ears; she ruled over his thoughts.

One day late in the evening, when the rains held off, he walked up to Bara-*bazaar* to order provisions. The fog had dimmed street lights; he walked with firm foot, slow from fear of slipping over sodden road. On his way home instead of taking the straight Mall road, he veered to Flats. The rain came in drizzles; he left his umbrella unopened; he enjoyed his tread over the wet gravel. Not until he had advanced up to temple of Goddess Nanda *Devi* he grew aware of his having sauntering too far in foul weather.

Two women streamed out of the gate; one was thin and fair of complexion, other plump and of wheat. His heart stood still. Surely Lalita and Har Preya had recognised him before he had them. He gazed at them from behind until both were merged into the fog. An impulse enjoined him to dash and overtake the two sisters, but his sense of pride defied it, helping him preserve his self-respect. He swung round and tramped homewards; Lalita kept burning his heart.

CHAPTER - XX

Uncle's health kept deteriorating from the beginning of the rainy season. In May and June some brightness had come upon his face; but soon his twenty years old asthma tightened its grip on him. His spasms of cough lasted overlong, when his face and neck was covered with film of perspiration; his body felt cold and lifeless. In a month he was reduced to a mere skeleton. Aunt nursed him night and day, disallowing Desh to share the burden of her work. He wondered where from she had picked up demoniac energy that she could live without rest. She fed uncle with her own hands; administered him medicines; stroked his back when asphyxia seized him. Her devotion for him was exemplary; it seemed incredulous that such a wife should have nagged at her husband all through his life.

During his examination of the heart by the physician, uncle failed to open his eyes even once; he seemed in coma.

Faltered Desh, "Will he get over his illness ?"

The physician silently walked to the verandah. Desh repeated his question.

He looked with wooden expression in his eyes at Desh. "Not many days can be survive."

He retreated to his room, his heart oscillating inside his chest. Since his childhood he had been accustomed to hearing his uncle cough at all hours; never had it occurred to him vaguely that this ordinary looking symptom would one day take him away. Desh was a stranger to death; he saw now its might that would break forever the companionship between him and his uncle. The lost memories from his childhood whirled up in his mind. During festivals uncle bought him, in his childhood, abundant sweets and toys. But he was hard too. Once for killing a nestling he commanded him "Go to *Siva* and seek his pardon." When he was in school, a boy bullied him. His uncle instead of bringing the matter to the notice of headmaster, advised him, "Pray to *Siva*."

Now Desh was a different person from his childhood; he looked with scorn at the oleograph of *Siva* resting on the mantelpiece. In spite of him a short prayer escaped his lips for the safety of his uncle. As a reaction to the prayer he had said in mistake, he lifted up the charming, gilt-framed, oleograph of *Siva*, prepatory to sending it crashing to the floor. But an uncanny fear gripped him; recollecting himself, he replaced the *Siva* to its former place. Then he began to despise himself for his act of cowardice; and to make amends, he demoted the *Siva* to his bath-room. It had stayed in his room from fear of uncle. Poor thing; he would never be able to leave his bed, let alone walk up to Desh's room to know where had *Siva* disappeared from there.

Next morning he found uncle asleep; he lay perfectly motionless with his eyes closed. Desh was surprised that in less than twelve hours the news of his committing sacrilege had travelled up to his uncle.

He said in his deadened, guttural voice, "Who is there ?"

"It is I". Desh seated himself at the bottom of his bed.

"Desho; Desho", uncle's voice was full of anguish.

"Yes, elder-father."

"I have brought you up as my own son."

Desh tried to restrain his tears. Slowly uncle's face began to work. "You are turning an enemy of *Siva*; you have thrown him into your bath-room."

"No, I am no enemy," he protested.

But his uncle disbelieved him; he had been watching his behaviour over the years.

"Elder-father; I am no enemy of *Siva*; I am a positivist."

"What is this unheard of thing?"

The *atma* of his uncle was perched high on a leaf, ready to take wing. Desh let his eyes travel over his shrunken body, thin as thorn.

"Desho; son; my time is near." He took a long pause to catch his breath. "In the flush of youth, you might stray into the wrong path, but some day or other by my blessings, you shall come back to the right."

Suddenly tears filled his uncle's eyes. Desh squirmed from fright for he had never seen him weeping; he felt sure, his uncle was suffering deep disappointment in him. His eyes too filled up.

x x x

Uncle was sinking fast; treatment was useless, but they held on to it out of sheer habit. As the news of his critical health went round, friends and relatives began calling on him; women in the day and men in the evening. All tried to soothe Desh and his aunt, and talked of the omnipotence of *Siva*. He was all merciful; Desh and his aunt should repose full faith in Him. Treatment was meant for the satisfaction of one's mind; it never saved the dying, for the time of everyone was predetermined by the *karma* one had performed in one's previous life.

To Desh listening to friends and relatives was a irksome job; but it pleased aunt. Like them she believed in the invocation of blessings of *Siva* for effecting cure of asthma than in medicinal treatment. She commissioned the snub-nosed priest to recite a lakh times over the short, Sanskrit prayer addressed to *Siva*. Though a dried up man, the priest exhibited remarkable energy in him. In a state of fast, he sat cross-legged in the *puja*-room, his sing-song resounded all over the house. He took a week to complete the task; each day at the end of his duty he placed flower petals upon the crown of uncle that he had collected from under the miniature phallus of *Siva*, decorating the *puja*-room.

Some heat was generated between the priest and aunt when she paid him his remuneration.

"What, this is about half," he complained.

"You will remain a greedy fellow," she retorted. "How can I pay less when I want to save Desh's uncle?"

"My father sent me to Banaras to learn *Sanskrit* rather than English and made a poor priest of me; otherwise I would have been in high position today, a *sahib*."

"Now *sahibs* are gone; time for people like you is coming."

The priest cast a suspicious glance at aunt. "Seems prestige of English will stay a long time."

Watching death hovering over uncle put enormous strain upon both aunt and him. Spasms of cough left him almost dead; it seemed any moment his heart would stop, his *atma* free from prolonged suffering. How well he had stood it over twenty years, without mentioning of his ill-fate; only he associated his asthma to his *karma*.

Parting with uncle would be sad, indeed sad; still he welcomed it. Death alone could lead him into peace and beatitude; his illness was beyond treatment. No one believed he would survive a couple of days; so often he came to the verge of death, but mysteriously enough he dodged its grasp.

"Your uncle might get well," mumbled aunt.

"Life is a mountain of pain for him." He folded his lips over his teeth, still tears broke into his eyes.

Aunt slumped upon a chair, wailing. The paroxysm lasted some minutes.

"Go", she requested in long drawn out accents, "Put these flowers on the feet of Goddess of the Rock. She will send your uncle Her blessings; he was Her great devotee."

Aunt roused him from his melancholy mood. He was star of uncle's eyes; a prayer by him in the temple would save his uncle. He might regard the proceeding as useless, but if he loved uncle, he got to obey his aunt.

"*Arree*; Desho", her voice rose in hope, I forgot to tell you to look out for Kailash Giri; if you bring ash, given by him, your uncle is sure to get new life."

Desh was acquainted with the name from his childhood, but he had never caught *darshan* of the renowned *sadhu* credited with mystic powers. Rumour said that he wandered to Nainital once in a few years and circled about the temple of Goddess of The Rock. A skinny man with matted beard and shock of hair, he spoke in ironical words resembling the naivety of a child. Few had met him. If he applied ash on the forehead of a dying patient, the latter regained life. He could penetrate the past of men and foretell their future. Once whenever Desh entered the temple, his eyes looked out for the figure of the *sadhu*. Now, he felt pleased, seeing nothing there; he executed the commission of aunt, peering at the Goddess, leaving out the prayer. By habit he picked up few flowers from the bottom of the shaffron Rock and carried them home as token of Goddess's blessings for uncle.

Over the years aunt was used to seeing uncle pulling through crisis after crisis in his illness; she expected him do the present one too, however severe. The snub-nosed priest calculated, on having a look at his horoscope, that malignant stars, Saturn and Moon, would turn away their glances from uncle after two months; hardly a long dangerous interval of time. Then winter would set in; aunt would take uncle over to Allahabad. There the warm climate and holy-water of Ganges would jointly help restore his normal health to him. Aunt's optimism stilled Chitra's anxiety to paying a hurried visit to Nainital for securing her interests.

One day aunt was cooking food in the kitchen when uncle signed him to lower his ear to his mouth, his voice being inaudible even from a yard. Asthma had cut his power of speech.

"Son, I have not long to live," he gasped even as he slowly transferred his eyes to the door joining the room to the kitchen, "I want to tell you something." He began to pant; his whole body writhed from the agony of breathing. "I made my will a year ago; it was done by your brother-in-law without knowledge of your aunt."

He had bequeathed half portion of the bungalow belonging to him to Desh, besides ten thousand rupees cash. Since his aunt would live with him, money was useless for her. However she owned fifteen thousand rupees worth of gold ornaments that he had been buying her all his life from his savings. He had deliberately forgotten his daughter, in his will, on whom he had bestowed a dowry of ten thousand rupees, at her marriage. He expected aunt to leave all her gold ornaments to her.

Uncle went into a coma. Desh shuffled to the verandah; blackening clouds over the skies deepened his sorrow. His uncle would survive three or four days. How kind and good he was to

Desh. A less charitable man than uncle would have refused to pardon him for his scepticism. His uncle bore him unselfish love that would not alter whether he was a sinner or no; but he was dying an unhappy man, all on account of him. There was still time left to express his remorse. He might hold opposite beliefs than his uncle, but these should not temper Desh's love for him.

The whole evening Desh fixed himself by the bed of uncle. Excepting for an occasional twitch over his face, he lay motionless. The rain fell in torrents with mighty roar; it seemed season's heaviest day.

Uncle opened his eyes. "This noise."

"The rain,"

"Desho, son,"

"Yes, elder-father."

"Can you accept my blessings, son?"

He put his head on the feet of his uncle. "Have I become so distant that you cannot bless me."

"Desho, I thought you would reject blessings from one whose beliefs are different from yours."

"I shall always be needing your blessings, elder-father."

"*Siva* give you the best in life, son."

He felt his eyes were swimming in tears. The difference in the beliefs of the nephew and the uncle themselves straightened out; the prick in his conscience had suddenly gone away.

Presently uncle's body shook from a fainting-fit; twisted out and felt cold. A shiver ran down the spine of Desh; he rushed to kitchen to fetch aunt. Though it was eight O'clock, she had left unlighted the *chulha*. Her eyes looked weary; she seemed to be getting over a fit of crying."

"Aunty, you did right, not to cook food; who eats tonight ?"

The downpour of rain matched the night of death. From a neighbour's house he rang up sister and Shanker, and sent for the two nephews and the snub-nosed priest. Everyone ran up to catch the last *darshan* of uncle. The priest at once put through ceremonies common before cremation. First he put few spoons of holy Gangese water, from a bottle kept in the house, into the throat of uncle. Next he brought a cow; sprinkling holy water on its tail, he made it touch the hand of uncle. Now one of the nephews with snub-nosed priest started chanting an important chapter from Geeta; it softened the grim atmosphere bound with death. It reminded the listeners that soul was indestructible, unborn, eternal. As a man casting off worn out garments takes new one, so the dweller in the body casting off worn out bodies enters into others that are new.

Uncle's death provided sister and Shanker occasion to meet, when the two were craving for each other. Excepting coming to uncle's room once, both seated themselves in the parlour and kept talking in whispers.

In the small hours of night uncle's face fell to one side; aunt hiding her eyes in the hem of her sari rent the air with her scream. One of the nephews and himself lifted uncle from the bed and placed him upon the floor.

"When the soul flies away" said the priest, "The body made of earth should return to earth."

A glorious bright morning marked uncle's funeral. Sobbing, aunt assumed widow's character by putting out her nose-pin and string of black beads; and by breaking away all the glass bangle on her wrists. Desh went into mourning by getting his head tonsured.

A charted bus carried the corpse, shrouded in blood-red shawl, to Kathgodam, with friends and relatives making up the funeral cortege. All the way Holi-*wallah* Belwal led the regular dirge :

"Only *Rama's* name is true."

Members of the cortege responded.

"Speak truth, death awaits you."

The lusty singing of Belwal and others over-powered Desh; his uncle's words kept resounding in his ears, "This world is *maya*".

"We brought your father here too for cremation," informed Belwal, "How beautiful is this place, chitrasheel."

There the wooded mountains flattened into plains. Over against the bank of the river, meandering through the valley, was located the cremation *ghat*, with a hoary *Siva* temple.

"Your uncle was a religious man", went on Belwal, "That is why we have a bright day after such a rainy night."

x x x

Desh had expected Chitra to visit aunt in her hour of distress to comfort her; but she was negligent in her filial duty. Her queer behaviour was in keeping with aunt's veiled hostility towards him. On the morning of the thirteenth day of uncle's death, when the mourning period was over, she opened up her heart.

"I am going to Allahabad day after tomorrow, Desho."

"You aunt." He was shaken.

"I will live my last days with my daughter on the banks of Ganges in Allahabad, meditating on *Siva* and your elder-father."

"What will people say ! Am I not your son that you should live with your daughter. Elder-father wanted that you should live with me."

"I have made all arrangements for going; so Chitra has not come."

A bullet passed through his heart, inflicting upon him as severe a pain as on the death of uncle.

"But aunt, you ought to live in Nainital."

"Desho, son; I love you; but I must go."

Two days devil-of-packing rode upon aunt; she did all personal effects belonging to uncle and herself. She refused to leave behind to Desh even an useless article purchased by uncle; but she despised herself if she happened to touch any article done by his father. So complete was her partition of moveable property.

On the scheduled day, Desh with sister and relatives accompanied aunt to motor-stand. The sub-nosed priest was escorting her to Kathgodam, where her son-in-law was joining her.

"You will always write to me," sobbed aunt.

He felt a pressure in his throat.

"My Nainital is finished to-day."

"Why say so aunt; you would be coming here to do the first death *saradh puja* of uncle."

"If I do not come here, you do it at Allahabad."

Sister, the two nephews, and himself bid aunt farewell by touching her feet.

As the bus vibrated into motion aunt shook with a paroxysm of crying.

"Desho, son; do not forget me." Her voice fainted away as she receded from them.

With his arms behind him, he walked homewards in silence; aunt had dealt him brutal injustices. He came into himself as sister jogged him.

"Do you know why aunt left Nainital so hurriedly." Desh glanced sister with stony eyes.

"When she knew from your brother-in-law that uncle has made a will to disinherit Chitra and herself, she was filled with rage. She thought you were a low-down; you got it done secretly from her."

"I am not guilty," he protested in hard tones." I never knew about uncle's will; I am not guilty if uncle loved me so much more than Chitra."

CHAPTER - XXI

Desh held himself aloof from Ramlila, or gaieties as pictures, boating or riding, to mourn the death of uncle. His unhappiness was exaggerated by his loneliness. The half portion of the bungalow with uncle and aunt, remained always shut. A domestic kept his house. In the day he attended law-courts; in the evening he occasionally received Shanker to bear him company; or read law books from his father's library. Sometime he saw uncle in dreams, ill and emaciated. At night he often felt that his uncle still tenanted the adjacent room. Sister advised him to transfer his residence over to Hamilton, but he preferred to stay on in his own bungalow to cherish the memory of uncle.

One day returning home late from law-courts, he saw a lean figure of a woman standing in the verandah. He took her for a client. As he stepped near, he recognised her; his heart stopped .

"*Arree*, it is you Har Preya sister. "He greeted her by joining the palms of his hands.

She looked pale and subdued.

"I could not come before, "she tendered her apology, "To meet you in the death of your uncle. I thought you will be seen in Thandi road."

"I never go out since uncle's death; come in." He unlocked the doors of the drawing-room.

"Let us sit here in the verandah."

Desh blushed. It was indiscreet of him to have led her into the house, when he lived alone.

"In your short hair and black cap, you do not look like your oldself."

He cut an apple into slices; Har Preya picked only one.

"Every one admires your uncle for his love for you," She said with an effort." I guessed you would be lonely; by meetings others your sorrow would be lightened." She paused. "Come this evening."

Har Preya startled him into awareness of Lalita. The illness of uncle had turned his thoughts away from her. In June in his meeting with her, Har Preya had told him that Lalita disliked visiting Nainital; she was trying to forget him, remove him from her heart; instead of exchanging a greeting with him that foggy evening near Goddess Nanda *Devi* temple, Lalita had cut him.

Har Preya was waiting for him in her front room; her right leg crossed over the left, joggling in restlessness.

"I thought you are not coming," she heaved a sigh. "After returning from your house, I cooked for you *pakoras*; you came so late that they have gone cold."

He surveyed the room in one glance. Only a fortnight had passed since *Diwali*; but it lacked the brightness of the previous year. No multi-coloured paper lanterns, flowers or chains decorated it. A sole image of Goddess Laxmi with Krishna, a fresh purchase of recent *Diwali*, stood upon the. mantelpiece below the photograph of the mother of Lalita and Har Preya. He glowered at it.

"No sigh of *Diwali* in your house."

"What *Diwali* in these circumstances," she replied in flat accent.

He glanced her with expression in his eyes, "I do not get you."

"It was the will of *Devi*", she exclaimed.

It seemed him that Har Preya had called him with some other motive than to work off the gloom of his bereavement.

"It was the will of *Devi*" she repeated.

She was bringing in Lalita; he felt a twist in his heart.

"Jagdish is in Agra mental hospital".

A tear broke out of her eyes.

He jumped up on his feet; and stepping over to the mantelpiece, he tilted his head forward against it. As the news sank into him, involuntarily his hand caught his face across his closed eyes.

"Poor Lalita! oh *Siva*; oh *Siva*; oh Goddess; oh Goddess !"

He resumed his seat on the high-backed chair. A heaviness closed in upon his senses, benumbing his wits. His head dropped sideways as his eyes got rooted to the pattern on the carpet.

"Desh; drink tea; Desh"

The voice was so familiar to him, rich and deep. He pulled himself together; he took in Lalita in a white-*sari*, occupying the chair of Har Preya.

"Desh; drink tea, Desh."

The voice trickled into his ears, caressing them. It sounded as sweet as never before. She wore herself a trifle thinner, than the previous year.

"Desh; drink tea, Desh"

Lalita shut her face in her hands to stifle her sobs; her body kept jerking from her suffering.

He consoled her, "When did you come from Ranikhet ?"

"Since when you saw me about the temple," she answered through her tears.

"Three months now; why did you not send for me before ?"

Har Preya had over again thrown them together, or the two would have remained separated all their lives. Leaving Lalita alone with him, she had disappeared into the inner regions of the house; she expected him to win over Lalita by the seductiveness of his bearing and conversation. But a strange, uncanny silence had fallen over, sewing his lips.

He made an attempt at conversation.

"How far is Ranikhet from here ?"

"Very far."

"How far you are from me ?"

"As earth from stars," she transferred her eyes on the refreshment on the table. "Desh, drink tea, Desh"

"It is gone cold."

Speechless, he kept setting with Lalita, oblivious of time; she exuded on him divine happiness.

"I am very sorry for you," he expressed his sympathy.

"It is all my *karma* of previous and of this life."

He had over-extended his meeting with Lalita; she scraped her feet on the carpet. He put on his great-coat to protect himself from chill in his homeward journey at night.

Har Preya popped in; she seemed to be eavesdropping from the next room.

"Do not stop coming," she prayed.

He went off his meal that night; his appetite had been impaired by the unexpected sight of Lalita, her coming back into his life. It seemed that he had parted from her on a mere squabble a few days before, than a whole year. It had fallen out of his memory that she was the very woman who had not only shut herself from him, but had also refused to give him a hearing; he was too humble to remember his grievance. She had over again caught him in her trap, and there was no pulling himself loose from it. The dying fire of her love, in his heart, blew up and spread over his whole body; burnt it.

But from the next day he began feeling disappointment in Lalita. "How far are you from me," he had said, "As earth from stars," she had replied.

Few days later, receiving a letter from Har Preya, he dismissed the hitch from his mind.

He entered the lane after sunset. She was knitting a red-sweater for Balu.

She whispered, "Why did you not come without my letter ?"

"I had not the courage."

"It is hard on me; sometimes I have to get ready Lalita, sometimes you."

His sense of vanity got the better of him. "How can I come, if Lalita does not like meeting me?"

Har Preya requested him to understand Lalita, so that he could forgive her. Everyone's eyes in the lane were levelled at her; Lalita was watched.

"But we want each other," he said stoutly.

"Lalita cannot think like you; she is a woman."

He put his hand to his cheek, in the pose of contemplation. Har Preya disappeared into the inner rooms as Lalita brought him *chai* and took a chair opposite him. As on the previous day, she wore white-sari; she looked weak.

He had rehearsed at home the dialogues he would speak out to her; he would let her know how he had craved her moment by moment; wherever he went, in *bazaar* or law-courts, his eyes searching and searching her. Then the thought that she was married filled him with depression. He would warn himself that she had flown away from Nainital and his life; still the flame of her love kept burning in him; it could never die.

Now he sat silent before Lalita, unable to open out his heart to her, a clog having struck in his throat. He wanted to complain to her, but his power of speech had deserted him. The uncanny silence had seeped into the room; he felt himself on the verge of ecstasy.

"Desh, you have not taken *chai;* you do not like made by me."

"Why should I not ?"

"Because," a tear glided down her cheeks, "I wronged you."

"Let us not talk about it."

"Will you ever forgive me ?"

"Dear Lalita." His eyes were blurred in tears.

His attention passed to her rounded hands and full lips.

"I like you more now," he admitted," "For you are thinner than before."

She gave a sad smile. "If you knew my life."

"Then tell me."

Her head hung sideways, Lalita's eyes were fixed on him. Over again the uncanny, thick silence enveloped them.

Desh frequently saw Lalita. In the beginning he had rejoiced at her coming back into his life. He loved her as a moth did the flame. She seemed to have taken such perfect control of the nerve-centre of his mind that he lost the capacity to perceive the shadow of Jagdish between himself and Lalita. Slowly he grew aware of him. Often he was reminded of Jagdish when she happened to talk something of Ranikhet. Her love hurt him; the unalloyed happiness she radiated on him got mingled with pain. He wanted to forget her, cast her away from his thoughts and life. He began a losing struggle against her. For few days he forced himself to stay back at home, but then his longing to meet Lalita overpowered him.

Inquired Har Preya, "Why did you not come ?"

"I was unwell."

Har Preya glanced him with reproach in her eyes that said, "I do not believe you."

She walked into the interior rooms, leaving the two to themselves. Lalita wore a white-sari. It touched Desh that she had taken to the widow's character.

He pointed his finger to her sari. "Why now you are always so plain."

"What's wrong with it ?"

"You are not wearing gay colours."

"He is in mental-hospital."

Desh was stung to the quick. "Jagdish will get well."

"If my *karmas* are good !"

He was surprised to know that Lalita kept fasts; every day she rose early and took a bath with cold water before her morning *puja*; the snub-nosed priest helped her perform it; or she read important chapters from Geeta. Occasionally she went to Goddess of the Rock.

"You should think of your comforts."

"Do not talk like this, Desh." she said in a harsh tone.

The more Desh turned over and over in his mind his love of Lalita, the more he felt that he loved her as he found her. Whether she wounded him or no, her image remained engraven in his heart; immutable, permanent. He craved her from the depths of his being.

Conversation went haltingly with Lalita; occasionally he sat with her through the evening, hardly exchanging more than few words. A stubborn, uncanny silence pursued him and Lalita, and he rejoiced at it. He longed to pass his hand over her round arms and imprint a resounding kiss on her lips. But she sat few yards away from him; it was scarcely possible to caress her.

He signalled her, "Sit here, beside me."

She gave a grunt accompanied by a negative shake of her head.

"Come Lalita, sit by me,"

"I will go away from here."

His plan suffered a shipwreck. Lalita was an enigma to him, but he kept trying to advance on her. Once he was late.

"Look at your watch," she exclaimed.

His face lighted up with happiness.

Few days later he delayed himself on purpose. He wanted to get sure, if she felt troubled by his behaviour.

"You are again late."

Her cuckoo voice dropped as nectar into his ears.

"I am waiting two hours for you," she continued.

A tremor passed through his limbs; he fetched a sigh of joy.

And she never allowed him to go away without drinking *chai* prepared by her own hands. Since he disliked metal-tumbler, she had bought a china-set.

"Why," he said, "You do not make a cup for you."

"I shall drink chai with you in next life."

He let the cup poured for him go cold. "I hate your chai and you." His breathing quickened in anger.

"Desh, do not make me more unhappy."

Her eyes filled up and overflowed and she made no attempt to hide her tears.

"I am sorry Lalita," he was filled with shame. He raised the cup to his lips.

"By being an hour or two with you, I thought I would be able to forget myself."

It fell to this lot to cheer her up.

"The pictures are shut for winter," he said, "Or I would have asked you to see them."

"With you" she pouted her lower lip.

"Then let us go on a trip of Bhimtal."

He saw the chance of sitting by Lalita's side in the taxi. She would be really left alone with him. He would hire a room in the state managed bungalow. No one there knew whether he was a bachelor or no; Lalita and himself would pass off as a married couple. In the day the two would wander to the cluster of lakes around Bhimtal, spending hours in boating or picnicking. In the evening Lalita and he would together cook food. What a happiness ! Beyond words.

"I entreat you, grant my request."

"What has happened with you?"

"Come along with me to Bhimtal; you will forget yourself."

"What has happened to you, Desh?"

He brushed aside her refusal. He would apply himself to breaking her obduracy; he could do it. Every evening she impatiently waited for him; her sorrow was lightened by meeting him. Above all, the tone of her voice indicated that she valued his company.

"If you just change your thinking," he said one evening, "You can become a happy woman overnight."

He was afraid that his advice might fire her up. But she gave a short, whimsical laugh. He was surprised.

"If you had listened me once," he declared, "How happy would become your life and mine too."

"Desh," she looked him in the eye, "I too wish to walk the way you want me to."

"What holds you?"

"Let us not talk about these things," she pleaded, with a wave of her hand.

He remarked a slow, imperceptible change coming over her. She never grew impatient with his new fangled notions as she had done at the beginning. A conviction had grown in his mind that he would win her over; it was only a matter of time. He needed to use subtle tact and broad sympathy with her.

He asked, "You never go out anywhere except Goddess of the Rock."

"With you," she shook her head with joy.

"No, no with me. That I shall never suggest; I mean with your sister."

"Where should I go and why, for people to laugh at me?"

"It will cheer you up to climb Cheena peak."

"Who knows I may go away to Ranikhet." Her lips broke into a wistful smile.

Though he had tried all his wits to change her mind, still he failed; but he would never give in, any way. He would enliven her by his talks on all manner of subjects. If he would widen her interests, he would succeed with her. She was daughter of a *vaisya*; business world should hold special fascination for her.

"How is your father's shop ?"

"Nainital is growing, so it trade."

"All cities are growing after independence; look Delhi."

"I have never seen Delhi."

"It is a charming city," he continued.

"There are Red Fort and Kutub Minar."

"There are also big hotels and restaurants where a cup of tea costs several rupees."

Lalita raised her eyebrows in surprise, "I wish to know the taste of such a costly tea".

"Then come along with me to Delhi."

She giggled, "With you," she burst into an uproarious laugh.

Desh had failed in his stupendous task, but he had succeeded in dissipating melancholy thoughts from Lalita's mind. He felt pleased with himself that his endeavours were showing some results. She was looking cheerful.

"I shall knit you a sweater," she volunteered one day.

His ears burst open.

"Tell me the colour," she added," I shall get the wool from the *bazaar*."

"You cannot buy for me," he shook his fist. "I cannot accept a sweater whose wool is bought with your money."

"Am I so distant from you; it is for you I live with Har Preya at night."

Lalita seemed taking some trouble for him; she was making him a gift; but he would make an issue of it.

"No, I cannot wear a sweater made by you."

"Why ?"

"Because you do not go out with me."

He had put an impossible condition; but he would stick to it.

"I wish I could come with you, Desh. Some day, who knows, I might."

"Why some day Lalita; why not tomorrow?. We could go somewhere, to Cheena peak."

"If I should go with you ever, it shall be Delhi, where no one knows us."

"Then why not there."

She grinned. "You do talk as a child."

He felt he was sighting his goal; he would be reaching there any day. But Lalita shocked him.

She asked, "Why do you not marry, Desh ?"

"You do talk as a child," he retaliated.

Over again he was defeated, while the flame of her love leaped up in his heart. But he would never lose hopes; some day she might steal away with him to Delhi. She would then come over to Nainital forever, breaking herself free from Ranikhet.

x x x

After meeting Lalita, he returned home late one evening in January in the biting cold wind, shivering all through the way. Next morning he felt himself feverish. By the evening his temperature rose up and his head split with pain. He wanted to send for Shanker to nurse him in his illness, but he was away, gone as every winter to the farm of Inder. The necessity of seeing

Lalita in the evening had prevented him from visiting sister, and now it seemed selfish of him to intimate her of his illness. For some days excepting liquid diet, he took no treatment, and lingered in bed. He received a letter from Har Preya expressing her bewilderment and concern at his sudden disappearance. She wanted to know, if he had changed his mind. He sent her a reply.

"What does she mean," he asked himself.

Next evening soon after nightfall he heard repeated knocking on the front of his bungalow. No one had called on him at this hour since the death of his uncle. Desh was at a loss to guess as to who should be his visitor. The doors of his room were pushed open, and the two sisters burst in.

He was taken aback; his heart came to his mouth. In his agitation he sprang up clumsily from his bed.

"Keep lying Desh," piped in Har Preya." You are weak."

He obeyed her. She helped him tuck in, but his heart knocked inside him from happiness.

The sisters drew chairs near his bed. He noticed their faces were drawn from nervousness.

"How you got courage to come out to see me."

"I may not have come; but she wanted to see you." Har Preya shifted her eyes on Lalita, "We could not know from your letter how ill you were."

"But were you not afraid of coming ?"

The sisters' faces brightened into smile. His question was normal. I was only after long argument between them that the two could take the decision to see him; but their hands and feet swelled when they came to acting on it. Harassed with anxiety, the sisters dressed themselves by four O'clock in the evening; but by five their hearts began sinking with fear. If even one man in their lane saw the two going to Desh's house, the sky would tumble upon them. But after sunset Lalita was seized with longing to meet Desh; the two set out.

"And no one saw you in the way."

"We did not come straight," told Har Preya, bubbling with laughter. "We went first to temple of Goddess of the Rock; then to Tallital; then we turned upwards to your house."

"And", interposed Lalita," I kept my eyes backward and forward to see if anyone was taking note of us."

He teased them. "If someone had seen you coming here, it would have been the thing."

But Lalita's attention had moved on from his talk to his room that had remained neglected since his uncle's death.

"You have no servant."

"I have one but he is out, or I should have given you *chai*."

"I go to the kitchen," joined in Har Preya.

"But," he ejaculated, "Remember Lalita does not take *chai* with me."

"I should in your house; this is my first visit."

Har Preya had whisked off the room before Lalita had finished speaking. Desh understood that she wanted to leave her sister alone with him.

"Come Lalita, "he signed "Sit by me."

"I have come to see you in your illness."

"I know."

Lalita climbed to her feet, sidled over and stood behind him.

"You look so weak; you could not even shave. Why did you not ask Har Preya to send you a doctor ? Why did you not take treatment ?"

"If it will be in my fate, I shall get well. What is the use of treatment !"

He wanted to show her contradiction between her beliefs and advices. Bit by bit he expected to change her.

"If I told you that myself, I did not mean we should not act."

He was aghast. She seemed normal as himself. "I thought you only believed in fate."

"I put best of my efforts into a thing that I should do; but I know there is fate also. *Arree* ! Leave these talks; you are so weak."

Leaning over him, she thrust her hands from under his ears and locked his neck in them.

"You have temperature."

The feel of her soft palms sent a wave of heat through his veins. The fondling touch of a woman was an unknown experience to him, by far of the woman he loved. He was enraptured.

"I never thought," he stammered, "You care for me."

"You are unjust to me Desh, if you regard me as not a human being."

Lalita resumed her seat with the coming in of Har Preya, who brought tea in a shiningly clean set.

Lalita came and faded away as a dream. A while he distrusted his senses; he tried to recollect himself. She had surely sat on the chair beside him, and had inquired after his health; then she had held his neck in her hands. The news of his illness had upset her so much so that she at once rushed to see him, blinking at public opinion. He knew Lalita's heart, it was with him. Now he needed to convert her mind, for gaining victory over her. "By increasing her love for me, I can do it." He said to himself.

After his illness, Desh spent an hour in wearing his garments, one evening, to impress Lalita.

She was knitting a sweater in expensive, grey wool. "You are not doing it for me," he said with emphasis.

She shock her head to poke fun at him. "I will not wear; I will not wear done by you; reply now."

"My reply is same; I will not wear."

"Why, when I have fulfilled your condition. If I have not gone out with you, I have visited your house and taken *chai* with you."

There was force in her argument, but, if he would bow to her, he could never hope to win her.

"Visiting my house is not equal to your going out with me to Delhi."

On a sudden she tossed off her knitting-work on to the wall, and, in a flash of rage, stamped away into the interior of the house. Presently he overheard her crying. He felt ashamed of himself.

He decided to put off seeing Lalita some days to let her get over her indignation. He blamed himself for his lack of tack and poise, even after his initial success with her, when she had visited him and took a cup of *chai* with him. He was asking for trouble when he was making her an unceremonious, hasty suggestion of a trip; rather he should have waited for it drop out of her lips.

He had expected a letter from Har Preya inquiring about the reason of his withdrawal from Lalita's society. But there appeared none; he was tortured with anxiety. Had the sisters brushed him aside from their thoughts; shut their doors on him.

One morning he received a letter; colour went out of his face when he saw it from aunt than Har Preya. She had wanted him to visit Allahabad than mouldering in the winter of Nainital. "Had Lalita not come in my life, I should have surely gone," he told himself.

He scarcely went to law-courts these days. Some of them had shifted to Haldwani, the town in *terai*, while others had suspended work, for magistrates fixed their tours in January. He was mostly free and read whole day law-books basking in the sun. One day while he was reading an article on the Constitution of India, in the making, his attention was drawn by the sound of steps approaching him from behind. Before he could turn round to see, Har Preya had stood over his low-chair.

She rang out, "Why did you not come ?"

"Sister", he pointed her an adjoining chair.

"I shall take my seat later; first answer me why you did not come ?"

"I am ashamed of myself," his eyes remained bent to the ground.

Everyone some time or other happened to injure the feelings of a near and dear; but one never lets a quarrel to cause a break. Desh's return to Lalita had infused life into her.

"I know, if you were not there, Lalita would have never met me again."

"What happiness it was seeing you in my house; everything looked as if nothing had happened. Lalita was not married. She became so fond of you and so cheerful."

"And it was to make her forget completely her past, I asked her to do a trip with me to Delhi."

"How could she come like this?"

Har Preya always left them to themselves, undisturbed, that Desh could propose to Lalita. She was pleased to note that he was making advances to her younger sister; gradually rubbing away the circular grooves in her mind. Always his visit filled her with joy. Har Preya began to see for her younger sister a new world being opened by Desh. Then she felt scarcely sorry for the exit of Jagdish; in matter of fact she was pleased at his getting insane.

He remarked, with feigned sympathy, "You should not say so."

"Why should I not, if Lalita gets you for him. First time I failed, but I should not now."

"But no man is there to back you; you might fail again."

"Hun", Har Preya uplifted her forefinger, "My father might not like this, but I hope to bring him round. He is not that old type. And father of Balu is with me."

Desh conducted her to the gate. He promised her that he would resume his visits. Har Preya had made herself plain, opening her heart to him. She wanted Desh to marry Lalita, if he loved her and valued her company. Har Preya's plan involved divorce for Lalita in future.

When he had met her, after her return to Nainital, he was surprised to see a Lalita in woe, come down to the state of a widow. Her fresh glimpses blew up the dying flame of her love in his heart. He was lost. So long as he could meet her, it was all the same to him whether she loved him or jeered at him; his hungry eyes drank her serene beauty; his ears sweetened on her cuckoo voice. He burnt for her night and day; he craved to make her his mistress. He kept making suggestions to her of a trip to Delhi, without prefacing it with a proposal. Not only he considered marriage unnecessary, but also revolting. No man in his brahmin circle would solemnize it with a divorcee girl. If Desh did it, he would expose himself to ridicule; people would point their finger at him. He winced.

Few days later a letter from Har Preya complained of his unfulfilled promise to her. Lalita had as well scribbled a line in *Hindi* in greeting. He wished it was in English. Anyway her unseen hand round and neat, rekindled her bitter memory; she seemed to have made way into his bones and hardened there. He beat his hand upon the arm of the chair, he sat in, to disengage himself from her, but she breathed with him, and moved with him. He carried on a struggle with himself; he slept over the reply to Har Preya, but she was a tenacious woman; she wrote him over again. However, he had once for all rejected Lalita as a wife; with all his passionate love for her, she was unsuitable for him.

His silence had troubled Har Preya so much so that she called on him early one morning while he was still in bed. His hair was ruffled and his eyes carried a brooding look in them.

"You have changed Desh," she intoned dropping into a chair.

He edged over to the dressing-table; rubbed his eyes clean, and passed a comb over his hair. He disliked her visit. She was persecuting him; he need to avoid her. While he was putting on his dressing-gown, he saw she was sobbing, hiding her face in her inexpensive white-shawl, wrapped over her inexpensive, white-sari.

He said tamely, "What is the matter?"

"If Lalita were dead today, how happy was I".

Her low, piteous moaning, interspersed with curses, accused him for shirking his responsibility.

"I could not come, because I was not well."

She uncovered her face, regaining self-control.

"You are lying; you are lying," she fumed. "You do not want to marry Lalita; I had such high hopes from you. I thought you were so educated, good, and modern."

"But, but society."

"Then why you came to my house when you lacked courage to marry Lalita. Why is our government making Hindu Code Bill when young people cannot act on it."

Her inflamed countenance, savagely contorted, whipped him with fright.

"I thought we could secretly meet, without marriage."

She gave a grunt. "You want to make Lalita your keep; I would see Lalita dead than allow such a thing." She marked her words by the gesticulations of her hands.

He added coaxingly, "What is the harm?"

Har Preya gave a roar of passion. "If only I had known you are a coward, like everyone, I should never have allowed you to see Lalita again."

He felt hot with shame; he put his hand on his face.

"You misunderstood me; actually it is not society. How can I marry a girl who will be a divorcee ?"

"You are very educated man; you also think like everyone." There was no edge in her voice.

"I shall think as everyone."

She gave him a speculative glance." "Where is your education ?"

He looked into her eyes.

"Your education must tell you, a woman is just like a man."

He listened her tense, keeping his mouth shut. He saw light of wisdom in her words.

"If man can marry again and again, why cannot woman ?" She repeated.

He had forgotten to warm the room by switching on the electric heater. Har Preya had undertaken an early morning walk to his house, and was shivering from cold.

As she walked out, he followed her. Sun touched the two with its animating warmth.

She inquired in a resigned tone, "Do you love Lalita ?"

"It shall last until there is sun," he swore, raising his hand.

"If your is true love, you shall not think of her past."

"I will not."

"It is with this hope I came here, sat with you alone in your room that you are my future brother."

He felt the storm of love raging in him, wild and elemental, urging him on. He perfectly understood now why kings abdicated thrones for a mere woman, and why men committed murders or suicides. Whether Lalita would be a divorce or no, he craved her. To sit by her was to attain bliss; if her cost was as heavy as marriage with her, he would simply pay it off.

x x x

As he climbed the dark, tortuous stairs so familiar to him, a flood of peace and happiness burst into his heart. He had triumphed over Lalita; he had reached his goal.

"Desh," she sighed, "You forgot me."

Her rich voice in her sadness sounded penetratingly sweet.

"I am sorry for my absence," he said with inflection of remorse in his voice.

"I apologise for my rudeness," she broke off.

The uncanny silence seeped in on them. Whole evening Desh remained sitting with Lalita squirming, unable to call up enough courage to speak out his proposal of marriage. When Har Preya entered the room to supply them coffee, she winked at him to go ahead.

"You have again to come to my house, Lalita," he quavered by way of making his proposal.

"Is it not enough that I came once?"

"You were in such a hurry then. Come with leisure."

"I wanted to see your house, every room and article."

"Come tomorrow."

Next day he dusted his room and tidied it up. He tastily disposed empty vases and a sofa-set, kept in one of the rooms, into his own for receiving Lalita.

"It is so nice and warm here," she commented, entering.

A big fire on the hearth had softened the severe winter in the room.

Lalita surveyed him in his modish, brown-suit uncovered by his great-coat. He looked her with self-conscious eyes that said, "I am handsome; I am rich, I am in for a big career." He felt sure that she would readily accept his proposal.

"You are late; you again came round Tallital."

The sisters looked at each other meaningfully and simultaneously grinned, indicating that they would always make a detour to reach him.

Har Preya excused herself to let the two to themselves. She wanted to help his domestic in making *chai*.

"Come Lalita," he signed her to his sofa, "Sit by me."

"I like the fire,"

He felt himself awkward; it was a nuisance that his heart fluttered inside him. His tongue felt cold in uttering out his proposal. But he could do it. He struggled to his feet and walked over to the hearth and poked the fire. He needed time to gain manliness.

"Why", he let fall, "You always wear white-*sari*; is there no other colour left for you ?"

He stood over behind her.

"This is the colour for me," her voice trailed off.

An uprush of emotion choked him. His hands instinctively slipped down her ears and held her neck tight.

"Let go Desh; let go."

Her breathing quickened. She made a mild, abortive attempt to pull her neck free of his hands.

"Your fingers," she pursued, "Are playing with my string of black beads."

It hurt him to feel the token of Lalita's fidelity to Jagdish, round her neck.

"You snap it off and wear a new one for me."

"This is not worn, a second one."

"But why;"

"Even dolls made wedding vows, before God of fire, I am after all a human being." Tears had moistened her eyes. "And you know Ramlila; I saw you there in the crowd."

"But what has all that to do with us?", remarked Desh.

"Do not hurt me Desho; do not hurt me; recall to yourself the widow ceremony of your aunt."

Her tears dropped over the back of his hands; he dried them with his handkerchief.

"It was not in my *karma* to be your wife."

"You can again be my wife," he protested, "These are not old times."

"Let us remain what we are."

His hands behind him, he pottered up and down the room, pensive and frustrated.

Har Preya re-appeared with loaded tea-tray, nibble on her feet and hands.

"These are hot *pakoras*", she shrilled, "Eat quick or they will get cold."

As she poured the tea and passed on the plates, she went on humming a film song. He let her enjoy herself, undisturbed by hints of failure of their joint venture to win over Lalita.

"I knew from the snub-nosed priest", resumed Lalita, "There is a large beautiful picture of *Siva* in your house."

Desh chuckled. "What makes you remember it."

"I want to see it."

Not only had she turned down his proposal, but was openly mocking him. He was exasperated. He sprang up as a lion, and in a jiffy produced the *Siva* oleograph from his bath room.

With snakes coiling about His neck and arms, and strident in His hand, *Siva* gazed at them, august and serene.

"His place is not in the bathroom," rebuked Lalita.

She bowed to *Siva*, snatched him from Desh and placed Him upon the mantelpiece. In an access of fury, he grasped at *Siva* for dashing Him on to the floor. Lalita anticipating his mind stared him with such ferocious eyes that he gave up his attempt. Defeated, he resumed his seat on the sofa.

A second rebuff from Lalita opened up his healing wound; he once again determined to resist bringing her name to his tongue. He broke off his visits to her, but he dare not degrade *Siva* to his bath-room. He still nursed, in the inmost recesses of his heart, hope that one day Lalita would return to him, repentant for her cold, inhuman behaviour towards him. If she found then, *Siva* missing from his living-room, she would refuse him again, turning away from him.

It took him little time to realise that his determination was frail as a straw. A letter from Har Preya shook it. She warned him that Lalita was far from an easy victory. He should have expected thorns on his way; but these should embolden him, move him to heroism and self-confidence than despair. He should continue meeting her.

"That day," remarked Lalita," You frightened me."

He had thought that she would grumble for avoiding her since her visit to his house. She would tell him that she had been waiting for him, alert to catch the sound of his steps; she had been counting his name day in and day out as beads of rosary; she was much too sorry for having hastily rejected his proposal. But Lalita made no such assertion of love for him.

He drawled, "Why were you frightened?"

"I had never imagined that you would ask me for marriage," she went on, "You are very good to me; I know you can do much for me."

She held him in a steady, immobile gaze.

He pleaded, "Then accept my proposal."

"You do not understand." A tear moistened her eyes, "You do not try to understand me."

That evening he came away early from his meeting with Lalita. It was time late in March. The air was free of chill; there was noticeable traffic on the roads. He kept trudging up and down the Flats, until he had not tired himself out. He settled upon a bench, staring street lights reflected upon the lake, as an insane; a mood of utter despondency having overtaken him. Lalita still remained an obscure, impenetrable enigma. He cursed his fate that had over and over crossed his path in life against hers. How he wished he could cut himself loose from her; invoke some supernatural power to release him from the bonds of an ill-fated love. He grew unmindful of time until a dull headache roused him to his environment. His bones felt stiff and cold as he tottered homewards, hungry and sleepy.

But Lalita dwelt in him. He was crazy, besotted by the intoxication of her love. The other person that came to his thoughts, after Lalita, was his dear uncle, whose memory uplifted his spirits and brought him peace. He had wished to see him married and happy, but Desh had defied him. If his uncle were living now, he would have fulfilled his wish, if not for his sake, at least for the sake of banishing Lalita from his mind. If his uncle knew of his present state of wretchedness, he would have wanted him to bury himself into *Geeta* and meditation of *Siva*. "I do not understand you, "he would have replied to him.

But when one evening Har Preya visited Desh and took him with herself to her house, he dare not cross Lalita.

She inquired, "Why did you not come this month ?"

"I was trying to forget you, Lalita," he admitted.

"Do you hate me ?"

"No, never."

She gave an ironical laugh.

Lalita was wearing a *choli* with short sleeves; her bare round arms agitated him. He longed to feel them, pass his hands over and kiss them.

"Come to a trip of Delhi", he prayed. "You will forget your loneliness."

"I am already forgetting; I need not visit Delhi for it."

"How ?"

"By going to Goddess of the Rock."

"Can I accompany you ?"

"No, no", she shook her head.

"I plead."

"*Achha*; look for me in the temple tomorrow evening."

He walked home in high spirits. If Lalita refused to accompany him to Delhi, she would meet him in a temple. Since he had known her after her marriage, strange and invincible, he had covered a long way; a tremendous change seemed coming over her. She could be persuaded to marry him, but slowly, in few years perhaps. He needed to call up all the tact and patience in him.

She had appointed the time after sunset. He loathed the summer for its lengthened days. He made a round of temple much before the right time, and lightened his waiting by throwing pebbles on the lake. Lalita appeared earlier than he had expected her, fast on her feet. A devotee, a lad with thin face, preceded her. He looked to be a student, who bowed to the Goddess to help him pass his examination. Having said his prayer, he bounded off to Tallital.

Desh followed Lalita into the open-air temple. She wore white-sari and *choli*. He had come to like this plain colour on her. He felt ashamed of himself that even in the hallowed atmosphere, he was conscious of her feminine charm.

Offering red and yellow flowers, she went down on her knees. The grotesque, shaffron, Rock Goddess with far away expression in Her bold, silver eyes, towered over Lalita, indifferent to her whisperings.

"You did not pray, Desh," She asked.

" I have, "he lied,

She rubbed her finger over the shaffron pigmented Goddess for making mark on his forehead, above the nose. She repeated the proceeding on her own.

"You do not come with me."

"It is almost night; no one can recognise us."

"No, you have not to come with me. We can meet here, inside the temple."

He felt at once indignant and pleased with Lalita; pleased at her getting adventurous, but indignant at her quick dismissal of him, without allowing him slightest chance to accompany her to Flats. But the odds seemed in his favour; he was advancing on her. She was showing signs of a radical and permanent change.

It was the pleasantest time of the year. The city was packing up with tourists. In noisy streets and shops, neon lights dispelled the night; summer excited Desh with vague feeling of merriment, lessening his sorrow.

He met Lalita in the evenings at the temple of Goddess of Rock, but never beyond few minutes; never he accompanied her on her homeward journey.

"You have prayed," she asked always.

"Yes," he lied.

One evening she made him stand before her to see how he said it. He did it with extraordinary fervour. She was pleased with him in as much as she permitted him to accompany her across the unfrequented Thandi road to Flats. The two walked in silence. His heart stopped when they came near the green summer-house.

"Let us sit in there."

"What strange things you talk about." She ground the words in her mouth.

Unaffected by her reprimand, he added, "Probably I did not pray so well that you would have sat with me in the summer-house."

"Probably."

"Then I shall try my best tomorrow."

He came home as though he was converting himself from a heretic into a religious. He laughed as a fool as he rehearsed, in front of the oleograph of *Siva*, the prayer that had been initiated into him by his uncle. He recollected the statement of Shanker, "If you cannot change the woman you love, she does you."

Next evening at the temple, closing his eyes, he went down on his knees; his palms joined under a reverential bow.

"O Goddess," he recited, "I your devotee, am fallen at your feet ... lift me from worldly *maya* to *nirvana*."

"I like your prayer very much," remarked Lalita.

Her eyes sparkled. As she picked up her *puja*-basket for making a move, she signed him to follow her. His mind agitated, he tried to keep steps with her, wondering whether she would bypass the summer-house or no; but he praised his stars as she walked in there without his having to request her. He seated himself by her side as clumsily as he had done with Champa.

"You are so silent,"

"I have gone too far with you," she said with a note of constrain in her voice. "I should not have walked with you like a *memsahib*."

"From tomorrow I shall wait for you here."

"This is better."

He had solemnly promised himself that, no sooner Lalita entered the summer-house, he would take her sculptured arms in his hands, feeling them a long time. But now his eyes remained glued upon the waves below him; he felt himself a faint-heart.

"You like the coloured lights reflected upon the lake," he asked.

"No, I like the sound of bells coming from the temple of Goddess Nanda *Devi*."

He nestled close to her. He called up all the pluck in him for putting his hand round her waist, but in vain. The feat remained unaccomplished.

"Do not touch me." She glanced at him with red eyes.

Though he had met Lalita several evenings in the summer-house, he had remained as far from her as before; whenever he tried to nestle close to her, she sharply reminded him that he was taking a liberty with her. The more she held herself away from him, the more his desire for her grew keen. He began to discover that meeting her was a torture; she tore through his heart as she rebuked him. He was sinking into the morass of helplessness; he wished he could take his life with his own hands so that he could finish off with Lalita. But he shuddered at the very idea of a violent end of himself. In these miserable moments Har Preya's words echoed in his ears and buoyed him up. "Be a wise man Desh; ignore the refusal of a perverse woman." He would once again propose to Lalita.

"You never come near me," she warned, as she seated herself on the bench in the summer-house.

"But I want you to be my wife."

"I will never come here to meet you," Her voice sounded deadened and shaky.

"How long should we meet like thieves?" He nestled close to her.

Wrapped in thought, her eyes set on waves below, she was totally unaware of her shoulder touching on his own.

He asked again, "Shall you be my wife ?"

A weird, hard look in her eyes plunged him into terror. But within moments he was lured away by her corporeality, female and solid. He slipped his hand round her waist and held her tight; she made no effort to pull herself loose from him. Her face a mask, she gazed vacantly the lapping waves below her. He passed his hands over and over the mould of her arms, soft and ravishing, but no sooner he squeezed them, she was roused.

"Stop this," she whispered.

He crushed his shoulder against hers; he kept squeezing her arms with his hands.

"You stop this," she pattered out, her body shaking, "I will go away, never to set my eyes on you again."

His power of restraint had left him. His cheeks and ear tips felt hot and his heart pulsated with superhuman delight. He folded her in his arms and smothered her with kisses on her lips, on her cheeks, and on her eyes, turning deaf to her muffled protestations and curses, "You beast, let me go, let me go."

She pulled at his hair to free herself from his embrace; she dug her teeth into his wrist.

"Oh", he cried opening up his encircling arms.

With a wrench she tore herself loose from him, and, springing on her feet, flew away.

Mortally ashamed and wounded, he tried to pull himself together. A mountain had broken over him. He buried his face in his hands and cried aloud. All was over between him and Lalita. He was thoroughly shattered. He longed for a bottle of liquor and a box of cigarettes to drown the agony in his heart.

x x x

Some days afterwards fell the monthly *puja*-day of death of his uncle. He waited from the morning for snub-nosed priest to conduct it, but he never showed up before noon. Desh was forced to absent himself from law-courts; he was irritated.

The priest's face was twisted with grief. "Lalita delayed me." His voice proceeded from his nose than mouth.

"What nonsense:"

"I never tell lies. She made me help her do a long *puja* this morning; before her departure."

"Where to ?"

"Ranikhet. She is very good; she gave me so much money as my fee and charity," he minced the words. "Poor thing; such ill-luck so soon after marriage."

"When she returns, she shall give you a lot more money."

"She says she will never come back to Nainital."

That evening Desh over again demoted the *Siva* to his bathroom. He went to the market and purchased for himself choice brand of whisky and cigarettes. He wished some companion had shared the joy of his dissipation. He tipped till late into the night, fully conscious all the while of the fateful, unavailing love of Shanker and himself for two insensate, unworthy women.

CHAPTER - XXII

Lalita's return had forced Desh to neglect Shanker and his sister. Since his evenings were engaged, he went to see the two on Sundays or holidays. When Shanker inquired reason of his delayed visits, he told him that he was studying law-books. Shanker trusted his statement; Desh guessed his friend was far from a shrewd man. He kept silent on his fresh adventure with Lalita. He feared that his sister would sneer at his wanting marriage with a divorcee girl; Shanker would join her. When one day Lalita flitted away from Nainital, he was glad that he had been saved from looking a fool in their eyes.

Suddenly his evenings had come free. In the beginning, out of a sense of shyness, he held himself away from Shanker and sister; but it seemed difficult for him to shut himself at home, cast down and forlorn. He wanted a convivial atmosphere, merriment and fun, for dispelling the gloom from his broken heart. He turned to Shanker.

He looked up at Desh with searching eyes over the book he was reading.

"You have stopped reading law," he asked innocently.

"I am trying to forget it", Desh remembered Lalita.

"Funny boy." Shanker's corner of upper lip stirred with his habitual, playful smile.

Champa's unexpected arrival disturbed the conversation between the two friends.

"How are you Desh?" she greeted in a low voice. Her face looked pale and overcast. She at once addressed herself to Shanker. "I have something important with you."

"Go ahead."

She threw an agonised glance at Desh. "I will come other time." She clambered to her feet and walked away.

She was obviously in distress. Desh blamed Inder for it, but Shanker disagreed with him. Inder's liaison with Champa had lasted for about a year, when he turned over gifts to her in ornaments and saris. It seemed both would get on smoothly, but before long Champa changed her stance. She thought that Inder had gone mad on her, little knowing that he was an unparalleled rake. She wanted him either to marry her or part with her. He told her that he was a married man with children; it was difficult for him to take Champa as his wife; she would grow rich by keeping on as his mistress. The more he tried to appease her, the more she showed herself stiff and unrelenting. At last his patience with her got exhausted from her constant nagging, "When will you marry me ?" He flicked her off as fly from milk.

"Champa should be sorry for her behaviour," went on Shanker. "Now Inder in wealthy. His father is dead. Everybody is sorry here in Nainital and in Rasalgaon. Narendra Pratap was a religious man."

He stayed with Shanker till late in night. It was amusing to see him pour drinks for Desh, while abstaining himself. Shanker told him over dinner that he was eager to make a new break in his life by starting an agricultural farm. Inder had bought a chunk of land measuring five hundred acres in *terai*, situated several hundred miles from Rasalgaon. But he had left it untilled. He never heeded his father, who kept warning him that the old, feudal order was vanishing; he should try to fit himself in the new one. Of late a change had come over Inder. He often remembered his dead father and repented his follies. He mentioned Shanker of his debts to him and earnestly wanted to pay them off. Since he had moved to Rasalgaon to manage his property there, he offered his land in *terai* for sale to Shanker.

Desh inquired, "Shall you buy it ?"

"Inder owes me ten thousand rupees; he is asking me just forty for the land, house, and a tractor, though the whole thing is worth much more. He says I am his friend."

"Then you buy it; it is cheap."

"I have not made up my mind. It is late; we shall talk the matter over some other day. It was nice of you to have come to dinner after so long."

Shanker accompanied him out to the road. The two perambulated under the neon-lights; Desh smoking cigarette after cigarette. The weather was enlivening with the tenderness of May in the air.

"You did not go to see your sister," pointed out Shanker at last, while taking his leave from him. Sometimes you should remember the poor thing; bring her out of the house. I have not met her, I do not know for how long."

The pathos in the voice of Shanker was apparent; there was no mistaking it.

x x x

A day later, Desh toiled up the climb to his sister's house; he was seeing her in the evening since after the death of uncle. He was forgetting her; he wondered how he grew indifferent to her silent suffering. He would plainly tell her, from his own experience, that she was sailing in a boat without destination. She should elope with Shanker, or she would spell ruin to two lives, one to herself and another to Shanker, following the example of Lalita.

In the *puja*-room sister was crouching on the floor, posed in meditation, below the picture of *Siva*. Desh seated himself noiselessly in a chair. Presently he saw tears gliding down her ivory-white cheeks. He was touched.

In a while Miranda and Sanjeev, thundering over the stairs leading to the upper storey, bustled into the room. Sister was disturbed in her meditation; she rose to her feet and took a low-chair. The junior sister and brother crowded their mother from two sides. Of the two, Miranda seemed to be a devoted child to her mother. She snuggled her head into her mother's breast.

"Let us go down to Flats," she requested, "Uncle has come after so long."

Sister suggested her children to take the gardener with them for a walk. With reluctance Miranda complied to her mother.

"Your daughter loves you; you should go out with your children as other mothers do."

"I should have gone with them," sister paused, crossing her feet over the other. "Perhaps I am not a good mother."

Sister was never in love with her husband; but she had adjusted herself to her circumstances. In the beginning of her married life she believed that one day she would come to love her husband. She tried her utmost to feel it. She managed the house as a frugal and industrious wife. She herself went to *bazaar* to make purchases, and as well did savoury dishes. But her husband neither appreciated her house keeping, nor her cooking. Then she tried to charm him by her gay-coloured saris and looks; still he remained cold to her. In desperation, she started taking interested in his legal work; she read out him old rulings, or hunted them in books. But he disliked her proffered help; he took it as encroachment into his profession. Sometimes he taunted her that she should present herself in his behalf in law-courts. Eventually she began to live to herself.

"That is all the more the reason, you should love your children."

"Both resemble their father,"

He understood the life of sister clearer than before. He was undeceived that her suffering was caused by a hopeless love. If he was a broken heart, he still amused himself; as a lawyer he met a dozen men in law-courts in a day. But the life of his sister was robed of happiness, desolate; her children were constant painful reminders of the failure of her married life.

He asked in a strained voice, "Why you do not go away with Shanker ?"

His question forced a pale smile on her lips, under her delicate nose. Suddenly he felt a rush of indignation in his heart for his father, who had married off his lovely sister to an indifferent looking, undersized, self-centered man.

He repeated his question, "Why do you not go away with Shanker ?"

"Desho, you do not understand me."

The words of Lalita resounded in his ears; he felt hot with anger.

"I have to consider the names of my father and father-in-law. What shall people say, if I run away! And I must always remember my religious upbringing".

"But how long can you suffer."

"Whatever it is; I have also to think of Miranda, whom I like, though sometimes I feel I should elope with Shanker, far, far from here. If something had happened to give me that strength."

In her weak moment he saw a chance of dominating over her, bringing home to her futility of her suffering.

"You are killing yourself and Shanker; one day you shall have to change your path."

"So long *Siva* is over me, I do not hope to give in."

His sister seemed as far from his influence as Lalita.

"Your education is lost in you; I wish something had happened to change you."

He was playing the role of Har Preya. He was trying to fire his sister with the spirit of revolt against the old order. And unknowingly he gave out the secret of his finding Lalita and losing her, a second time over.

"I am so pleased, Desho," she gave a brilliant smile. "You are saved, if you had married a divorcee, you had to leave Nainital."

"But you can do, what Lalita could not."

"If I was she, very young, with my husband gone insane and with no children; probably I would have married again. Her case is excusable, not mine."

As with Lalita, so had he failed again in regenerating his sister; in infusing into her a new social awareness. He believed only a miracle could now stimulate her to live life than destroying it.

He stayed with her till late into the night, out of a sense of guilt for neglecting her. She was pleased that the break in his coming to her was temporary, caused by the recurrence of Lalita. She talked of pictures and visits to Shanker.

"I did not see Rama Nath," he remembered, "This whole evening."

"I turned him out a fortnight ago. He had become so disobedient."

x x x

Desh learnt from Shanker the purpose of Champa's visit to him. She had sought help in getting appointment as a tutor to the children of Heera Lal, elder brother of Shanker. She went to Arcadia, on getting free from her school, in the evening. Gradually Heera Lal started paying attention to Champa. Often he sat through the lessons that she gave to the children, and offered her tea or coffee before she departed. He invited her to pictures; presented her saris and sandals. On his paying her much higher fees than had been agreed upon, she was startled. She refused to accept the excess amount of money.

"Do not get troubled; I like you."

Champa frowned. "I will not teach your children anymore; I am not a cheap thing."

Recently she had gone through her sourest experience of life with Inder, who had held out to her false hopes of marriage. She wanted a husband than a philanderer.

"I will make you my wife," promised Heera Lal.

"Do it first."

Though he was earnest, he was hard put to it to go through the ceremony in hurry. He belonged to a joint-family; he needed to consult his brother. She should wait until he had not found a suitable opportunity for speaking the matter over with Shanker. Champa trusted him and liked him all the more for his frankness.

One Saturday, after pictures, Heera Lal abruptly invited her to dinner. Through out the evening he had showed himself unusually sober and gentle. When Champa felt her father would be worried over her delay, if she accepted it, he ran a domastic to her home. Before and in the course of the dinner, Heera Lal requested her to give him company in his drinks, but that she refused. On his growing importunate, she sipped a drink to please him. But he remained unsatisfied. He persuaded her to toss off drink upon drink. All she remembered later was slipping out of his bed-room by four O'clock in the morning, tottering home, weak in legs and dishevelled in hair. Next day she inquired of him as to when he would marry her. He laughed her question away. She stopped giving lessons to his children. For two months, she went to Arcadia only to press Heera Lal to marry her, but all in vain. On discovering that months were coming into her, she was seized with panic.

"I must do suicide," she cried.

But he remained unaffected by her threat. The more she shed tears and entreated him, the more unfeeling and dastardly Heera Lal grew. He point-blank told her that she should stop persecuting him, or he would call for police protection against her. Turned helpless, she narrated Shanker, between sobs, her story, reposing her head on his feet. He promised to talk to his brother to marry her, whose conduct infringed Shanker's sense of justice and propriety. The blood rushed to his face in anger; he sent up message to his brother that he was seriously taken ill. Heera Lal dashed over to see him. He saw Shanker hale and hearty with Champa sitting beside him, with her head low.

"*Arree*, Shanker," exclaimed Heera Lal, "You had given information that you were ill."

"I am ashamed of you," growled Shanker.

Heera Lal tried to go back on his pledge of marriage; he offered to pay a lump sum to Champa besides looking after the management of the abortion.

"You got to marry her," Shanker thumped arm of the sofa. "Or I will advice her to file maintenance suit against you when the baby is born; and I will ask for partition of our joint-property."

"Then I will marry Champa".

Champa fell on her knees and placed her head between Shanker's calves and cried a long time. He neither tried to disengage himself from her, nor consoled her. He knew she was happy.

"Today," she wept, "By your help I have corrected my mistakes in life."

Champa's wedding with Heera Lal was performed in the absence of fanfare of brass instruments. It was his second marriage and she was an elderly bride. The simple background suited them all the more, when it was an inter-caste marriage.

On the occasion of her wedding, Champa arranged an at-home at Arcadia. She had resigned from her job, and had invited her former colleagues in the school, friends and relatives. Sister, Shanker and himself occupied one table along with the wedded pair. Though Champa poured them tea and passed round plates, she talked self consciously. Her slow, demure gestures indicated that she had been undoubtedly affected by her brilliant marriage.

Sister sipped tea in a joyous mood, exchanging smiles and jokes with Shanker. She seemed genuinely happy that her old friend was at last married off.

As Desh was parting from her, Champa flashed a mischievous smile on him. He wondered whether she loved Heera Lal or no; but she would as time passed. He was fair of complexion, glib of tongue, and rich. His vice of drinking hardly mattered. Over the years Champa had hunted for a man who owned a mansion and enjoyed a big income. Until luck did not give her company, she gambled on. She never faced in life the conflict of sister or Lalita.

x x x

Shanker was attracted by the life of a farmer that was characterised by romance with nature. In winter he often dined with Bhandari, whose land lay contagious to that of Inder. Shanker liked the smell of fresh vegetable that Bhandari himself raised. Everyday, either both went out on *shikar*, or on long walks around green and yellow fields of sugar-cane, mustard, and wheat. Shanker yearned sister were accompanying him.

"But this land," advised Bhandari. "Inder is giving you cheap; and you shall get in me a fine neighbour. If you manage it well, five hundred acres will give you much more money than your Empire store."

Desh had never got a chance to live in a farm. Shanker's talk aroused his curiosity. But he was afraid that he would lose his only friend in the world, if Shanker left Nainital. He tried to dissuade him from launching into a new type of enterprise, among strangers.

"Do not go to *terai*," he lit his cigarette. "In law-courts we mostly deal with criminal cases from there. Land has been given to refugees from the Punjab. You will not be able to live with them with peace."

"Bhandari is there to help me."

"You have always lived in a city; you cannot live in a jungle."

Unknowingly, Desh had concurred with Heera Lal.

He shouted, "We birds of Himalayas will be burnt to death by the heat of *terai*."

Pulling a long face Shanker came away from Arcadia. He disliked to quarrel with his brother over money for purchasing farm land.

"I am glad," said Desh, "You have changed your ideas."

"I have not done so."

A conflict operated in the mind of Shanker. He wanted to leave Nainital for good so that he could forget sister. He had come to feel that he had bound himself to an unrequited love which would plunge him into life long suffering. He had tried all his wits and exhausted all his patience to bring round sister to separate herself from her husband. He told her that she was a tyrant, who was pleased to see her victim tortured.

"I suffer more than you, Shanker," her tone sounded raucous.

"What is the good of my suffering; how long is this waiting ?"

"Wait on in this life, praying that we be married in next."

"You know, I do not believe in next life."

"Whether you believe in next life or no, you should have patience to wait for me all your life."

"Chandra, dear, I will wait for you all my life, but how am I to get that superhuman power."

"Through prayers, Shanker."

"You know, I do not believe in prayers." Shanker opened out his eyes.

"But, you can believe in the simple fact that lessening your desire, reduces your suffering."

Sister led him on *Geeta* way. When Desh came unexpectedly to his apartment that evening, he found Shanker with a copy of the sacred book. He slipped the *Geeta* under his cushion to avoid a useless argument with Desh. He was trying to attain a state of no desire; and as first step, he broke his habits of smoking, drinking, and seeing pictures.

"Now I suffer much less for Chandra; I can quietly wait for her all my life."

He was stunned. He believed Shanker was showing signs of mental illness.

"Any sense in your self-denial", asked Desh.

"I am seeing merits in it; I am on path to peace."

"You are taking nonsense. Let us go out to Flats."

Sometimes Shanker admitted that in all probability his rebellious spirits had gone dull, as through he was addicted to a drug. If he could get away from Nainital, he would recapture his old-self.

Desh declared, "Then be a farmer."

But Shanker loved Nainital. He was born there and wanted to die there. All his friends and relatives were scattered over there, and held him back. He had lived all his life in Nainital without a break; he could narrate all the important hockey matches he had played in. If he went to live in *terai*, he would be closing his eyes to the gay atmosphere of Nainital. In summer he would miss the gust of cool breeze of home, where tourist were lulled by the soft music of bands and enchantment of neon lights reflected from the lake. He would see himself climbing to tops of mountains, or sailing in boats round and round the lake. Then working in fields in *terai*, he would feel stab of dragger through his heart. He would be reminded of his costly suits, left neglected in his wardrobe, which had not only stood him in good stead in his Empire store business but also had accentuated his handsome looks in picture houses which he frequented. He would feel sorry for them.

"I am glad you are not going away."

"I might," drawled Shanker. "Only Nainital is holding me back."

"So you do not know your mind."

"Yes," Shanker pointed his forefinger to the sky, "You are right. Fate will blow me to whichever direction it likes."

Desh was touched. His brave friend was resigning himself to his circumstances.

"Your thinking power is weakening." added Desh.

"When emotion has taken such a hold of me, how can I think?"

"If you do not go away," forecasted Desh. "You will sink deeper into your melancholia."

Shanker's fair moustache jerked up with his playful smile; his eyes shining.

"O *Siva* take me away from Nainital," he cried, "Or I would become a *mahatama* one day."

Desh felt an indefinable emotion, deeper than sorrow, choking him. He lighted his cigarette.

"But," Shanker put his hand affectionately round Desh's neck, "I have not given up hope. I have a feeling that some day something will happen, when your sister will change."

"You are again talking nonsense; nothing will happen".

x x x

The rains came over again in streaks, booming over the high valley. The sky rumbled with flashes of lightening, as usual, at the breaking of monsoon. The scorched grass began to show itself green, and in courtyards flowering plants came into bloom.

The silence of summer inside the houses was broken by patterning roofs and guttural noises in the pipes. Mass of fog rose from the lake, surged, blotting the mountains around.

The murky, rainy weather, exaggerated the sorrow in his heart. He felt his uncle was sitting in the veranda, bent on his *Geeta*. He seemed alive; he still occupied the suite of rooms on the other side of the bungalow. Whenever he returned late at night, Desh suffered with qualm that his uncle would be waiting for him; harried by his delay. In the mid of night he heard spasms of his coughing. On uncle's monthly *puja*-day of death, he lay on the bed sleepless; his mind agitated with memory of uncle, who walked into Desh's room and took a seat on a chair in front of him. Now that he was dead, his soul could divine his nephew's thoughts, desires, and actions.

"Desho, you have thrown *Siva* to the bathroom; but it does not matter my child, if you bow your head to him."

"What for, uncle ?"

"For killing your desire."

"Why should I kill my sweet desire?"

"You need to kill your desire before anyone; Lalita is *maya*; she is gone forever from your life; you can never gratify your desire."

Desh's head dropped; his laden eye-lids fell over his eyes. He whispered, "O *Siva* give me peace." As he came into himself; his eyes slid open; he regretted for having surrendered himself, even though momentarily, to morbid thoughts. He poured a drink and sipped it in a long time; then he quickly finished several, but the image of Lalita remained engraven in his mind, unblurred by the somniferous intoxicant. He kept saying to himself, "I will not remain behind Shanker; I will try to purify my love for Lalita."

x x x

The dismissal of Rama Nath by sister upset the seeming harmony between and her husband, who had allowed her liberty to mix with Shanker, of course in his company. Desh was further aware of the strain that his retiring disposition had put upon sister. In point of fact he found no leisure in his profession. When Desh grew up, brother-in-law suggested him to take sister to pictures, marketing or just to a stroll. Wrinkling up his brow, he enjoyed listening to his account of the recreation from Desh. When Shanker came into the picture, he was sincerely pleased that sister had taken to him, and welcomed his company. Never once he suspected her to fall in love with Shanker. He absolutely trusted her, as every member in his caste, in which no wife was known to be unloyal to her husband. If brother-in-law, with all his penetration as a renowned criminal lawyer, erred miserably in his own case, it was only natural.

Rama Nath informed brother-in-law of the secret love between his wife and Shanker; he possessed all proofs. He gave a detailed account of the trip to Bhimtal. He further informed brother-in-law that Desh acted as cover, who carried messages, made programmes, fixed meetings of his wife and Shanker. The deception the brother practised by always keeping company with the sister, when Shanker was seen with her, secured her from public talk.

At first brother-in-law disbelieved Rama Nath, but as days went by, he saw truth in the revelation. He noticed that his wife remained unresponsive and cold towards him. She replied him in monosyllables, and slept away much before he entered the bed-room. She was as well indifferent to her children; neither she looked with alacrity to their needs, nor talked to them with the effusiveness of a mother. She discharged her household duties too in a perfunctory way; she neither bothered to suppress waste by servants, nor rebuked them for sloth. But the day she went out of the house, she was a different woman. She dressed herself elegantly, and seemed in good-humour when she returned home.

In spite of his poise and balance, for some days, brother-in-law went to law-courts as a half mad man. He strived to focus his mind to his work, but without success; it kept wandering from one frightening thought to another. Any moment the secret might trickle through the town to the country, ruining his legal reputation; people would talk a thousand monstrous things. His colleagues at the bar, though dare not openly heap ridicule on him, would laugh at his back; a jealous lot as they were of his success. And if he checked his wife from seeing Shanker, she might turn violent, act in a rash way, precipitating a scandal. He stood over a precipitous. To save his reputation, he got to cut off his wife from Shanker, but through some clever move, whose purpose would be unintelligible to his wife. He had to affect ignorance of her secret. For the first time in his life he needed his legal acumen to help himself.

On returning home from the at-home given by Champa sister, instead of joining her husband in the dinner, made straight for her bed-room. That night he brought in no news-paper with him; sister felt surprised. She watched him change his dress with anxiety. He kept contemplating, for some minutes, the photograph of his father before he opened his mouth; he wanted more children. He was finding himself richer day by day; his income from law was growing larger; his deposits in the banks increasing from interests. Two children were much less to satisfy his paternal instinct, when he could well afford to bring up a dozen. Furthermore Miranda and Sanjeev, to whom he was firmly attached, would slip away from his life, leaving him lonely. He wanted new children to keep him company in his old age.

"But", remonstrated sister amazed. "It was understood between us that we will have only two."

"The understanding that was made ten years ago can change, for life goes on changing."

"But I cannot share your feelings; you must see to the difficulties it will cause me after such a long gap."

In a jubilant mood, Rama Nath had sent a letter, though unsigned, to sister stating that he had settled his scores with her by giving away her secret love to her husband. It filled her with apprehensions; any day her husband would go mad with rage, when he would turn the house upside down. She had read of instances in newspapers in which men in identical situations had murdered their wives. She would fall on her knees, lay herself prostrate, seeking her lord's pardon; still he might kick her out of his house. He might lock her up in a room, and starve her to death, or he might kill her by slow poisoning. It was useless listing all the dangers she was exposed. She was worried; she had to be on her guard.

But her husband remained his former self, calm and imperturbable. He spoke in his natural way, and went as usual to his work. He never brought the conversation round to Desh, let alone Shanker. Only at night in bed-room he stoutly told her that he wanted more children. Then sister understood him. He would never betray his reaction to her love for Shanker; never would he overtly try to separate him from her. He was a formidable criminal lawyer; he would never dare challenge Shanker's supremacy on her over him; he would never come to an open fight. He was eliminating his foe by means of a stratagem. Sister saw through it at once; he was subjecting her to repeated pregnancies to get her mind and energies entangled with them; thoughts of Shanker would be crowded out.

If her husband had wanted to pass a bullet through her breast, she would have gladly offered it; or if he had ordered her to stop seeing Shanker, she would have promptly obeyed him. But he was trying to make her forget Shanker through travails of pregnancies. She was besides herself from dark, preternatural loathing for her husband.

"If you touch me", she snarled, "I will kill myself and you too."

He wrinkled his brow from a sense of shame mingled with helplessness. He watched her transfer her bed to the *puja*-room, without uttering a single word.

Asked Desh, "You mean you will not go back to the bedroom?"

"Never," declared sister.

Desh was astonished at the ingenuity and patience of brother-in-law, even though he had shown himself a mean and pitiless man. He wanted to hold sister to himself whether she loved him or no; he was unconcerned of the means he employed so long as he achieved his end. He would lay down his life than surrender sister to Shanker.

"Brother-in-law mentioned you Shanker ?"

"Never," responded sister, "Nor he shall. He cannot do it out of self-respect, or he would force me to plain speaking, when I would tell him, I love Shanker. In that case he could not stop me from leaving him."

"He is not much in love with you; why is he afraid of your leaving him?"

"Then where will he stand; how can he show his face to Nainital?"

Brother-in-law let his wife sleep in the *puja*-room, separate from him. He seemed to have accepted the change as normal. He wanted her to believe that he genuinely needed more children. If he forced her to return to the common bedroom, he would miss his aim; she might revolt, go over to Shanker. He allowed her to have her way so that she could be brought round, submit to him. He counted on the excellence of his stratagem, his trap. One day she would walk into it; he had only to bide his time.

"Your brother-in-law," remarked sister, "Is very clever; If Rama Nath had not sent me a letter, I would not have understood him."

"But you cannot live in a *puja*-room, always."

"You are right; but I am afraid of sleeping with your brother-in-law."

"Then take courage and give him up for Shanker."

"I shall think."

"No thinking. You do what I tell you."

"First Shanker should buy the farm; I cannot live with him in Nainital."

x x x

On knowing sister's mind through him, Shanker was borne away on the wings of joy. A far away look of a lunatic came into his eyes, and, for a few days his sleep and appetite were impaired.

"Desh," he cried, "I was never a happy man. In years I forgot Lucy. Then came this unfortunate love with your sister."

Now Shanker saw himself being blessed with a new life. He would turn into a hard working farmer; but he would not carry the burden of his new job alone. He would be assisted by Chandra, his wife. He would buy a jeep-car, and with her by him, he would roam about the *terai* forests, looking out for game. Some night the two might be prevented from returning to their farm. They would halt under a thatched roof of a peasant; cook a course meal; and sleep upon hay-mattress. They would like the change, sick of luxuries.

Shanker saw his brother Heera Lal several times, in a painful crescendo. The more he contemplated about farming, the more he wanted to go in for it. It suited his somewhat nomadic temperament. It was not a monotonous work, as looking after his trade in Nainital that was concerned with buying and selling. In agriculture he would be bound to nature, revelling with her in ceaseless productive activity.

"But Shanker", said Heera Lal sharply, " I can never let you go to *terai* to kill yourself."

Shanker sat out the objection of his brother.

"If your farm fails, we shall all starve." Heera Lal leered at Shanker as he poured himself a drink.

"It should not; but even if it did, there is Empire store."

"I thought you wanted to sell it to buy farm, or how can you begin it."

"I have come to ask you half the money from savings of Empire store income."

Heera Lal poured himself another drink, accompanying his action with a dazzling smile.

" Shanker you are not my brother but son; I cannot say untruth to you. All the money you have been giving me, I have been spending in this." He hoisted up the glass of drink.

Shanker's upper lip jerked up playfully. He knew his brother was working off a joke on him.

"I am needing money urgently," his face waxed tense, "I am too worried to enjoy your lies. Just give me forty-thousand; I do not ask for half."

Heera Lal burst into a guffaw. "Shanker, you are my son; but believe me there is no money. "His voice rang thick from intoxication.

Shanker looked up at Champa to give himself countenance. "I have been turning over to you so much all these years; there should be more than two lakh of rupees in spite of your spending."

"No, there is none; believe me; I am not joking."

Shanker's face blanched over from sheer misery; his head drooped to the back of the chair. He felt himself giddy.

He called up all the flattery in him to persuade his brother to divide the deposit in the bank. As head of joint-family, it stood in the name of Heera Lal.

"You were a fool," remarked Desh, "Never taking from your brother account of money."

"I never imagined," Shanker's voice broke from distress, "My brother will forget that we were one and not two; he will forget we belonged to one family. Naturally I thought our love was above money."

"You are like my uncle."

"But, when he made a will, he sensed times are changing; while I could not."

The gross dishonesty of Heera Lal led Shanker to demand partition of total assets held by the joint family, both moveable and immovable, including Arcadia, Empire store, bank-deposit; ancestral gold ornaments; silver-ware, carpets and furniture. But Heera Lal went on prevaricating with a view to suppressing his brother's equal right, for Shanker had brought in panel of elderly members of his caste to resolve his dispute with him. It consisted of Joga Sah and a few others. They set afoot negotiations with Heera Lal, but to little effect; he said oily words to them, promised to divide the property, but never fulfilled it.

"Heera Lal is a rogue", remarked Joga Sah, "You have to go to the law-court to get your shaɪe."

"Law-court," Shanker clenched his teeth to express his sense of horror. "The name of our family shall mix up with mud."

"Law-court is the only way."

Shanker hesitated to take legal action, even though he desperately needed money to buy farm land to make a home there with his sweetheart. Desh offered to help him in few years, when he attained twenty-fifth year. Until then, both in his father's and uncle's wills, his brother-in-law acted as executor. But Shanker was too impatient to wait. He decided to raise loan against Empire store than blackening the name of his father and forefathers by fighting with his brother in law-courts.

"Why," suggested Desh, "You are not taking help of Champa; you have been so good to her."

Shanker drew open his eyes as from sleep. He doubted whether she would like to settle the dispute between him and her husband, with whom went her interests. Behind the breaking of joint-families, separation between brothers, lay women. Until his second marriage, his brother had retained love for him; who knew if Champa had not altered it.

"There is no harm," insisted Desh, "In meeting her, once."

It was difficult for Shanker to get her alone; Arcadia was a prohibited ground for him. Whenever he ran against him in street, his brother turned his face away from him. His letter to Champa might be intercepted by him. Shanker deputed Dev Rama to keep a watch of the movements of his brother. One evening he informed him that his brother was away; Shanker dashed off to Arcadia.

"Why you gave up coming here," Champa lead him to the drawing-room as though he was a visitor.

He surveyed the maroon-coloured tapestry and upholstery that he had himself selected for decorating the room. He looked to Arcadia as his home, and had wanted furnishings there to be of superior order than in his apartment on the Mall road. And now he was feeling like a stranger in that very house.

"Your brother, and children have gone to the cinema."

She sat bolt upright on the sofa with her legs crossed; she looked perfect mistress of the house.

Then she took him around the house and showed him some of the improvements she had effected. All the broken glass-panes had been mended; new sinks and sanitary-fittings installed; old, stained furniture had been refurbished or changed, and new carpets and curtains brought in. But her hardest job, after her marriage, was to get the rooms dusted and cleaned up; in them had accumulated dirt from months.

"I am laying out a garden," she croaked. "I always loved flowers. And I shall not be spending anything on it; we have two servants; one I am putting to the garden, taking over cooking from him."

"This is real good idea."

"Yes, Shanker; servants can never give us good food."

He looked up at Champa with amazement. Too soon, after her marriage, she was imposing her seniority on him, by addressing him by his name, as wife of his elder brother.

Returning to the drawing-room, he lingered for a few minutes over the photograph of his father, flanked by his brother and himself, adorning the mantelpiece. Prominent eyes, the family lineament, was easily discernible in all of them. He came away without seeking Champa's support in his dispute with his brother. The photographs had worked upon him; he saw, in the background of events, his childhood and adolescence in Arcadia. He exchanged high words with his brother in hockey matches, when he played the ball wrong; but Shanker made friends with him over evening meal, when his parents laughed at his taking his game with the seriousness of contending armies. He was the younger son and his father reproved him for wasting money, but he was always joined by his brother in pressing new demands on him. Then the family was visited by misfortunes; on a sudden, his father died one night; the property was sold to pay off debts. Shanker felt love rising wild in his heart for his brother; he felt weight of self-confidence in his bones to start on a new enterprise and come successful. He would face the hard life of a farmer in *terai* than split up with his brother.

He received a message from Champa that she was visiting him, one of these evenings. She was sincerely trying to revive the old comradeship between the brothers.

"What can she do?" grinned Shanker.

True to her word, Champa came dressed gaudily in an olive-green sari. Shanker felt her heavy make up was out of keeping with the trying times he was passing through, when his own brother was turning his enemy.

"I like your tidy apartment," she seated herself majestically in sofa.

Since she had met him at Arcadia, she had been ceaselessly trying to bring his brother towards partitioning the joint property. Even children in Nainital knew that all the wealth in the family was earned by Shanker. In the present day world, few loved brothers with his unflinching devotion. Instead of complaining that his brother was a sponger on him, who wasted his money in alcoholism, Shanker had gladly passed on his savings to his brother, believing that he could lay hands on some of it, if need arose.

"I told your elder brother," she went on, in a cool voice, "Can there be a better example of a brother's love?"

On account of Shanker, Champa had quarrelled with his brother several times over and she would not stop until she had not united the two. His brother's behaviour had brought her shame. She had suspended visiting relatives, who blamed her for the family dispute, when she was not only innocent, but was also wholeheartedly trying to settle it.

"I do not want partition, if brother gives me money to buy a farm, I would not ask for anything more; I want to go away from Nainital."

"He will give you money," she said with conviction. "He has transferred it in my name in the bank even though he keeps saying there is none." She paused. "There is well over two lakhs."

For the first time, a ray of light came to the eyes of Shanker.

"But you shall not let your brother know that I gave you the intelligence about bank money, or our marriage would break up."

"*Arree*; trust me."

Champa disfavoured the idea of Shanker of dividing only the bank deposit; she wanted complete partition of moveable and immovable property. She advised Shanker to meet his brother the following evening, but not without warning him of his visit to Arcadia. Shanker should hide from him the fact that he had been seeing Champa. He should threaten him with speedy legal action, if his brother continued evading partition. Shanker should further tell him that he knew bank deposit stands in the name of Champa. The revelation would break the nerve of his brother.

"But," she ended, "You shall have to agree to partition that I would suggest."

Shanker had never looked upon Champa with much respect. She had defamed herself with Inder, not to mention others. Once she was well known in Nainital as a flirt. But the way she had shown herself a capable housewife and unselfish woman, she had secured a place in his heart.

x x x

Heera Lal was waiting for him in the drawing room. It was a rainy evening, foggy and somewhat chill. He had already started with his drinks.

"I am glad you have come".

Shanker seated himself in an adjoining sofa and probed his brother with an affectionate gaze; in his broad face and prominent eyes, he resembled Shanker. He wondered how his brother came to be diabolically selfish, wiping off the memory of their common childhood and parentage. Though his brother was older than him by several years, still in their younger days, the two had grown as friends, inseparable. Both had common hobbies and interests; both were fond of English pictures, hockey and chic garments. It was only when his work at Empire Store had increased that he shifted to the apartment there. Still until their mother was alive, he went to Arcadia every evening to take his meal. After her death, he gradually dropped that practice; and his brother was left to himself. It was only then he turned into an addict. Had Shanker continued staying in Arcadia, Heera Lal would never have ruined himself, before his eyes. A twinge of repentance shot through Shanker. In having absorbed himself with Empire store,. he had neglected his brother, let his character change, while his own had survived through time. He still loved his brother as before; he wondered at himself. Probably his bachelorhood was responsible for it, which had caused no emotional disturbance in his heart. And if he was not loving a woman now, he would not have demanded from his brother partition of the joint-property. But he could still suffer than fight his brother in law courts.

"I am pouring a drink for you Shanker," called out Heera Lal.

"I do not drink even casually."

"You have got to do it with me," whispered Heera Lal tenderly," "Let us feel we are going to play a match of hockey."

Shanker was touched. Breaking his vow, he pulled at the drink. His limbs shivering, he wanted to hug his brother, even though Heera Lal was practising dishonesty with him.

"What has come over you, Shanker? you this!" Champa walked into the room followed by a stupid looking, lanky servant, bearing a try. "I had brought you tea."

"Tea, tea; you always talk of tea." "Heera Lal moped his lips on the sleeve of his coat, "Today, sit with us and enjoy a drink."

Champa gave her husband a fierce look that silenced him.

"I am trying my best," she resumed, turning towards Shanker, "That he should give up this habit," She stood between the two brothers. "But if even you give him company, how can I be successful."

"I am doing it for old time's sake, "replied Shanker.

Pouring himself another drink, Heera Lal hoisted it to tease Champa. "I wanted Shanker to give me company so that I could remember our childhood."

"You do not give him his share, while you talk of remembering childhood."

Overpowered, Heera Lal glanced Champa with melting eyes. "Who is not giving Shanker his share".

"You."

Heera Lal crossed his legs, and coughed; he lighted a cigarette and gazed at coils of smoke.

"I was never against partition; all our property is open to every eye. Let Shanker make two halves, and take the bigger."

"But what about bank deposit," ejaculated Champa. "Two lakh and forty thousand rupees."

Shanker was taken aback by the strength of moral courage in Champa.

"There is nothing in the bank", replied Heera Lal in a dull, characterless voice.

Suddenly a tear oozed out of Champa's eyes; her face rested upon her cupped hands. Baffled and repentant, Heera Lal glanced awkwardly at Shanker.

Slowly Champa recovered herself; her hands fell down. She praised Shanker long; her husband owed every bit of his prestige, standing in society to his brother.

"I will do," promised Heera Lal in wooly tones, "Whatever you say. I will give Empire store to Shanker, and take bank money, and do equal halves of Arcadia."

"No you give the bank money to Shanker, take Empire Store and Arcadia."

"No, no; this is too much." Shanker's heart was bursting with joy; he felt he was soaring in the sky. "Bank deposit is enough; I want nothing more." He waved his hand. "But how can brother manage Empire store."

"This is my idea," Champa flipped her right forefinger on to her left thumb. "If your brother takes up Empire store, he will be forced to work. He will not sit at home with his bottle."

Heera Lal stirred uncomfortably. He doubted whether his wife was taking sense. He was coming on to fifty; he had lived a carefree life of a rich man who had spurned at work. How could he apply himself to business.

"Brother, Champa is right," agreed Shanker."

A few elderly members of the community, acted as witnesses to the oral partition of the joint property, legally binding on both brothers. Shanker still managed Empire store, for Heera Lal was lacking in self confidence.

"Champa", said Shanker, one evening to Desh, "Is trying to reform brother. One day, he may give up drinking, and start earning. Who would have thought she would be so good and wise?"

"Even I feel grateful to her, for being so affectionate and fair to you."

x x x

Desh was happy at the unexpected, quick settlement of the dispute between Shanker and his brother. His friend could at once start his farm in *terai*. Sister would separate herself from her husband so that she would marry him. Shanker and his sister would live in heaven; both had suffered too long.

"I have changed my mind," declared sister, with a far-away tone in her voice. "I am not going away with Shanker; I will die in Hamilton house."

Desh was aghast. His sister had shared Shanker's anxiety during his dispute with his brother. She thought he had made an irreparable mistake in trusting Heera Lal in matters of money. She had wanted Shanker to take legal action against him to get his share, for she doubted whether gentle and persuasive methods would succeed with Heera Lal. She was more concerned on her own account than of Shanker .She had decided to break herself loose from her miserable, married life; moving with Shanker to *tarai*. She was naturally delighted when the dispute between Shanker and his brother got settled.

"But Desh I am not going now with him to *terai*," she waved her hand.

It was the dread of her husband, who was wanting her to suffer repeated pregnancies, that had inclined her to elope with Shanker. Now she was retracting. Desh wondered how she would impose upon herself that restraint that would deny her the company of Shanker, when he was gone for farming to *terai*.

"Your fear is natural," he coaxed, "One leap and you have crossed over to the other bank of the river."

"No Desho: I can never do it."

"But, why? In years you made a decision, and when the time came, you could not act."

Sister gave him a sidelong glance as though he was talking nonsense.

"You are forgetting, I am a human being."

"Who has power of tolerance and self-sacrifices?", he said sarcastically.

"Probably."

"And seek desirelessness," he added in ironical tones.

But no amount of his persuasion or innuendoes altered sister's resolution. He felt giddy with anger; he saw Lalita again in his sister.

"But, if you do not live for yourself, you should for Shanker. He loves you so much."

Sister joined the palms of her hands in front of her breast to the print of *Siva*, hanging in her *puja* room. "It will show me the right path." Her eyes filled up with tears. "When I think of Shanker, I despise myself. How much I have made him suffer."

Sister highly esteemed him, for he was a rare person. Though Shanker's beliefs differed from her own, yet his patience with her was simply admirable; rather on her suggestion he was studying *Geeta*.

"Any one in his place," went on sister, "Would have given me up long ago than wait for me, without hope."

"You are very right," agreed Desh.

Teats streamed down the cheeks of sister; they were born of remorse.

"If you love Shanker truly, you should not make him suffer."

"Yes, Desho; I do not want him suffer. O *Siva*, O *Siva*, help me."

She was seized with a fit of crying. It was useless for Desh to try to comfort her, or advice her to break her marriage. She seemed to be another Lalita.

"But do not misunderstand me," she pleaded through her sobs. "I am not a coward."

Desh checked tears from overflowing his eyes. He was more distressed by the ill-starred love of Shanker than of himself. He lighted a cigarette and ranged about the flower beds, in front of Hamilton house; without seeing them in the dark. He wished to walk home, but his legs felt heavy as stone to carry him. He should make one more last attempt to convince sister of the futility of her life long suffering.

He walked back into the house. Brother-in-law, with his children and sister, had already started with the dinner. He was in good spirits; he often wrinkled up his brow. For the first time Desh heard him appreciate the milk and rice pudding cooked by sister.

"This whole year," he began, "I lost no more than three or four criminal cases; and it was not my fault if I did."

"You earn more than any lawyer in near about districts," remarked Desh.

The face of brother-in-law took soft, smiling curves.

"You will earn much more money and name, if you went to high-courts in Allahabad."

"I am seriously thinking about my going."

"When shall you go," broke in sister.

"I have not decided.

"Do it quick."

Sister and himself remained behind in the dining room, after brother-in-law, Miranda and Sanjeev had dispersed.

"I want to go to Allahabad," she announced.

"Then you have once and for all decided against Shanker.

"Yes,"

"This is self-immolation."

"I do not mind."

"You must think of Shanker."

"I will never show him my face."

"It will not help him."

"He shall forget me, when I go away from Nainital and he to *terai*." Sister wailed. "Shanker; Shanker; how I love you." She leaned her head against the edge of the table. "O, if I could run away with you; forgive me dear; forgive me Shanker."

He patted her back.

x x x

Desh kept struggling to forget Lalita, taking her as dead; for her memory awakened desire in him. He burnt to feel her arms and squeeze them; cover her face with kisses. He profoundly regretted his rash and unbecoming conduct at the summer-houses; he swore to himself that he would never go wild as that evening there with Lalita. But, with all his regret, desire kept smouldering in his heart. He was ashamed of it. "How am I to purify my love". He often asked himself.

"By removing desire," said the voice of his uncle.

He felt sweat breaking over his body. He limped to the oleograph of *Siva*, lying under a film of dust, in the bath room. Wiping it clean, he looked at it with mistrustful eyes. The voice of his uncle over against resounded in his ears, commanding him to pray. If it was living, Desh would have defied it, but the soul belonged to a dead. He was frightened. It seemed to have effected direct communication with his inner self.

A long time his uncle was ill. Himself and his aunt, nursed him between them night and day. He, never complained of the chronic asthmatic pain he suffered; it was his *karma*. So long as he lived, he was an enigma. Now that he was dead, Desh was awakening, understanding him. The scene of his death grew vivid in his mind; he heard the roar of the rain, and the chanting of the *Geeta*.

"Lalita is *maya*," the voice of the soul of his uncle kept saying.

The scene of his death caught Desh with fright. For shaking it off, he opened the *Geeta* himself, though he could not bring himself to read a line. He stood in front of the oleograph of *Siva*; silent as a statue; unaware that it was a moment for praying. But his action soothed him. He felt that the *atma* of his uncle was watching him, pleased. Only terror of death never left him, however much he tried to shake it off. Occasionally the scene of death got vague and blurred; different from the one of his uncle. It was death absolute; terror kept striking at his heart. He wished to talk the matter over with Shanker; he might cure him of his nervous disorder. But Shanker seemed an unfit person for seeking help; he might end up his life as a *mahatma*, who could tell. He might talk to Desh of detachment. But ah, he was craving for a sight of Lalita; feel her arms and plant full-blooded kisses on her face.

x x x

It was hard on Shanker to get over the deep disappointment at sister's refusal to elope with him. Until his dispute with his brother remained unsettled, he was in torments, all on accounts of her. Now his hopes were shattered. He could suffer nervous breakdown, or meditate on suicide. His love was hopeless-sister lived so near him; yet so far. His hand reached short of the cup, full of wine. Desh felt his case better; he had come to take Lalita as dead, flown out of his life and Nainital. In a way he was glad; he would never catch her glimpses.

"Do not be sorry for me," begged Shanker. "Some people are never lucky in love. First was that English girl; second is Chandra."

He had expected Shanker to express himself with bitterness; but he did nothing of the kind. He was a different man. He spoke in an unmodulated voice, with the serious mien of a *mahatma*.

"I love Chandra, and I will do so until my death. If I could not get her in this life, I would in next."

Desh pursued his lips.

"You, saying so."

"Yes Desh; I saying. I told you, once, that if you love a woman as passionately as I do Chandra, you begin to think like her, if you fail to change her."

He felt the power of Lalita working on him.

"Sister is going away."

"Where to ?"

"With her husband to Allahabad."

"To forget me."

"No, not to forget you. " Desh glanced intently at Shanker. "But to make you forget her. She knows she has given you great suffering."

Shanker twitched corner of his upper lip with his playful smile.

"I wish Chandra had thought of suffering she has caused herself than me."

Shanker's eyes filled up. He turned away his face to hide his tears.

"I tried hard," informed Desh with a tone of apology, "To persuade sister to give up the path she was taking."

" No Desh, you should not have spoken to your sister for me. I know you love me. "Mopping his tears, Shanker turned towards him, "You always wanted her to break up with Pathak."

"Wish something had changed her."

"Nothing will ever change her but death."

"Any way, you shall forget her when you go to *terai*."

"Desh, I will never forget Chandra. "His voiced was breaking. "Only I am changing as she wanted me."

CHAPTER - XXIII

The abrupt departure of Lalita to Ranikhet had mortally hurt him. If he had attempted to fondle her, in the summer-house, he was justified. Lalita loved him, he believed, and for the first time she was completely left alone with him. Though he felt penitent afterwards, he was nevertheless, full of anger with Lalita; it helped create for him illusion of her death. But in less than two months, his anger had cooled off, while the flame of her love leaped in him. Once or twice, he went half way to Har Preya's house to inquire after Lalita. He was curious to know whether Lalita would revisit Nainital. The grand *puja* at Ranikhet, calculated at removing the influence of evil stars from over Jagdish, should have come off. Who would inform him whether it had been answered by Goddess or no; whether Jagdish had returned to Ranikhet from Agra, or no. Desh was crazy with jealousy; but the truth remained, independent of Jagdish, that Lalita was lost to him. Often he walked to and fro the verandah of his bungalow, seeking company with the rainy weather that seemed to lend him sympathy and anoint his melancholy heart.

One evening the agonizing memory of Lalita goaded him to the temple of Goddess of the Rock. Instead of bowing and offering flowers to Her, he scowled at the silver-eyed Goddess as a magistrate did a criminal. He demanded answer from Her to his quiry; whether Lalita would be seen in Nainital or no. But the saffron pigmented Rock Goddess preserved Her eternal silence.

As he turned to go away, he was confronted by a bearded-man with pock-marked face.

"You want to know your destiny from the *Devi*", he quizzed in a brassy voice, "I can tell you that; show me your palm."

He threw a quick glance at the bearded-man. At any other place, Desh would have ignored him; but inside the hallowed atmosphere of the temple, he was impressed by him. *Mahatma* Kailash Giri might be disguised as a bearded-man.

"From your face I can tell you, your destiny; a beautiful girl will fall in love with you; you will marry her."

Desh could not contain himself for joy. The *mahatma* was blessing him his beloved Lalita. He at once unfurled his palms.

"You are very lucky." The bearded-man feigned to read them. "You will get fame and chance to travel in foreign lands."

"Anything more."

"You have heart of gold; give charity by handfuls, otherwise your wealth will fly away."

He took out a five-rupee bank-note from his purse, and handed it to the bearded-man who cringed on receiving a big tip. As Desh walked towards the Flats, he realised that he had committed a mistake in taking the greedy mannered, bearded-man for *mahatma* Kalaish Giri. He was sorry for the loss of his money.

x x x

As never before, the rains that year spilled over into winter; and the grey, ominous fog deepened the sorrow in his heart. He had lost Lalita; sister Shanker; what a fate ! Pre-determined probably. It distressed him meeting Shanker or his sister; soon the two would be separated. Sister had resolved to accompany her husband to Allahabad. In about a month, he would himself be making for there to perform the first death-anniversary *puja* of uncle, whose life reminded him of Geeta. He felt he needed its help too; if he wished to mitigate his sufferings. One day, he might find himself free from the bondage of Lalita.

One evening he got a letter. It came from Har Preya. It was about four months since summer-house incident. She had never remembered him during this interval of time. It was short with request for a visit; her son Balu being seriously ill. He was glad to get a chance to talk of Lalita with her sister.

As always he felt a slight shivering in his limbs, when he passed through the dingy lane. Jeewan Lal, the hulking goldsmith, was busy working at a golden bangle in his shop; he had given

Joga Sah intelligence of his courtship with Lalita, hastening her marriage with Jagdish. Narrow minded people lived in the lane.

"I was wondering whether you would ever come," Har Preya looked at him with glassy eyes.

"You have but to write me a word."

His eyes swept around, till they rested on the photograph of the mother of Har Preya and Lalita. Up from the mantelpiece, she seemed to look at him with a frown.

"Whenever I shall write you, I know, you shall come. Only my sister is a strange woman; she has never been good to you."

"This was all in my fate," he replied dryly.

Har Preya led him through a dark, narrow room, into another. It howed no better looks, excepting that it was over crowded with steel trunks. Balu was breathing with difficulty; in illness he looked fairer than his mother.

"He will get well soon." Desh felt the child's pulse. "There is temperature."

"This will never go." Tears came to the eyes of Har Preya. "How lovely is my little darling and *Devi* had him to give T.B."

Har Preya sank into Balu's bed; she was overcome by a fit of crying.

"Now in operation lies hope for Balu," she mumbled through her teeth. "Bhowali sanatorium doctors say so."

"When shall you take him there ?"

"In about fifteen days."

Suddenly he was aware of the presence of someone behind him; as he looked sideways, he took in Lalita, serene and aloof, in her unchanging white colour. His heart throbbed with happiness. Har Preya shepherd Lalita and himself to the front room; but she immediately sneaked in, leaving the two to themselves.

He inquired with nervousness, "When did you come from Ranikhet ?"

"Forty days ago, "Lalita's eyes were devouring him.

"Why did you not sent for me before."

"I did not know you were coming here today."

She expressed no regret for losing her temper in the summer-house; nor she saw that she had heaped humiliation upon him by running away to Ranikhet.

"I thought you will never come to Nainital."

"I too, But I love Balu and he is so ill."

The deep, rich voice of Lalita pierced deep into him. He intently listened her, fearing he might miss a syllable; but she broke off. And the uncanny, divine, silence engulfed the two, locking their lips. He sat with her long, without exchanging a single word; wondering what thoughts were hidden behind her gloomy eyes. If someone had told him that he had returned home from distant lands, he would have not to depart now.

"Come soon Desho," she glanced him with melting eyes". I wish I had never gone to Ranikhet."

At home that night he poured himself a drink and smoked off many cigarettes to dull the shock of meeting Lalita. He loved her as intensely as never before; an hour with her had obliterated the memory of all the sufferings that she had brought upon him. When he least expected to meet her, she was entering and re-entering his life.

He dressed himself meticulously next evening, in his new woollen suit, with the colour between the scarlet and brown. His hair had grown long; he groomed it carefully; he was out to impress Lalita.

"You came late", she suggested.

Pleased at the impatience of Lalita for meeting him, he waved to her. "Come, sit by me."

"Your play has started," she looked at him severely. "That is why I do not want to come to Nainital. Here I must meet you whether I wish or no, all on account to my sister. "She spoke in wooden voice." And you must behave with me like this; I do not know what you think of me."

"I am sorry Lalita; I will never misbehave."

She heaved a deep sigh.

His head bent down from uneasiness, he did not know which way to look. "I am trying to purify my love for you."

He repeated his declaration before it penetrated into Lalita.

"I am glad to hear you say so", she grinned.

But the sweetness of the evening had been soured. He had expected some change to have come over her; she should have been persuaded by Har Preya to turn to him, now that Jagdish could be regarded as a confirmed lunatic. She had got sufficient time in Nainital, since her return from Ranikhet, to decide something about him. Again she seemed a riddle to him. If he had to advance on her, he had to go dead slow, act in most unobtrusive manner. He would always regret his hastiness at the summer-house. He would wait until he had not thoroughly indoctrinated her, when she would herself want him to take her to a trip of Delhi. He was aware of having taken a formidable task on his hands, last time though. He had not lost all hopes; after all Lalita sometimes relaxed her principles for him.

He was surprised to see Lalita in good-cheer, next evening.

"Even though Balu was not too well today," she beamed, "I have cooked something for you." She handed him a small *thali* heaped with *pakoras*.

"Bring your cup and *thali* too, or how can I accept your hospitality?"

She meekly complied to him. He wished to sign her to take seat beside him, but he recollected himself; he would never force his love upon her.

"You are not eating," she intoned, "You do not like *pakoras*."

He listened her absently. His mind had been drawn by her chiselled arms and full lips. He craved to feel them, pass his fingers over and kiss her lips. With all his will to purify his love, he was giving in to temptation. He was sorry for himself; sorry for his failure to master his desire.

She nudged him, "Are you hearing me ?"

"I like *pakoras* done by you; very tasty they are indeed; so crisp; wish my servant could fry them as well as you did."

"Some day I shall come to your house, and tell him how to do them."

"Why some day?" Har Preya entered the room. She had been eavesdropping as usual from behind the door.

"Some other day," Lalita looked up submissively at her sister.

"We will come tomorrow evening," added brusquely Har Preya.

Next day he felt so agitated that he absented himself from law-courts. He washed the crockery himself, and took inordinately long time in decorating the vases with roses which had bloomed in the front of his bungalow. Much before evening he dressed himself smartly, and started pacing up and down the verandah. Following the summer-house incident, Lalita was not expected to return to Nainital. When he had taken her for dead, he had over again run against her; his fate was opening; he was slipping closer and closer to her. Her Preya wanted him to make proposal of marriage to her; but he would refrain from it; he would never let fall a word over trip to Delhi. By way of purifying his love for her, he would desist smoking in front of her.

It was an hour past sun-set. His back was aching from walking an hour over the verandah. Filled with disappointment he dropped on a chair, when he saw Lalita entering the gate. He dashed to receive her. She had come all alone; her face looked pale and careworn.

"Sister came with me near to the gate of your bungalow," she explained. "But Balu was very ill; she went away."

"O you are alone." He threw a seductive glance at her.

He seated her in his drawing-room. She surveyed the grand sofas, plush carpet, paintings and vases.

"I like your house."

"This is your too."

He stopped short; overt repetition of his proposal would have hurt her.

To express his sympathy, he asked, "How is Jagdish?"

"By my coming to Nainital you should have understood how he should be."

It was easier for him to win her to himself by playing a friend than a lover. "How strange was your fate."

"It is all my *karma*," she said in unbending voice. "I must have done evil deeds in my this and previous life; I am punished for them."

Desh glanced at her with cold, expressionless eyes.

"We cannot know of previous life; but Lalita in this you have done nothing evil."

"How can you say that; when I was engaged, I kept on seeing you, before marriage. "Her eyelids dropped from modesty.

There was little sense in his starting an argument with Lalita, questioning her beliefs. He would only irritate her.

Unmindful of time Lalita sat with him full two hours; she was in a lively mood and talked of indifferent subjects with interest.

"O my father !" seized with panic, she jumped to her feet. "I am so late. If someone sees me, where shall I go."

"You will come here." He underlined his proposal, in his advice.

"To you my difficulties are a joke." Her face was ashen from worry. "Are you aware that I am living in the world."

"I shall not let you go tonight", he mocked.

"You are going mad."

He had made a wrong move; Lalita might break through his siege.

"But you had to tell my servant how to make *pakoras*."

"Some other day; too late I am; what am I doing all this, I do not know."

"Have peace; you are not going to your father's house, but Har Preya's"

"Desh, how am I reaching home !" She wailed.

He helped her pull a veil over her face with her shawl so that no one would recognise her on the way.

"My servant will get you a rickshaw to uplake, from down the road. Cut though Flats to avoid the *bazaar.* Do not worry; no one will see you."

"You are wise, Desh," a ray of light came to her face.

He was pleased with himself. All through the evening he had exercised utmost restraint with Lalita; he had sat away from her, and at no moment had betrayed his love to her. Of course her coming, all by herself, had surprised him; but it reassured him of his success. Behind her seemingly adventurous spirit lay her sister Har Preya, he knew; and by degrees, she was contriving to bring Lalita closer to him. Out of excitement, he started beating his foot upon the floor of his room. There, one day Lalita would dance with him as his wife.

Next evening it was Har Preya, who softly unbolted the doors of her house for him.

"Do not come in," she whispered with a frightened expression in her face.

He glanced at her perplexed.

"Lalita is in inner room; she has not seen you. I shall tell her you are not coming, better she had go to your house. There she is alone with you; you get her ready to marry you."

He walked home aglow with happiness, wondering how he should win Lalita. He waited impatiently for an hour before he heard her foot steps across the verandah.

"I will never come here again." She tore off the sari veil from her face.

He looked up at her. "Why do you think like this?"

"If someone learnt I am coming here every day."

"This is why I tell you to come here for good."

She said, in a resigned tone, "This was not in my *karma*; your renowned family and you."

She had taken a sofa opposite him; he walked over and seated himself on its arm.

"I am so hurt, when you tell me that."

Lalita withdrew into herself, unaware of his presence. Suddenly he grew conscious of the uncanny, divine silence, pervading the room.

She sat by him, almost breathing upon him; and yet she remained unimaginably far off from him. He was forbidden to touch her.

He said disjointedly, "Can I put my hand round your waist ?"

"No," she replied curtly.

"This is so painful, to be with you."

"To me it is heavenly, sitting by you."

"Not even to touch each other."

"This was our *karma*."

"But why !"

"You have never understood me, Desho."

His eyes recurrently slid over her rounded arms; his ears strained to listen her deep, rich voice.

"If I just see you," she went on, "My heart is filled with such happiness that I cannot speak."

He kept out of talk that evening his proposal to her; it might enrage her. He wondered how he had come to love so passionately an odd woman, at once human and inhuman, at once loving and indifferent.

Next day was a Sunday. Having finished a late midday meal, he was turning the pages of the newspaper in his sleeping room when Lalita came up. He was surprised to see in her awakening of courage to visit him in broad daylight.

"Har Preya sister asked me to see you, for today is holiday; you should be in". Her face was drained of colour. "Sister will be coming here in the evening."

For reassuring her, he gave her an engaging smile. "You did well to have come."

"Last night I got no sleep", she intoned. "I do not know what is come upon me; why should I come here like this ? What has Goddess in store for me ?"

"Do not be a coward; you are on right path; one step more and this is your home."

"This is impossible," she declared with a tone of finality in her voice.

His sense of vanity was bruised; he cursed his fate that had tied his heart to such a woman.

"You are angry with me", she resumed.

"No" he pouted his lower lip. "You hope one day Jagdish will return, cured."

His words thrust into her, deep as an arrow. She knelt to his feet.

"You never understood me:, she cried, "You never understood me."

"I understand you too well, probably."

Encircling his feet in her arms, she sobbed hysterically.

"Ranikhet-*wallaha* will never get back his senses."

"Then why did you refuse me?"

"You do not understand me,"

He stroked gently her back. "On coming of Hindu Code Bill, you can take divorce, and marry again."

"Desho, I love you too much," she hugged his legs tightly.

The tears he had been himself suppressing, burst forth, rolling down his cheeks.

"Lalita," he slobbered, "I love you too much; one day this love shall take me away."

"Do not kill yourself Desho; do not kill yourself."

"One day this love shall take me away, sure."

Gradually her sobs ceased; so did his own tears. For long he stroked her back, she hugging at his legs.

"It is all right, if this love does me." She moaned, her head remaining buried into the hollow between his legs. "But it should not you. I know death is something soft; I have seen my mother passing away."

He let silence to plead his case with Lalita. The anguish of his failure lay too deep for words to express.

Presently she climbed to her feet and resumed her seat on the sofa.

"Desho," she said with a luscious roll in her voice.

"How can you live in this house all alone ?"

"This is my *karma*," he replied in an ironical tone.

"Desho," she paused. "Promise me one thing; you get married."

"I cannot obey you."

"Why do you love me so much Desho; this world is *maya*."

"Then why you love me too."

"Yes, you may be right. I only say than act on what I say."

Though she had waited hours for her, Har Preya never appeared. Lalita was annoyed with her sister; she scraped her feet over the carpet with impatience.

"My staying with you too long and all alone; this is no good."

"How ?"

"This leads to temptation; I held your legs in my arms; and put my head into them. I will never come here again."

"You are a strange woman."

"Desho; I am not strange; only you do not understand me."

As always, her voice sounded to him deep and velvety as never before.

"I will never come here again."

He guided her to the gate, and helped her pull a veil half over her face with her sari.

She took few steps, when she whirled round, and droped her veil.

"Desho," she burst out," I did not see the picture of *Siva* in your room."

"It is in inside the room," he mumbled, fear gripping him.

"You have put it in the bath-room again."

He was forced to nod.

"When will you put it back to your sleeping-room?"

"When I am married to you."

Returning to his room, Desh kept striking his knuckles upon his forehead from sheer misery. If Lalita were dead, he would have felt happy; he would have found himself free from an unrequited love; but so long as she lived, he was took weak to break himself loose from her. Either he should kill himself, or win over Lalita, at any cost. To alleviate the pain in his heart, he drank deep, till he fell unconscious.

Next evening Har Preya called on him. She declined to walk into the house; she was hurried.

She said sharply, "You did not propose to Lalita."

"I did."

"What has she to say ?"

"She would neither she would marry me, nor visit me."

"You come to my house and propose to her before me. I will prepare her to accept you."

A new ray of hope brightened his face. Har Preya would scold Lalita, or persuade her; but she would get her ready to marry him. She was firmly in Har Preya's control.

Har Preya spoke of his steadfastness to Lalita. She was exceptionally fortunate in meeting him; marriage with him would turn her sorrows into joys. She must show gratitude to Desh for the true love he bore her. None, who had been treated as she had done him, would have offered to marry her.

"You need not tell me all this". Tears filled up Lalita's eyes.

"Nothing is lost still," emphasised Har Preya, "Jagdish has spoilt nothing."

Covering her face with the hem of her sari, Lalita sobbed muffled sobs.

"Desh is like *Siva*, ready to marry you."

"I will pray to Goddess of the Rock; I will ask my mother to show me the path; tell me what I should do."

"Then do it tomorrow with Desh with you".

x x x

Next evening Desh waited for Lalita below the open-air temple, on the road. He had arrived there much before the appointed time. His heart was full of hope; one who had always rejected his proposal, seemed inclined to accepting it. He liked her shifting of responsibility of marriage upon the Goddess of the Rock. Only he feared her petition to her mother to help her lift the fog of her indecision. He felt that Lalita's mother was always opposed to him; she had advised her daughter to marry Jagdish than him. She might still want her to reject his proposal. But circumstances had changed to his favour. Mother should be loving her daughter, and must know that a second marriage would end her misery. She was likely to send her daughter to him.

Lalita appeared a little after sunset. She flashed upon him a brilliant smile.

"Am I late ?"

He looked at her in detail. Though she was wearing her usual white-sari and *choli,* she had for the first time bedecked herself with golden necklace and wristlets.

"Today you are looking cheerful."

"Why should I not; Goddess may give me permission to marry you."

Desh followed Lalita into the temple where both took off their footwear. As usual, Lalita lighted a cube of camphor for lamp, and struck ringing bells. Offering flowers, she knelt to the saffron Goddess, and keeping her eyes closed, prayed in silence.

No sooner the two left the temple, he queried with a tone of anxiety in his voice, "What did the Goddess tell ?"

"I just did my prayer," she informed.

"How will goddess send you her instruction ?"

"She will send it to my heart; or through my mother in dream."

"When will the goddess do it ?"

"Today, tomorrow, in a year, or never."

"Long waiting it is," he drawled.

Lalita said her prayers in the temple several evenings; at night she invoked the spirit of her mother; but neither she received any instruction in dream, nor heard the voice of Goddess in her heart. She let the suit of Desh pending. He wondered how she could possibly take a decision on him through occult ways. He suspected that Lalita was unsound of mind; and again, he began losing hopes.

One morning Har Preya called on him early, while he still lay in bed. Quickly he washed himself and changed. During tea Har Preya shed silent tears.

" Lalita will take a decision," he said, "She needs time."

Har Preya looked at him impassively even as she wiped her tears." "I think, we should not give Lalita time; she can take it against you." Har Preya paused, looked round to see if anyone was within hearing. "I have a scheme, there is a temple in Padambori, some miles off Bhimtal. Here *mahatma* Kalaish Giri is known to come; our mother also went to this temple to pray; whenever she was in difficulty. I will suggest Lalita to pray there too."

"So what ?"

"You go with Lalita to Bhimtal; stay there with her for a few days, and change her mind."

"You are wise," he smiled knowingly.

Lalita approved of offering prayers in the *Siva* temple, but she stoutly refused to be accompanied by Desh in her pilgrimage.

Retorted Har Preya, "You do not want him; you are making an excuse of prayers."

"No excuse I am making".

"First you shall take divorce from law-court."

"I am not thinking of divorce; I am constantly praying to see the right path; I do want to go to Padambori, but how can I without you?".

Har Preya reddened, "Have you brains? When I am taking Balu to Bhowali for operation, how can I come along with you. Take Desh with you; he will not eat you up."

"But if someone sees me with him", submitted Lalita, her eyes tense with fear.

"Who knows you at Bhimtal ?"

It took Har Preya a full day to convince Lalita that her trip to Bhimtal with Desh was safe. There both could live in state managed bungalow; they could tramp down to the valley, where was located the temple of Padambori. Being a stranger there, Lalita was secure from public eye. Their father Joga Sah would be easily settled; he would be told that Lalita was accompanying Har Preya to Bhowali.

As he descended the tortuous stairway, Lalita followed him. Impressed by her unusual courtesy, he turned round; she stood over him, her lips close to his; he burnt to hoist himself on his toes and plant a kiss on her lips. The passage was darkly lighted; he felt himself attracted by her female figure. He kept staring at her round arms and full breasts; he died to feel them, just for once. Her eyes too were focused on him; and he noticed in them an expression as he had never seen before.

"I can go with you," she declared in her sonorous voice, "To a trip of Bhimtal and Padambori; but only on one condition."

"Blurt it out."

"Promise; you shall never touch me."

"I do."

Desire had possessed him; he craved Lalita. Whether he spoke truth or untruth hardly mattered. The wistful expression in her eyes haunted him.

x x x

A party of five members boarded an evening bus. It consisted of Har Preya, her husband and son, Lalita and himself. All other passengers being unknown to them, the party felt at ease. The bus ran down the mountain slopes for some miles, before it drew up in front of a large, simple, white-gate. Har Preya, her husband and Balu, stepped out of it; and the *coolies* quickly removed their luggage. They seemed to have brought a lot of it.

"We shall be staying in the sanatorium for two months, you come here from Bhimtal." Har Preya winked at Desh.

He was surprised at her light-heartedness, when she was taking her only son for a major operation. Har Preya was sure of his success with Lalita; she was overjoyed.

During the journey beyond Bhowali, Lalita sat by him in the bus, abstracted and morose. He wondered whether she was not feeling sorry for having come out with him. As the bus raced down through pine forest, shaking in cool wind and golden vegetation in autumn, Desh was charmed by the rich landscape; but Lalita remained cold to it. She sat as a dead person even as the bus passed over against the Bhimtal lake, silvery in the setting sun.

From the bus-stand, the two walked up to the bungalow, where Desh had stayed with his sister and Shanker. The *chowkidar*, recognising him, bowed low. He had brought with him some utensils, crockery, stove, and provisions; he arranged the equipage of the tour in his room. While he lighted the stove, and put a kettle of water over it, Lalita placed cups and plates on the table. When the water boiled over, the two quarrelled over the amount of tea-leaves required for fusion. The sun set before the *chai* finished. Desh hurriedly lighted the lamp; Lalita bowed to the flame, representing the God of Fire.

She took up the task of cook. She peeled the potatoes and sliced them, and shelled the peas. Having cooked the meal, she broke from him for performing her devotions in her room. "You took a lot of time", he grumbled, when she reappeared. "Since you went, I cut a plate full of radish, and read four pages from a law-journal."

Overlooking his complaint, she put before him, on the table, a *thali* loaded with vegetables and *chapattis*. He waited for her to serve herself, before starting with the meal; but she sat away from him.

"Where is your *thali?*" He glanced at her amorously. "Are you not eating to night."

"I have never eaten on a table".

"You do it now."

"Both at my father's and husband's houses females follow males." She shook her head.

Desh looked at her quizzically. "You need not do with me what you do elsewhere."

Lalita submitted to him; she placed a *thali* for herself on the table. In the glow of the lamp the two kept eating in silence. An uprush of blissful joy clogged his windpipe. With Lalita food tasted unimaginably delicious.

"You are a matchless cook", he extolled, breaking the silence.

Lalita lifted her eye-lids, dropped from shyness.

After food the two consumed apples, for desert, Later he boiled water and made coffee.

"This is the first time, I am drinking it."

"You like it."

"It tastes something like fried groundnuts."

Having finished coffee, Lalita cleared away the *thalis*, and scrubbed them along with cooking pots, in the bath-room. Extending himself across his bed, he savoured a cigarette. He felt he was a married man with a hard working wife. As the first step towards winning Lalita, he planned to make conversation with her till late into the night.

She twitched up her nose as she entered the room. "You smoking."

"So long I have been resisting before you, but after the meal, I could not."

"It is time to sleep."

Abruptly she made for her room. Following her, he lighted the lamp there.

"You are frugal,"

"Yes; I put it off while going out after prayers."

He looked at her with an expression of entreaty in his eyes. "Can I sit in your room ?"

"I will be sleeping; so you should."

She cut him short. With bowed head, he slouched to his room. He heard her slam shut the doors of her own. Her sudden departure came as an anti-climax to the happiest day of his life. He regretted his smoking; he would try to suspend the habit so long as he stayed with Lalita.

Next morning he was awakened from sleep by the soft knocking on his door. Before unbolting them, he groomed his hair and flung about him his gay-coloured, dressing gown.

"Am I late in getting up ?"

"I have gone through my bath and morning prayers." She glanced at him with shining eyes.

She lighted the stove, and supplied him hot water. While he was busy with his ablutions, she made the breakfast. Before he dressed, she had done it. She seemed quick at her jobs.

He was surprised to see fried eggs on the table.

"You can touch these", he pointed out with his finger. "I wanted to do them myself."

"Of course, I do not eat them; but I can cook them; I do for Balu".

He had taken Lalita as a perfectly orthodox woman who looked with abhorrence on eggs as an article of food. He was mistaken in his understanding of her; she seemed responsive to new ideas and change.

She averted her eyes from him as she poured out tea, and applied butter to toasts with agile hands. He felt that she liked to work for him. The overnight happiness revived in his heart. He started bolting the breakfast; she following him.

"Hurry up", she prayed, "We have to go far on foot to Padambori."

"I am tired today," he made an excuse.

He wanted to keep Lalita with him as long as possible.

"I cannot live here long; and I might go to Padambori not once, but twice."

"Har Preya sister permitted you to live here a week."

After the day-meal, Lalita astounded him; she herself suggested that he should light a cigarette, if he desired.

"I thought, you are against smoking."

"No, I am not against anything."

He turned over her reply in his mind. "Then what stops you from marrying me?"

"Not your beliefs at least."

He felt Lalita was coming closer to him. If she lived with him as now, he could infuse into her modern, rational outlook to life. Every moment he passed with her was full of importance. Lest she might not go into herself, he had to keep her engaged with himself. The evening was free, as the medical officer, whom he had sent invitation to tea, had accepted it for the following day. He suggested her a stroll on the motor-road over the lake. She declared, "I will not go with you to public places, until I am not married to you."

"Then Naukuchia is the only choice."

Anxious to reach there an hour before sunset, the two sallied forth over a level eastward bridle road, passing through terraced fields, lately harvested, or ploughed over. Dogs barked; village folks turned their eyes at them with curiosity. The two doubted whether they were reaching the lake in time; when, on a sudden, they found themselves in front of it, with numerous corners, enclosed by low, wooded mountains. The tenuous clouds of autumn were dyed pink in the setting sun. They were carried away by the vision.

"Let us go into the lake," suggested Lalita.

Two boats were moored on the marshy bank. He looked out for a boatman, but finding none around, he himself pulled out one; Lalita took an oar from him.

"Ply it carefully, or the boat will sink us", he teased her.

She said airily, "I am not the daughter of my father who is afraid of death."

The two leisurely rowed the boat towards the middle of the placid lake. As it approached about there, they dropped the oars; the boat kept gliding on its own momentum. Lighting his cigarette, he started counting the corners of the lake, for which it was well known.

"Desho" Lalita put her foot over his.

His eyes twinkled as he looked at her.

"Desho, if you were always with me."

"Lalita, dearest, I am always with you. It is you who have to make up your mind."

The boat had come to a stop; only it rocked in the waves. White homing birds flew over them; from over a mountain floated in shouts of a herdsman driving cattle out of the woods.

Lalita put her right arm on his shoulder. "I wish you were always with me; I love you so much."

Her eyes were swimming in tears. To comfort her, he threw his hand over her shoulder. A shiver passed through him as he saw as never before, the strength of the unknown spirit hidden in her that held her away from him.

"Make up your mind Lalita; our lives will be different."

She pressed his shoulder with her hand, "This is why I have come with you so far to pray."

"Can you not accept me without prayers?"

"No."

"If the result is against me ?"

He pecked her hand; she gave no demonstration of distaste.

"I will act on it."

"Can you not decide without prayers ?" He kissed her on the cheek.

"No."

He kissed her on the lips. She offered no resistance. He kissed her again on the lips. She was absent-minded to his caressing; her eyes were glued to the fading pink on the skyline. It was useless entreating her to give up the expedition to Padambori. He kissed her with the intolerable anxiety of a lover whose sweetheart was dangerously ill; the prayers might snatch her from him. He was filled with dejection as he smothered her with kisses. Slowly and imperceptibly darkness had gathered up over the lake, when the two roused to it.

"Row the boat fast, but with care. " Lalita surrendered her oar to him." You have not to get yourself drowned; though it is different with me."

He tugged the oars hard over the lake; and, with skill, saved the boat from being trapped in the marshy bank. But if it had capsized, the two would have felt equally glad; they had lost or found each other in the enchanting lake. As they picked their way, the strident croaking of frogs sounded musical to their ear drums.

"The couple is safe," he pronounced.

"Desho, I feel my prayers will give me you."

With shivering fingers he unlocked the doors of his room; rowing through marshy lake in night had tired him out. He put off his coat and shoes, and within a minute fell asleep. After a while, he rose with a shriek.

Lalita inquired with a tone of anxiety, "What has happened ?"

"I saw a strange dream. While you came away, I was left behind in the lake, in night."

The aroma of spices pervaded the room. Lalita was always an excellent cook with vegetarian food.

"You should not have kissed me," she complained between two morsel of *chapatti*.

"Why ?"

"Because I am not your wife."

"Why should you have put your hand on my shoulder."

"You are right; I am equally responsible for the sin."

While he took food with his right hand, he placed his left on her shoulder. "There is no sense in your prayer. Let us go from here, not to Padambori, but to my house in Nainital."

"You never understood me."

"I have never understood you as another woman."

Lalita inquired sharply, "Who is she?"

"My sister Chandra."

After meals, he retired to bed. He was tired out by rowing the boat. He wished that he had taken a few drinks to deaden the pain in his limbs.

"You are not looking well." Lalita seated herself at the bottom of his bed. "Let me massage your legs."

He permitted her; himself he wanted to experience the feel of a married man in illness.

"You are odd; you would not marry me, but behave in a way as my wife."

"I do not want to have too many regrets, if I cannot marry you."

With her hands nursing his feet, her negative reply hardly bore sense. It was only a matter of little time when she would accept him. Instead of himself, he let silence to speak for him.

Quietly he piloted her to the doorway of her room for the night. Before parting, she stared at him with the same wistful expression in her eyes that he had seen at Nainital.

He was torn between desire and apprehensions. He had better kill himself than lose her; he wanted her from the depths of his *atma*. And it was dangerous, allowing her chance to offer last prayers, at Padambori. He got to make her cancel the exercise. He faced life's job; but it was not unpractical. Lalita had let him kiss her; and there in Nainital and that night she had looked him with amorous eyes. Still he was uncertain of himself; if he misunderstood her, he would lose her, all on account of his haste. He dreaded repetition of the scene of summer-house, she had enacted. But he was lucky; he had received the support of Har Preya. Victory was again in sight.

Next morning Lalita, during breakfast, insisted on starting to Padambori.

"I am still tired," He lied again, "From overnight rowing."

"Promise, you shall come tomorrow." She cast a suspicious glance at him.

"I cannot promise anything." He paused, tapping the spoon on the top of the dining-table. "How can you expect me to accompany you?"

"Why not?".

"Accompany you to the *Siva* temple where you may decide against me."

"Then I go to Padambori alone."

" Lalita," He glanced at her with appealing eyes." If you leave me after your prayers, where have I to go; I will end my life." He delivered himself in well measured tones.

"Do not say so, Desho," she implored in her deep rich voice. "You are a man". She paused. "If I decide against you, I will never again show you my face so that you can forget me; I say on oath."

"Then you shall go back to Ranikhet."

"Yes, I will go back, praying for his recovery". She reinforced her declaration by rapping her fingers on the edged of the table. Suddenly tears welled up in her eyes. "Do not foresee the result of my prayers; do not talk ominously; let me say prayer in peace. Do not talk ominously today, Desho."

x x x

Dixit, the medical-officer, was expected that evening. He wished Lalita to look trim in some of the golden ornaments and red-coloured sari, she had brought with her for the occasion of prayers. Though she stuck to her white, she fulfilled first part of his wish. He was pleased that Lalita valued his sentiments.

Dixit was visible in the bungalow after sun-set, two hours past the appointed time. Desh had fidgeted about the verandah, regretting his mistake in inviting a tardy guest. Dixit shook hand with him coolly; but his simple, cordial manners touched Desh. He introduced him to Lalita as his wife.

Dixit excused himself for the delay. He was an overworked man; he was returning form paying a call to a dying patient in a village situated three miles off. He wore a high-necked coat and baggy, grey trousers of thick material. He looked countrified. Constant walking over mountain roads had shrunk his fleshy face, bulging out all the more his eyes.

While he had been engaged with Dixit, Lalita had vanished from the room. He was perturbed by her behaviour. He looked out for her in the compound; but seeing no sign of her, he turned into her room. She was huddled over her bed, sobbing in darkness. He was taken aback.

"What is the matter?", he articulated.

"Why you lied to the doctor that I am your wife."

He slipped his hand though her waist. "Are you hurt ?"

"Yes."

"You do not understand things. What will the doctor think of you and me, if he learns we are not married." He pecked her arm. "The *chowkidar* would have suspected us unmarried, from our taking two rooms, if I had not told him that you are ill these days."

"You go; I am coming to serve tea."

Lalita had instantly understood him; she had begun behaving as his wife. He whistled from delight as he walked back to his room.

"You seem to have changed;" resumed Desh blandly, "How simply you are dressed since I saw you last year."

Dixit slowly passed his hand over his temple with some pride. "Yes, I have changed quick though. Before coming here, I had seen villages from far; now I live among them. I have begun to understand them; their poverty, ignorance, and superstitions. Many many five-year plans might be needed to change them."

"You are very right."

"Probably I am not right; I am posing to be a great man, when I say I have understood villages; I have not. I do not know why people there are poor; why they do *jagar* to cure diseases."

Lalita had laid tea on the table; but Desh had been too absorbed in the enlightening talk to make it. At last Dixit, who had been wanting it urgently, poured it out himself. Lalita sat quiet through tea; not once she let slip a word from her lips. Dixit was slightly troubled, embarrassed by her reserve bearing, though he relished the salty refreshments prepared by her.

"Like you, my wife is a good cook", he addressed himself to Lalita. "She is out of Bhimtal, or I would have invited you for the evening meal."

For the first time her lips parted with a faint smile. "If you enjoy vegetarian food, come tomorrow evening."

Desh accompanied Dixit out of courtesy beyond the compound of the bungalow. The latter declined invitations from tourists. Secondly evening-meal tasted vile without drinks.

Desh agreed. "I will arrange for that too."

"I keep whisky," ejaculated Dixit." I shall bring it with me. But there is your wife. How will it look?"

Desh caught at his hand. "My wife is frigid; please make her drink."

"I see; I will get your job done."

Desh as surprised by the quick invitation Lalita had made to Dixit. He tried to guess the reason behind her warmth to a new acquaintance.

"I wished your guest had come again," explained Lalita without his inquiry. "He serves patients."

Desh was hurt by her veiled reference to Jagdish.

x x x

The daughter-in-law of the *chowkidar* had been running a temperature for about a month. He was treating her by performing *jagar*-ceremony that night. Since Desh's sister on her visit to Bhimtal had wished to watch it, the *chowkidar* invited him.

"Show your daughter-in-law to Dixit, who is not gone far from here," he advised, "Than fixing *jagar* for her."

The *chowkidar* gave a vague smile of disapproval. He slowly transferred his eyes to Lalita, who had been listening him with concentrated gaze, for her opinion.

"I will go to see it," she interposed with glimmer of a smile on her lips."

"This is a big event," the *chowkidar* joined the palms of his hands under his bowed head. "Your coming to my hut to see *jagar*; you are unlike city-*wallahs*; you are a great wife."

"It will be wonderful, Desho", she exclaimed.

Lalita was excited; she glanced provokingly at him during meal. A quiet woman, she surprised him by her voluble expressions on *jagar*. But she actually startled him, when, after having taking an hour in getting dressed, she stepped out of her room in a blood-red, brocade-sari. She had neatly parted her hair down the middle of her head, and had, for the first time, applied perfumed oil to her hair, and fixed a red, round *bindi* on her forehead.

She gave him a sparkling smile. "I had brought this sari to wear after prayers at Padambori, in case *Siva* permitted me to marry you."

Lalita walked with such jaunty steps that he held her hand whenever a puddle or depression came in the path. The roar of men accompanied with the beating of *dholak* proceeding from a nearby village, indicated that *jagar*-ceremony had begun. The *chowkidar* was impressed by the presence of a distinguished looking couple in his small, stone house. His face crinkled up in the wave of nervousness that had swept though the ill-clad crowd, in the front of the house, squatting around a bonfire, built on logs. A grey-haired drummer with a parrot-nose and cheek-bones showing though his skin, threw a sharp look at Lalita and him, from his high seat, but not for a single moment he relaxed the tempo of his playing the *dholak*. Though Desh held himself calm and unruffled, Lalita was touched by the suspense of the situation; her face was suffused; her eyes were levelled at the drummer who played the *dholak* with feeling, alternating the tempo high and low. Neither he was a consummate drummer, nor an unskilled; he was one out of the ordinary. Slowly he played the *dholak* louder and louder, varying the tempo in quicker succession. Then in patois he started singing verses narrating feat in battle of a chieftain, apotheosized as a deity. No sooner had he finished singing, he thundered the *dholak*, oscillating from head to foot. It seemed land under him was shaking from quake.

The old peasant whom Desh had known from his previous visit to Bhimtal, jumped off the crowd, and advanced towards the bonfire. Every part of his body shook as he staggered round and round it; his eyebrows kept fluttering above his wild eyes; his hand jerked and swung, groped. He wore white-*dhoti* down his waist, and a caste-mark on his brow.

"*Memsahib*," declaimed the *chowkidar* to Lalita, "Over Godhan has come the deity."

Several men one by one jumped off the crowd, and filed past him, aping his bodily movements, gestures. While circling the bonfire. Godhan stopped before the drummer, turned square, and let fall a couplet, depicting deed of valour of the chieftain. The drummer, lowering the tempo on the *dholak*, responded by singing yet another couplet. Having finished it, he played the *dholak* with fury. Godhan, uplifting and gesticulating his hands, blowing sounds between a wheeze and whistle, started jumping and trotting round the bonfire, keeping menacingly close. Aping him, his disciples followed him. The crowd whistled, gave discordant sounds, hissed. The savage dance roused in the crowd primitive instincts of fear and worship.

"O deity, show us your powers," petitioned the *chowkidar*.

Dipping into the bonfire, Godhan brought out a miniature axe with red-hot blade. Flourishing it to the crowd, he chuckled; made discordant noises as he passed the red-hot blade over his hands and legs, and licked it with his tongue. Coming out from his performance, whole and unscorched, he whistled in self-satisfaction. Then he passed the axe to his followers to imitate him.

"Godhan and his companions," Lalita looked at Desh, "Has the deity in them or they would have burnt themselves."

A lone woman with her face veiled in head-cloth, crouched farther from the bonfire. Godhan leapt to her and with the sacred ash of the bonfire, made a finger-mark on her forehead.

Towering over her, he blessed her. "You will get well. Should you fast one month, light wick in village temple one month, sacrifice later two goats, you shall get well."

The daughter-in-law of the *chowkidar* prostrated herself at the feet of Godhan. The *chowkidar* as well bowed to him, and showered flower petals over him. After her another woman took her place, awaiting Godhan or any one of the possessed men, following him, to bless her.

The *chowkidar* whispered to Lalita, "If you have any problem; anything to ask about, take the place of the woman there," he pointed out with his finger, "The deity in Godhan will solve it."

Lalita beamed. She glanced at Desh with inquiring eyes.

"Desho; I shall go; I shall ask the deity to give me you."

He was seized with panic. In case Godhan advised her to reject his proposal, he would lose Lalita, once for all. She would go back to Ranikhet. Seeking blessings was a risky business.

"No Lalita", he ground the words in his mouth. "No; you will not pray to a petty deity, but to the supreme *Siva* at Padambori."

"But the deity, Goddess of the Rock, *Rama, Krishna* and *Siva* are one and the same. Let me go; let me beg the deity you."

"Godhan and his companions", Desh sprang to his feet as a lion, "Have no deity in them; they are ordinary men in hypnotic trance."

He felt himself too cowardly to release Lalita. He carved his way through the crowd, dragging Lalita with him. The *chowkidar* entreated him to prolong his visit, but he turned deaf ears to him.

As Lalita and he waddled through the compound of the bungalow, he protectingly held her shoulder in his hand. She took no umbrage to his gesture and readily sat down at the edge of the verandah, on his suggestion, than getting into her room. For the first time in his life he felt he had looked into the mysterious firmament, powdered with stars; for the first time he breathed the autumn breeze heavy with the scents of cucumber and pumpkin vines and upturned earth in fields. For the first time flitting dots of bluish lights, in the glow-worms, roused him to the beauty at night.

"I would have been yours now, Desho," cried Lalita, "If you had allowed me to pray to the deity in *jagar*."

He was overcome, deprived of the power of speech. He was accustomed to sitting with her in silence. He kissed her neck; he put his arm round her waist, and kissed her on the lips.

"Let us sleep in the very room tonight." The suggestion escaped his lips in spite of him.

He felt she was staring him through darkness with soft and liquid eyes.

"Come, we sleep in the very room from tonight."

"I am not married to you," she remonstrated.

"What difference does all that make?"

"Desho, you never understood me."

Before separating from her for the night, he passionately kissed her; despite her beliefs, he had undoubtedly won her over; her red-sari, with wistful expression in her eyes bore it out. He recalled of his indescribable, long struggle with her. How hard it had all turned out to be; twice, fate dodging her from his grasp. It had over again flung her upon him. He heartily thanked it for its kind gesture. Future seemed to open up a new path, strewn with flowers, over which walked his wife Lalita in step with him.

Next morning Desh rose with a sweet, warm spot in his heart. He put off Lalita's demand for visiting Padambori, without difficulty. There seemed hardly any reason for hurry. The *chowkidar*, who would have remained awake in the night attending *jagar*, had not turned up at the bungalow. He had been fixed by Desh for accompanying Lalita in her march to Padambori. He was glad that he was easily putting her off; he felt sure that she would come to accept him, between two and three days at the outside, without the help of prayers. He eagerly awaited the nightfall for sitting with her under the stars and kissing her.

"I have to tell you one thing," he warned, during breakfast.

Lalita had maintained a silence from the morning; occasionally she glanced him with furtive eyes.

"Remember, not to behave before Dixit in such a way that he suspects you are not my wife; or he shall not think well of us."

Lalita blushed; she avoided looking him in the eye.

It was the longest day in the life of Desh. Several times in the evening, he went out of the compound of the bungalow to look out for Dixit. When he appeared, Desh held his hand a long while, before indicating him a seat.

The three talked of the mild autumn season, which Lalita adored for its important festivals, *Dusshera* and *Diwali.*

Before serving the food Desh took Lalita aside to the verandah.

"You know," he whispered, "The doctor refused tea even though he was tired."

"Why ?"

"Because," he peered into her eyes through darkness. "He must drink in the evening."

"Let him drink; I do not mind; after all its only a habit."

He put his hand on her shoulder." The doctor will ask me to keep him company," he stammered.

Lalita remained stock-still.

"What should I do ?" He passed his hand over her forearms.

"If you like, you can."

"My drinking would turn your prayers and thoughts against me."

"No."

He locked her in an embrace; she leaned her head on his chest.

"We are forgetting our guest," he said.

Dixit poured out whisky for Desh and himself from a bottle that he had brought out of his portable-bag. Lalita winced as the fumes of the alcohol assailed her nostrils.

"Please do not pull a face," Dixit glanced awkwardly at Lalita.

She screwed her eyes. "Does not your wife tell you that you should not drink?"

Dixit burst into a staccato laugh. "My wife keeps me company."

"You are spoiling your wife."

"No; drinks makes life gay."

Before sipping it, Dixit clinked his glass on that of Desh. Lalita started doing water in protest.

"You have never tasted it, still you condemn drink."

"I need not to do it."

"If you have never known the feel of drink, how can you condemn it?"

"Yes," struck in Desh, "You are a coward if you condemn a thing without knowing it."

Lalita looked challengingly at Dixit, who poured her a glass.'

"No, I will never touch it," Lalita shook her head.

"You are simply a coward," Dixit turned to Desh. "You are a henpecked, weak husband, or your wife dare not disobey you."

Lalita stamped out of the room. Desh overtook her in the verandah, and blocked her way.

"Dear, *dekho*," he murmured tenderly, "Keep my honour."

"But how can I drink?"

"Then I got to tell the doctor that you are not my wife."

She inhaled an audible breath.

"Save my honour before the doctor, dear. There is no harm in your drinking. If you condemn a thing, you must know of it, or you are a hoax."

"*Desho* !"

"Come now Lalita, you are a brave woman."

She crawled back to the room, Desh preceding her. By the time the meal finished, she had emptied a tall glass of whisky, even though she kept raving, "This is a nasty thing; you wanted me to drink it; see, I have done it."

Her face flushed and burning, she clambered to her feet, and made to her room, but knocking against Desh's bed, fell across it. As he left, Dixit winked at him.

When the chance, he had for long been seeking, came his way, he found himself unmanned from a twinge of nervousness.

To give himself support, he lighted a cigarette. He mustered up all the courage in him. "Lalita."

Neither a word slipped out of her lips, nor a tremor passed through her body. She had shut her eyes with her hand.

" Lalita". He shook her.

He sat down over against her; slowly he sank his chin into her neck. "You are conscious ?"

"Yes, all the time."

"Why are you not removing your hand from your eyes ?"

"I hardly looked at you the whole day."

He covered her arms and face with ravishing kisses; he understood her.

"I have never seen a woman," he sighed.

x x x

On waking up in the morning, he realised that he had over-slept. He swung his eyes, expecting breakfast on the table. But he was no trace of Lalita about his room.

He wondered how his friends and relatives, and citizens of Nainital would take his marriage with Lalita. But he would boldly face them. His sister and Shanker should approve of it. It might induce them to review their own decision to separating from each other. But his marriage was a complicated affair; taking divorce would entail long waiting, how the time would weigh on him.

He washed and dressed himself; still Lalita remained sleeping. To allow her more time, he lighted the stove and prepared the breakfast. Then he tapped at her doors.

"Get up darling," he crooned. "It is past ten."

He tapped at the doors a shade louder. "Get up darling; it is already late; tea is ready."

Failing to draw a response, he repeated his tapping.

"I am not joining you," rang out Lalita's strange, peevish voice. "Finish *chai*, then do your bedding and packing. We are starting for Nainital."

Bewildered, he slapped his breast.

"Going to Nainital, just now, I do not get you. You have still to do prayers at Padambori."

"I have done over with my prayers."

He was familiar with the spice of abnormality in Lalita's mental make-up. He felt pleased by her sudden desire to return to Nainital. She had decided to marry him without the fuss of prayers. While he kept whistling during break-fast to proclaim his victory, Godhan entered the room.

"Be seated," he accosted.

But Godhan remained standing. "Some days ago an old lawyer gave a public speech; I asked him to remember me to you; I am so pleased to see you in *jagar* last night."

"Yes, he is Sunder; he told me about you."

"Has he been sent to jail ?"

"Why ?"

"He gave such a fiery speech. He said we should overthrow the congress government; it is starving the people."

Desh grinned. "Why should Sunder be sent to jail; we are not in British India."

"I see, I see." Godhan tilted his head. "Then our government is a good one; but it is not doing everything good; it is making law against untouchability. How am I to get the deity in me, if I take food and water from the hands of *dalits*."

In a white-sari Lalita followed him to the motor-stand. The corners of her eyes were showing tinge of red. Maintaining her silence, she handed him a telegram, which she had received, when he was a sleep. It had been sent from Bhowali in the morning, and ran as under:-

Balu died on operation table. Going Nainital. Har Preya.

He rolled the telegram sheet recalling the shape of a long cigarette, and stuck it into his mouth. He was fond of the child and had expected him to recover from his illness. He saw now Lalita's behaviour quite normal and sane, in cutting short her stay in Bhimtal.

As Lalita and himself took seats in the bus, Godhan walked up and bid him farewell, but Desh's attention had been caught by a lanky chap who seated himself behind him in the bus.

First he failed to place him; slowly he recollected that the chap had preceded Lalita and himself, in one of their visits to the temple of Goddess of the Rock.

Lalita sat through the journey in silence; occasionally she surveyed him with the frightening eyes of a lunatic. At the Nainital motor-stand, no sooner she jumped out of the bus, she scampered off to her home. Her abrupt parting hurt him, but he readily excused her; Balu's death had upset her.

On his way home, he ran against the old physician who attended on his uncle. He gave Desh a nod of recognition.

"Not seen you for long," he said condescendingly.

"Been keeping good health," replied Desh crossly.

He looked into his mail that had accumulated during his absence from Nainital. One letter came from his aunt. She had given him the date, falling after a fortnight, of the death anniversary ceremony of his uncle. She had requested him perform it with the help of the snub-nosed priest at Allahabad.

That day he stayed at home. He wanted Lalita to recover from the shock of death of Balu. He expected Har Preya to be in bad shape; poor thing, she was an unusually devoted mother who had nursed her only son since before she knew Desh. How grateful he felt to her; without her help, he would have never discovered Lalita, and won her.

Next day he waited eagerly for nightfall. He looked out for darkness from old habit to escape notice of the inhabitants of the lane, though now he could have easily broken it. No longer gossip mattered, when he was marrying Lalita.

Har Preya was resting in bed in the front room, covered in a quilt. Her face looked tear-worn and blanched.

"I was expecting you yesterday," she glanced him with listless eyes.

"I had not the courage to see you."

She jerked up the quilt that had dropped down to her waist.

"He was ill for so long." She paused. "I was prepared for his death; I always try to follow the *Geeta*," she broke off.

Her eyes filled up and ran over; she began to wail. "I knew he would not live; he was so lovely, my Balu."

Her anguish was contagious; his eyes were turning misty from a tear.

She let drop the quilt in which she had buried her face. "We were not worthy of him; he was so intelligent and lovely; my Balu."

He wondered whether Lalita was present in one of the interior rooms or no; his eyes were athirst for a sight of her. But making inquiry after her seemed awkward. He let Har Preya's fit of crying to pass over, before he took his leave from her.

"I shall come, some other day."

"No; come tomorrow evening."

From Har Preya's house, he took a detour to his own, round the temple of Goddess of the Rock, below which he stood a minute. Paying homage to Her in childhood in company of his uncle how he believed Her to be all merciful. Now in night, she struck him with an unintelligent terror. Instantly he fled off as though a spectre was on his heels. His heart was still knocking inside him even after he had put on the light of his room; he seemed to hear the coughing of his uncle two rooms away. He knew he was labouring under a hallucination; his uncle was dead for about a year.

Next evening, though a cloud still hung over her face, Har Preya seemed to be rallying from her depression. She felt strong enough to sit up on bed; the puffiness over her eye-lids had too lessened.

"You look better today", he began.

She ignored his point. "You are late."

"I want to avoid daylight." He plucked at his neck to hide his embarrassment.

She gave him a pale, deathly smile. "Now how does day light matter; everybody here knows you and Lalita lived together in Bhimtal. The lanky chap who travelled with you from there to Nainital is brother-in-law of the fat Jeewan Lal of our lane, and you know his tongue." She paused. "It is for this reason I want every thing to be rushed through; my anxiety for Lalita has turned away my thoughts from Balu."

Public eye would no longer restrict his freedom with Lalita; whenever he liked and wherever he chose, he could meet her; he sucked in his lips from joy.

"Lalita", he said emphatically, "Is my responsibility; you do not worry."

"I know, you will never change."

She interlocked her fingers, striking a pensive attitude.

"Nobody can point finger at Lalita, when I shall be marrying her." He clasped the sides of the chair he was occupying.

A ray of light came into Har Preya's eyes. "I am suffering less on account of Balu, when I think I have brought you and Lalita together. If Balu was not going to Bhowali, she would not have gone with you to Bhimtal; and when she returned from there she cried so hysterically; she was not herself. I consoled her; I told her soul never dies, I see Balu's soul around the house."

"Had you had any talks about me?" he asked with a tone of anxiety in his voice.

"Yes; I asked her whether she had decided to marry you."

"What did Lalita say ?"

"I have decided was her reply."

"Is Lalita here ?"

"No; she is looking after father."

He had been overtaken by misfortunes. The news of Balu's death was followed by publicity of Lalita's trip to Bhimtal, in the company of Desh. Har Preya advised him to begin seeing Lalita, at her father's house, in the capacity of her prospective husband so that her honour and reputation in society was restored.

"How will your father take it?"

"He wants to meet you. He never had courage to marry Lalita a second time; but Bhimtal has put the matter very far."

He was dying to meet Lalita, listen to her deep, rich voice. The knowledge that Joga Sah would welcome his marriage with her, fortified Desh in his nocturnal venture into Joga Sah's house. Climbing with firm foot a flight of stairs, he tapped at the doors in the second storey. Pushing them open, Joga Sah threw an anxious glance at him. His greeting him, in the character of his prospective father-in-law, gave him quite a shock. Following him Desh walked into the very room he had waited on Lalita, with his suit. As his eyes riveted on the large-size portrait of the mother of Lalita, hanging on the wall, Desh felt, for the first time, that she was smiling down on him. He took it as a good omen.

In a feeble voice Joga Sah started recounting his misfortunes. Desh was touched by seeing tears in his shrivelled face.

"I had never known sorrow," he went on, "Until the death of the mother of Lalita and Har Preya." He glanced up at the portrait on the wall. "She was a Goddess. When she came to my house, I had not a broken earthen-pitcher. She brought wealth and luck to me. With her death everything of this house is breaking; I feel so lonely." Tears fell down his cheeks. "I can never think of a woman as faithful to her husband as she was to me, whether I was rich or poor."

"The world is *maya*," slipped out of Desh's lips.

"Yes," replied Joga Sah in an undertone of pathos in his voice. "I read the *Geeta* every day; I am getting the fruit of *karma*, I have done in previous life, for I have done no evil in this to be punished."

Feeling bored with Joga Sah, Desh yawned. He had waited overlong for a glimpse of Lalita, keeping his eyes fixed on the closed doors, leading to the inner room, at which he had stubbornly knocked that fateful evening, about two years before.

"Lalita, daughter," shouted Joga Sah, "Come out."

He resumed his talk. He had always prayed for sons; but, gradually he had come to treat his daughters as such. Now their tragedies had brought him uninterrupted sorrow in his old age. "Sometimes, I think, Shanker's bachelorhood is good. He has no one to worry about."

Desh gave an inane, dim smile accompanied by a look at his watch to indicate his restlessness for Lalita.

Joga Sah walked over to the closed doors, and called out, "Daughter, what is the delay; Desh is here."

A few minutes passed without any response from Lalita. Joga Sah gently tapped at the doors. "Desh is here for long." He kept tapping at the doors. "Lalita open the doors."

Having unsuccessfully tapped at the doors, he set his ear at them; silence harassed him.

Desh sidled over, and called out, "Lalita open the doors." Before knocking them, he waited few moments. He knocked on at the doors, and rattled them.

"Now do not disturb her," advised Joga Sah. "She will not open them."

Desh gave him a look of inquiry.

"Lalita is a very modest daughter", he declared, "She will not open the doors before me and meet you."

"It means I should not come here."

"Har Preya's house is the better place for you to meeting her."

He agreed to Joga Sah. His vanity was bruised, while his ache to meet Lalita had been aggravated. At home, he poured himself several drinks.

x x x

Next morning as he was dressing for the law-courts, he felt someone had entered his room. He gave a sidelong glance to his visitor, over his hands, busy doing the knot of his tie; he took in the snub-nosed priest.

"It is good, you have come." He opened out his arms in a gesture of welcome.

The priest seemed downcast; his eyes looked stony and moist.

"I am glad you have come. Aunt has remembered you in her letter."

The priest fixed him in his immobile gaze.

"Can you not talk; I am getting late for law-courts."

A tear fell from the eyes of the priest." No one knows His ways. The world is *maya*."

"What is the matter."

The priest's frame shook with sobs." Lalita is gone."

"Hun; To Ranikhet again."

Nodding in dissent, the priest raised his hand to heavens as tears rolled down his cheeks.

Desh gave a short laugh. "You are mocking me."

"No, no; I am not mocking. "The priest reinforced his statement by flattening his palms.

Desh fell down upon the sofa nearest him, and rested his cheek in hand. "*Arree*; *Siva; Siva*;"

Early in the morning Lalita left the house, telling her father that she was going to meet Goddess of the Rock. With her she carried her basket containing *puja* things. At the temple bowing to the Goddess, she made a shaffron mark on her forehead that matched well with her blood-red, silk-sari she wore. As the rays of sun touched the peaks of Nainital, she disappeared into the lake, leaving behind her basket in the temple. A bearded, young man, self-styled as an astrologer and fortuneteller, who happened to come early for morning *puja*, dived in and swam under the water, and with in minutes, tugged her to the bank. In spite of his prompt help the Goddess had called Her devotee to Herself.

At once the news had blazed over the city; father, sister, host of relatives dashed towards the temple.

Unmindful of his wet cheeks, Desh jumped to his feet, crying disjointedly, "I must move off."

"It is late," the priest continued, "The cortege should have reached Chitrasheel in Kathgodam."

"Why have I been stopped from paying respects to her ?"

"Your presence would have spoken ill of Lalita to the world." The priest's eyes again filled up.

The bile of an indescribable exhaustion flowed into his mouth; he felt his legs had refused to move. With his hand over his eyes, he remained lying on the sofa, unaware of the passage of time, day light, or himself.

"Lalita! Dear Lalita," he wailed. "Where are you? Dear Lalita."

A voice in him answered, "She is merged into the Goddess; she is merged into *Siva*."

"Lalita, where are you; I love you, I love you very much."

"You lie," remonstrated a voice. "You wanted her to gratify yourself."

"Lalita", tears streamed down his closed eyes." I love you beyond this life, for the soul is indestructible; I will ever keep loving you, however many times I take bith or die."

His body shook with a violent jerk; his eyes slid open.

In his hands and under his arms, he carried off, in one turn all the stock of his whisky bottles to the bath-room, and throwing them upon the floor, shattered them. One sacred deed performed, he applied himself to another by crushing all the cigarette-boxes which he possessed, under his shoes. "I will never touch these evil things," he pledged to himself.

He restored the oleograph of *Siva* from the bath-room to its original place on the mantelpiece of his living room. Joining the palms of his hands in front of his breast, long he kept his head bowed to it.

In a state between waking and sleeping, he remained in bed the whole day; occasionally faint moaning escaped his lips. He wished someone had given him company, alleviate the sharp pain in his heart. He recalled his sister; she should be coming along any moment to silence the storm in his life. Lalita had opened up his eyes; he considered his sisters decision to accompany her husband to Allahabad as a right step towards finally breaking from Shanker.

None called on him. In the evening his domestic served him meals in his living room, but he retched at the very sight of it. Through the night, he kept murmuring to himself, "Lalita, dear where are you? My love where are you?"

An hour or two before dawn, he heard the mellow chanting of *Geeta* by the snub-nosed priest, filtering out of the room of uncle. Suddenly terror of death loosened its grip on his heart; he felt it was something soft. In months he pushed open the room of his uncle, who at once holding Desh's hand, took him to the *kirtan* hall. Desh joined him in beating cymbals, rolling, oscillating, inspired. Then he saw he was a boy; uncle led him to the chariot of Rama; he bowed to it with excitement. Next he performed *arti* in the *puja* of Satyanarayan; his heart was throbbing with ecstasy.

In the morning he felt fit enough to walk up to the bathroom and wash himself. tea refreshed him somewhat; when his domestic brought him a telegram. It cleared the mystery over the absence of his sister and Shanker in his hour of sorrow. It had been transmitted from Kichha, the previous evening and ran as under :

Shanker and I have made home here; come and see.

He crumpled the telegram in his hand, before throwing it away. "What a shameless act by my sister," He reddened with anger. "Shanker betrayed me."

In the evening he received a letter from his brother-in-law, sent through a messenger. He had confirmed the telegram of his sister, whose sudden departure to Kichha hardly surprised him. Though his wife had separated herself from him, in spite of living with him in the same house, still he had never suspected that one day, she would elope with Shanker. He was retained in the law-suit, occurring among illiterate and backward people, over desertion of wives of their husbands and vice versa. Now he was shocked to realise that times were changing, when his wife had followed their example. For few years he had been mulling over moving to high-courts. Now he felt himself too disgraced to live in Nainital. He wanted Desh to precede him to Allahabad, and take a suitable house on hire for him. Of his two children, Miranda missed her mother, while Sanjeev calmly accepted her parting. The post-script expressed surprise at his wife's leaving behind her, excepting a few saris, all her personal effects, including her golden ornaments gifted by him on the occasion of wedding. He never quite understood the reason of his wife's contempt for wealth.

With his brother-in-law he too would quit Nainital. The ringing of bells, floating from the temple of Goddess of the Rock, would plunge him into gloom. The enchanting lake would never attract him; rather it would awaken in him poignant memories.

x x x

Next morning while he was occupied with packing, he was troubled by a visitor's knock on the front doors. He was no other than his friend, lawyer Belwal.

"You will not mind, please, my doing packing as well as talking with you."

Belwal followed him into his livingroom; his eyes were drawn by the oleograph of *Siva* upon the mantelpiece.

"Seems you are taking away everything to Allahabad." Belwal paused. "You will be coming here in summer."

"Not for a long time."

"You would not take it ill, if I say ..." his voice sounded mellow.

'No."

"My niece's proposal was made for you through your uncle."

Desh lifted his eyes in an effort to recollect. "An engineer's daughter."

"The very one; it still stands."

Desh resumed putting the law-books in a large steel-trunk. His heart was too full to continue an untimely talk. Belwal understood him.

"It is all right; we shall be writing to each other. But remember my niece is M.A. in English.

"Reads English novels," flung out Desh.

"Quite so."

He had known two women intimately; one was his sister and other Lalita; what a difference lay between them.

"Your niece would not suit me."

"Why ?"

"I do not want a girl like my sister."

"I see," Belwal slapped his shoulder. "You are greatly mistaken; you have based your notions on school and college. We in India read the same English books that are done all over the world, and now we are going to have similar types of laws on marriage and divorce as in western countries; but so long we are brought up in homes with *puja, kirtan* and *Geeta*, we shall remain what we are."

Belwal limped through the maze of law-books over to Desh, and affectionately put his hand on Desh's shoulder.

"I shall not disturb you in your packing." He touched the crown of Desh with his right hand, and blessed. "May God give you kind thoughts."

Gayly dressed, Champa surprised him by her presence in his house. She tried to dissuade him form proceeding to Allahabad; Desh should look upon her as his own sister in place of Chandra, for, with Shanker's departure, she too had lost a brother. Her husband, Heera Lal, had taken the change in his brother's life with mixed feeling. Though he was pleased that Shanker would be taking for himself a wife, he strongly disapproved of a divorcee. Champa seemed to be pleased at the scandal over his sister; she might be harbouring a bit of jealousy for her friend. Dev Rama, the domestic of Shanker, had refused to accompany him to the hot climate of plains; he was distressed having to leave his old master. Now he worked with the district magistrate Desh had met in Bhimtal.

The two nephews helped him purchase the bus ticket. A mile before Kathgodam, as the mountains disappeared and the bus entered the plains, Desh felt warm even though it was time close on to winter. He put off his woollen coat. Like Dev Rama he too wanted to live in mountains; he was sorry having to leave them behind. At the railway station he found his train allowed him, before its departure, two hours to refresh himself. He walked into the dingy refreshment-room with walls decorated all round with oblong looking-glasses. He was surprised to see Bhandari, occupying a middle table, bent on an omelette.

"*Arree*," chuckled he. "When did you arrive; I was waiting for you at the station." A deep, heart warming smile flashed on his face." Then I thought let me eat something; I was hungry."

Desh started him, wondering how Bhandari came to know of his movement.

"I was sent here by your sister. She had received a telegram from her husband that you are going to Allahabad today. He wanted her to talk over, on his behalf, divorce and other matters with you."

Desh tossed his head backwards to cut short Bhandari. He signed a waiter, with tipped moustaches, and ordered tea.

"No," interposed Bhandari in his powerful tone. "Full meal." He turned to Desh. "You look weak; your sister suspects you are starving yourself." He glanced up at Desh.

The waiter brought a non-vegetarian meal; Desh got it changed to vegetarian. He ate heartily; he had gone without food at Nainital, he had lived on tea and biscuits.

In the first-class compartment, which Bhandari and he occupied, they were the only two passengers. While he stowed his heavy luggage, Bhandari luxuriated a cigarette. He felt like smoking one himself, but he quickly suppressed the desire.

"I am greatly pleased," began Bhandari," With your sister."

He exclaimed, "Pleased!"

"Quite so, " Bhandari pulled long at his cigarette." And she is so beautiful; but she is more modern than beautiful."

"Modern ! That modern without a soul."

"Why bring in the soul? For a really modern man, it just does not exist."

"If there is no soul", Desh pouted his lower lip", "There is no re-birth; no flowing of life", he paused, "No *karma*; no *niravan*."

"Yes, yes, yes" Bhandari ejaculated, "You are talking sense. This is exactly what your sister understood in a flash before leaving Nainital."

Her children had made for school; so had her husband to the law-courts, when she received the tragic news. A violent shock swept over her. Immediately she scribbled off a letter to her husband, informing him of her decision to proceed with Shanker to Kichha; she could no longer bear to live away from him. She requested him to pardon her by not taking, excepting divorce, any unsustainable legal action. As she was parting from her children her heart went out to them, whom she would always want to meet. Having completed the letter, she put in some of her saris in a suit-case, and emerged out.

Shanker went mad with happiness; at first he disbelieved Chandra. Hurriedly he packed up his clothes, some utensils in few trunks; did the roll of bedding; and, in a short while, he with Chandra set forth on their journey.

"I do not know," Desh waved his hand, "Why they did not come to see me at Nainital."

"Your sister feared, if something happened, she might change her mind. She was not very sure of herself then."

"One day, she shall repent her hasty decision."

"No, no, no," Bhandari thumped the cushion on the bunk. "She will never do it. She only regrets the delay very much." He lighted another cigarette with the butt of the first. "Your sister is a smart woman; in a short time she has completely made her home. She knows internal decoration and cooking. Both your sister and Shanker are so happy; and both make such a wonderful couple. Really *Bhagwan* had made one for the other."

After sunset the train whistled off; once or twice Bhandari reminded him that in less than hour they would be reaching their destination; and in a short time it was steaming into the dimly lighted, small, station of Kiccha.

"I am bringing *coolies,* your sister and Shanker". Bhandari at once detrained. "You start throwing out your luggage; the halt here is very short."

Leaping to the door, he slammed it shut. At once he pulled down the shutters over the windows, and switched off the light. Presently he heard knocking on the door.

"This is the very compartment", Bhandari shouted.

Bellowed Shanker, "No lights; door, windows shut. Are you sure ?"

Desh keenly listened to the hurrying steps over the platform. He was delighted at having kept eluded the search-party.

Bhandari knocked on the door "By God, this is the very compartment."

Burst out sister, "You are very right." She knocked on the door. "Desh I have come to see you." She desperately knocked at the door and windows. "Desh open the door for a minute that I may see you; you are not my brother, but son." She was overpowered by a fit of crying. "Have I become so unworthy of you." She kept banging on the door with her fist.

In some moments the wheels carried him away.

The compartment of which he was the only passenger felt warm. He slid open the shutters; cool October breeze rushed in. Without putting on the light, he unrolled the bedding in darkness over a bunk. Too late, he had resurrected himself; he was overcome. Long he gazed, through the barred window, the mysterious firmament powdered with stars. Lalita dwelt among them.

Indian Words Incorporated in the Concise Oxford Dictionary (new edition) Used in the Novel

Allah	Atma	Attar	Avtar
Bazaar	Bhagwan	Bhajan	Bidi
Bindi	Brahmin	Burra	Chaat
Chai	Chapatti	Choli	Chokra
Chowkidar	Chuddar	Chulah	Churidars
Chutney	Coolie	Dal	Dalit
Dharamshala	Devi	Darshan	Dharm
Dholak	Dhoti	Dhyan	Diwali
Durzi	Dussehra	Ghee	Gulab Jamun
Gur	Guru	Hakim	Halwa
Hindi	Hindustani	Holi	Ji
Karma	Kashmiri	Khaddar	Kirtan
Kishmat	Kumbh Mela	Kurta	Laddu
Lakh	Maharaja	Mahatama	Maya
Memsahib	Namaskar	Nirvana	Nobobs
Paise	Pakora	Pan	Pashmina
Puggaree	Puja	Pujari	Pukka
Pundit	Purdha	Puri	Raj
Rajah	Rasmali	Rickshaw	Rupee
Ryot	Sadhu	Sahib	Salaam
Sanskrit	Sari	Sarkar	Shikar
Tabla	Terai	Thali	Thug
Upnishad	Vaisa	-Wallah	Yogi
Zamindar	Zilla		

Indian Words

ACHHA	Very well, all right.
AREE	You see; mark of exclamation.
ARTI	Circular or to and fro movement, with a bow, of flame of camphor or greased threads, in front of idol, to mark end of worship.
BILAYATI	Made in, pedigreed in, England.
CHHICHHI	Fie.
CONGRESS	Most dominant political party before and after independence.
DEKHO	Look here; you understand.
GAYATRI	A popular prayer in Rig Ved.
GEETA	Philosophic treatise combing code of conduct followed as much by Hindus as the Bible by Christians and Koran by Muslims.
GULAL	Red powder.
JAI HIND	Greeting most popular immediately before and after independence.
KALIYUG	Following good, reign of Evil.
KRISHNA	One of the two most worshipped avatar of Vishnu.
ROLI	Thick mixture of brick-red powder in water used in puja and auspicious occasions.
RAMA	One of the two most worshipped avatar of Vishnu.
RAMAYANA	One of the two great epic poems of ancient India, narrating the life of avatar Rama; the other epic being Mahabharata.
RAI BAHADUR **RAI SAHIB**	Titles in British Raj for Indians.
SAHIBLOGS	British officers.
SATYANARAYAN	An avatar of Vishnu.
SIVA	Most worshipped, is one of the three supreme deities. The other two being Brahma and Vishnu.
SWARAJ	Self-rule, independece.